Will at the Tower

Pete Hartley

Copyright © 2018 Pete Hartley

an un**easy**book

ISBN: 978-1-7312-7313-0

To David

Foreword

This novel is a development of a play first performed at Hoghton Tower, Lancashire, England in February 2010.

I am grateful to Sir Richard de Hoghton who permitted the performance to take place in the very same space as that used by his ancestor's players; to Melissa Peter who encouraged and facilitated the production; and to the *uneasy theatre* cast and company for the staging of it, especially my chief collaborator Andrew Brindley. Thanks also to the two long-suffering proof readers of this version of the tale.

The scope of a novel is much greater than can be encompassed in the *two hours' traffic of the stage* so the theatrical story has been significantly expanded, characters added and the plot developed.

One brief note before we start: the spelling of *Bradshaigh* has been modified to *Bradshaw* to ease the imagined pronunciation. The latter spelling is found in some sources. The Elizabethans were inconsistent in the construction of their surnames, as we shall see.

This is unquestionably a work of fiction.

Parts of it are true.

Pete Hartley

February 2016.

Prologue

"I want him dead." Eliot leaned back. "I want William Shakespeare dead."

The smaller, fatter, older man toyed with his cup of wine. "He's sixteen."

Eliot's stare remained fixed on the candle flame on the table between them. "I'll kill him myself if I have to."

The fatter man pushed the debris of his dinner to one side. It was his turn to lean back. He breathed and sighed before he spoke.

"We'd better find him then."

Pete Hartley

ONE

The shadow of a dream

Will knew he was waiting to meet a very dangerous man. He was happy to do so. The decisions that he had taken during recent weeks had shaped the rest of his life. Sixteen years he had survived, and he was now content if he lived for but another sixteen hours. It was likely that he would not stay long in this world. Furthermore, he envisaged a very painful death. He would endure it. He would survive it, not to walk on English soil but to feel Eden beneath his feet, and to shake the punctured hands of martyred saints as they welcomed him into their elite assembly. He, William Shakespeare, son of a Stratford alderman, glove maker and sheep dealer, would become a priest. In doing so he would be deemed a traitor and would have to play cat and mouse for as long as he could, but capture would come, and torture, then slow public death, then resurrection, then perpetual ecstasy and unending glory.

This was what he told her as she got dressed.

Martha was unimpressed. "Don't come preaching to me," she said.

"I'm gifted at it," said Will tugging at the inadequate tuft posing as a beard.

1

"Says who?" said Martha, stuffing her shirt into her skirt.

Will extracted the shards of straw from his own shirt and tugged it over his head. "Mr Cottam," he said. "And he should know. But he says I am all pipe and no tune."

"I think I might agree with that," said Martha.

"And so I will need to go abroad and study. And then come back, save you all, save my soul, die a good death, and live happily ever more. How does that sound?"

"Sounds like a dream," said Martha and without a thought she stepped from the edge of the barn attic and fell to squat on a stack of straw below, then she dusted herself off once more and went about her business, leaving Will Shakespeare to his lofty thoughts.

Three days later, an hour before midnight, he was sitting at his father's table with the most wanted man in England. That man passed a document across the table and Will watched as his father signed each page of it.

"Keep it safe," said the visitor.

John Shakespeare nodded then folded and patted the paper. The visitor looked at Will.

"This man knows the way?" he asked.

"He's been once before," said John.

"I went with Mr John Cottam," said Will. "Our schoolmaster. His brother is . . ."

"I know who his brother is," the visitor said. He smiled. His weathered cheeks wrinkled readily. This was a man on the verge of his middle years. Will doubted he would see them through, and he seemed to know that. The way he had spoken that night told of a man who was eager to do as much as he could before his scarcity of time ran out. He was not running from the inevitable, but playing with it. His eyes had the joy of the hunter and the vigilance of the hunted. He looked into Will's soul. Will celebrated the agony. The Queen's men hounded this fugitive, and Will was going to accompany him for perhaps one hundred and fifty miles in the full knowledge that they would be going much further than that and may never come back.

The visitor smiled. "You are convinced in your mind that this is the path for you?"

"I am," said Will.

The guest turned to his host.

"And you, John? Is your mind at peace with this?"

John Shakespeare looked at his eldest son. "God gave him to me. The least I can do is give him back."

"Are we leaving tonight?" asked Will.

The visitor smiled more widely and shook his head. "Tomorrow, or the day after that. I need to see some of your mother's family."

Will nodded. He understood why.

The visitor stretched and cheerfully tapped his tummy as if to congratulate it on the supper it had just received. He was tall and strongly built. "So clean your boots, get some rest, and rehearse our route."

"I can remember it," said Will. "And Mr Cottam has made me learn and recite the turns and stops."

The visitor turned to Will's father. "Is it direct?"

John shook his head. "It's safe," he said.

"Safety doesn't interest me," said the visitor, "Expediency is my priority. But for young Will's sake safety is, without doubt, the best option."

"I don't need safety," said Will.

His father swallowed a grunt before it had chance to degenerate into a snigger. He regarded Will with a look of amusement that rapidly deteriorated into despair. Their guest spoke.

"Oh aye you do," he said. "Do not wish your liberty away. Nor mine. The game is to do as much good as we can before others make it that we can do no more. Our ambition is not served by surrender."

John Shakespeare said, "You'll be much safer in Lancashire. They're all of the old faith there."

"Not all," said the fugitive.

Will would not be leading the journey all the way to Lancashire, he had never been that far. He would be the guide for just the first twenty-five miles following lesser used footpaths and lanes, then others with local knowledge would take the lead, providing a chain that would pull Will a hundred and fifty miles from home.

"The situation is much better in Lancashire than here," said John. The big families are holding on. And the further you are from London the better."

3

At that moment the door from the street burst open making both Will and his father jump. It was Simon Sedlow, a corn merchant known to Will's father and someone that Will knew to be fundamental to the secure movement of their visitor. He sat with them. Will's mother brought beer, smiling broadly as she put it on the table before him. Simon kissed her with his eyes. "All is in place," he said, pushing his hat back a little. The candle light showed the recusant grey hairs not quite hiding among the majority of black ones. "A safe bed awaits you."

"Thank you Simon," said the visitor.

"It's only a few doors away. The night watchman is occupied, so he'll not trouble us. Is your business here concluded?"

"Just about," said John. "How many will be in the party with you and Will?"

"Whatever Simon advises"

"I've two good men" said Simon. "We think your presence here is unacknowledged, but just in case we are wrong we'll send an entourage by the main road, following the route you might be expected to take. I will be part of that group. We will divert late in the day and join you at your destination. Meanwhile my men and Will here will guide you along a more benign path."

Will felt inflated and overburdened and hid both behind the plainest face he could muster.

Simon leaned forwards. "Father, there is danger at every corner."

"We can trust in God." He turned his attention back to Will. "And we will do that, won't we Will?" His irises glowed golden through the candle halo.

Two days later boy, priest and two of Simon Sedlow's men set out on their journey and three days after that they were lost.

Will's departure from Henley Street was beneath the first hint of dawn and had followed another sleepless night. It would have been far too risky to depart during darkness when the night watchmen might be alerted, so he sat up in the parlour while his siblings came in staggered succession to say their farewells. All of them were his junior. Gilbert was the closest in age, and hence in familiarity, and he made as much fuss of the event as he did of his brother, constantly checking his pack, the quietness of the street, the weather, and the portents in the gaps between the clouds. Joan was very quiet; on the cusp of adolescence, she frothed with excitement but settled to a seriousness that became almost haunting in its silence. She stared at him through moist eyes, actively storing his image in her memory. Richard, only in his seventh year, hugged his big brother with the joyous pain of their countless play fights and giggled his goodbyes not really understanding their possible permanence, and then was dispatched firmly but kindly to bed. Will looked in on him just before he left, and at the same time placed the softest of kisses upon the brow of the youngest, Edmund, swaddled in his cot and dreaming of the first steps that he had taken only a few weeks earlier.

Then there were the two household servants. They kept respectfully in the background though both stayed up right through the night partly out of friendship and respect, but in part too because their mood was not conducive to sleep. Walter was the apprentice nearing the end of his seven years and while his journeyman's licence was within sight, Will's departure made his tenure at Henley Street much more secure in the short term. Walter had never hidden the satisfaction he felt that Will did not seem cut out for glove making, but at the same time being only three years older than Will the two had stitched a strong bond. Walter had encouraged Will in his religious vocation, and not just for selfish reasons. Will could tell that Walter too had leanings towards the priestly life. What he lacked, thought Will, was the courage. The two embraced even more strongly than brothers and Walter swallowed his farewells.

Will embraced the other servant tightly too, though this cuddle hid secrets. Though tight in grip it was brief in duration, with Martha being careful to present only her cheek and not the lips that she had shared in secret. She too, was slightly older than Will and had contributed to his education both willingly and cautiously. He was grateful for her lessons. "When you're ordained, say a Mass for me," she said. "By then I'll be in need of a few, I'm sure."

Will sniffed and smiled. He tried to put true tenderness and gratitude into their hug, but she was anxious for it to be brief and to break from him.

Will's thoughts turned to another woman. Anne Hathaway was eight years senior to Will. She was not as convenient as Martha, but had been just as obliging. He had wanted to go to see her to make his farewells, but no one was to know that he was leaving, so farewells would have to be relayed. He had asked Martha to do that very special favour. The expression on her face had been priceless, but she vowed to do his bidding. She was that kind of woman.

Will's father was quiet all night long, sitting by the small fire, making slight remarks about thrift in trust, caution in judgement and generosity in faith. "Pray a lot," he said.

"I shall," said Will.

Will's mother fought a failing fight with tears. She was a resolute woman. Her background and her inheritance had given her a confidence and a resilience to more than match her husband. When they had wed, John's standing in Stratford had been high, but even so Mary had been a much admired catch. Since then she'd supported him valiantly through the variances of business made much worse recently because of their determination to remain loyal to the old religion. In addition, she had produced eight children, two of which had not survived infanthood. To say farewell to her eldest was bad enough, but for him to be setting out on such a dangerous adventure was almost unbearable. Will gripped his mother by the shoulders, kissed her crown, and told her all would be well.

"I give you back to God," she said. And that was the last he heard before Gilbert opened the door and let him out.

He was met at the town boundary by Simon Sedlow who quickly introduced two others of his household, one was already vaguely known to Will, but the other was a stranger who spoke with a Welsh inflection. Sedlow went back into town, hooded against the morning chill and also against instant recognition. The town gates were open and the beginnings of the traders' bustle were in motion, so the rendezvous went unnoticed and the three set out with calm confidence.

Will was immediately relieved of his responsibility as his companions led the way, though it was by the lesser route that his schoolmaster had suggested, and one that Will knew fairly well.

The Welsh sounding lad was named Oswyn and he worked with Simon Sedlow's livestock as a herdsman. The other, the one Will had seen before was Allen, Simon's stepson, his mother having married a second time after the death of her first husband from winter sickness during Allen's first year. Will found Allen to be truculent and ill at ease with his role. He said he disliked travelling. Oswyn was more outgoing and open to conversation. He was closer in age to Will and had an easy and infectious sense of humour. Will enjoyed talking to him, and listening to his peculiar intonation. They passed only a pedlar and his apprentice on that leg of their journey.

By afternoon they arrived safely at their first lodgings, the home of William Catesby at Lapworth. It was there that Will met again with his auspicious companion who had arrived the night before. A Mass was said that night though only the close household attended. Their celebrated secret guest conducted the ceremony and gave the sermon. Will was captivated and captured, and placed in even greater awe that he was now to be entrusted to serve this man who was so fervently wanted by both his friends and enemies. He feared he was scheduled for another night without sleep but the fact that he had been awake for two days and had walked twelve miles put paid to that fear.

The following morning as they prepared for the next part of their journey, Catesby organised a group of his household to stage a diversionary exit. Their departure was given much fuss, while Will, Allen, Oswyn and the priest slipped out through the orchard and down to a river which they followed upstream to a ruined house that Will recognised. Will's confidence soared, he took the lead and strode out in high spirits.

Their journey that day was simple and entirely secret. The route was easily charted and they met no one. They located the second safe house, a lodge of a compatriot of Catesby. Their hosts were anxious but gracious and the travellers slipped in at dusk and out at dawn without fuss. They slept simply but comfortably on makeshift beds by the parlour fire. They were fed generously but no ceremonies or sermons took place, though Will's companion said prayers and gave blessings, and listened in private to the confessed sins of those who asked him to do so. And so another night was peacefully passed and the next morning Will once again led the way but some hours after noon their progress was halted by the sound of hooves, and shouted commands.

Allen turned pale and demanded they fled from the path and diverted into the woodland. The priest advocated calm, but Allen would hear nothing of it and insisted that they swiftly put considerable distance between themselves and the riding party. Oswyn said they only need take cover and wait, but Allen was spooked by the sounds they could hear that suggested the strangers were well-separated and being methodically vigilant. This was a search party, he declared.

They were in ancient forest of mixed woodland with a myriad of minor paths and tracks occasionally cut by more heavily worn lanes. They moved swiftly, penetrating further into the forest. The shouts did not intensify but neither did they diminish and it did sound as if the group were engaged in something other than simply travelling to a destination. Under Allen's silent instructions, Will's party veered further and further off course. Eventually panting and sweating, they squatted amid deep cover and waited. After only hearing the natural noises of the wood for a prolonged period they attempted to retrace their steps only to discovered that they were lost. Will said that he thought he could lead them back to the path and he attempted to do so, but failed.

Will was embarrassed and apologetic, but his esteemed companion would hear none of it, and quickly silenced the curses of Allen. They squatted on the trunk of a fallen tree. Will was despondent now, and tired, and even questioned that they were heading in the right general direction. It would be dark soon and the thick woodland was not an ideal place for them to spend the September night.

His companion refused to allow their spirits to falter. "If we can't find ourselves then her majesty's agents won't find us either," he said.

Will shrugged and accepted the goatskin flask that Oswyn filled from a nearby brook. The water within was peaty and sweet. In town they never drank water, and they had brought some ale with them, but the afternoon had been warm and they had drunk it all. Their journey thus far had been straightforward. Two safe houses had provided beds, and now a third awaited them but they had no notion of in which direction it lay.

Something laughed: a crow, a jay, or a pheasant.
The older man surveyed the light beyond the foliage

above them. It would be dusk within the hour. "Well," he said, "we have three options. We persist on, we try again to retrace our steps or we bed down for the night."

Will did not like the sound of the third option and neither did Sedlow's men. There was the threat of rain in the air and already the day was decidedly cool. Allen had drawn his dagger and was testing its point on the bark of their bench. He was in a deep sulk. Oswyn stretched his legs and tapped one boot against the other dislodging biscuits of mud. He smiled cherub-like. "Looks like we're stuck," he said.

The forty-year-old seemed to be relishing their predicament. "Let's make a shelter," he said.

The priest chose a place where an immature willow fought for sunlight with other woody sapling bushes. He craftily intertwined their branches and got Will and the others to gather windfall boughs to mix into the weave. By the time it was dark they had fashioned a rough half-dome with its curve against the prevailing draught, and insufficiently artificial to draw attention but condensed enough to offer some protection if rain came. They wrapped their cloaks around themselves and sat close. They would wait out the depths of the dark and make a move at the first hint of pre-dawn.

"What's a Welshman doing so far from Wales?" the priest asked.

"Went to market and never went home," he said. "Didn't like home much. Who does?"

Will did. "Been lost before?" he asked hopefully.

"Not sure I've ever been found," said Oswyn. Best thing to do, is pick a path and follow it. They all go somewhere in the end."

"Ever been robbed?"

"Never had anything worth robbin'."

Allen murmured, "Except your life."

The wood seemed at once empty and full.

Will felt he was totally threatened and absolutely secure. His youth empowered him to be blunt. He spoke to the priest. "Did you consider rejecting your mission?"

"Obedience is obedience. A vow cannot be conditional."

"Yet, you will fail."

"Failure is the only success. Isn't that the message of

9

our saviour?"

Will searched for the thinnest stripe of despondency in the creases of joy covering the face of his friend, but he could not find one. "Is it true that your students pinned the word 'martyr' on your door in Prague?"

His superior smiled even wider. His eyes twinkled. "And I left it there."

Will chewed a shard from his thumbnail and spat it out. "Aren't you scared?"

For the first time the older man's face shed its glow. "If I wasn't scared I'd have taken the word down, because I wouldn't have understood it. I know what's in store, Will. I came back to this country horizontally – across the sea on a boat - and I will leave it vertically." He clutched the teenager by the wrist. It was arresting. "And by association with me you run the risk of the same fate."

The other two men were listening carefully but their silence signified their unease with the discussion. Will too, had found a point of insecurity.

"All boys dream of battles," said Will. "I've always thought of the night before."

The wood was now as dark as it would get.

"Think instead, of the day that follows," said the priest. "Everlasting day."

Some beast, deep in the forest, moaned and demystified the image that the hopeful martyr had implanted in his disciple.

Talk was spent for now and they made themselves as comfortable as they could in the hope of finding sleep. They wrapped their cloaks about their heads and curled like unborn children to trap warmth. The older man used his satchel as a pillow but took care to ensure the strap was fed beneath the cloak and under his arm. Will copied the idea. The priest said out loud a lengthy litany in Latin invoking the intercession of saints. Will understood the majority of it, with just a smattering of terms and a few of the saints' names alien to him. He echoed some of the structural responses his voice merging with the music of the priest's praying tone. They induced a sense of sanctified enchantment that was warm, elevating, and at variance with the chill September air that turned their prayer to mist as they spoke. Allen blocked his ears. Oswyn stared at nothing.

Against the odds they all found sleep.

Will awoke to see his companion's satchel swinging clear of the ground whilst suspended at an angle because only one side of the shoulder strap secured it. The other side had been sliced and the stub dangled down. The bag was open and some of the precious paper contents were in the grip of the man who held the bag. He was a short, swarthy, stocky woodsman. As well as the bag and the papers he clutched a long-bladed hand knife typical of the kind kept by those who coppiced trees. Will instinctively grasped for his own bag. It was safe and still on his person. The priest was awake and sitting up, though not yet fully animated despite what must have been an alarming wakening. Only now did Will start to try to sit. A boot prevented it. The second newcomer was strong in similarity to the first. He too, was stocky and weathered, and his style of dress suggested that he was an artisan who plied his trade in the woods. Despite not being tall, his position inside their shelter meant he was bent over with his curly grey hair pressed against the willow dome.

It was dawn, but only just.

Will's awaking had only brought the smallest acknowledgement from the man with the knife who, after the briefest of glance at Will had returned his attention to the priest's papers. He was standing outside of the semi-circle of their shelter and two or three yards from them. He drew an affected breath exploiting the authority that the situation had thrust upon him.

"These look like . . . very . . . important papers," he said. He toyed with the sheaf, shuffling between pages, but something about his manner told Will that though this man could see the words, he was unable to read them. "They're not what we usually find on poachers."

Will now realised that there was a third man, large in build and heavy in purpose, he had his knee in the small of Allen's back forcing him face down in the mud. Oswyn was nowhere to be seen.

The priest was rubbing his beard and eyes. "We're not poachers."

"What else would you be? In my lord's forest before

11

this hour?"

The priest opened his arms in invitation. "Where is our quarry? Where the tools of the poacher's trade?"

The thief stuffed the papers back into the bag. "If your traps are set, they'll not be on you, will they?"

Allen spoke up. "We are not trappers, we are travellers."

The man kneeling on him knelt harder.

The leader spoke. "You can't travel this way."

"We are lost," said Will.

The second man pressed his foot harder on Will's side. His voice was older and throatier and with a watery wheeze to it. "You're lost all right."

"Normally," said the first man, "we just . . . deal . . . with poachers."

The priest ran his hand through his hair. "We're not poachers."

"You're not anything. Except fodder for vermin." He rooted deeper in the satchel. "There's no purse in here."

The second man removed his foot from Will and in one smooth move whipped back Will's cloak to reveal where a purse was tied to Will's belt. Will clutched it tightly to him. The second man now drew his long wood-knife and Will, in defence, drew his small dagger and began to stand.

"Whoah, whoah, whoah!" cried the priest to halt the scuffle before it started. The second man stood off, the first sighed as if to signify that this was some tiresome routine formality. The priest calmly got to his feet and emerged from their shelter. For a moment he was blatantly the tallest of their number, but having stretched his spine as he would on any mundane morning he leaned back against a tree. His matched the feigned indifference of the satchel thief and this gained him some control over the conflict. "Can we just be clear? Do you rob us in your own name or in that of your lord?"

The thief had to consider this inquiry. He came up with a clever reply, or at least his face suggested he thought so. "We rob you in our name, and kill you in his."

Allen blended a groan and a squeal.

"Why in his?" asked the priest.

"It's his estate that you violate. He pays us to preserve it. Where's your purse?"

Somewhere in the wood a woodcock crowed.

"I don't have money." He pointed lazily at Will. "He'll give you some."

"I will not!"

The second thief rattled a chuckle.

The priest carried on. "If we will freely give you our money before you kill us, then we'll have saved you one sin."

Something very difficult was knocking at the door of the first thief's brain. Will could see him struggling with it. Will, on the other hand, was several steps ahead in the mental arithmetic of their predicament. He felt sure his holy friend would not fight, and Allen was clearly in no position to do so, therefore no matter how skilled he proved to be in applying the point of the dagger he held, in all likelihood the thieves would win the bout. The only way through seemed to be via a terrible gamble. If he betrayed his companion he could deflect an immediate attack. The priest was a huge prize if he was delivered alive to higher authority. It would not save either of their lives but might delay their deaths. Would there be any point in that? Of course there would. They each wanted to die a martyr's death. Killed for a few shillings at the hands of greedy woodsmen was not a highway to heaven. Will could not die yet, with all his sins un-counterbalanced by courage. He resolved to make the best of this dilemma but before he could speak, his holy friend had played a similar move.

"By giving you our money we may buy all of us some time," he said. "After we die and before we meet the almighty."

Will immediately understood the supreme skill of this remark. The priest was making a subtle reference to the time the thieves might spend suffering in purgatory as a consequence of their sins, and he was now watching for their reaction. The notion of purgatory was excluded from the state-imposed protestant religion, but still held true by those of the old faith. Will wondered if the subtlety of his friend's speech would be lost on the simple woodsman. What the priest taught him in this tutorial was that the woodsman was not simple. Will would never forget that. The first thief was halted by the priest's remark. He froze for a moment then returned his attention to the papers in the satchel. Whilst he seemed to exhibit the same inability to read them, he was drawn to certain individual words. He looked back at the priest.

"These are important aren't they?"

"They are to me." There was a long pause. "And to you."

The two principal thieves drew close and muttered. After a moment the first addressed them again. "Where were you going?"

"North," said the priest.

"You shouldn't have come this way. Not without my lord's say."

Will spoke up. "Who is your lord?"

"Do you not even know whose land you tread on?"

Will said: "This is the Arden Forest."

"And I am a forester of Arden. So you have your answer."

"Then please, deliver us up to your lord."

"I fear you may be too hot for his hospitality." The thief fastened the satchel again and sank for a moment into his own thoughts. "Perhaps I don't want to be the one to bring him trouble. Perhaps we can best serve him by dealing with his trouble for him?"

"He won't thank you," said Will.

"He won't know."

"He will," said Will. "Because he is expecting us."

The young man knew what he was doing. In his estimation there was no alternative. The woodsmen had worked out what they had in their laps. They might not know who the priest was, but they knew he was a priest. They hadn't rushed to their knees and offered their help, so even if they were of the old faith they still saw Will and his friend as a source of immediate gain rather that long-term salvation.

"Why would he be expecting you?"

"Because," said Will, "I am of his family. My mother is Mary Arden and she is second cousin to your lord."

"Then why didn't you just ride up to see him?"

"Why do you think?" said Will and glanced at his companion.

It was fully light by then and another dawn gave an added pallor to the woodsman's face. He signalled to his compatriot who let Allen stand up and cough the soil and leaves from his gums. Will put his knife away, and two hours later they were inside the manor at Park Hall, and Edward Arden had rewarded his liegemen with coins comprising rather less than the contents of Will's purse. The poor men went away contented, especially the first thief, who left the hall with his master's gratitude ringing in his ear, and a sheaf of the priest's papers tucked inside his shirt.

TWO

Fair fruit

Will had never met his mother's second cousin before because he wasn't at home when Will had made his first visit. Even if he had been, Edward may not have deigned to greet him. The Arden family was extensive, and even more so if all the illegitimate branches were taken into account, and Will's standing was somewhat removed from that of the proprietor of Park Hall.

Edward Arden was a very important Warwickshire figure and, like many others, he was subject to the peculiarly cruel pressures brought to bear on those forced to choose between faith and state. In truth there was no choice. The state was the faith. Anyone at odds with the Church of England was at variance with England herself and hence vulnerable to accusations of treachery, especially as some of England's chief enemies were Catholic nations. This was especially testing for those who saw this life as a necessary trial to be endured in order to secure everlasting joy in the next. The alternatives were to deny the Queen and suffer now, or deny God and suffer for eternity. Edward Arden was the head of one of the few families that could trace their lineage right back to Anglo-Saxon England,

and their loyalty to the old Catholic faith was just as long and hence Edward could not harbour any thought of breaking it. He was a wise, strong-spirited man, not yet forty, and a willing player in the secret fight against the religious oppression by the state.

Will's father had fallen foul of the local authorities over his reticence to comply with religious directives. Consequently, the family suspected that their Henley Street home was being watched. That was why their most precious visitor had to be smuggled in and out at dead of night. Similarly, the other 'safe houses' were periodically watched. That was why they had devised a convoluted plan for their journey through the county. For the most part the plan had worked, but their chance discovery by the woodsmen cast questions over their safety. The men were in the service of Edward Arden, but gossip could spawn a thousand poisoned tongues. Their stay at Park Hall would be short. Nevertheless, a Mass and a sermon would go ahead. Both were strictly forbidden.

Allen was directed to chambers close to the kitchens where he was reunited with his stepfather when he arrived by horse later that day as prearranged. Nothing more was heard of Oswyn and no one seemed overly concerned, except Will who had valued their unfolding friendship.

Will's companion retreated into the private chamber set aside for him and spent some time praying and preparing to preach. The priest hole where he might hide should they be surprised by the agents of her majesty's government was close to that room. Meanwhile Edward delivered Will into the company of one of his gardeners. Initially this introduction perplexed Will, but he trusted his host's judgement.

"This is one of the wisest men I know," said Edward. "Hugh, this is William, my cousin's son. He came with our chief guest. Show him the garden and set the signals." He turned to Will. "Hugh can be trusted absolutely. Absolutely. Tell him anything, and mark him well."

At first glance Hugh seemed senior to Will by a good many years but Will soon realised that was a false impression. This man was only a little older, yet he spoke with a calm authority that rang of considered wisdom and he moved with the pedestrian rhythm usually evident in those well-rooted in the autumn of their life. He wore a straw hat to shade him from the

September sun and his gardener's attire was cheerfully ingrained with the stains of his occupation. He was entirely genuine in his manner, yet his speech and movement seemed at odds with his age and this led Will to form the opinion that there was a performance being played.

"William," he said, and placed his hands, dusty with dry soil, on Will's.

"Will," said Will.

"Will. Come, let me show you all. Meanwhile tell me about yourself."

So Will told him. He felt no compunction about this because he entirely trusted the word of Edward Arden, and the gardener's greeting had a warmth and penetrative quality that immediately lifted Will's spirits. They walked the walled garden heady with herbal aroma and heavy with fruit, some of which was being harvested. Will informed Hugh of his Stratford childhood and how his father had been a successful businessman trading in leather goods and also in property, land, livestock and, surreptitiously, in wool.

"Ah, wool," said Hugh.

"Yes, wool," said Will.

"Help me with these will you?" There were a number of fence staves stacked in the northern corner of the walled enclosure. They moved six of them to the south side.

Will hesitated slightly then told of how his father had fallen from grace because of his reluctance to comply with certain directives involving worship.

"Ah yes. I did hear of that," said Hugh.

"You did?" asked Will, confused as to why a gardener some thirty miles from Stratford would be so familiar with the town affairs.

"Take a basket will you? We'll bring some apples. They left the walled garden and entered a small orchard of stunted but heavily endowed apple trees. "Just the larger ones," said Hugh, and they began to pick the fruit.

"Trade rapidly declined," said Will.

"Ah yes," said Hugh. "Trade: a many branched bush."

Will struggled with the metaphor, but didn't dwell on it. "And then there were fines."

"Fines. Fruit of the self-righteous."

"Aye," said Will pawing then rejecting an under-

18

developed apple. "Things were much more difficult. I had to leave school early. Father needed me at home and besides, school is expensive."

"Ah, school," said Hugh. Will waited for the metaphor, but it failed to germinate.

"I wasn't much use in the workshop. My hands haven't the skill and my thoughts are much travelled."

"That's education for you."

"Is it?"

"Soil for the soul."

Will considered this. He wasn't sure, but he smiled broadly and went on picking. He explained to Hugh how his father's standing in Stratford had remained subdued in direct contrast to the respected position he had once held, and how this fall had tainted the esteem of the whole family. He had been particularly saddened to see the decline in his father and vowed to do what he could to rebuild his pride.

"How?" asked Hugh.

"By being the son he would want me to be."

The gardener regarded his helper with a reflective squint.

Will considered his reply. "By following his example."

The gardener contorted his face further. "So by replicating that which has made him sad you aim to make him glad?"

Will snapped a pippin from its tenacious branch. "I will be devoted to that which I know to be true," he said hoping that the non-specific sense of what he spoke would satisfy his inquisitor. It didn't.

"And what do you know to be true?"

Will's silent response seemed to satisfy the one who heard its absence.

"That will be enough," said Hugh. They went back towards the garden but instead of entering it Hugh led Will down to the southern corner of the wall. "Wait here," he said putting his basket down. He disappeared but returned a few moments later with a short ladder and a smaller basket. He filled the small basket with apples then placed it on top of the wall.

"It's a signal," said Will.

Hugh nodded making his straw hat rattle slightly. "The apples in that place tell that our fruitful guest is here. Inside the wall, the staves give the hour."

"Six," said Will.

"Of the morrow," said Hugh. We'll have the Mass, hear the preaching, break the fast, and then you must go. So we only have today to talk." Will's confusion deepened. Why was it so important that he should talk with this gardener? There was something about their conversation that felt slightly awkward. It seemed preordained. Hugh had taken one of the larger baskets and was heading for the house. Will collected another carrier and caught him up.

They took the apples to the kitchen which was hot and busy as preparations for a worthy dinner were getting underway. Hugh snatched a clutch of currants and passed some to Will. The chief cook saw the crime and scolded him with language worthy of the punishment of an hour in hell. Hugh laughed and leaned down to the side of the fire to find a small copper pan into which he scooped a small stack of smouldering embers from the base of the fire. They made their way outside again.

In the fields hay was being harvested. High on a rise close by a fire had been made ready. Hugh took his embers tipped them into a clutch of straw and lit the fire. They stood and watched while it took hold. "Now all who need to know will know," said Hugh. "Those within the house and those further away. They will know that the priest is here and will say Mass in the morning."

"And can you trust them all?" asked Will.

"The estate is loyal," said Hugh.

Will recounted their escapade with the woodsmen.

"You can't trust everyone," said Hugh. I don't recognise the men you speak of. They could be imposters. It's easy to say you are loyal and local if you know a few names." Hugh moved around the fire stack to be on the upwind side. "Your father is loyal, and so are you." He looked across the conflagration and directly into Will's eyes.

Half a field behind Hugh a rabbit broke cover and pelted over the scythed hay to vanish at the roots of a hawthorn hedge. Vagrant wisps of smoke curled in the combination of crosswind and up-draught found Will's face and tortured his cornea.

Hugh took up a stick and lifted the base of the stack to encourage more air to be drawn in.

Will altered his position and pummelled his eyes.

"We will welcome all who wish to hear the Mass. Some people have more than one face. You either have to trust everyone or no one."

"And you trust everyone."

"No, I trust no one, but I love everyone, because that is what my god tells me to do."

"Can you love someone that you do not trust?"

"If you have to trust someone in order to love them, you don't love them."

"So should we trust the woodsmen who brought us here?"

"No we should not trust them. But we must still love them. Even if they betray us. Could you do that Will?"

"I would find it very difficult."

"Which is why you must study."

"Study what?"

"To be the person to make your father proud. To be a priest. That's what you want isn't it?"

"Who told you that?"

"You did."

"Did I?"

Hugh gripped Will's arm and gave him a friendly shake. "Yes." He prodded the fire.

There was more smoke than flame.

THREE

Vaulting ambition

Frances Thursby liked to be on top when her lovers died. She had lots of lovers and they died a lot. She liked to die too but they often failed to provide the same service to her as she did to them. They did, however, provide her with lots of information. Frances made a very good living by dealing in information, which was just as well, because her family had long disowned her and ostracised her, so she had to survive somehow. She did more than survive. She took a horse from one lover, a set of fine clothes from the next, a surname from a tavern show and a Christian name from a churchyard, and off she set. From the outset, some four years previously, she had been determined to forge a life that was not dependent on the protection or charity of others. It had not always been easy, but with time she became more skilled. When it suited her, she dressed, lived and travelled as a man, but this deception could be set aside on some occasions as she became more proficient at manipulation. It remained, however, a useful means of getting into the inner sanctum of male domains without questions being asked.

She built up a network of associates, some were lovers,

most were not, but all grew to appreciate her expertise at sourcing and supplying whatever they needed. She traded in far more than gossip. She would buy and sell anything if there was a market for it, and so her transactions would range from leeks to livestock. She had a nose for scandal, slander and suspicion, consequently by 1580 she was well aware that there was a much feared secret network of Catholic traitors at large. She knew that a major campaign had been launched from Rome, and that knowledge of the enterprise could win esteem and favour for those who had it, and that meant that they were very happy to pay for it.

   The man beneath her died quickly, much to her relief. Furthermore, he had no interest in satisfying her, which was an even bigger relief because she wouldn't have to fake it. He was portly, well over fifty, had fewer than ten teeth and breath that smelled as sweet as an August gutter. His hair, a sickly mix of grey, white and yellow, was well-receded. An oily sweat gave a greasy sheen to his head. She dismounted from him and got to work with the bed sheet, wiping his seed from her groin and his saliva from her cleavage. Through him she had a line to London. He was a man of considerable private means and lived in one of the larger town houses close to the centre of the bourgeoning market town of Birmingham. He was a recognised burgess and had one or two minor official functions in the town. More importantly from Frances' point of view was that he had both business and political connections in the capital. She suspected these were not as grand as he made out but nevertheless they seemed genuine. Sometimes he would spend as much as two or three months there, and the next time she saw him he would have gifts and gossip.

   His primary business interest was horses, and not just any horses, but particularly fine horses, and now that their usual formality was out of the way that was where his interest lay. She had no deal to strike in livestock that day and that was sure to annoy him, but she gave it little thought because she had something more valuable to offer.

   He was still panting.

   "I've got something to show you," she said.

   He was puzzled by this, because he'd seen her arrive and she'd ridden up alone and without any significant baggage. "Where is it?" he said. "What is it?"

She rummaged beneath her pile of clothes on the floor to find the saddle bag she'd brought upstairs. She unfolded the document and passed it to him. He hitched himself more upright in the bed and the folds of fat on his paunch overlapped the sheet.

The September air was cool. She slipped on her shirt as he held the document very close to his face scanning the text so nearly that he could have sniffed the meaning.

"Where did you get this?"

"That's my business."

He snatched the paper away from his head and fixed Frances with a severity she had not seen in him before.

"Someone in your family?"

"I have no family."

"Someone in Birmingham?"

"I want to know what it is"

"You have to tell me if you got this from someone known to me."

"I'll tell you all about it, if you agree to buy it." She got out of bed and began to put more clothes on.

"Where are you going?" he asked.

"There's someone else who'll be interested in that," she said drawing up her stocking.

"Who would?"

"Now Philip, you know I don't betray my confidences." She pulled the other stocking to its gartering-place, just below her knee.

"No, no," he said. "I know you don't."

"I need to understand what it is."

Philip returned his near-sighted focus to the ink. "It says . . ."

"I know what it says. I want to know what it is." She stepped into the men's hose that she wore to facilitate rapid riding.

Philip scanned down to the edge of the sheet. "There must be other pages," he said. "It's incomplete."

"I realise that. So he'll not want to pay much for it?"

"Who won't?"

"Now, Philip." She took her leather belt with its purse strap and sheathed dagger from the floor and laid it on the bed, then slipped into the stylish doublet she sported and began to lace it to the hose. He was scrutinising the paper again.

"I'll buy it off you."

"Philip!" She paused in her lacing.

"But as it stands it has virtually no value."

She knelt on the bed next to him. His skin was dappled with the nodules of age and peppered with goose-pimples. "I'm selling its history," she breathed. "But I can't agree a price until I know what it is. The problem is I think its value may be falling by the hour."

He nodded. "This has come from abroad. There are only a few people who could have brought it. And they have a very high price on their heads."

Frances smiled very widely. "I think I know who brought it. And I think I know where he is."

Cold ham so late would not normally be her choice, but Philip had the food brought up to persuade her to stay until morning. He slipped on a shirt, a jerkin and some stockings, and sat at the table with Frances.

"Parsons is the golden hind," said Philip.

"Who's he?"

"Jesuit priest. Ring leader of the invasion. We don't know if he's in the country but he's not been seen by our spies abroad since spring. He'd fetch a tidy sum if you knew who to sell him to. But an even bigger prize would be Campion. They're probably together. Though on reflection, that would be foolish."

"There were two travelling together, I was told," said Frances. "And one or two liegemen."

"Both of an age?"

Frances gave Philip a glazed stare and chewed her meat.

"In the name of Christ!" he swore. He put his knife down, wiped his fingers on his kerchief, and went around to the far side of the bed where he kept his strong chest. He returned with a purse from which he spilled a number of coins onto the table. He made a small stack next to his own plate. It was five times the amount that Frances had paid for the document. Philip pointed at the pile with his knife. "But I need to know everything."

"So do I," said Frances.

"Were they both mature?"

25

"No. One was a youth."

"Then you may have one but not the other. Or it may be neither. But whoever it is may lead us to one or other of them. Only someone of their ilk would carry a document like that. The content is very Campion from what I know of him, but in any event, it's Catholic, it's seditious and it's evidence that they are at large locally." He tore a crusty corner from the bread. "This isn't just business you know. This is direct service to the Queen."

Frances' tone was colder than the ham. "It's just business."

"You'd go far at court."

Frances laughed loud and deep. There were so many layers of absurdity in what he'd said that she couldn't help herself. She would like to go to London but she had no intention of going anywhere near any court, unless the price was right. Philip was content to ignore her outburst and refocus his thoughts on the matter in hand.

"The youth could be a novice, or probably just a guide or companion, said Philip. "Describe the mature man."

"I didn't see him."

Philip waved small circles in the air with his knife. "Tell me what you were told."

"Tall, striking appearance, a man of bearing and charm."

Philip chewed more slowly. "Sounds like Campion."
"Who is he?"

"A turncoat - which is why he is so valued. Well, one reason. The other is he's famous. Even the Queen is a fan. Well, she was."

"Why?"

"Very clever man. Brilliant speaker. Son of a bookseller. He debated in front of Elizabeth when she visited Oxford and his clever wordplay won her over. In fact, he's impressed two queens. He also charmed Mary when he was but a boy. Initially though, he was of the proscribed faith. Even became a Deacon, but then switched horses. Went to Ireland, and then to the continent. All over the place. Prague. Rome."

"And he's back in England?"

"Rumours are strong. He's an ordained Jesuit too. They are the worst kind - pernicious to the root. Edmund

Campion is English to the core and so clever with words there's no way they'd leave him to go to seed in Italy. There's a mission. He's their Hotspur."

"It's a death-wish mission."

"They're not scared of death." Philip sliced another leaf of ham. "But I don't reckon they fancy dying much."

Frances sat back in her chair and rinsed her mouth with the Rhenish wine her host had served up. Philip Gyfford was promising to be lucrative again. This was why she maintained her links with him. Despite the distasteful bed-sport and the pomposity and posturing that she had to endure, her visits usually turned out profitable. As soon as she'd chanced on the document she knew that he'd be the man to give the context, and he had. She eyed the pile of coins still on his side of the table.

"Well, my lord Philip, do you want to purchase the whereabouts of this Campion fellow?"

"We don't know it is him. Personally I'd let him run for a bit."

Frances looked quizzical.

Philip explained. "He has to eat and sleep but he can't risk staying in one place too long. We can pounce and get the rat, or follow him, note his fellow rodents, and skewer a shipload of 'em."

"How much money is there in trapping these . . ."

"'*Traitors* is the word you're looking for. A lot. You can get several hundred just for turning in your next door neighbour, if they're going to the wrong church."

"As much as that?"

"And it's on the rise. Twenty pounds per person, per month. One third to the state, one third to the poor of the parish, and one third to the informer. Though I've never known the poor to get their share as of yet."

"That doesn't add up to hundreds."

"Oh yes it does, because they don't change their religion or their practices. They just pay up. Several have gone to ruin. I know one or two personally. In Warwick. And I also know one of their neighbours who did very nicely out of his report."

"Is that the kind of neighbour we're told to love?"

"Don't spare your sympathy. These people are allied to

Spain. Parsons is the spearhead of the Spanish invasion of England. Mark my words. Him and Campion are of a new order: Jesuits. They are the pioneer regiment of the Pope's plans to take this country. France and Spain will help him. Maybe Ireland too. Maybe even Scotland. We are surrounded Frances. There is a new terror being trumpeted, and Campion is its herald."

"Well I know where he was this morning and it is my guess he is still there tonight. So it makes little difference whether you want to pounce or pursue. You'll need to move fast."

"And knowing where you live and your haunts, it doesn't take a magician to predict that what you are about to confirm is that he is at Castle Bromwich. Park Hall. Especially as Edward Arden is known to be clinging on to his Catholicism."

Frances leaned forwards and wet her lips with the wine. "You're an honest man. You wouldn't take goods and not pay for them."

He belched. She ignored it. He opened his purse again and dipped his fingers in. "You'll stay 'till morning?"

"I might."

He added another coin to the pile by his plate and slid the stack across the table towards her.

She managed to get the rest of the bottle of Rhenish down him so he collapsed, contented, on his bed. It was too late to leave as the night watchmen would be about and the town gates shut, so she was compelled to sit by the window and watch the blanket of cloud as it skimmed the roofs. It gave her time to think. Philip Gyfford had given her a lot to think about. She'd been aware of the religious tussle tearing at the heart of her country but hadn't fully understood the wider perspective of the threat that secret priests brought with them. She knew the document she had bought had value but only now appreciated just how great that value was.

She ate some of the leftover bread. Philip snored. A shower came and soaked the town and made the night doubly dark. She snoozed and when she woke the sky was starting to soften in the east and the first movements on the streets could be heard. Shortly after that dull thuds and sharply scolded barks signalled activity below, so she gathered all her things and made her way through the wakening house to the stables at the back. She watered, superficially groomed, bridled and saddled her gelding. Two stable lads came in, but they were familiar with her and gave her no attention, at least not when she was looking. She led her horse out, mounted up, and trotted off along the wet and unevenly cobbled street. Once she was clear of the town she urged him to a canter. She hadn't far to go. Thanks to Philip she was richer not just in pocket but also in knowledge. She knew of someone else who might want to make a purchase. Why sell something only once when it can be sold twice?

Philip Gyfford was ambitious, but only for his survival and to guarantee a certain security of comfort. He played the game of propriety with sufficient skill to sustain the respect of Warwickshire society. He liked to be well thought of among the preening classes and be respected and valued by those in authority. There was no doubt that come morning he would make his way post-haste to Charlecote just outside Stratford, the house of Thomas Lucy who was a prominent anti-Catholic enforcer. Gyfford would have his reputation bolstered and his loyalty noted.

Frances cared little for that. She had turned her profit and a handsome profit it was too, and now she was ready to turn another. This deal would be more entertaining. Gyfford was an old, philandering, self-preserving, stumped-up lackey. Her next customer was young, spirited, flamboyant and fun. He was also a confidence trickster, rapist and murderer.

Frances' horse was a chestnut gelding she called Jake. She couldn't push him too much on the morning she left Birmingham as she'd ridden him hard they day before to get to the town by nightfall. It had been late afternoon by the time the woodsman had sold the document to her. The deal with Philip Gyfford had been satisfactory but to make more money she would need to keep moving. He would be doubly annoyed when he woke, because she was not there and because she had taken the document with her. She cared not and laughed out loud at the thought of him. She may choose to never see him again. He was tiresome and unpleasant and this new line of business might open up a whole new network of interesting traders.

She varied Jake's gait: sometimes a walk, sometimes a

rising trot and for very brief periods a canter. She reached Solihull by mid-morning. The landlady of the inn where he lodged was sour and cantankerous. How should she know where he was or how long he'd been gone? He'd be back. She didn't know when.

Frances arranged some feed for Jake and installed herself in her quarry's room. She wondered what to do. The longer she waited the less value her information would have. The priest in all likelihood was still at Park Hall. He could still be apprehended or, as Philip Gyfford had said, it might prove even more lucrative to track his movements and secure a string of convictions for harbouring him in addition to claiming the main prize. She knew the man she'd come to see would be attracted by that. If only he was here.

The tapster came to see if she wanted anything to eat or drink.

Frances blinked the remnants of the thought she'd been contemplating from behind her eyes. "What's your name?"

"Ellen."

"Do people often stay here?"

"It's an inn."

"Here. In this room."

"Mr Eliot's stayin in this room. He's been stayin here for two month."

"There's a second bed over there."

"That's temporary. This other fella."

"What other fellow?"

"I dunno. Some gentleman friend of his."

"How long was he here?"

"Came day before yesterday."

"When did he go?"

"I thought he was still here. Till you came."

"And Mr Eliot?"

"He comes and goes."

"Does he have many visitors?"

Ellen thought about the question. "Not that I've noticed."

Frances nodded and smiled.

Ellen said, "Women, you mean?"

Frances said, "Women or men."

"Not that I've noticed."

Ellen picked up the trencher and cup from the floor. Frances went over to the window.

"Do you know where they went?"

"Why should I know that?"

Frances shrugged. "Men talk."

"He don't talk to me. Not much."

Frances eyed her, trying to borrow Eliot's perception. Buxom and beddable.

"So are you stayin?"

Frances nodded. "Bring me dinner, and stable my horse."

Ellen put the cup on the trencher and held out the palm of her free hand. Frances paid her and the girl went downstairs.

Frances was annoyed because she had probably lost the chance of a sale. If Eliot did not return soon her information may have severely diminished in value. She decided to stay and wait to see if he came back either that or the next day. She'd had enough riding for the time being and wanted some time to think. Ellen brought her a pie, a not very appetising apple, and some ale. She ignored the fruit but once she'd finished the pie she did the only thing she could do under the circumstances, and fell asleep.

In her dream she was bridled, except the bridle was far too thick and wouldn't go in her mouth. The leather covered not only her mouth but also her nose, and whoever was harnessing her was pulling ever tighter. She could not breathe. It was not a harness, it was not a bridle, and it was not a dream. It was a glove, a leather glove. She opened her eyes and met the rapier stare of George Eliot.

"Why, in God's name do you have to dress as a man?" His free hand was busy with what should have been her bodice, but was instead, a doublet.

She smiled beneath the glove. He peeled his grip from her mouth and kissed the blood back into her lips. She took his tongue onto hers and ran her fingers into his hair dislodging his black hat. When he pulled clear of her she arched her neck towards the door.

"What's the matter?"

"I was told you had a guest."

"He's downstairs." Eliot kissed her again. He fumbled

31

more with her jacket.

She grabbed his hands and stopped him. "Where have you been?"

"Here. I wrote to you and told you. Where have you been?"

"Very busy. I have been to Lincoln."

"Lucky Lincoln." He forced his tongue back inside her mouth. He was cider flavoured.

She gripped both sides of his head and eased him from her. She took all the energy from her tone and spoke simply and quietly. "I have something of great value to share with you."

"You have," he said, "and you have shared it many times. Let's share it again." He tried to reinstate their love wrestle but she held him still and with a firmness that gave the gravity her message required. He eased back. "What is it?"

She held and stretched a silence and then said, "Campion."

He thought. She could see his mind whirling behind the deadness in his eyes that she found inexplicably beguiling. She felt sure others, especially other women, must be chilled by his eyes, but for some reason she found them exciting. They hid a unique danger and she found that threat exhilarating, perhaps because she had faced it and survived it. The thought she had put in his head paralysed him, and once he had completed it he sank into a relaxed yet charged readiness.

"Campion?"

"Campion. I know where he is."

"Where?"

"What's he worth?"

Eliot took a moment to consider his answer. "Whatever you want. If you can deliver."

"I always deliver."

He didn't smile. "You are sure you have him?"

"I know where he was yesterday, I expect that he is still there today and perhaps will be there tomorrow."

"I don't believe you."

Frances unhooked the buttons on the front of her doublet, reached in towards her bosom and drew out the document she had sold to Philip Gyfford. She handed it to Eliot. He read a few dozen words then leaped for the bedroom door, swung it open and yelled down the stairs "Rondel!" He sank back against the door jamb. "Rondel! Rondel!"

Frances got off the bed, strode over to Eliot, pulled him inside the room, shut the door and leaned him against it.

"Campion is not for sale, George. Campion is for sharing. Half and half."

"Third."

"Half."

"Not possible."

"Why not?"

Footsteps on the stairs. The door behind Eliot moved. A voice. "George?"

"James."

"James?" asked Frances.

Eliot moved Frances to one side and opened the door. "Mr James Rondel. Frances Thursby."

Rondel was a sturdy and slightly under-proportioned young man. A foot taller and he'd be an admired specimen with his curly blond hair. He was dressed as a gentleman though his leaf-green outfit was not in pristine repair. He smiled at Frances. "Ah, George has spoken of you."

"I'm sure he has."

"Delightful suit."

"Thank you."

"A finer looking gentleman I have not seen."

Frances cracked and then dismissed a smile.

Eliot rattled the paper in his hand and beckoned Rondel into the room. He closed the door. "She knows where he is."

"Who?"

"Campion." He passed the paper to Rondel, then spoke to Frances. "We've been on his trail but not been able to find him. We know he is somewhere in Warwickshire."

"That's true," said Frances.

"She wants half," Eliot told Rondel.

"Half of what?"

"He has a point. We are doing this for our country."

Frances looked at Eliot and matched the stare he was able to give her. "You're doing it to stay alive. I know your history Mr George Eliot. But don't tell me there will not be a reward in this. Turn Campion in and the favours will follow - and a great reward. Half must come to me."

"It has to be thirds. James is our key. Mr Campion and his kind will trust Mr Rondel."

"I'm not interested in thirds," said Rondel. "Do what you like with your part George, but my half is all mine."

"Ah," said Frances turning two steps of a merry dance across the room. "So this honorary reward is already halved. Well two halves of nothing is nothing. I have the whole. And I know where I can sell it. So I'll wish you good day."

She made for the door. Rondel did not move aside but grabbed Frances and turned her arm behind her back. "You've nothing to sell my new friend, and everything to give."

Eliot shouted tersely. "James!"

"What?"

"Don't. She has friends in sharp places."

"Oh yes? Where?"

"Here." Eliot tapped the hilt of the dagger on his belt.

Rondel considered what to do but his consideration was cut short by Frances' heel which connected abruptly with his testicles. At the same time, she broke free of his grip and with one simple move drew her own dagger.

"Frances!"

She ignored Eliot and moved towards the crumpled gentleman, gently swaying the point of her weapon. "If I want half, Mr Rondel, I will take half of whatever I want."

Rondel found his own richly decorated knife and now there were three blades being brandished. Eliot took control. "Hold! Hold! Cutting each other will not help us to split the difference." He took the apple that the tapster had brought Frances and cut it into four. "One quarter each," he said. "And the last quarter we settle with dice. That way we have equal chance of having half."

Everyone seemed equally unhappy with the arrangement and so a truce and a tenuous deal were agreed. Knives were sheathed. Rondel sat awkwardly on the bed. Eliot ate four quarters of the apple. "So where is Campion?"

"Park Hall," she said. "Castle Bromwich."

"How far?" asked Rondel.

"Ten miles," said Eliot.

"We could be there by dark," said Rondel, still breathing carefully.

"And do what?"

"Well, first of all, find out if he is there."

"And if he is? We'd need an armed force and some authority if we were to take him."

"That's my meaning. First we have to know for sure. Once we have confidence there's any number of people we could turn to for force of arms."

"We'll not get near. And we'll certainly not get in. Our best bet is to catch him on the move. And move he will. But where to, and when?"

"We will get in," said Rondel suddenly much recovered. "There is someone who will vouch for me."

"Who?"

"He served my father for nigh on three years. He watched me grow up. Last I heard he was in the service of Edward Arden."

Frances was puzzled. Eliot read her face. "James is the knave in our pack," he explained. "His family are Catholics." He watched with dark pleasure as Frances solved the equation of the two men before her. "Birds of a feather," he mused, "turn together."

Someone downstairs laughed uproariously. Others joined in. Meanwhile in their room nothing was said, no one smiled. Low sunlight caught the dust in the air near the beam where the writing parcel had been. Frances knew the depravity of Eliot and now saw the wantonness of his accomplice. She despised his treachery but understood it. This new knowledge redefined the syndicate she had just joined, not changing it, but sharpening its profile. She was in cruel company. These were unpredictable men with flexible principles. There was added danger in what she was doing and that excited her.

Eliot looked out at the fading light. "If he's there they'll barricade the place at dusk and be doubly dubious of uninvited visitors."

"We'll have an invitation," said Rondel, "just as soon as I can speak to my man there. But you are right. Night is not the best time. Dawn. That's when the Mass will be, if they are to have one. They'll do it early and put him back on the road so that he can find another roof before dark. That's if he hasn't already moved on." He looked at Frances. "That's if he was ever there."

Frances picked up the document from the bed. "If

Campion wrote this, then yesterday morning he was at Park Hall." She folded the paper and put it in her saddle bag.

"I thought you were going to sell that to me," said Eliot.

"I might," she said. "When the time is right and the price is agreed."

Eliot kicked his boots off. "Well, at dawn we ride for Park Hall." He looked at Frances. She took his eyes. "James, good fellow," he said. "Go downstairs and have a brace of beers will you? And when you come back up, knock before you come in."

FOUR

In the catalogue

It was the second time that Will Shakespeare had heard Edmund
Campion preach. On both occasions he had been stunned,
enchanted and transported. Nevertheless, he wished he would
stop soon.

Campion had conducted the majority of the Mass and
had left his sermon until the end. This was a prudent move.
Lookouts were posted and would signal any distant sign of
trouble, the believers would disperse and priest, vestments and
sacred artefacts would be hidden. There were over a hundred
persons gathered by Will's estimate and he seriously doubted
that they would be able to convince any raiding official that they
were there for any other purpose than for conducting forbidden
rites. The inquisitors would not leave unsatisfied. They would
tear the house apart until they found the priest, who with his
host, and a good many of the guests, would face harsh
punishment. It would be unlikely that Will would escape
unscathed.

What amazed Will the most was that Father Campion,
by constant reference to the peril that they shared, demolished

that danger and made it a cause for celebration. He had the ability to speak to a crowd and make each individual feel that he was talking directly to them. The contact he made was resonant and singular. Will had never heard that quality of communication before. It moved him overwhelmingly and made him think.

"Each of you is a chalice," said the priest. "Each of you is a vessel. You all contain the precious blood. The vessel can be crushed. The vessel can be broken but the blood cannot be broken. The blood cannot be anything other than precious."

The congregation was silent. They were in the great hall. The morning was cool but the sun cut through the tall windows and with so many people in a relatively confined space, the air was growing uncomfortably heavy. No one complained. No one murmured. Everyone listened.

Will realised the enchantment came not just from the vocabulary that Campion used, but also from the delivery he employed. His eyes were seldom still, except when a phrase induced rapture. On such moments Edmund would stop speaking and stare as if he saw a saint, or the Virgin, or even Christ himself, there in the room, among them and aside from them. Consequently those immortals were there, with them.

"He will welcome all of us," said Edmund. "He will welcome you. He will congratulate you for preserving his precious blood."

Will corrected his thinking. It was not *as if* Campion saw Christ, he *actually* saw him. Will watched a man who could see God standing in the air just above Will's right shoulder. Will did not look for himself, for that felt somehow sacrilegious. He could see a man who could see God, and that made him feel immortal. The moment would pass. Campion was not yet beyond the human; he could only suffer the joy of rapture in small doses. Eventually he had to look away. He had to close his eyes. He had to recover. At that point the congregation would cough, shuffle in their chairs or redistribute their weight where they stood. Then the priest would speak again, and his eyes would be alive once more, sweeping around the room, finding the soul of every person, re-establishing contact, rebranding union with those same eyes that had just seen their supernatural saviour, eyes that had seen the smile of God.

It was with considerable relief but also with

disappointment that Will witnessed the service come to an end. The vestments and sacred objects were hidden and the room rearranged for its usual purpose. The family lingered and chatted while Father Campion went upstairs to hear confessions. Once Will realised that the number wanting to confess was very nearly the total number that had attended Mass, his pulse rate soared again. However, Edward Arden had been both benevolent and canny enough to lay on a breakfast for all, under the guise of a harvest gift to his estate workers. This idea was barely plausible, as the harvest was far from over yet and it was a Thursday, which was not normally a day for major celebrations, but Will considered the scheme preferable to simply having everyone milling about aimlessly if trouble came. He normally wouldn't be so pessimistic but the encounter they had had with the woodsmen played heavily on his mind.

There were three or four neighbouring families of note that had made the dawn journey from their own homes. The majority of the remainder were in the service of the Ardens either in the house or on the estate. Hugh the gardener was there and Will scanned carefully in search of the woodsmen they had encountered on their way there, not really expecting to see them, but hoping he might because that may negate the danger that he imagined they posed. Most of those there were comfortable within the company of the others but there were just a handful of persons with whom the host family was unfamiliar. They had, of course, been carefully challenged on arrival, and their answers must have satisfied Edward Arden's staff or they would not have been admitted.

One figure in particular troubled Will. He was a dapper gentleman. Obviously a man of some means and good taste, he sported clothes that seemed new and well-cared for. He wore a black hat, cape and doublet, and his trunkhose were slashed with slices of contrasting grey matching his stockings. His shoes were buckled. The reason he had caught Will's attention was because he had noticed his arrival. Hugh had been summoned to vouch not for him, but for his companion who was similarly attired, though not quite as finely, and in green and brown. Both these men sported fashionable knives upon their girdles, each was elaborately decorated, though Will thought the second man's dagger was the finer. This person was known to Hugh, they recognised each other and spoke warmly, though with due deference on Hugh's part. This pair of visitors did not go to confession but went straight to the breakfast that was spread in the great hall once the Mass was over. Will sought out Hugh and found him modestly attempting to be inconspicuous towards one corner of the hall, neither eating nor drinking. Will was munching on a game pasty.

"Not eating Hugh?"

"I'll confess first," said the gardener. "There's more space in the stomach once you've emptied the soul."

Will sniggered and chewed. "I must admit; I will digest more easily once all these people have gone."

"Some will stay the day," said Hugh.

Will nodded. That thought did not bother him. He turned, putting the man in black and grey behind his left shoulder as he faced Hugh. He used the pasty in his hand to surreptitiously direct Hugh's gaze. "Who's the grey-stockinged fellow?"

"Mr Eliot," said Hugh.

"And who is Mr Eliot?"

"A friend of Mr Rondel."

"Mr Rondel?"

"I worked on his father's farm. Gloucester."

Will casually turned back letting his gaze sweep the room so as not to draw attention to the principal focus. "And Mr Eliot is an Arden man?"

"Not by birth. He's staying in Solihull."

"How far is Solihull?"

"Ten miles."

"They set out early."

"Wouldn't you, to hear Father Campion?"

Will decided that he would. "How did they know he was here?"

"Word was passed."

"Widely?"

"Not widely, young sir. Selectively." Hugh shuffled a little uncomfortably. "If you'd be so kind Master Will, I'll join the confession queue."

"Of course."

Will stood aside. Hugh went upstairs. Will contemplated as he worked on finishing his pasty. When he looked up Eliot and Rondel were coming towards him.

Rondel had a curious smile, half gracious, half condescending. "Young Master Arden, we believe?"

Will did not correct him, after all he was not completely incorrect.

"I am of that family."

Eliot dabbed his lips with his kerchief and ran his tongue round his teeth. "Auspicious family," he said.

It was not the word that Will would have chosen. "We take pride in our heritage," he said, feeling suddenly elevated to speak on behalf of the Arden fraternity.

"And so you should," said Eliot.

"Shackled by the times," said Rondel.

"Not so much by the times as by the clock makers," said Will.

Rondel and Eliot shared a patronising smirk of approval.

Rondel asked, "What did you make of Father Campion's address?"

"I've heard him speak before," said Will.

"I was enthralled," said Eliot.

"Mmm," said Rondel.

"How did you know he was here?" asked Will.

"Hugh," said Rondel.

"Hugh?" said Will.

"Hugh Hall. The gardener."

"He sent word?"

Eliot cut in. "Word was sent. We knew father Campion was due."

"You were delayed," smiled Rondel.

"Only a day," said Will. "Hardly a delay."

"Precious cargo," said Rondel. His smile stretched but somehow failed to activate the muscles round his eyes. He took the liberty of grasping Will by the nearest shoulder. "William . . . isn't it?"

"Will."

"Will. I'm sure you'll get you to your next destination on time."

"I'm grateful for your confidence."

"Where are you headed next?"

Will drew breath to reply, but he was prevented by an interjection. It was Simon Sedlow.

"Gentlemen, just to advise you that Father Campion is hearing confessions for just a short while longer, if you'd care to take your place in the line."

The compatriots hesitated, with each seemingly waiting for the other to reply. Eventually Rondel spoke. "We'll take our places."

"Good," said Simon. The pair bowed and withdrew.

"Mr Sedlow," said Will, "I wondered where you were."

"I've been watching from the gallery," said Simon. His face was set with concern.

"Wonderful sermon," said Will.

"Get your things together," said Simon, "I think it will be best if Father Campion moves on soon. Sooner than we intended."

"Very well," said Will and started to finish his drink. "Easy, my young friend. Be all urgency but promote lethargy. Take your time, but be ready to go at a moment's notice on my sign. The problem is Father Campion is too good a priest. He will want to hear everybody. If he's not careful he'll extend his ministry and truncate his liberty."

Only now did Will see the depth of concern in the lines on Simon's brow. It reawakened the foreboding he had felt during the Mass, and that realisation heartened him. His instincts were in tune with those of Simon Sedlow, someone he admired. Perhaps he was the right person to accompany Campion after all. However, he was also wise enough to realise how foolish he would have been had Simon not interrupted him, a point that Sedlow now reinforced.

"Note, Will, that these people are welcome to the ministry they receive here and now, they are not welcome to know of Father's future whereabouts, no matter how god-fearing they may appear to be." He looked into will's pupils with a penetration that was at once both reprimand and encouragement.

Will smiled and took both meanings to heart.

"Now," said Simon, "I must speak with Hugh, the gardener."

The confessions went on into the afternoon. Only then did Edmund Campion eat. He remained in keen demand with Edward Arden's higher status visitors wanting to converse and hear more wisdom. Campion was eager to oblige but his host was considerate and escorted him to rest in a bedchamber before tactfully encouraging his guests to consider making their way home. Will was standing by to depart at any instant, but Campion refused to be hurried. Will became more uncomfortable. To make matters worse he noted that Edward Arden was at odds with Simon Sedlow. Despite the danger, their host wanted to make the most of his chance to harbour the celebrated cleric.

It had always been part of the plan to travel by lesser known routes, but they would also have to use major roads and ways. When in transit Campion would revert to a previous alias as a merchant, and Will would be his apprentice. The wealthier householders would furnish Campion accordingly. This was not difficult for Edward Arden as he and Campion were of a similar build. The priest was therefore kitted out in Kendal green. Will was given a slightly newer cape than the one he had brought. It was black, a little heavier than his own, and to his irritation, a good match with the one Eliot wore, though his was of a far finer weave and finish.

The decision was taken not to risk another night at Park Hall, so they left in the mid-afternoon and travelled just a few miles to a lodge on the estate where a tenant who had been to the Mass gave cramped accommodation to all four travellers. Edward Arden provided two horses which, along with Simon's mount, had been ridden to the lodge by two of his servants and an openly belligerent Allen, whilst the party of Will, Campion and Simon had slipped out from the garden and made their way by a separate route on foot. By this means it was hoped that anyone observing the Hall would take little note of the departure of the horses and miss completely the exit of the principal players. The lodge was a stark contrast to the luxury Will had briefly enjoyed at Park Hall, but it was only for a few hours, as they rose and were on their way before sunrise.

So it was that the Friday morning saw two well-dressed gentlemen and a boy trot through the low-lying dawn mist heading for the north road. The way through the woods was narrow and so enforced single-file riding. This suited Campion who said he would absorb himself in prayer as he rode. Will was assigned to bring up the rear and told to scan behind frequently and alert the others at any hint of the presence of strangers. Once they found the road, riding abreast became possible, but

Campion still insisted on spiritual diversion, riding a few lengths behind Simon while Will retained his position at the rear. From time to time half-lines of Latin would float to him as the flat melody of a monotone plainchant.

And so they continued all of that day. They met no one during the morning. They dismounted about noon to divide the loaf Edward Arden had given them and drink from a river. Campion declined his share of the bread. In the afternoon they encountered other travellers, but all were going south and keen to keep moving. Simple pleasantries were exchanged, but no questions were asked. They mostly walked their mounts, only seldom rising to a trot. By late afternoon they were close to the edge of the Forest of Arden and, at a crossing point, Simon took them off the northern route and led them down a lesser-used way for a mile or more. They came to the house of a yeoman farmer where a simple message from Edward Arden ensured an instant welcome.

As they were settled and food was being brought to the table Simon leaned close to Will and whispered to him. "I must return to Stratford in the morning. Your host will take you to the next house. Soon you will leave Warwickshire and so to Shropshire, Cheshire and Lancashire. It may be a long time before we meet again Will. When we do, I expect that you will be ordained."

Will thought that he may even be resurrected. God knew what must transpire for him in the meantime. He would pray. God would grant him courage, of that he had no doubt. Well, only a small one.

Giles Colby was the yeoman farmer in whose house they spent the night. They rode out with him at dawn. He guided them over his meadows and through his woods to a quiet path between two field boundaries. Their road ran straight as a carpenter's rule and slightly uphill into a lingering morning fog. It was all wondrous to Will who was much further from home than he had ever been.

Simon Sedlow had left them at dawn. With Simon and Allen gone Will was now free of all ties with his home town save those he held in his memory. With no certainty that he would ever return he felt the pangs of severance much more intently than he had when setting out from Henley Street a week earlier. Then he was buoyed by an effervescent sense of purpose. Now he was enclosed by a pale fog and had no clear vision of what lay ahead.

Eventually, the sun rose sufficiently high to lift the moisture and reform it as wispy clouds high above their heads. About the same time, the track they had been following reached the brow of the pasture land. Looking back, they could just see the farmstead where they had spent the night and at the same time realised that they were blatantly exposed and hence they quickly made their way down the far side of the hill towards a place where the path forked. Instinct told Will to take the left route, because it led more quickly into an area of cover, their guide, however, took the more exposed route. Will cast his eyes right around the panorama, relishing this new image of England. Suddenly a small movement caught his attention.

Behind them, perhaps a mile or more away, three riders were following at speed.

FIVE

Sweetest bud

Frances Thursby knew exactly how conception worked. It had never worked with her and she rode that luck, or more likely that curse. It wasn't the first time she had taken George Eliot's seed inside her and she doubted it would be the last. She hoped it was just his seed and not his child. She didn't want any child, but only God knew what Eliot's child would be like. Frances didn't devote much time to God. A tiny part of her asked if God would approve of the work she was now doing, but she quickly reasoned that God's approval seemed to manifest itself in very unpleasant ways, judging by the executions she had seen. She didn't seek God's approval but now sought instead his so-called servant, and in that respect she was doing very well.

It was she who had woken the others well before dawn on the day of Campion's service at Park Hall. She awoke unusually hot and took a moment to realise that it was because there was another body next to hers. She rose and dressed and drank small beer whilst checking the signs in the sky. At the first hint of greyness she roused Eliot and then Rondel. Neither was keen to shake off sleep but she made them. Once he realised where he was and with whom, Eliot tried to pull her back into bed, but she would have none of it.

"Get up!" she urged.

She knew that any activity at Park Hall was likely to be early in the day and they had ten miles to cover which would take an hour or more. They bribed the gatekeeper at Solihull to let them out even before sunrise so they had a head start and arrived at Park Hall with exhausted steeds just as the last of the locals were getting there. Realising immediately what was afoot a small amount of crafty chatter gleaned the necessary confirmation.

"Hurry on my friend," Rondel called down to an elderly man and his wife.

"We'll be there soon enough."

"How blessed we are," declared Rondel.

"That's the truth," the man said.

Rondel tipped his hat in a way that acknowledged the old man and sent a prearranged signal to Frances watching further up the road on the edge of the woods. She took a path that by-passed the entrance to the Hall walking her horse nonchalantly in the direction of Birmingham. Meanwhile she saw her companions challenged at the gate and made to wait while Hugh the gardener, who was known to Rondel, was summoned. Once out of sight of the hall she waited to see if her associates would re-join her but they didn't which meant they had either been apprehended or admitted. She tethered her horse a short distance away, so that even if he was discovered she might still evade detection. Then she settled down to chew on grass stalks and watch the tightly shut doors of Park Hall.

Nothing happened for a long time.

Eventually the gates opened and a small amount of activity was evident but very few people left during the morning. Around noon the flow increased and Frances came to the conclusion that the gathering had consisted largely of those who lived and worked within the confines of the immediate estate. She took closer note however when parties of relatively well-attired visitors rode out. Any one of those groups may have contained her quarry for all she knew, and she wasn't foolish enough to think that Campion might be dressed precisely as had been described by the forester from whom she had purchased the document.

Suddenly her instinctive predatory aptitude kicked into

life. It was a trio of horsemen. They were clearly servant class and her equestrian experience told her that they were most likely riding unfamiliar mounts. It was a gamble, but her instincts were seldom wrong. She quickly recovered her own horse and followed them carefully and at a distance.

They did not travel far and it was not hard for her to keep mostly out of sight around bends or in dips in the lane whilst still keeping track of their progress. They came to a small timber-framed farmhouse, handed over their horses and went inside. Frances took to cover again and waited. Only an hour or so later three men walked into view from the far side of the house and Frances felt a surge of satisfaction. She knew that she had her first sight of Edmund Campion. With him was a youth as described by the forester except that he was wearing new clothes. She didn't know who the third person was, and she didn't care. This was her prey.

That night she slept rough. Fortunately, the weather remained dry, but the air turned cold and she became numb with pain in her fingers and feet. She had nothing to eat, was low on small beer, and did little more than snooze intermittently, but in the morning she was rewarded with the sight of the three men who had arrived on foot, leaving on the horses that she had followed to that place. Her instincts once again had won the reward, but now she had a stiffer challenge. This threesome would undoubtedly be more careful than their lackeys had been. If they saw her they might bolt, or worse confront her. One might be saintly, and the boy a novice religious, but who knew to what the third man might resort in their defence. She was hungry and weary and yet could not risk undoing all the good she had done by letting them go. Somehow she had to get word out to Rondel and Eliot, and there would be no point doing that if she lost Campion. She had to surreptitiously trail her prize.

She wondered if Eliot and Rondel were making any attempts to trace her. It would be unlikely that they would have any clear idea which routes to explore, and knowing Eliot's temperament, she had no doubt he would be angry that she had not done as agreed and held her position overlooking Park Hall to report on what she had seen. She didn't care. She enjoyed making him angry.

Towards the end of the afternoon the road came to a minor crossing of ways and here the soil was deeply pummelled and she was worried that she had lost the hoof prints she had been following, but she found their pattern leading off down a small lane that led eventually to a farmhouse. Once again her instincts told her to be cautious, and the moment that she saw the property she moved out of sight and then tried to assess if this was their destination for the day. After a short while, she caught sight of three horses being turned out in the paddock behind the farm and she knew for certain that their riders were inside. She did not fancy another night sleeping under the stars and wondered if instead she should ride through the darkness and try to rendezvous with Eliot. Either way sleep did not seem to be scheduled, and she was exhausted. She sat on the floor at the foot of a hornbeam tree and closed her eyes to clarify her thoughts and the decision was made for her because when she opened them again, the atmosphere was sapphire blue, the moon was up and Jake had wandered off.

It didn't take her long to find him. He had wandered through the trees to a neglected field with a broken gate and was happily grazing. Close to the gate was a dilapidated shack. It may have been a small dwelling once but the cloven-printed ground told of more recent use as an animal shelter. It had no door, and one small window, but the roof was in good repair and there was hay piled in the corner. She recovered Jake and with a little encouragement brought him inside and watched enviously as he chewed on the hay. She made a bed in the straw, lay down and slept.

She was awakened intermittently by Jake stomping or snorting but managed to get sufficient rest to recharge he mind, though she was chilled and hungry. She chewed and old crust from the saddlebag and wriggled life back into her limbs. She took Jake out just before first light, then recovered her position a reasonable distance from the farm, to watch for the priest to appear.

Almost immediately there was activity in the yard. A rider emerged and trotted up the road towards her. The sound of his approach unsettled Jake and he whinnied.

"Shh!" she spat.

The light was too poor for her to determine clearly who the person was, but the closer he came the more convinced was she that it was one of the three that she had trailed the day before. He rode straight past, his horse slowing to a walk as it encountered the more awkward and narrower twists of the lane as it rose towards the main route. Even at that pace it was only moments before he was gone from sight and she was left in some doubt as to if it had been the person that she suspected.

She settled to watch the farm again. It came to life only slowly with women opening the hen houses, feeding dogs, bringing wood and swilling out piss pots. Smoke from the stacks grew in volume and thickened. Shouts went up. Coughing was heard. Labourers set out for the fields. She heard more shouts from the direction of the orchard and imagined and feared what might be being said, but it all came to nothing so she was probably wrong. She could smell cooking.

As the light grew, so a mist rose and her view became less clear. This gave her a dilemma. If she moved closer she risked detection, but if she stayed put she might miss the departure of her target. Of course she could not know whether or not he would depart that day. He might stay there for several nights. If he was going to move on this day he would surely do so soon, so she needed to see the gate. She would have to move. She turned to return to Jake and found her path blocked by the man she had watched ride past.

For a moment neither he nor she moved or made any sound, then he spoke to her.

"So, sir. What would your business be?" His sword was drawn but he held it casually.

"To find my bearings," said Frances.

He paused, then said, "At this hour?"

"Is there an appointed time in which to become lost?"

"Where is your company?" He paused again. "Sir?"

"My horse is over there."

"He is your company?"

"I need no other."

The man extended his longest wait yet, and then said, "You're not a 'sir' are you?"

"I am what you see."

"A woman, dressed as a man, alone in the night."

"I think you'll find that day has broken."

"Watching." He tapped the tip of his sword against the toe of his boot. "Spying."

"And who are you?" She leaned against a tree to feign confidence. "Sir?"

"What business is that of yours?"

"A friend of those in the house?"

"Let's go and ask them."

Frances drew her left arm close to her doublet to mask the position of her dagger. "I was going to seek their charity," she said. "To put me wise and guide me on my way."

"I'll introduce you," he said easing to one side but keeping his downturned sword to his fore.

"Why, thank you." She bowed slightly, then beamed a killer smile at him. Her charm caught him unawares and she saw the pleasant startle in his eyes. He smiled back, his instinctive response suppressing the threat in his gaze. She drew close surreptitiously as if simply veering in the motion of passing before him, then she slowed and almost stopped. "I think I know you," she said and leaned closer.

He looked unsettled and puzzled and jolted into alertness, but it was too late. Her blade was in his belly. Then it was out; then in again through woollen cloak, the fine fabric and horsehair padding of his doublet, his shirt, undershirt, skin, and between two ribs, to puncture his lung.

SIX

Self-mettle

Will gave the shout. "Ahoy!" he called. "Three in pursuit!" And he kicked his steed into action, rising to a gallop and passing his companions while they were still looking back. Fortunately, the track opened out ahead and an obvious escape route presented itself. Will felt proud at seeing the opportunity and yelled to the others, "This way!" He looked over his shoulder to find they were hardly moving, their confused horses jostling and stomping as the hunting trio drew nearer. He was puzzled, but his mount had risen to the gallop and he was concentrating hard on keeping in the saddle and guiding the horse around hazardous depressions in the ground. He couldn't decide whether to pull up, or curve back towards his friends or to keep at full pelt for the thicker woods ahead and seek safety there. Self-preservation won the day and he pounded on.

As soon as he was under dense cover he slowed right down then stopped and turned his horse to look back across the glade. To his horror, he saw that Campion and Colby were already surrounded having hardly moved from the point where he had left them. He could see now that there were many more than three in the pursuing party. There were at least half a dozen circling them, with some looking in his direction, and two more cutting wide arcs around the glade as if to pincer him. There was no plain path for him to follow. He broke into an instant sweat and to his dismay realised that this was a sickness from the belly of blind fear. Where was the calm courage of the legendary warrior? Where was the firm resolution of the hero? Why was he not brave? Why hadn't he stayed and defended his compatriot? Why hadn't he grabbed the bridle of Campion's horse and taken it with his, to a place of greater safety? Why wasn't he even now fighting a rear guard action, cutting down his champion's captors and liberating God's lieutenant? Instead his knees and ankles prodded and jabbed a reluctant horse while he pulled her mouth this way and that. He made no worthwhile progress through the woods that were every bit as dense as they had looked when he had craved their cover. Soon he was aware of other riders close by. One skirted the edge of the woodland, the other was already within it. His cowardice found new audacity and he slipped from the saddle and took to weaving away on foot.

His imagination raced ahead of him, picturing his adversary, duplicating him, trebling him and meeting that trio face on, swords unsheathed and with their scruples suspended as they savaged into him. But he was low, the cover was close, and on foot he had both flexibility and speed, until he ran into thorn-ridden shrubs, cutting his face and snagging his fine clothes. A small struggle made him free and he ran again.

In the end he was captured not by hands or blades or impenetrable undergrowth but by words.

"Master Will!" "Master Will, wait! Wait!"

It was not the meaning that he trusted but the tone. He broke cover and stood where a shaft of sun, shining like God's blessing, burned through the branches above to make a halo a few feet from him.

A rider, still in his saddle, stood his charger before him. "Master Will, Father Campion is needed back at Colby farm. And so are you."

Will recognised the man as someone he had seen at the farmhouse the night before. His slight smile was kindly, but it baptised Will in a Jordan of shame.

Simon Sedlow was lying on the board that formed the table on the trestles in the centre of the hall at Colby Farm. A cushion had been placed beneath his head, his cloak and doublet lay in a pile on the floor, and he had been bandaged with bed sheets. A blanket was over him but one arm was laid over the top to meet the hand of Edmund Campion.

It was the table at which Will had eaten the night before, and at breakfast only a few hours earlier. Now the meat was warmer, but only just. Simon had a pallor that said death had already taken up residence and was simply waiting impatiently for life to vacate the body. Blood had been cleaned from the floor and the board, but despite rigorous padding and binding, more was seeping from beneath him. He strained for every breath but the effort that he made was feeble and his attempts to breathe were separated by longer and longer gaps. He was not responding to the quiet voices of those gathered around him. Campion gripped his hand and quietly incanted a Latin litany. The dozen in the room waited for him to render up his spirit whilst harmonising with Campion's sentiments that Simon should live on either in this world, or the next.

No one spoke above a whisper. Movement within and without was muted. Occasionally ignorant animals would proclaim their indifference from a distance, but even those sounds seemed to have a unique timbre as each one may be the last of their kind that Simon might perceive.

Campion did not look at the subject of his prayers. His eyes were closed and it was as if he existed in the veil of a trance that was mid-way between England and the realm of those who were pure soul.

Will felt an urge to shift the pillow from under Simon's head, place it over his face and gently smother the life from him. This was not because he wished the man any ill, quite the contrary. He hardly knew him, but liked him immensely. He found him generous, gracious, god-fearing and genial. He didn't like to see him strain for life so arduously when it was clear that no hope of survival was left. Everyone could see this, including Campion, who prayed for the swift acceptance of Simon's soul into the glorious heavenly throng. Eventually, it was almost as if Simon simply neglected to take the next breath, and thus the next breath was never taken.

It was not the first death Will had seen and it would

not be the last.

All in the room knelt and more came from the kitchen and the yard and this impromptu choir joined with the priest in a ceremony for the soul of Simon Sedlow. And so the Colby household had gone from alarm, to panic, to prayer, to vigil and then to prayer again. Once that was done the women and the labourers went back reverently to their tasks while their seniors moved on to hushed but frenetic planning. A pair of riders was to be dispatched to take the news to Stratford, but Colby ordered that this must wait until the next day as he needed the manpower at home until then. Simon's body was removed into a parlour and the board on which he had bled his last was rigorously cleaned. It was decided that Campion must return to his journey but Giles Colby was rattled, and insisted that the next phase must now be taken under cover of night. It was too late in the day for the party to reach the next safe house before nightfall and the killing of Sedlow had shown that they were under surveillance.

Will was told that a farm labourer had discovered Simon sprawled on the track leading to the gate. He had heard his calls from within the morning mist and had seen no sign of the assailant, who by that time must have been well gone. Simon had said one thing: "She was a spy." He had said this several times in the hearing of the other labourers who came from the farm in response to their colleague's call. He had been taken straight into the yeoman's house while riders were sent to to bring Campion back.

Giles Colby feared the worst, that Father Campion was being trailed and that he was now implicated in his protection. Giles was steady and wise, however. He knew that night travel was both the safest and the most dangerous of all. He would lead a party of eight men in addition to Edmund and Will. He would arm them all. Campion protested that this was too much fuss, but he acquiesced. The priest was profoundly moved by the death he had witnessed, knowing that it was he who had caused it to happen.

Colby's wife, daughters and servants saw to it that a fortifying dinner was given to all towards the end of the day. Will perceived a mood of adventure as misfortune turned to resilience in the face of shared danger. The small impromptu escort troop was bonded by nothing more than a shared sense of purpose. It was a conspiracy of kindness and he was part of it. They left two hours after sunset.

Will's embarrassment returned as soon as they rode clear of the farm, after all they were retracing the path they had taken that morning and very soon reached the point where he had misread the movement of Colby's men who had set out to bring news of the attack on Sedlow. Will felt ashamed. Apart from his foolishness, the moment had called for maturity and bravery and he had only displayed childish fright. In that respect he was his own prime witness and from that moment Will felt he had become two people, and one was detailed to spend his life spying on the other. He was a traitor unto himself.

Colby insisted that the party would go the whole way to their charges' next destination. The company fell quiet but they were far from silent, and the drumming of their horses' feet would send a signal as to the size of their party. All but two of them were armed with swords and the light percussion of that metal gave a reassuring high note to the symphony of their motion.

The moon was up, and in the middle of the night they came upon a sight both magical and diabolical.

It had not been a major monastery, but with the moon being low in the sky, the silver shadows accentuated the thickness of the stone of the chapel walls and swelled the bulk of the pillars, deepened the arches, and redefined the symmetry and tranquillity of the cloister. Fifty years had passed since the property had been raped as part of King Henry's purge. The monastery itself was more pitiable precisely because it retained the trappings of its former grandeur. It had a presence that proclaimed pride, pious devotion and penitence. Every shape spoke of prayer. Doorways, window gaps, and even the broken masonry were reminiscent of hands joined in praise, in supplication, in apology, in atonement. Now pagan nature had reclaimed the site. The walls were clad in creeper, the pillars were purple-veined in moon-coloured ivy, and young trees, already mature, spread their own panes into and through the places where sacred stories had been illuminated by stained glass.

The party stopped. Campion was silent. He stared at the wreck of the church and his entourage gathered around him. No one felt compelled to speak and it was as if their silence was both commentary and communion. Will attuned to the mood effortlessly. The combination of place, people and education infected his senses. Their horses stomped and jangled their tack as they bowed their heads not in prayer but in attempts to graze.

Will had been told at length of the sacking of the great religious houses by King Henry and now he could see for himself the consequences, though he could only imagine the human suffering that had accompanied the pillaging. Much greater pain came from the knowledge that the sight before him was not a monument to the past but a memorial of the carnage yet to come. He had picked his place in that pain.

Will could be a custodian of God's own grace. As Campion had said in his sermon, he could be a chalice of precocious blood. He could secure souls for God. He felt sure that that was the reason that God had given him such a gift for the understanding, application and invention of words. He had enchanted himself with the adroitness of language that had blossomed during his adolescence. His schoolmaster had heard it, acknowledged it and fostered it, and at the same time the teacher, by nurturing both sapling and gardener, had grafted the wood to the carpenter. They were nailed together with growing thorns.

Colby was respectful but his patience was not without boundaries. They still had a good distance to go, and he was mindful that, despite being derelict, the ruin lay on a well-used highway. This was not a place to linger. He spoke to Campion and the priest made a prayer in Latin and then traced a yard-long sign of the cross in the air to bless the site. His escorts tunefully murmured their amen and all took to the road again.

A tawny owl and his wife negotiated across an acre.

Some of Colby's men were becoming unsettled. They had ridden further and longer than they anticipated, and as the night curved towards dawn the chance of detection grew slightly stronger, so the combination of weariness and apprehension tempered their enthusiasm. Wit withered into muted whinging. Their horses too, were starting to tire, and where beast and rider were of a similar disposition their shared attitude became blatant. Each protested in their way and curses found their reply in shaken bridles, tossed snouts and snorts of indignation. Their train became stretched and fragmented. Colby swore openly and loudly at them. Way ahead, Campion was upright in his saddle, an effigy of effort.

Colby's determination paid off. The sky brightened and day was on the verge of breaking as their destination came into view. Everyone was greatly relieved, with the exception of Campion who retained his air of detached devotion and presented an expression of indifferent pleasure when their target house was spotted. Colby's men were much more demonstrative. Some sighed with relief, others swore their gratitude. Will allowed himself the luxury of echoing the sighs audibly and the swearing inaudibly. He longed for refreshment and a chance to grab some sleep.

It was a pity, then, that the householder refused to admit them.

SEVEN

Single spies

Frances Thursby had not knowingly killed anyone. She still hadn't. She suspected that the man she left in the mist-cloaked woods would by now be dead, but she had no way of being sure. Not knowing that he was dead was the same in her mind as not having killed him. If he died when she was not there, then how could she have killed him?

She could not waste time wrestling with guilt. Her immediate priority was to put a mile of mist between herself and her victim. This meant retracing her steps, for riding past the farm was not an option. Once she estimated that she had covered a safe distance she reduced Jake to a walk and considered her alternatives. She had now lost her point of vantage on the person she presumed to be Campion. She swore at that. His general course seemed to be north and even to Frances' ill-informed mind that looked to make sense, because the north had a reputation for a much stronger Catholic allegiance than England's heartland held. So what? She could not scour the northern counties on the chance that she might cross his trail, and the land there was reputed to be a wilderness. She had never ventured further north than Staffordshire.

Another factor was that she was weakened. She had

been on the road for two days, managed mostly only short sleeps, and been nourished by a limited diet. Her desperate encounter with her victim had been fuelled from her animal reserves but now, as the rush of heightened awareness subsided, she felt both nauseous and weak. By far the most tempting prospect for her now was simply to abandon this task and put it all down to misfortune, but she had once been told that she would make her own misfortune, and she had decided that if that were true, then she would make misfortune and give it to others. Resurrecting that prophesy prompted a plan. There was something positive, though awkward, that she could do, and that was what she did.

Philip Gyfford could not disguise his anger, but moderated it with his expectation.

"I turned the place upside down," he said. "In case you'd put it out of sight. It's not a paper that can stand sudden discovery by unscrupulous people."

Frances knew he was lying so she lied in reply. "I was half way to Castle Bromwich before I realised I had it on me."

"I don't believe that," he said. "You took it and sold it again."

"Then how come I have it with me now? "She pulled the paper from within her shirt. "I've brought it back to you."

"Took your time."

"I had him Philip. I have seen your Jesuit spy."

Philip put his armchair against the door of his parlour and sat in it. He hoped his vacant lap would be invitation enough. "How do you know it was he?"

"I don't. I followed him for three days. He held some kind of court at Park Hall. People came and went, the place was set with watchers, the gates secure. When he left they set up a diversion, which I followed, and then I saw him myself when he met up with his horse."

"Describe him."

Frances swallowed some of the Rhenish wine that Philip had given her. She looked at his empty lap and kept her distance. "He's tall. Well-dressed."

"Is that all?"

"We were not introduced."

"Where was this?"

"Close to Park Hall."

"What then?"

"Two days later we were further north, near Watling Street, to the west of Lichfield."

"Then?"

She drank another mouthful. "I lost him. In the mist."

"Which way was he going?"

"He wasn't. He was in a farm house. Substantial. Yeoman at least I would say."

"In a mist?"

"A mist came down and before it lifted, they'd put men out. I was in danger. I was seen, but fled into the fog. I couldn't risk going back. I had to let him go."

"When?"

"This morning."

Philip eyed her. "West of Lichfield. On Watling Street."

"Not on it. Mile or two off it."

He ran his hand over his mostly bald pate. "Could be Colby," he said. "He's Catholic."

"Have you been to Sir Thomas Lucy?"

"What – and confess the robbery?" he said with a pointed look at the document she held.

"And confess the robber?" She teased.

Philip shrugged. Frances smiled, not in endearment, but smugly.

"I'll go tomorrow. Provided you leave the evidence."

Frances let the paper slip to the floor. "It's yours."

Philip let it lie, but not for long. When he rose to collect it, Frances slipped into the arm chair, the chair that only he as the head of house should occupy, the only chair with arms. She was the chairman and she enjoyed the elevation. He took the paper closer to the candle to ensure it was the correct one. "There's an implication here that they might establish a seminary."

"A what?"

"A school, for potential priests."

She thought about the suggestion. "That would be very dangerous," she said.

"Yes. It would."

He put the paper away, she didn't see where and she didn't care.

"Where will he go?" she asked.

"Anywhere. Who can say? North probably."

"Yorkshire?"

"He has that option. But there's nothing to stop him turning to any quarter." A draught from under the door lifted the debris of the heads of herbs sprinkled on the floor. She saw Philip watch them swirl as he turned his thoughts. He turned and leaned on the side board. "Do you want bread and mutton?"

She smiled.

He came to move the chair resting his hands upon its arms and trapping her in it. He kissed her at the corner of her mouth. She tolerated it for three flickers of the candle flame disturbed by his movement, and then she slipped her face away and eased him to one side so she could stand. He moved the chair and left the parlour to call for the food. She sat in an armless chair and turned over the latest perspective. A missionary and a school of priests. What price for that?

When he came back she said, "How can we find him?"

Philip replaced the armchair at the head of his table and sat in it. "You want this prize very much don't you?"

"Perhaps I will go to see Sir Thomas Lucy?"

"I don't think that would be a good idea."

"I'm sure you don't."

"He'd like the look of you, of that I have little doubt. And he'd relish your news, though . . . my . . . paper will please him even more. But as for finding the man; he would have no better idea than we."

"And what's your best idea?"

Philip blew a breath through rubbery lips. "If I were he, I would go north because it would give me a better chance of doing what I am sent to do without losing my skin. The man must have a death wish in him or he wouldn't be here at all, but he wants to prolong his liberty, otherwise his mission comes to nought."

"Who will know where he is?"

"Where he is, is no use to us. You have proved that. Because by the time we get there he is already gone."

"That's why we need to know where he is going. So

we can get there first," she said.

"Others may make those decisions for him."

"We can question those in the places where he has been."

Philip shifted his weight in the chair, sitting more awkwardly as if attempting to ease some inner discomfort. "Yes, well, Thomas Lucy knows all about questioning, but his methods may also prove pointless because whilst you can make people say whatever you want, that doesn't include making them tell what they do not know."

"Who will know?"

Philip adjusted his posture again and sighed as he thought. "Who was in his party?"

"It changed."

Philip snorted softly.

Frances went on, "But there was one constant. As the paper-seller reported. A boy."

"Ah yes. And how old? In your estimation."

Frances gave a slight shrug. "Fifteen? Too young to be his guide."

"And too young to have been trained as a Catholic spy. Which means it is unlikely he has come from abroad."

Frances' face briefly outshone the candle. "He's from Arden."

"What?"

"The forester said that the boy said he was related to the Ardens, through his mother."

"Well, it's a slim thread my dear, but it could be a silken one. If anyone knows where that boy is destined, it will be his family. Find an Arden who is no longer called Arden and if they've lost a boy, then they might know where he is, and hence where your reward lies."

A servant brought bread and cold mutton. Frances was very tired and felt doubly so after she had eaten. She knew where she would have a bed for the night and she both craved and detested the prospect. But at least as she did what she must, she would have something distracting to contemplate.

It took Philip Gyfford less than a day to discover the family connections of the Ardens. This was very good news for

Frances because it meant she only had to spend one night with him. Furthermore, he was able to equip her with some local knowledge and details of recent recusant activity in the area.

She used her usual ploy of travelling as a man. It was far easier for her to get a room at an inn when in that guise. And so she took up residence in Atwood's Tavern in High Street at Stratford. She implored the landlord's advice and from him she learned a great deal about where she might purchase good gloves and negotiate a deal for wool. A good price might be forced from one John Shakespeare, the landlord reported. He dealt in both commodities, and his fortunes were not as buoyant as they once had been.

It was also the landlord that unwittingly named the person she had knifed and in doing so stabbed her with the even sharper blade of culpability. All the talk was of a Stratford man called Simon Sedlow and how he had been killed by an unknown assailant miles to the north, near the edge of Arden forest. The gossip was rich in speculation because the facts were much clouded. His family were not saying why he was so far from home, but the rumours swarmed around possible secret activity. Many in the town were much moved by his loss, and several of them were known to have sympathies with the old faith, including John Shakespeare.

Frances soon got to know John. Presenting herself in her true gender, she purchased a pair of gloves and, despite his reservations at discussing a major commercial deal with a woman, she managed to persuade him that she was acting on behalf of her sick father and he invited her to sit at the table in the hall of his house on Henley Street. She slipped off the new gloves and put them on the table.

She quickly had John captivated. She knew how to snare any man. It was easily done. She looked deeply into his eyes, and let him look upon her where ever he chose. She let him catch her catching him, as he made his appraisal of her, and then she signalled that she did not mind. All the while they discussed the price of wool. The glover's workshop was from their sight but always in their ears and the odour of the stale urine used for the treatment of the leather was ever-present, though John's wife had done her best to cloak the smell with the scent from lavender besoms fastened to the walls. Martha came in with the beer. The younger children wandered back and forth, looking with strongly scrutinising stares, and uncertain how to relate to her. Joan, who was eleven and in rehearsal as an adult, stood rigidly upright by the door until a nod from John sent her out of sight, and six-year old Richard with his finger hooked into a semi toothless mouth, giggled and swung on his father's arm. John sent him running to find his mother with a playful slap on his behind.

Frances happily secured the conversation to the topic of families, and soon she knew the names of the entire household, including the one that John had not mentioned: William.

It was an accidental remark by six-year-old Richard that gave her the opening for which she was searching. A tiff was flaring in the parlour, most of which was muffled, but in response to his mother Richard shouted "Our William!"

"William?"

John hesitated a little, but seemed to know that there was no point in hiding what had been uncovered. "My eldest," he said. "He's gone to find his fortune."

"Can he not find it in wool?"

"Not at your prices."

They both laughed.

"Where is he looking?" she asked.

"We haven't heard."

"Yorkshire wool is weaving itself a reputation."

"Do you have any?"

"I may go and test the worth of it. I'll keep an eye out for your son. Is there a likeness?"

"More in soul than in face."

"Strong in faith then."

John's eyes flashed fear. She reassured him.

"Do not fret. I never let a man's conscience trouble the negotiation of business."

John shifted in his seat. "I am what I am."

"What else could you be? Except what you were. I've been told of your troubles. I know the reasons. They hold no weight with me."

There was a silence and she could tell that John was uncertain whether or not to question her. She played her next move. "The old ways are the best."

John was still hesitant so she played the card that

Gyfford had given her. "Shottery is close to here isn't it?"

"What of it?"

"I was told of Richard Debdale."

"We know the family."

"He's in London's Tower."

John nodded.

Frances whispered. She always found it best when she was lying. "I pray for him."

John's face lightened. "We all do."

"Not all."

The cloud returned. "No. Not all."

"I doubt it will ever be all again." She watched the reckoning wriggle across John's face. He was trying to work out whether or not he could trust her. She leaned forwards a little, softened her inflection and spoke slowly. "At least, not in this life. All we can do is hold firm. And to do that we need all the help that can be given by brave men."

John nodded but kept his counsel. She knew he was still uncertain. Gyfford had told her of how John, a man of measure in the town, had lost his prominence because he had been indicted for not adhering to the religious requirements. His customers had dwindled for fear of too close an association and he faced obstacles in the wool markets. The prospect of hardship was on the horizon and he was effectively under house arrest because to appear in a public place would leave him vulnerable to debtors' claims and prosecution. No wonder he had given his son to aid the cause so readily. That son was the beacon she sought. He would lead her to her prize, but she could see that John was not going to betray his son's whereabouts easily.

"They say Richard Debdale of Shottery gave certain items to John Cottam, the schoolmaster."

"He gave them to Thomas Cottam. John's brother."

"Ah," said Frances. "And what of this Thomas Cottam?"

"He too was arrested. Like Debdale, he'd been abroad."

"And taken to the Tower?"

"And taken to the Tower."

"And John Cottam?"

"What of him?"

"Can he stay the schoolmaster?"

"There's talk he may go back north."

Frances locked all the muscles in her face to prevent the glee she felt at this information. She made an interested sympathetic face encouraging John to talk on.

"He is a good schoolmaster. My son spoke well of him. When he . . ." John ran out of words.

"School fees are expensive," said Frances.

John nodded and shadows washed his face.

Frances was doing well, but all she had learned she already knew from Philip Gyfford and the landlord at the inn. She felt she was getting closer to that which she sought, but experience had told her that the prey is most easily scared away when the prospect of capture is closest. She must tread carefully, but did not know where best to place her feet.

Young Richard came running in to destroy her opportunity, but Martha was hot on his tail and she ushered him out.

"So can I interest you in Yorkshire wool?"

"I'd need to see it first."

"Well, I'm intending to go north next week. I'll see if I can bring you some back."

"You do that. Is there anything I can take for you? A few words for your son?"

"I doubt you will chance upon him."

"I'm willing to go out of my way."

"You won't find him in Yorkshire."

"Won't I?"

"No."

She waited for elaboration, but it didn't come. She considered a direct question but knew that might sound too persistent. She tried a different tack. "Well if I can't speak to him, I'll speak to heaven on his behalf."

"Thank you. We will pray for you."

Those prayers will be wasted she thought, but smiled and said, "Too kind."

"That you may find good wool at poor prices."

They laughed. Frances reached across the table and softly grasped John's rough hand. "Where can I find safe sanctuary in the north?"

John returned her touch by taking her hand in both of

his and for a moment she thought she might have hooked him, but after a long-drawn breath while he ordered his words, he said, "I have no knowledge of that part of the country." He let go of her hands. His movement signalled it was time for her to leave. She made deliberate joy apparent as she donned her new gloves.

She left John Shakespeare's house disappointed, but knew her next step. She strolled thoughtfully down Henley Street, and asked to be directed to the schoolhouse.

EIGHT

Infirm of purpose

Colby did his best to negotiate, but the porter was having none
of it. The master of the house was sent for but he refused to
appear. Instead the porter was joined at the high window by
other menfolk some of whom held staves in an unmistakeable, if
understated, threat. No mediation could be entertained. No
welcome was possible. The travellers must go on their way.

"Do you know who we are?" yelled Colby.

"Why do you think we won't admit you?"

"Does your master make this change of heart plain
before God?"

"Who says it is a change of heart?"

"Well it's a change of practice considering what I
witnessed here last year."

"You'll witness another kind of practice unless you get
on your way."

"These men have travelled . . ."

"Leave it Giles, leave it," said Campion quietly, then he
raised his voice. "We thank you for listening to our petition.
Offer your master my blessing."

"He will decline it."

"That is his choice. I will intercede for his soul."

"He'll take care of his own soul thank you."

Colby spoke too softly for the men above to hear. "He's already done that."

Campion had turned his horse and was riding away. The others followed.

Will held back and watched Colby as he grappled with a problem of such magnitude and immediacy that his face looked as if it would simply rupture. His men were so weary and worn that they were in open revolt. They were not prepared to ride on further, and they could not contemplate returning home without some rest and refreshment. They followed the track that traced the bank, moving a few hundred yards downstream until they reached a place where an arch of pebbles described the inner curve of a bend in the flow. They dismounted and let their horses graze and drink. Campion washed his face and dabbed it dry with the inside of his cloak. He came over to Colby.

"Where now?"

Colby shook his head. "The only place we could risk is another twenty miles."

Will filled the gap that followed. "How did they know we were coming?"

Colby shrugged, Will shivered, Campion drew a deep breath slowly.

"Let your men rest here. Then send them home by the most direct way. Give us the directions. We will go on alone."

Will saw his chance for redemption. "Tell the directions to me. I will remember them."

Colby ignored him and spoke to Campion. "I will not leave you unprotected."

Campion glanced upwards. "I am never without protection. I am always safe. My time for danger is already determined by he who decrees all. If it is now, it will be now. If it is not now, then it will come. Tell us the way to our destination, and then you can go home whenever you are ready."

Colby shook his head and nodded towards his unhappy men. "They'll stay with you or they'll have no home to return to. And that's what I'm just about to make clear to them."

Campion blocked his way. "No. I forbid that. Let me speak to them."

Will and Colby followed him as he went to join the escort party. Sensing Campion's approach, they shuffled and made nervous jokes, holding each other's attention with their eyes and not looking at him until they had to, and even then some kept their eyes on the river, or the pebbles at their feet.

"My friends," said Campion, "I want to thank you for your company and your protection. Do not think that I do not recognise what risk you have taken by seeing me safe to this place. I know your master gave you no option, but that does not diminish the courage you have shown. I do not count your bravery any less because you were compelled to come. You have done that which you were asked to do, and done so nobly. I will not forget it. I will send you home now with all my blessings and with the promise that I shall not fail to intercede for you with him that grants all freedoms, in the hope that he might jail you in his heart. Think not of us. We would not wish to be taken with any one of you who would not wish to be taken with us. Let me bless each of you in turn, then go with my love and in the knowledge that I will pray for you."

Then Campion went to each man in turn, spoke his name, and made a personal prayer in English and gave a blessing in Latin. After that they failed to regroup but each person claimed his own space by the river bank. Then Campion asked that Colby dictate the route to their next safe house to himself and Will. Colby refused. He dismissed his men and told them to take the most direct way home. He made no threats or conditions and stressed that they were without obligation, and they were to take the message that he had ridden on. Campion, Will and Colby mounted their horses and began the next phase of their journey. And, without exception, all of Colby's men rode with them.

No further complaints were made, and for some reason the day's ride was simpler, easier and merrier than the night-time trek had been. They were gentle with their horses. The animals were awkward, frequently noisy, and made slow progress but even they seemed to understand that the trudge must be endured. Everyone feared that the next house would present the same change of heart as the last one had, and that once again the door would be barred against them, but it wasn't. They were welcomed warmly, fed generously and bedded comfortably.

Will never forgot the effect of Campion's speech at the riverside. He marvelled at his technique. He noted the pace, pitch and timbre of his voice, the way in which he used his eyes and the firm gentleness of his touch as he embraced and blessed the men and grinned sincerely as he shook their hands. By dismissing them, he recruited them. By freeing them, he captured them. By empowering them, he harnessed their power.

Little ceremony was given to their first day at that place. They were given beds early and everyone slept soundly. By chance Will and Campion were the first to wake and they found each other by the fire in the hall where kept their conversation muted.

"You won them over, yesterday," Will said.

"Not I," said Campion. He raised his eyes to heaven. "Him."

"You took a risk, dismissing them."

Campion wrinkled his nose and twinkled his eyes. "Life is risk." He yawned, took a poker and provoked the fire. "Just knowing me puts you at risk."

Will knew the correct answer. "At risk of heaven."

"There's many paths to heaven Will. And they need not be this treacherous. Take the safest road is my counsel. Only go the dangerous way if you travel for others' sake."

"I travel for your sake."

"Oh no Will. Do not travel for me. I do not travel for me. If I were journeying just for me I'd be on that safe road, I warrant you. I do this for my lord and his flock. For them, Will. For them."

"Then I do it for them also."

"You're not yet of an age to make that vow, Will."

"Am I not?

"No, boy, no."

"And what age do I have to be to make such a choice?"

Campion put the poker back on the rack by the hearth. "Of an age when you can abandon all desire to see your next birthday."

"I am that age."

"No you are not. You are a good boy Will, but you fall short of being a man who knows his mind and is sure of the security of his soul."

Will saw memories in the smoke. "I know what things my father suffers and I know what my mother's family have suffered, and I've heard and seen things done that turn my Christian stomach."

"Exactly it, my boy, exactly so. You're driven by revenge Will, not by redemption."

"I want to be like you."

"My God, boy, that's the last thing you should want."

"Why?"

"Because God made you different. If he'd wanted you to be like me, he'd have made you like me. He hasn't, so don't aspire to it. Be as he has made you." He looked at Will and waited for their eyes to connect. "Or that into which he will turn you."

"I didn't mean that I should be you. I want to do what you do."

Campion released Will from his gaze and turned his attention back to the fire. "Wait 'till you see it done, before you subscribe to that."

Once more Will drew on his education. "What greater thing can there be done, than to bring my true lord back to his English people?"

"He never left them, Will, he never left them. What we are about is bringing the English people back to their true lord. And that, they say, is treachery. And one of us boy, will hang for it."

"Then they can hang us both. Though you will need the thicker rope."

Campion chuckled. "That is an ill-crafted jest."

"It is not ill-crafted and it is not a jest."

"Do you really know what you are saying? Are you really ready to pledge your life? To forswear felicity, liberty, and life itself?"

"I am. And do so promise that to you now. Why do you laugh?"

"Because you give me great joy, my jester, and there'll be time enough for weeping."

The whole party stayed at that lodging for three days. Then Colby and his men went home and a new escort was provided and Will and Campion rode on. In that way the pattern was replicated and the duo slowly wended north and west. At each point no one knew more than one stage in the path ahead. That was by far the safest way and it gave Will a great sense of security. Only he and Campion and a handful of others knew their ultimate destination.

Just he, Campion, John Cottam, and the members of his father's household, and he knew he could trust each of them absolutely.

NINE

Breeching scholar

John Cottam, the schoolmaster at Stratford-upon-Avon
grammar school, was not attracted to women. Frances formed
that opinion very quickly. Once upon a time she had considered
that she could make a fool out of any man. That was a decade
earlier when she was in full bud and with sufficient experience of
seduction to know what to do, when, and how quickly. Men
could treat her badly, very badly, but she knew how to get her
revenge in first. By the time they'd had their way with her she
would have what she wanted from them. Sometimes she simply
wanted to test her skill; the bigger the challenge the greater the
gratification. John Shakespeare represented a big challenge and
he was there for the taking. He'd had his prominence and fallen
from it. He was a deflated and demoralised victim. He craved for
the respect he'd lost but would settle for any similar adulation,
especially if it was dressed up as the love of a much younger
woman. She would have trapped him, and he would have given
her the information she needed, but it would have taken time
and probably required a prolonged build-up of gradual trust. So
she switched her attention to John Cottam, but her charms had
no effect. She rapidly realised he was impervious not only to her
allures but to those offered by any of her sex.

Cottam's disposition did not mean that Frances was helpless. She was a practiced businesswoman who could hold her own with the toughest rival. Those with whom she traded on a regular basis knew she would drive a hard bargain. They knew also what she expected of them in terms of quality, quantity and delivery on time. Anyone who dabbled in dubious practice did not fool with her a second time. She was obdurate with tricksters and adroit with the honest. She had a wide range of techniques and an astute nose for selecting the most apposite method. There were other ways she could work on Cottam and she was wise enough to play that hand from the outset. She was disappointed when he proved unaffected by her finest flirting, but she held her course steady, and having failed with the heart and the groin, she prepared to engage with his soul.

They were in the school room. The boys had been sent out for dinner but it was nearing one o'clock and they were waiting to be readmitted.

"My sister will be much heartened by your information, Mr Cottam. I shall relay every word with great care."

"When does she anticipate taking up residence in the town?"

"When, and if, a suitable property can be found, and when and if she can persuade my brother to finance it."

"How recently was she widowed?"

"Just over a year ago. Children grow so rapidly. Her son has such a quick mind. And perhaps a dangerous one."

"Dangerous?"

Frances now brought her performance prowess into play. She breathed shallow breaths, gently bit her lip and flashed her eyes this way and that, as if some danger might be close, but all was done with restraint and entirely naturally. "His father suffered persecution, Mr Cottam."

Cottam employed a pause then said, "For his faith?"

Frances nodded and looked for some anchorage in his eyes.

"He was martyred?"

"Not directly, but I'm sure the penalties gave him great strain. Financially he was completely broken. His pride shattered. His heart broke."

"My condolences."

"His son is given to emulate him. I feel he is drawn

towards ordination. He is far too young and lacks education. He needs the right kind of tutor. Mr Shakespeare said you are that man."

"Did he?"

"You taught his son?"

"That is true."

"From what Mr Shakespeare said his son and my nephew seem to share a very similar disposition."

"Well, perhaps I will meet him soon."

"I hope so. Would this be the place to begin that saintly path to priesthood?"

She could see that Cottam was both terrified and energised by her topic.

"Europe is the place for that," he whispered.

"He's too young for France."

"France?" He was testing her.

"Or Rome." She passed.

He traced the scratches the boys had made in the table with his forefinger.

She employed a phrase suggested by Philip Gyfford. "My nephew needs education before emigration."

He smiled. "There is talk of a preparatory seminary."

"A what?"

"A school where boys can be prepared. We . . . I have heard rumours to that effect."

"In Warwickshire?"

Cottam smiled briefly then looked concerned, and she feared that she might have overplayed her hand. So she changed tack. "I'm distressed by what I have heard of your brother."

Cottam's gaze hit the graffiti-scarred table. "Yes."

"And Mr Debdale. From Shottery."

"These are difficult times."

"And this is a difficult shire."

"I think all shires are much the same."

"Easier in the north, I hear. Where you come from."

"I doubt it is much easier there."

"Lancashire – is that right?"

"Yes."

"Where, precisely?"

"The boys are due back into their class. And I must keep strict time." He filled the remaining conversation with pleasantries and ushered her out. The line of boys, some no more than six or seven, and others twice that age, filed in. Once in the schoolroom they were orderly and silent, but several of the senior ones had scrutinised her and made indistinct remarks to their comrades who grinned and giggled.

Now she was in the doorway and he was smiling his farewell.

"I may be travelling in Lancashire, Mr Cottam. I may seek refuge in friendly houses. Mr Shakespeare has given me a greeting for his son William. Would you like to add to that message?"

This offer caught the school master off guard. His deferential disposition faltered and he was locked into instant and deep thought. At that moment she knew she could secure the deal she sought.

When she left him, she had a message for Will Shakespeare. She also had an address where he might be found.

"He's too ill to talk to you, and if I were you I wouldn't go anywhere near him. I'm terrified that whatever he's got I'm going to get too." James Rondel leaned against the doorpost of the entrance to the Red Lion Inn, chewing on a stalk of barley straw and watching the September traffic in the street.

"What's his sickness?"

"Who knows?"

A boy brought Rondel's horse to the front of the inn and he began to secure his few belongings to the saddle, transferring them from a small stack in the doorway. Frances pushed past him and went up to Eliot's room. He was in bed, pale as a frost and hot as an oven stone. His bed sheets were drenched. She called the tapster and played merry hell with her until fresh sheets were brought.

Rondel came to see what she was doing. Frances stared at him sharply. "You're just leaving him?"

"Well I can't cure him. I've settled my bills downstairs, with interest. They'll keep an eye on him."

"A blind eye by the looks of it. If you walk out of this inn you walk out of any deal with me."

"I don't recall any deal." He smirked, bowed slightly, and left.

She stayed with Eliot for nearly a week. For three days there was little change, except that he cooled and stopped sweating. He slept almost continuously. She managed to get a watery broth down him and some sips of small beer. He made not the slightest acknowledgement that he knew her.

Frances surprised herself with the way she had set aside her mission and devoted herself to Eliot's care. Prior to that week she had thought of him primarily as business contact and a casual lover. There was a tertiary image of Eliot the scoundrel, the dabbler with danger, the rogue who lived fast and fenced with fate. Seeing him so ill, shook her in a way she had not experienced before.

The fourth day brought a near miraculous transformation in her patient. He awoke to full awareness and complete cohesion. He was very weak and felt very cold but within a few minutes he was entirely rational and lucid. He was anxious to get up and about but Frances forbade it. Ellen, brought gradually more substantial food and by the breakfast of the sixth day it was clear that Eliot was out of danger, though he remained weakened in his limbs and plagued by a persistent chesty cough.

During the two days of wakefulness Eliot and Frances spoke a great deal. He told her all that had happened at Park Hall, and how, once Campion's party had slipped away, the other guests were distracted for a while with entertainment by Arden's musicians. They had left as soon as they could, but there was no possibility of them locating Campion. They looked for Frances but she too, had disappeared.

Frances in turn told her tale, though she kept some details to herself. She did not mention stabbing the man she now knew to be Simon Sedlow. She told him of her trip to Stratford and of John Shakespeare's family. She told him of her meeting with the schoolmaster Cottam. She did not tell him what Cottam had told her. She would keep some details to herself. She would retain the advantage that she had won.

Once George had realised who it was that was caring for him, his face had softened in a way she had not seen before. There was sincerity in his eyes that seared to the depths of hers in a way she had not experienced previously. His tone of voice had a music to it, born of gratitude, of debt, of incredulity. His smile, though lacking strength, was easy and warm and devoid of the desire it had always previously expressed. His yearning for her was still there, that was clear, though it was muted by his disposition. She told him she was leaving for Lancashire.

"Lancashire."

"All the signs are that is where I will find Campion."

"Well I am coming with you."

"Don't be an idiot. You are not well enough."

"Of course I . . ." Eliot erupted into a prolonged fit of coughing.

"I will need your help," she said once he had stopped. "But I don't want to lose any more time."

"Lancashire is huge. How will you even start? And, if you do find him . . ." Another burst of coughing. "He'll move on before you can get anyone to move in. Just like . . ." More coughing. "Just like he did when he was here in . . ." Coughing. ". . . Warwickshire."

"Do you know what a seminary is?"

"A what?"

"It's a school for priests. They're going to start one. Here, in England."

"They wouldn't be so . . ." Three coughs. ". . . foolish."

"Not a full one. A starting school. A place for gathering boys, testing them, training them, before shipping them abroad."

Eliot's eyes were widening and finding a fire she had not seen during his illness. "You have to wait for me."

Frances shook her head. "You can follow."

"And how in God's name will I find you?"

"Wigan, Preston, Lancaster. They mark the spine of the county from south to north. I'll leave notes there. At the inns closest to the markets. It works. I've done it before. We'll have a code."

"A code?"

"Secret marks. We'll agree it now. Get your pen."

Eliot protested but soon realised that he had no option. They agreed their code. Then they spent an hour in the kind of closeness that only sealed lovers know. The closeness that transcends the need for words or even for touch. A closeness forged in terms that cannot be spoken because they are known too deeply. Then Eliot watched Frances Thursby as she put on her man's attire.

As she rode away from the inn where he lay wrapped in his blankets, she knew for the first time in her life that there was a man who would, without doubt, follow her. He would, without doubt, find her. Ahead of her was another man, and she knew too that she would, without doubt, find him.

TEN

A truant disposition

Will's first glimpse of Hoghton Tower was the sight of a stone
crown upon a wooded mound. All he could see was a silhouette.
The hill was stretched to his left pointing towards the place
where the sun had settled into the sea which, he was reliably
informed, was only a few miles away. Will had never seen the
sea. The hill fell away much more steeply on the eastern side
where it was heavily wooded, and it was towards that wood that
they were heading.

They had been met that afternoon at a small safe house
some six miles to the south. Now there was sufficient moon to
lay a silver hue on the land and the absence of cloud revealed a
star cloth against which Will could delineate the shape of his
ultimate destination. Dominic Arrowsmith, a local man, had
been with them for two days and they were being led by Jerome
from the tower. He was very warm in his welcome. His
handshake was firm, prolonged and energetic. His eyes glowed
with goodwill and he declared himself to be both thrilled and
honoured to meet Campion. He exuded confidence and made
Will feel that he was in good company and he was eager to
complete their journey. They had been a full month on the road.

Their passage through Staffordshire and Cheshire had been largely uneventful, though there had been a couple of close escapes. They had not remained more than three days in one place.

Will had learned a great deal from his mentor and on an intellectual level he felt supremely confident. There was no one from whom he might have learned that would have held greater authority than Campion. He was the master of religious rhetoric. After all, he had once been an authority on the opposing point of view, so when it came to arguing the logic of his faith he could not be caught out by the counter argument. Will was hungry for that knowledge and consumed it with relish, but despite that there was a part of him that felt uncomfortable. He had the bizarre feeling that he was going in the right direction but on the wrong track.

Jerome led them down silent lanes until they dipped into the valley of the Darwen river. They followed its western and southern bank as it curved around the foot of the escarpment where the tower stood. Several tracks led this way and that but Jerome ignored them all until they came to a well-defined route from a fording place. Their mood was buoyant. They were almost there.

There was a sudden tumbling rustle. Jerome snapped into a crouch and signalled his charges to do the same. A form was lurching out of the tangle of undergrowth. Will caught a glimpse of a slender figure wielding a hefty pike.

"Ahoy!" came the shout and the apparition accelerated towards them. Will instinctively reached out and grabbed Campion's forearm.

Jerome stepped forward and called, "Tom! Tom!" and then more quietly "Tom! it's Jerome, from the Tower."

The aggressor slowed and halted. Will could see him a little more clearly. His hair looked long and grey, his face thin, aged and drawn. The pike was but a sturdy staff, sharpened at one end.

"Tom, it's Jerome, from the Tower."

Tom looked cautiously at them. Dogs were barking not far away.

"Jerome Sir?"

"With friends for my lord."

Tom stood to one side. "Poor Tom is merry."

"Be merry Tom."

"But cold."

"Light a fire Tom. You have plenty of wood."

Over Tom's shoulder Will could make out a simple hovel of stone and wattle. Next to it was a substantial pile of foraged wood.

"Plenty," said Tom.

"Make a fire," said Jerome. He patted Tom on the arm as he walked past.

Campion shook his hand and blessed Tom, which seemed to mystify him.

"Hello," said Will and smiled.

Tom stared back with wide eyes and pursed lips. "Tom is cold," he said.

"Make a fire," said Will.

They moved on. Tom stood his ground.   Dogs barked intermittently.

The climb was steep but only short and soon they were at the curtain wall of the tower and made their way to the turret of the gatehouse. There was a short wait while Jerome was happy that nothing untoward was evident, and then made three sharp raps on the gate. Dogs erupted into barking. Reprimands were shouted and they quietened. The gate was unbolted and the two travellers and their tiny entourage were admitted.

The dogs barked again and the porter admonished them more. He tipped his hat, then took it off and bowed before Campion, who took his hand, straightened him up and embraced him.

"This is Rowland, the porter," said Jerome. "If you ever find him sober, let me know."

Campion laughed and turned to present Will.   "Master Will, my apprentice."

Will nodded at Rowland. The porter grinned back. "Master Will," he breathed. Will tasted strong ale in the air.

The gate was barred behind them. The dogs barked again. The porter barked back at them and they settled for growls. The new arrivals crossed the first courtyard towards the impressive keep that was surely the eponymous tower, but they were whisked swiftly through this to the inner yard and across to the great hall on their left. As they entered that they were met by a small feminine form. Jerome presented his companions and as the woman stepped back to indicate their welcome the firelight caught her face and locked Will's lungs.

"This is Ros," said Jerome.

It was not as if she was classically beautiful, Will would never have said that about her, but she had a special radiance; an aura that seized the whole of Will's attention. He instantly knew the pain of love, and what's more he knew that he knew it for the first time. He thought he'd known love before but now he realised that he hadn't even been on cordial terms with it.

She gave a slight bow to Campion and respectfully averted her eyes from his, but she looked straight into Will's soul unwittingly mauling it.

"Come over to the fire," she said.

"Thank you," said Campion.

Will followed the glow.

"Wait here, if you please. " She left the room by the door beneath the minstrels' gallery. Will watched her go and Campion watched Will.

Jerome settled himself on the end of the bench at the table. Dominic Arrowsmith joined him. Campion remained standing and Will remained entranced. He took two deep breaths and began to regain normal levels of awareness. For the first time he took in the impressive size and décor of the great hall. It was not possible to appreciate it properly in the light from the fire but even in that muted illumination he could tell it was recently constructed as it had several fashionable features. There were two towering bay windows that stood opposite each other, timber panelling ran the length of the walls, and the screen beneath the gallery was bold and ornate. Will sensed that there might be a person watching them from the gallery, but it was too poorly lit for him to see into the corners there.

Campion stood to one side of Will and embraced him.

"Well," he said. "We've made it. We are here. Your new home Will. At least for a while."

Will let his pack slip to the floor next to Campion's. "How long?"

"Mmm?"

"How long here?"

Campion wrinkled the bristles around his mouth. "This moment, and the next."

Will looked at his mentor askance but the priest just

repeated himself.

"This moment, and the next."

Will sensed another movement in the gallery. "This moment and the next," said Will, not knowing why he had echoed his master, and still not grasping what he meant by it.

Logs cracked in the grate. Beyond the windows tawny owls were talking.

The door in the screen opened and the full skirt, elaborate bodice and puffed sleeves shouted the status of the lady who entered. Ros returned with her, much more dowdy in dress, infinitely more radiant in appearance.

Campion bowed his head "My lady de Hoghton?"

"Mr. Edmunds." Elizabeth nodded gently and while doing so quickly surveyed everyone in the room. "Or may I call you Father?"

"Edmund is my name."

"Welcome to our house."

"Thank you my lady."

"And who is this?"

"A man of learning."

"Indeed?" Elizabeth eyed Will and presented a smile that was beyond sincerity.

"He's learning how to learn. Master Will. William Shakespeare."

"I know the name. I have heard it. Your father is a glover. Warwickshire."

Will said, "Stratford, my lady."

Elizabeth nodded slowly. "We trade in alum. A necessary agent of the glove maker's art, I believe."

"You believe correctly."

Elizabeth held a small breath before saying, "I hope so. I hope so." She sighed and then breathed freely again. "We have knowledge of your father. How fares he?"

"Business is tidal. He puts his trust in the Lord."

"And therein lie more penalties. He has been fined for not attending church."

Will heard himself speaking before he had time to consider whether or not he should. "If only gloves changed hands as swiftly as gossip."

Campion cut in sharply. "Will! Mind your tongue."

Elizabeth laughed slightly. "Let me reassure you

Master Will, the whole of Lancashire is not awash with gossip regarding Warwickshire glovers. There is a network. We had to know who was accompanying our most precious visitor. And I had to be sure you were he."

Will felt himself redden slightly but held tightly to his esteem. "I am he, my lady." He flicked a glance at Ros, catching her unawares and scoring eye contact albeit only for a second or two.

Elizabeth walked a little further into the room drawing closer to the fire and ensuring that everyone heard the detail of what she was about to say.

"We feel it best that you are not he, whilst you are here. Shakespeare is not a common name in these parts. My husband suggests Shakeshaft, which is far more common."

Campion selected a droll expression to bracket a knowing twinkle in his eyes. "There you are Will. You are common."

Everyone, bar Ros, laughed a little.

"Whatever my lord desires," said Will. "I am my lord's man."

Elizabeth's smile widened, seeming slightly more sincere. "That you are. Can you sing?"

"Sing, my lady?"

"Sing."

"Aye. I can sing."

"Then our singing boy you will be. Can you play?"

"Play? Play what my lady?"

"Whatever my lord commands. The fool, the villain, the hero."

"Oh – play!"

Campion remarked, "It's a simple enough word, Will."

"I have never played, my lady, but if my lord commands it I will play."

Elizabeth clasped her hands together. "Then that's what you are whilst you are here. Should anyone ask the reason for your residence, then the answer is you are to join my lord's players and you are a player and a singer. Tomorrow I shall introduce you to Fulk."

Edmund turned to Elizabeth. "And am I to be so costumed?"

Elizabeth found another short laugh. "I fear you are

87

too famous, Father. Should your audience arrive, then we have a place for you out of sight. I will acquaint you with it in good time, but first I must acquaint you with my husband. He is upstairs. Good master Will, will you wait here? Ros will bring you some bread and ale."

Will fired Ros his best love look. "Then I will gladly wait, madam."

Ros took Will's look and deflected it to the floor.

Elizabeth turned to the others there. "Jerome, take Mr Arrowsmith to the kitchen and see he is refreshed and provided with a bed for this night."

"Aye, my lady."

Arrowsmith smiled and bowed. "Thank you my lady."

"Thank you Mr Arrowsmith."

Campion went to him. "Tom," he grinned. They shook hands and Campion chanted a tiny Latin blessing.

Elizabeth led the way out under the gallery. "This way Father Campion."

Will said his thanks to Tom Arrowsmith, then fired another love look at Ros. It missed.

Will was left alone amid the gently dancing shadows cast by the firelight. He decided that this hall was every bit as grand as any he had seen on his journey including that of Edward Arden's Park Hall. He began to reckon up the number of properties he had visited during his month on the road. He resolved to sit and write a list, but then instantly realised what a dangerous document that would be. He found a strange joy as well as terror in that insight. What power words held. If he had pen, ink and paper he could sit down now and write his own death warrant. That was frightful. He wished he was illiterate.

He had been given a disguise and a new name. He liked that. He enjoyed the tales of those who had adopted aliases, and Campion had a compendium of those. So he had a role to play. That would be fun. He had seen troupes of players in Stratford and always greatly enjoyed their exploits. Some of them had been intimidatingly talented, but he could rise to that. That thought put a very broad smile on his face. He caught his reflection in the window. He looked pathetic. He felt his tummy wobble and before he knew he was laughing out loud at the sight of his own silly face.

Something moved.

Will glanced at the gallery. Nothing there. Something flew past the outside of the window, or it didn't. The fire settled. The oak beneath his feet creaked. The door under the gallery opened.

A woman came in, older than Will but younger than Elizabeth. She was cloaked against the cold so Will found it difficult to detect her status. He stood his ground and bowed slightly to be on the safe side of respectful.

"And who is this?"

How should he answer? Was he already under alias? "Ah . . . um . . . a player."

"A player?"

"A singer."

"A singer."

Will rocked slightly from foot to foot. "A singer and a player."

The woman regarded him dubiously. "Which?"

"Both."

"In whose service?"

"My lord de Hoghton."

The woman moved further into the room, gravitating towards the fire. "Then we have something in common, for I too must do as he says."

Will edged towards her. "Are you a singer?"

"I used to be."

"Used to be?"

"I have not sung these last twelve months."

"Why not?"

"For I am not disposed to singing." She stared into the fire for a moment then turned her attention back to Will as if expecting a response.

Will shrugged. "If my lord commands it you must sing."

"How so. How so. And if my lord commands it you must play."

"I must and I will."

"And do players and singers arrive under darkness these days?"

Will turned towards the window looking for inspiration. "If the sun has set."

"Dipping and dodging the night watchman lest he sees

you and locks you up?"

Will cockily rested a foot on the woodpile at the side of the hearth. "If the night watchman watched me I would play the free man."

"And what name would you give?"

Now the answer was in the floor of the fire. "Jack Frost, Jack in the Green. What name would you give?"

"Queen Mab. Bringer of dreams. Tormentor of those who sleep easy in their beds."

This remark unsettled Will but also seemed to give him the key to be more at ease. This woman had a more angular face than the one that had just bowled him over, but despite its severity of shape it had a youthful lure and she had a life in her eyes that was somehow at odds with the regret in her countenance. He felt she was searching for a rapport and he was glad to offer it. He liked the sheen in the tiny strands of hair that had slipped from her bonnet. He leaned slightly towards her.

"Is that why you are about at this hour: to distribute dreams?"

She twisted her lips awkwardly, then said, "Nay. To avoid them."

"Is that possible?"

"Nay again. Queen Mab is a fertile midwife and a murderer. Mab has poisoned night's balm. Mab has murdered sleep."

"Queen Mab has?"

She looked directly at him. "The queen has. The queen. I have trouble sleeping as do others in this house. Our bedtime prayers simply serve to remind us of our persecution and keep us awake." She slipped her hands from beneath her cloak and reached out for the warmth of the flames.

Will said, "You have smooth hands."

"And you sing a false tune . . . Jack."

"Will."

"Will."

"Will."

She said, "Shakespeare."

He said, "Shakeshaft."

"Shakespeare I was told."

"Shakeshaft, I was told."

She spread the warmth around her palms and rubbed it

into to her wrists. "Shakespeare, Shakeshaft: it matters little. Willy Shakespeare. I'll wager you were teased at school. Willy Shakespeare. Were you teased?"

He had been, mercilessly, but he shrugged the memory away. "That's what school is for: teasing out."

"And they taught you playing did they Will?"

"They taught me singing."

"You've come with Mr Edmunds. Mr Campion. Father Campion. Well, Will? What's the matter? Can you not trust me?"

"I cannot trust myself."

At last she smiled. "I have played with this player and I am sorry. I am Jane. Daughter of Thomas. Of this house."

"Lord Thomas that has gone abroad?

"Far abroad. He died there this summer gone."

"Dear lady I am sorry . . ."

"So am I, but it won't bring him back."

"I am also sorry that I have not shown you due deference, respect and honour. I wasn't sure who you were, I should have introduced myself from the start but . . ."

"Do not be sorry. I do not deserve your deference."

"That is true of most who do demand it."

Jane sniggered and he saw a warm smile for a moment. "True enough. So why does a secret priest need a singing boy?"

"To keep his spirits up?"

"Sounds like a good reason."

"I am not a singing boy. Well, except when I sing. I am Father Campion's companion. I am his pupil."

Jane turned her back on the fire putting her hands behind her. "Saints preserve us; you'd better learn your lessons quick. He teaches a treacherous profession. If you are found in this master's form you could be clapped in capital detention. If I were you I'd develop a truant disposition."

"I hope I am too obedient for that."

"Obedience is but weakness disguised as strength."

Will was taken aback by that remark. "Obedience?"

"Aye."

"It's in the Bible."

"So is sodomy."

"My lady?"

"Or so I am told. I haven't read it. I have little Latin."

91

"I have less Greek."

"How do you know?"

"I don't. I was just trying to make you feel better."

"Why?"

"I could teach you Latin."

"Not if I don't want to learn."

He liked her feistiness and the way she played tennis with his wit. "I could teach you to want to learn."

"How old are you sir?"

"Of an age when I can abandon all desire to see my next birthday." He wasn't sure he believed this anymore and he hadn't had time to consider why he might have doubts on the matter.

"What?"

"I believe I am older than I look. And I believe you are too."

Jane turned back to face the fire. "That remark could be flattery or insolence."

"Or simply true, in which case it is neither."

Will knew that he was seriously overstepping the mark of protocol, but he was enjoying the flirtation too much to back off. She didn't seem uncomfortable or insulted.

She said, "I think there are many years between us."

"And I think there are far fewer."

"Kind words. You are well studied, my student priest."

"There is a great deal more I need to learn."

Will refocused on the fire and saw in it the memory of the lessons he had learned about the everlasting torments of hell that were handed out to those who died with sin on their souls. A silence must have stretched because he was suddenly jolted back to the realisation that Jane was staring at him.

She said, "I had a brother who thinks as you."

"Had?"

"Had."

"He is dead?"

"No. But he is not free to visit us."

Will worked out her meaning. "In prison, for his faith."

"Aye, exactly that." Then it was as if she had read his thoughts for she said, "He has wasted this life by thinking too much of the next."

How quickly the mood of their conversation had changed thought Will. What had triggered it? His moment of absence? She must be mightily perceptive to see through his posture and into his thoughts, or was it that she too was preoccupied by thoughts of the eternal? He began to see the nature of the shadow that was jailing her humour, and he saw too the noble anger that fuelled her fight. Here was an aged youthful beauty of spirit. It engaged his inclination to debate.

"This life is the journey, surely your brother is wise and brave to give priority to the destination." He felt most pleased by that speech. Jane was unimpressed.

"Think not too much of the next world Will, think instead what you desire from this one."

Will was stunned by her dismissal of his grand idea and fell back on his learning from Campion. "All I desire from this world is the opportunity to show that I deserve the love of God."

"I didn't ask you what you desired from God, I asked you what you desire from this world."

Their game of wit had collapsed into disarray. Or was it just that she was outplaying him? He found a simple truth. "To see the sea before I die."

"Hmm. You'd better hurry. The tide is turning against us."

With that remark she served up a silence that said the game was over, and Will was not at all sure who was the victor, but Jane had won a part of him. He felt injured, uplifted, brow-beaten and dangerously inspired. This woman had a magnetism. There was a new energy at play with his spirit and he found it irresistible. The door opened.

Ros returned with bread and cheese on a platter and ale in a pewter cup. She placed them on the table close to the fire. "Supper, sir."

"Good thanks."

Jane pulled her cloak more snugly around her shoulders. "Well, I'll leave you to your nourishment. We'll talk more on the morrow."

"I hope so." He watched Jane go with regret. For a moment he had been sandwiched in a young man's bliss, and half had now gone but Ros was still standing there so his soul did a little jig. She, however, looked downcast.

"Is there anything else you require?"

He noticed that with Jane gone from the room, Ros had dropped the 'sir'.

"Nothing at all."

Ros started to go. Will stopped her with a question.

"Ros?"

"Aye?"

"Do you know Jane's brother?"

"Not well."

"Is he not of this house?"

"He could not inherit Hoghton, for he is a priest and in prison for his faith. Jane has watched his promise come to nothing but pain."

"Did you serve her father? Lord Thomas?"

"My lord has always been his brother."

"Alexander."

"Aye."

"Are there others?"

"A half-brother, also called Thomas. At Brinscall south of here. Never comes here. Never seen him."

Will tore a corner off the bread. He wanted to continue the conversation but Ros did not seem disposed to remain. She lingered for the briefest moment then left Will to his food and his thoughts.

The fire settled.

Distant owls hooted.

ELEVEN

Players

Will fell asleep with his head on the table in the great hall. He was woken by the strong gentle hand of Edmund Campion. The shock of it meant that he reacted instinctively flinging his arm out and sending the pewter cup tumbling across the board and clattering to the floor. Luckily, it was empty. Campion recovered it and set it back on the table whilst Will shook off the delightful confusion of his dream of which he could remember little except for a spectral hybrid of Ros and Jane.

"This way Will," said Campion softly.

Will followed Campion who in turn was following Ros. They crossed the courtyard where the sharp air of the clear night nipped them, and then entered the southern range and Ros took them upstairs where another lively hearth welcomed them into a spacious chamber. A sturdy bed stood proud. Close to it, a mattress and blanket had been placed on the floor.

Ros proffered her goodnights. Will offered a warm smile, she returned a cold rebuff.

"The bed is yours," said Campion, but Will was adamant that it was not, and quickly spread himself on the mattress on the floor. He threw his bag to one side and pulled the blanket over him. He heard Campion settle himself to prayer and knew he should join him, but worshipping the image of Ros was far too tempting. He was asleep before Campion had petitioned his seventh saint.

Three moments later he was awake, it was full daylight, the fire was out and Campion had been replaced by a youth with long curly hair, a nose borrowed from a raven, eyes set slightly too close together and a jester's grin. He was sitting on Campion's empty bed.

"Good day," declared the stranger.

Will licked the lethargy from his lips, then croaked, "Good day." He cleared his throat and said it again. The youth slipped from the bed and in a movement that was half creep and half dance he placed himself within reach of Will and extended a hand.

"Fulk," he said. "Fulk Gillom."

Will took his hand. "Will Shakespeare," he said.

"Are you sure about that?"

Will was sure. Then he wasn't. "Will Shakeshaft," he said.

"You are a sound sleeper," said Fulk striding athletically to the window.

"What's the hour?"

"God knows," said Fulk.

"Where's Campion?"

Fulk surveyed the clouds and then the courtyard. "Ever been to London, Will?"

"No."

"Winchester, Worcester, or Wales?"

"No."

"Me neither."

"I've been to Warwick."

"Been to Lancaster?"

"No."

"I have. Lancaster is good."

"What's good about it?"

"It's steep."

"Oh."

Fulk turned his back on the window and did two and a half perfect, and near silent, forward rolls to land on Campion's bed. He lay there face-down and soundless for a moment then lifted his head and said, "Think he'll make it to sainthood? Your friend?"

"I think he already has."

"He'll need to die first," said Fulk and rolled onto his back.

"I think he already has," said Will. "In his head. That's why he's not afraid of death."

"Hmm," said Fulk, and then he said it again more tunefully. As he finished the note he flexed his tummy skywards then flicked himself upright to balance on one leg on the edge of the bed. This was unsuccessful but he slipped to the floor to land with no more noise than would a cat. He then did two cartwheels to finish sitting on the floor close to Will. "He's with Sir Alex - your prematurely dead priest."

Will nodded his head in acknowledgement then rubbed his eyes.

Fulk continued, "I'm to teach you acting. But first I am to give you breakfast."

"Good," said Will but didn't move. "How many players are there here?"

"Just the one."

Will raised his eyes.

"But there are three more at Lea and you will make us five. Seen much playing?"

"Enough," said Will.

"You can never see enough," said Fulk. "And there is your first lesson. Never make them feel they've seen enough, because if they do, they'll not want any more."

"You are Sir Alex's men?"

"We are. Two were even Sir Thomas's men. Andrew has been here some six years."

"And you?"

Fulk flexed his eyebrows. "I have no history. Come and eat." He skipped away humming a tune, and left the room. Will found his shoes and followed him.

After a quick but filling breakfast of porridge, Fulk took him to all the parts of the house that he could. The property had been extensively rebuilt recently and it was well appointed and fashionable without being as ostentatious as some of the houses

Will had seen. It was centred around a much older core and upon longstanding foundations and the property and its estates were well established in local and regional culture. Will quickly realised that he had arrived at a place of some importance and influence. Fulk took him to the top of the great keep. The day was cloudy but clear and a strong westerly wind tugged their hair and sharpened their faces as they peered into it.

"Is that the sea?" said Will.

"Well, it's the coast," said Fulk.

Will stared. All he could make out was a grey band. To their left was the low rolling landscape that Will had crossed on his approach. To the east and north were distant hills. It was much more comfortable to look in that direction with the wind behind them, but Will was keen to focus on the suggestion of sea.

Fulk raised his voice against the blow of the air. "I don't think you should say you've seen it until you've heard it."

Will digested that advice and then said, "How do you know I haven't seen it before?"

Fulk let the wind blow his curly tresses across his face, then skipped around the man on watch and retreated backwards down the spiral steps presenting a storytelling face that said follow me without the need for words.

They made their way from the keep and into the north range at the first floor level. After a couple of kinks in their route they emerged onto the minstrels' gallery of the great hall. Fulk instantly slipped to his knees pulling Will down with him. They peered through the spindles of the balustrade. Beneath them Campion sat at the table opposite Elizabeth and next to a hunched figure whose face Will could not see because he had his back to them. He wore a heavy blue and black coat, richly stitched and sporting a grey fur collar. His flamboyant black and grey feathered cap hid his head from view. Fulk took Will's sleeve and drew him close enough to hear his whisper.

"Your patron."

"Alexander?" mouthed Will.

Fulk nodded.

Will looked again, but all he could see was a great bulk of a man as sculpted by his garments. He heard his voice however. It had the weight of confident authority but there was also fragility. It was powerful, but aspirated, giving it a wet acoustic and a sense of expended effort. "You are a brave man to have carried these with you."

"I want to leave them here," said Campion.

Elizabeth recoiled visibly, then found control and edged back into a dignified posture. She tried to find pleasure and honour in her face but it was shadowed by a veil of fear. A silence hung in the air punctuated only by the tortured logs of the fire cracking. Alexander scanned the documents.

"We have safe places where we can keep them for you," he said.

Elizabeth stared horror into her husband's eyes but he wasn't looking at her.

Campion said, "I would want to compile more documents before I move on, if you are willing to accommodate me."

"Of course," said Elizabeth, slightly too slowly.

Alexander smoothed the scroll beneath his hand. "Father Campion, let this be your home."

Elizabeth beamed frozen warmth.

"Well," said Campion, "I have a mission. The flock is wide and dispersed but the saddle makes an unsteady desk. What is said is dead as soon as it is heard. What is written speaks on every time it is seen."

Alexander grunted his agreement. Elizabeth tried to smile hers.

"I must leave written accounts. I need a little time to put my thoughts down."

Alexander caressed the paper again. "Your time is ours to give."

Campion extracted more paper from his satchel. "I have others. Documents from Rheims, from Douai and from Rome."

Elizabeth yelped. "Rome?"

"Directives from the Holy Father himself."

"What - in our house?"

Elizabeth looked upon them as she might the entrails of enchanted vermin.

Campion said, "The Pope himself will know of the sanctuary you have given."

"And who else?" said Elizabeth, more in fear than in inquiry.

"And then, of course, there is the matter of the seminary."

"The what?" asked Elizabeth.

"There has to be a place, here in England, where young men can be schooled and seek out the path to priesthood."

This was clearly news to Elizabeth whose countenance was now beginning to colour as if it faced the fire. "We have held a school, of course. But schooling in writing, in reckoning, in music and in domestic arts, - and in scripture and its message; but a school for, for, priests, for . . ."

"Soldiers of our saviour. Crusaders for Christ."

". . . in our house would be, would be . . ." She looked at her husband.

Alexander raised his hand, reminding Will of Elizabeth's gesture the night before, but this hand was more authoritative and calming. He said, "This is a safe house."

Elizabeth struggled to restrain her anxiety. "No house is safe. We can trust no one."

Campion said, "You can trust in the Lord."

Elizabeth was unconvinced but unable to disagree and forced straws at which she might clutch. "My husband will need time to consider your proposal Father, so shall we . . ."

"It was his idea."

"What?"

"Or so I was taught by the schoolmaster at Stratford."

Elizabeth was burning a glare into the head of the household, but he was only interested in the papers before him. He ran his fingertips over the ink trying to feel the soul that had stirred the hand that had moved the pen.

"From Rome?" he said.

"The one beneath is from the master of Douai. The school so generously supported by your late brother."

Alexander's hat bobbed three times. "Douai, Rome and. . . ?"

"Rhiems. The cathedral."

Alexander shuffled the sheets slowly testing the texture of each one.

"I have heard much of your library," said Campion. "I cannot wait to see it."

"Elizabeth will show you." Alexander gestured a dismissive wave in the direction of his wife who brewed a storm behind her eyes then stood.

"This way, Father," she said. "This way."

Fulk gripped Will's arm tightly to keep him still as Elizabeth and Campion passed beneath them. Then with super slowness he led Will from the gallery.

At the table, Alexander savoured his scripts.

"Shall we go and bother Rosaline?" proposed Fulk as they crossed the courtyard.

"Rosaline?"

"Ros."

"Sounds good," said Will.

"Thought you'd say that."

"Do you spend a lot of time hiding in the gallery?"

"It is a most profitable position Mr Shakespeare-Shakeshaft. And yes, Ros is plum isn't she?"

"You were there last night when I arrived."

"Had to get the measure of my apprentice." Fulk spontaneously inserted a complete circular twirl into his walk, just the once.

"Your apprentice? I thought I was Campion's apprentice."

"No doubt you were once your parent's apprentice?"

"A poor one. I have more interest in hands than gloves."

"Smooth hands - like Lady Jane's? Ros's are rougher."

Will wondered if Fulk was speaking from observation or experience. They had arrived at the kitchen door. Fulk turned abruptly and set out back the way that Will was still coming. "Stop up the access!" he sang quietly and reaching across Will to his opposite arm he twirled him round so that both had a new direction and neither had broken their march.

"What's the matter?"

"Agony."

"Mmm?"

"Agnes the cook. We can only bother Ros when Agnes is not there and she is. She usually is."

"Do you often bother Ros?"

"All the time."

"Is she ripe?"

101

"No she is sour. Come on, we'll go to one of the barns and start our acting."

Will's first acting lesson turned out to be a fencing lesson, or rather demonstration. Fulk recovered a pair of short but sturdy hazel staves from the rear of the barn and challenged Will to duel. Will was keen to show just how proficient he was but he quickly understood that there were new rules to this match. Fulk's moves were slickly evasive in defence and flamboyantly deft in attack. This was no violent exchange but rather a dangerous dance. When Fulk had outmanoeuvred Will several times he laughed raucously then patted his adversary on the back and set about the serious business of teaching him co-operative fencing which looked dangerous but was choreographed for the entertainment of the onlooker. It was in strong contrast to anything he'd done for many months and Will was genuinely thrilled to learn the tricks of their interplay.

After several bouts they lay back on the straw which was springy and prickly having recently been piled there.

"Have you always been a player?"

"We all have Will. We all are."

Will thought about this.

Fulk stood up, back off a little and braced himself. "Some of us are applauded, others are booed off the stage." He flexed his knees then leaped into an airborne backward somersault to land nimbly back on his feet. Then he ran and leapt to on a stack of hay. "In the end we all exit through the trapdoor." He rolled back on the hay and disappeared into the depression behind it. "Until," he said still out of sight. "We come back again." He reappeared with arms splayed wide and decorated with random straw strands.

Will sniggered his approval. "Do you mean as ghosts?"

"Nay," said Fulk, slipping back to the floor and brushing the straw from his person. "In the bellies of worms, then of pigeons, then of pies, and then of princes."

"I'd never thought of that," said Will.

"The only way to be a king is to die at court. The worms will make you royal."

"Did you work this out yourself?"

"I am mortified that you may think I did not."

"I just wondered if you learned it from another."

"Who else is there to learn from?" Fulk took a straw

stem and with a pronounced posture, he lunged at Will as if to slay him. The straw struck home close to Will's heart and promptly bent in half. Fulk sat at Will's side. "If you are to be applauded Will, you must listen with your eyes and hear with your heart."

"He heard that from me," said a soft strong voice.

Will turned to look over his shoulder and saw the radiance that was Ros, standing in the barn doorway. The daylight behind her blurred her frame and diminished the detail of her face.

"It's true," said Fulk. "She said it first."

"Which part?" asked Will.

"The eyes and the heart." Fulk leaped to his feet and then niftily onto the bale opposite.

"And the bit about the worms," said Ros.

Fulk bowed in concession. "Ros knows a worm when she sees one."

"His is still waiting to be a worm," she said.

Fulk gave a little squeal and executed another backward somersault but this one crumbled into an ungainly tumble and roll.

"Master Will," said Ros, "Lord Alexander wants to meet you. I'll take you."

"She won't," shouted Fulk from the floor. "She never does."

Alexander de Hoghton had an armchair in his bedchamber. It was set close to the fire which was well banked making the room more than warm. Nevertheless, Alexander still sported his thick coat and hat and Will could tell he had several layers beneath that. He looked stocky but Will suspected that though he had once been so, much of what he now presented was wadding rather than useful weight. His face was large but looked like it had been larger. His skin sagged. His full beard merged into the grey fur of his collar and it was difficult to discern where one ended and the other began.

"So, John Shakespeare's boy."

"Yes, sir."

"Bring the seat."

Will followed Alexander's point and saw a stool by the

window. He brought it closer to his host, but sufficiently far to restrict the scorching effect of the fire. Alexander seemed almost oblivious to the heat, wrapped in his many layers he looked pale, yet as Octobers go, this was not a cold day in Will's estimation. He had seen age and illness before and knew this to be both.

Alexander had slipped one of his shoes off and he stretched that foot towards the fire flexing the ankle to feel more of the heat on his sole.

"Do you know my father, my lord?"

"I know of him."

"And he of you, my lord."

Alexander's beard made a small smile. "Missing him?"

"Yes sir." This was neither true nor a lie.

"You will," said the old man. "When he is gone."

Will listened with his eyes.

"So, I have spoken at some length with Father Campion. I expect that you have too whilst you have been journeying here."

"I have, my lord."

"And it is your desire to follow him?"

"It is."

"Brave boy."

"Thank you, my lord."

"It is I that must thank you, my lord."

"Sir?"

"Be a priest my boy, and there is no greater service you could do me or mine."

"I'm glad you think so, sir."

"I know so." Alexander rubbed the arch of his un-shoed foot against the edge of the hearthstone. "Help the poor, boy, help the poor. And he who needs the greatest number of servants is the poorest of all."

Will's eyes heard the weight of the meaning.

Alexander coughed slightly twice. "How are you at your prayers?"

"I thought I was diligent, sir, but then I saw Father Campion."

"Don't be dispirited," said Alexander reaching for his shoe with his toe. "He's done a lot of it."

"He has." Will wondered if he should kneel down and

help Alexander with his shoe, but then he saw he wasn't trying to put it on, he was just toying with it.

"Don't be fooled boy. Campion doesn't say his prayers."

"Doesn't he?"

"He lives them."

"Ah."

"When you think he is praying, he is simply practising what he will do. It's the doing that matters. Anybody can mutter." He flicked the shoe from his toes, flexed his free foot, sat back further in his chair and regarded Will with a look of pleasure and admiration and leaned towards him. "Praying will get you nowhere, William. When you pray you rely on others, when you do you need no one else."

Will heard this with his ears. His heart wasn't listening.

Alexander went on. "Pray for me William." Will was about to point out the contradiction in what his host was saying, but Alexander elaborated. "There's nothing you can do for me yet. Others can, and by God do I need their help. Pray for me won't you?"

"I will." Will made a quick prayer there and then so that his promise was fulfilled almost before he had made it.

"When you can do something for me, then replace the praying with the doing."

"I will," said Will.

"I'll be dead by then and need it all the more."

Now Will's heart was alert. It heard every word.

That evening Will ate dinner with Campion, Elizabeth and Jane round the table in the great hall. Alexander remained in his room. They were waited on by Margery a middle-aged servant who was seldom far from Elizabeth. Conversation was stifled and polite and played out as a kind of card game. Elizabeth was in control and Campion considerably followed suit. Jane tried to subvert the rules but won nothing. Will was the compliant beginner playing only in accordance with the prompts he was given. Their talk was of their travels, but of places and people not threats, dangers or narrow escapes.

Elizabeth concluded by announcing that the other members of Lord Alexander's acting troupe had been sent for from their other house at Lea. It was expected that they would cover the ten miles the next day, and they would then inaugurate Will into their next play, which they would give in honour of Father Campion in a few days' time. She also confirmed that Will's other function would be as tutor to the household. Will asked who it was that he would be charged with educating.

Elizabeth masticated the venison in between her jaws and took a drink of wine. Then she said, "Well you can start by improving Jane's Latin."

Jane sent her eyes to heaven and went on eating.

Elizabeth said, "We must make Jane as erudite as we can prior to her marriage."

"Marriage?" asked Campion cheerfully.

"Jane is betrothed to James Bradshaw of Haigh Hall."

Will smiled but his heart had plummeted and he wondered why. He and she were separated by insurmountable strata, and he felt no especial affinity towards her. But he saw the look on her face.

"Great joy," declared Campion.

"For whom?" asked Jane.

Silence struck and resounded. Elizabeth breathed deeply and destroyed it.

"James Bradshaw is richly endowed and truly handsome."

"Sarah Brindle's bay horse is richly endowed and truly handsome but I don't want to marry him."

Elizabeth flushed crimson but breathed deeply and spoke calmly. "I could learn to love Mr Bradshaw."

"Any woman could. That's because a woman's love is a duty, and like any duty it can be beaten into you. We can all learn to love if it hurts enough."

Elizabeth stared death at her step-daughter. Campion slipped a smooth tone into the conversation.

"When will the wedding be?"

Elizabeth said, "It is yet to be arranged, father. No banns have been drawn up."

"Ah."

The remainder of the meal felt strained. Jane said nothing more except to excuse herself as soon as the food was done. Elizabeth was edgy and falsely jovial. She played out the politeness as long as she could, then she too withdrew. This left

Will alone with Campion amid the warmth of the evening fire and the feeble light it threw in conspiracy with two candles on the table. Will felt no compunction to be formal.

"Edmund?"

"Will?"

"When will you leave here?"

"Within the week."

"How long do you expect me to stay?"

"Until I come back."

"What if you don't?"

"I will."

"I wonder what the other players will be like."

"As good as you can make them."

TWELVE

Words, words, words

Will went to bed to find that his bed was not there. It had been moved to a room in the north range beyond the great keep and overlooking the outer courtyard. Most of the servants were lodged in this area and he was now bedded close to Fulk in a room where three more places had been made ready for the players from Lea. The room, when fully occupied, would be cramped but for now the players' mattresses were stacked against a wall so there was a reasonable space for Will to stretch out on his bed on the floor. The meal had been hearty and Will slept well.

When he awoke the next morning it was barely light. Fulk was up and gone. Autumn was closing in, extending the nights and bringing a blanket of dampness to the start of day. In general, people slept longer in the darker half of the year, but Hoghton was a busy place and the working day could not be compressed. As yet, Will had no appointed tasks so he lay there for a while adjusting to his new accommodation and considering his new commission. He remained saddened by the prospect of Campion's departure but heartened by the fact that he would remain in the same household as Ros. Rosaline. Rosaline. He said the name over out loud to listen to its music. He liked the tune.

He then considered what he knew about his new responsibilities. His roles were multiplying. He was to wait upon Campion's return and all the while pursue his vocation of studying for the priesthood, whilst also learning how to act, and schooling Jane. He wondered just how good her Latin was. He did not baulk at tutoring her. She was charming and attractive and he had enjoyed their first encounter when she had gently sparred with him verbally. There was a clear demarcation between them with respect to their roles and social status, but Jane had seemed relaxed about that when they met. She had not appeared enamoured by Elizabeth's directive that she should take lessons from Will however, so that might make their meetings uncomfortable.

There were aspects of Elizabeth's demeanour that interested Will. There was a front and a falseness to her disposition. His meeting with Lord Alexander had felt much more unaffected and there was a clear sincerity to his new lord's attitude. He felt that he had dealt with the genuine person, whereas with Elizabeth so far he had only seen a persona. She was presenting a performance and she may not be aware that she was doing so. The performance was therefore doubly interesting for Will, because it was both false and true.

Eventually the randomly assembled noises of the working day stirred Will. He pissed in the bucket then made his way to the kitchen. A stocky woman with large hands was there. He suspected that this was the dreaded Agnes, the cook. Ros was also there. She gave him sticky porridge and suggested he ate in the small dining hall nearby. She didn't give him a smile.

Will ate the porridge and helped himself to bread and ale from the table there. Fulk found him. "Campion wants you," he said. "He's in Lord Alex's library; upstairs, north range, next to the keep. Soon as you like."

Will chewed slightly more swiftly. "Are we to learn more acting today?"

"You are."

"Are you to teach me today?"

"I have to help with the hedging and coppicing."

Will looked at him sceptically.

"We don't just play you know." He switched his tone

to one that was mockingly deferential." Not in this part of the realm, my lord." He backed away with exaggerated obsequiousness. "This servant who is your master will find you later when your master who is our servant is finished with you. If there is light in the day and strength in the limb we may find time to play." He slipped away grasping Ros' buttock as he passed her. She lashed out with a cloth. Fulk skipped as if enjoying the whip. Agnes yelled something indecipherable, and Fulk folded his arms into chicken wings and clucked his way into the yard.

Will considered replicating Fulk's assault on Ros, but decided against it. Instead he took his bowl back to Ros and thanked her. She took it without even the promise of a smile. He asked her where the library was and she replicated Fulk's directions. He had hoped that she would show him the way.

When he walked into the library he almost fainted. It was not a large room, but Will had never seen so much paper or so many books. Some were bound in leather or vellum or thicker paper. A few even had embroidered bindings and covers. The majority were flat piles, simply stitched or bound. There was a very large quantity of scrolls stacked in shelves upon shelves. In the centre of the room a board had been set up on trestles as a simple table and there sat Campion peering closely at a page of a volume. Some of his own documents were close by, and Will spotted a pair of thick, heavy spectacles. The lenses were secured in a v-shaped frame which allowed them to widen or narrow like shears. He picked them up and held them astride his nose. The Latin text on the table swelled up as if breathing. He chuckled.

"Aha!" said Campion.

"Morning Edmund."

"A task for you Will."

"Very well."

"There are pens and there is ink and Lord Alexander has generously gifted me paper." The priest patted a small pile of brand new paper. "Now," He reached into his satchel which was on the floor by his seat. "You'll have heard of my brag?"

"You spoke of it to . . . who was it? Sir Edward Fitton wasn't it?"

"Ah yes."

"It is your boast."

"It is my permanence. Or part of it."

"May I read it?"

"You may do more than that. You may copy it.
Several times. I have given all the copies I had bar this first.
Everyone wants one. Paper is precious. If you will make me a
new half dozen, I can distribute those and they can spawn more
copies and my words might reach those who cannot hear me."

"Of course," said Will.

He set about his work standing at the table. To begin
with his attention was drawn by the document before him.

*I have come out of Germany and Bohemia, sent by my superiors,
and adventured into this noble realm and my dear country for the glory of
God and the benefit of souls. I thought it like enough that in this busy,
watchful and suspicious world, I should either sooner or later be intercepted
and stopped in my course.*

Will wrote neatly, carefully and minutely. He knew the
cost of paper. He knew he must use as little as possible but fill
almost all the available space on each sheet. However compact
he could make it, the paper could be carefully cut to fit.
Furthermore, if he made it small, it could be more easily hidden,
and hidden it most certainly would be.

*Wherefore providing for all events, and uncertain what may
become of me, when God shall happily deliver my body into endurance, I
supposed it needful to put this into writing in readiness for your Lordships to
give it your reading.*

This was Campion's confession. He was completely
resigned to his arrest. Will looked at his friend, busy with his
own document, consulting references, and writing something
new.

*I trust I shall ease some of your labour. For that which otherwise
you must have sought for by practice of wit, I do now lay into your hands by
plain confession.*

Will's pen paused at the word *wit*. Did he mean word
play? Did he mean manipulation? Did he mean torture? Would
this paper spare Campion pain? In the short term perhaps, but it
would secure his demise beyond doubt.

*I am strictly forbidden by our Father that sent me, to deal in any
respect with matter of State or policy of this realm.*

Will had heard his mentor many times stress to their
helpers and associates that they must always assert their
patronage of the country and their loyalty to the crown. The
Jesuits and their supporters were not spies or traitors. They

111

were missionaries.

Many innocent hands are lifted up to heaven for you daily by English students which beyond seas gather virtue and knowledge and are determined never to give you over . . .

This referred to Will. The future Will. Will the priest, Will the missionary.

. . . but either to win you heaven . . .

Yes, that's what he could and would do. He would save souls. He would win heaven for them.

. . . or die upon your pikes.

His nib dug into the parchment. It stuck there. He extracted it, blew the minute shards of paper flesh from the point and carried on. He tried to write without taking every word to heart but concentrating instead on the shape of his letters and the alignment of his words. Transcription became transfusion, however, and the ink entered his pores and set his pulse racing.

. . . and never to despair your recovery while we have a man left to enjoy your Tyburn . . .

Enjoy! Enjoy? Enjoy Tyburn – the place of execution. What a choice of word. Enjoy. Will trembled as he carved it into his work.

. . . or to be racked with your torments or consumed by your prisons. The enterprise is begun; it is of God, it cannot be withstood. So the faith was planted: so it must be restored.

When he made the second copy, the impact on him was even greater. The shock was gone but the meaning resounded. By the third it began to dull. Its potency would never leave him but the repetition was assuaging the pain. He was able to write complete sentences without consulting the original. He was beginning to own the message.

His admiration for Campion had not faltered at any time during their month on the road, and reading his brag only served to bolster that veneration. It did, however, resurrect two concerns that he had not entertained whilst at home. The first was if he, Will, could sustain the heights of self-sacrifice so exemplarily demonstrated by his idol. The second was a nagging question regarding the mind of the man he idolised. He appeared to occupy a state beyond anything he'd ever seen in anyone else. Was this grace? Was this the special power that God gave to selected individuals? Or had the man found a kind of madness?

Will's hand began to ache in reminiscence of his grammar school days. He had to pause more frequently. Occasionally he sneaked a scrutiny of Campion. The great man was entirely engrossed in the world of his words. He worked in near silence. Infrequently he would mutter, pronouncing phrases that were difficult to decipher, or issuing breathy brief bursts of Latin prayer, but mostly their only audible accompaniment was the scratching of their pens, and the distant thuds, door slams and shouts of the tower bustling through its day.

The task that Campion had set Will occupied him all of the morning, and by the time he had finished he was both weary and hungry. He went to the small dining hall where there was bread and cheese and ale, but to his disappointment no Ros. When he returned to the library there was no sign of Campion or of the work that either of them had done. He felt that he had a legitimate reason for being there and hence lingered and examined many volumes. Some were much easier to read than others. Some, he suspected, were very old, though it was impossible to say when they had been written. He considered how many words the library might contain, and could not come to a confident conclusion. He wondered how many would ever be read again and arrived at a much smaller estimate. Libraries were sanctuaries. They were sacred. They were shrines. They sanctified the words, but they did not keep them alive. They kept them dead.

"Ah!" The proclamation was damped by the acres of rolled and folded paper. The voice belonged to Fulk. "Ros was right."

"Was she?" asked Will. "About what?"

"Your whereabouts. She said you would be here."

"I am. "

"You are. The players have arrived. They want to meet you. They are in the great hall. Come."

It was with some shock that Will realised the daylight was already shedding some of its intensity. The afternoon was old. He'd been seduced by the library and the day had slipped away. No matter; he'd revived a few dead words.

The other three players were much older than Fulk, who was

close to Will's own age, though he liked to present the impression he was more senior.

"So this is the Warwickshire boy?" said a stocky individual, small in stature and with a good deal of grey hair except on the top of his head. To Will he presented a vision of Fulk forty years hence.

"This is he," said Fulk. "And this is Piers. Chief player at our feast."

"And at our famine," boomed a deeper voice from over Piers' head.

Fulk's hand tumbled skyward in a courtly flourish. "Solomon the wise, and the very, very, and quite unnecessarily, tall."

Solomon was indeed exceptionally tall. He was one and a half times the height of his leader. Fair, shy of forty and with a tightly curled beard, his benevolent face might have belonged to God the Father, or a cloud caught between sun and storm. He crouched a little and slipped his hand under Piers' armpit so that Will could shake one hand but seal the acquaintance of two persons.

The trio was completed by a third fellow. His form was on the fat side of sturdy and the flexible side of stodgy. Sitting on the bench by the table he cradled a lute as if it were an extra bowl of his being. The three together offered an emblem of entertainment just by their appearance. Their attitude exuded an invitation to be amused without the need for anything to be said. The apprehension that Will had felt prior to meeting them was instantly banished and replaced by eager anticipation. He wanted to be one of them.

Piers stepped to one side while Solomon extended towards the rafters to recover his full stature. "Fulk says you passed the playing test."

"I wasn't aware that I was taking one," said Will.

"Absolutely right," said Piers. "That's the only way to prevent you from cheating."

Will couldn't work out how he might have cheated. He wandered towards the fat man who was stroking the strings of his lute so gently that almost no sound escaped. He made his next strum slightly stronger and the chord celebrated their handshake. Will looked back at the horseshoe of actors studying him. He shrugged. "He taught me some fencing moves. That's all. That's far from playing."

"Was it pleasurable?" asked Piers.

"Very."

"Then it was playing."

Will sniggered, and so did everyone else.

Piers recovered his cup from the table and took a swig. "Know any songs Will?"

"A few."

"Give us a song."

Will protested with a pant of breath and an involuntary gesture. "What song?"

"Whatever song you want."

Will struggled for time to remember a tune and hence made little sense. "I don't know what song you would want."

Solomon giggled. "Hear that Warwickshire in his lungs!"

The others laughed.

"Say a song you know," said Piers. "*The Fox will Come to Town?*"

"I know that."

"Give him the tune, Andrew."

The fat man strummed a sequence on the lute.

"Aye, that's the tune," said Will.

Everyone laughed gently. Andrew played again, paused and nodded Will to come in. Will sang.

> *"Tomorrow the fox will come to town*
> *Keep, keep, keep, keep, keep!*
> *Tomorrow the fox will come to town*
> *Keep you all well there!*
>
> *I must desire you neighbours all*
> *To hallow the fox out of the hall*
> *And cry as loud as you can call*
> *Whoop, whoop, whoop, whoop, whoop!*
> *And cry as loud as you can call*
> *O keep you all well there!"*

Fulk smiled and frowned, Solomon grinned and clapped, Piers whistled and Andrew slapped the flat front of his lute. Will suspected there was a blush about his face but he felt

115

that he had mostly mastered the melody.

Piers put his cup down and turned to his compatriots. "Was that singing? What says Solomon?"

The bass notes reverberated. "Solomon says the song was sung."

Piers rooted in a sack beneath the table. "Well Fulk says he can fence, Solomon says he can sing, and I say . . . can he speak?" He produced a scroll secured to two short wooden staves. "Ever seen a player's part, Will?"

"Never."

"Then I give you your lines."

"Lines?"

"Aye. Lines."

Will took the scroll and unfurled a short section by twisting the handles about which it was wrapped. He saw mostly lines. Straight lines of ink were drawn across the paper with just two of three words at the end. Between these were sections written out in full. Piers came close to point at the paper. His breath was not good, but Will disciplined himself not to react.

"These are your words," said Piers pointing to the paragraphs written in full. "And these are what you must listen for." He indicated the three of four words at the end of the drawn lines. "They will give you your cue to speak. So you learn it all and you listen. When you hear those words you say the ones that follow."

Will looked at the paper. "Who will say these others?" he asked pointing to the short clusters of words that were not his.

"Does it matter?" This was said in a way that precluded a response, so Will didn't give one. Piers walked back to his cup. "That is your part of our play. We will play it tonight."

"Tonight?"

"Tonight."

"Play it for whom?"

"For us."

There was some relief in that. "How much should I learn?"

"You should learn your part. All of it."

Will wound his hands in opposite directions until all the paper was unravelled. The scroll stretched his full reach and sagged into a slight bow. Andrew struck new chords. It was a melancholy tune.

Piers drained his drink. "See you at dinner," he said.

Will took the script to the room where he was lodged. There was no one else there. He read through the paper from start to finish. It was called *Nobody at Home*, and as far as he could surmise, he held in his hands only a short section of the play. His role was called Pod, and he seemed to have been well cast as a witty young man. He was talking to an evasive and upset young woman called Willow. His task seemed to be to comfort and woo her. He could play that part surely? He would think of Willow as Ros and that would be his impetus to learn the lines and give them good life. A third character came in towards the end. This was Hardwicke, the girl's father. The scene would only take a few minutes to play, so it would surely only take a few minutes to learn. In that he was very wrong. By the time dinner was called, he knew less than half his words.

Almost everyone was gathered for dinner. The family was there, with their guests, together with the players and many other senior servants. All these were served in the great hall while more labourers were seated in the small dining hall and given a share. It had been a very active day and lots had been at work on the estate in preparation for the short days and long duress of winter which was not far away. The meal was not a formal occasion and Will gained the impression that while it wasn't routine to feed the majority of the household in this way, there were probably other days on which this arrangement was put into practice. The food was simple but flavoursome. It was a vegetable and pork stew. Will found a place across the table from Fulk. His new friend looked at him knowingly.

"Learned your lines Will?"

"Some."

Fulk laughed slightly and chuckled.

"When and where will we play it?"

"Probably in the barn. When Piers calls it."

Will looked along the table to where Piers was in animated conversation with Campion. He caught Will perusing him and gave a little wave with his wedge of bread whilst remarking something to Campion. The priest grinned and gave

Will an encouraging wink. Will acknowledged them both, wished he could hear what they were saying and went on eating. His nerves were getting the better of him and damaging his appetite. As soon as he could, he slipped away from the meal and went back to his lodging room and his scroll. The light was completely gone now. There was no candle or fire in there so he wedged himself against the window but the night was mean, keeping its moonshine beneath the horizon and wrapping its stars in bulbous clouds. He went in search of a flame, anxious to learn his words but fearful that the players might not be able to find him and wrongly deduce that he was scared by the ordeal. He went outside and walked the inner courtyard. Although there was no natural light he found that in the open the contrast between the ink and the parchment was enough for him to determine what he had to learn. He walked back and forth and found that the movement and the rhythm of his walking helped his memory. Suddenly he was confronted by Ros.

"What are you doing?" She was clutching a stack of bowls.

For a moment he was stunned. Then he was severely tempted to say one of Pod's lines attempting to seduce Willow, but only the coarsest would come to mind and her solemn face didn't offer a ready receptacle for the sentiment, so he stumbled to a stammer. "L . . . l . . . learning my words."

She gave a slight laugh and a willow frond of breath condensed close to her face and ghosted into invisibility. Her smile was equally short-lived but the glimpse of it was branded onto the inside of his brow. He thought of something to say but she was already gone from him and a quarter of the way across the courtyard. "Love the words," she called.

"What?"

She turned but did not slow, walking backwards while she repeated her advice. "Love the words." Then her face was gone again and all he had was her alluring form drifting into the dark and through the door.

"I will," he shouted.

Turning back to his task he found that his mind was even more addled. The character he had to play readily found words and brought them to the fore effortlessly, yet he who had so much more to say could not find his own. He managed to learn a little more, and then Fulk appeared bearing a small simple lantern.

"How is it," he declaimed as he crossed the yard, "that Ros always knows where you are?"

"If only she did," said Will.

"Come on," said Fulk and set off for the outer yard.

"To where?"

"To the barn."

"I don't know it yet."

"I'll help you."

There was utter blackness in the barn but Fulk tied his lamp to a dangling string and it gave a poor pool of bronze illumination over a small circle of floor.

"Put the paper down. People who read their thoughts speak only from the mouth and not the heart."

Will thought this was a spontaneous remark but then recognised *and not the heart* as his first cue. He cast aside his scroll and said his response. "But you must hear these words from Jed."

Fulk raised the pitch of his voice and adjusted his posture by arching his back and stretching his neck. "There is not one thing that Jed should say to me."

Will froze. "You are Willow! You are Willow!"

"That's not your line," said Fulk sinking back into his own stance.

"You are playing Willow."

"Well who did you expect?"

Will said nothing.

"Who had you imagined?"

Will said nothing.

Fulk adopted his feminine form again, hitched up his voice and said, "Put the paper down. People who read their thoughts speak only from the mouth and not the heart."

"But you must hear these words from Jed," said Will.

And so they battled through as much as Will had memorised which was about two-thirds of what he had been given. Then Fulk helped him memorise some more. Only a few lines remained. "Look," he said, "get the sense of these last ones and force the end words into your head because they are our cues. As long as you can hit those well, we can keep the play playing."

"Right," said Will and they worked on that with Fulk also putting in the lines of the father of Willow when he entered the scene.

"You know those as well," said Will.

"I know them all Will. I've played this play several times. Now from the beginning to the end, no stopping, move towards me when it feels right and only when you are speaking."

And thus they did it. And for the first time it had life and energy and credibility. Will found himself loving the words, which brought Ros' advice and hence Ros back to his mind and the image of her stoked his passion higher. At one point Will infused a little too much enthusiasm but Fulk calmed him with a gesture and by the pace of his reply. When they reached the part where Willow's father entered, the line came resounding out of the darkness, and Piers stepped forwards into their dim circle. Will did not allow himself to be thrown by this and kept going. Somehow he got to the end, and when he did so a burst of resounding music sprang forth and two hearty voices sang from above the bales of hay.

"Hey ho, nobody at home
Meat nor drink nor money have I none
Fill the pot Eadie."

Then there was a chorus of clapping and Andrew and Solomon slipped down the straw to join them. Everyone laughed and Solomon slapped Will between his shoulder blades.

"Am I a player?" he asked.

Piers took him by both arms. "You are a Pod," he said. "And you will sprout."

THIRTEEN

Nose-painting, sleep and urine

After the private performance in the barn the players took Will back to the great hall. Many of those who had eaten there were still in the room, talking and drinking. A chill had fallen outside and the room was warm with the fire burning cheerfully. All the family had withdrawn and there was no sign of Campion. Will was plied with a lot of beer and he chatted freely. Everyone was relaxed and in good humour and Will became glued to the conviviality until he could no longer ignore the annoyance that his bladder hurt very badly. He couldn't be bothered wandering off to the privy so he staggered out into the courtyard and pissed in a corner.

"I hope it rains tonight."

He wet his hand as he tucked his penis away whilst cranking his neck to look over his shoulder. Ros rocked there, wrapped in a shawl and with her arms folded. He wiped his hand on his doublet and turned to face her. She wasn't rocking. He was.

"Do you live out here?" he asked.
"I don't live anywhere," she said.
"You're too lovely to live," he dribbled.

121

She sneered a snort. Her phantom breath lingered longer than it had earlier.

He reached out to grip her and draw her closer but he underestimated her proximity to him and his hand swung short of her.

She breathed more disdain.

He wanted to say so much but could not think what even the tiniest part of it might be. A drip of urine, warm then suddenly very cold, was running down the inside of his right thigh. He wrestled with his brain. A thought came. "I loved my words," he said.

"And where are they now?" she said whimsically.

His brain threw him. "In the barn," he said.

This remark made no impression on her at all. Her face remained almost impassive apart from the layer of contempt that she had crafted so exquisitely. Her face was so tight and so soft, so straight and so curvaceous, so pale and so rich, and so plain that it was perfect. Her hair, fair by day but black in this light, was the gold of the night where its outline caught the feeble glow from the fire beyond the window. Will wanted to sing her a spontaneous sonnet, but said instead, "I loved my words."

"And where are they now?" she said again.

"In the barn," he said.

"Gone."

"Gone?"

"Gone, like all the girls you will love."

"No, no, no, no, no." He reached for her again but once more failed to grasp anything other than futility.

Her silence and her stillness were so superior.

"Why are you here?" he asked.

She thought for a short time which was long enough for him to ask her again.

"Why are you here?"

Her eyes inclined upwards to find a thought. "Ask those that made me."

He realised he was leaning against the corner of the courtyard and the seat of his pants would be wiping the wall that he had decorated with an arch of urine.

"I will," he said. "I will ask them, if you tell me where they are."

"I can't tell you who they are," she said.

"Ah."

"But I'll wager my life on one truth about my father."

"What?"

"I'll bet he told her he loved her."

"He probably did."

"And where is she? And where am I?"

"You are here."

"Yes."

"Wrapped in your loveliness."

"You are sitting in your own piss."

"No I'm not. I'm standing in it."

"Willy Shakeshaft!" she said disparagingly.

"Shakespeare!" he said proudly using the nobility of the suffix to propel himself away from the wall and towards her.

But she was gone. He'd made the mistake of blinking and within that blink she'd sidestepped his stagger and slipped from his view. The night took her. She might not have been there at all and he grasped at that hope, the hope that she had not seen him smear himself with his own stale, but then the night tapped him on the ear and he heard the door she'd gone through close.

He needed to piss again so he replenished the puddle he'd put in the corner, then he went back to find the happy huddle of merriment but found instead a hoop of reverence with Campion at its focal point. Everyone was kneeling. Solomon gently tugged Will to his knees and so Solomon stood a mile high even without the aid of his shins.

Campion was praying quietly. Will could make no sense of it. His ears heard every word but his mind only listened intermittently. He felt slightly sick.

The praying was mercifully short. The gathered voiced a collective amen. Many left. Others bedded down. No one objected to their staying. Will went with Solomon back to their allotted room.

"Do I smell of piss?" he asked Solomon.

"No more than the rest of us."

Will woke with his head four times its usual size and eight times as heavy. The pain was worst just behind his eyes. Something was lodged there and was pushing at his corky eyeballs to persuade them to pop out. They refused and swelled up so that they must stay in. The blood in his brain had turned to iron and slapped at his skull with any slight move that he made.

"The last of the harvest is on Will, we all have to help," said Andrew as he carefully suspended his lute from a roof beam by reattaching its strap.

Will sat at the breakfast table in the dining hall and ate nothing. He sipped a tipple of small beer. His state provoked much kindly ridicule. He tried to leave when all the others had gone but only made it as far as the door post against which he planted his forehead.

"Come on you." It was Agnes, the cook. She spoke gruffly but there was kindness too and when she gripped his biceps there was a pleasant pain. She took him back to the table and sat him there. "Stay put. I'll send Ros."

How could joy and horror be so wholly blended? How he craved to see Ros but how too he dreaded it. She was being sent to him. There was hardly a state in which he could charm her less. He was incapable of formulating anything resembling an apology, or an excuse, or declaration of contrition. All the flattery that he had rehearsed would be demoted to puerile platitudes. He looked pathetic. He considered throwing his undrunk cup of small beer over his hose to hide any possible smell of last night's urine. Fortunately it was just out of reach and his head refused to let him move. He folded his arms on the table and cushioned his pounding skull upon them. He closed his eyes.

When he opened them again someone was gently shaking his arm. He saw the hand. The fingers, buried in the folds of his sleeve were the best fingers, and they were in the best place.

"Come on," she said. It was the best voice. They were the best words. The feel of her hand on his arm was the best sound, and the noise of her voice was the best touch. He lifted his head and his lips followed several moments later after they had detached themselves from the table where his saliva had stuck them. As his head found a plane somewhere close to vertical the room swelled and slopped in the bucket of his brain. He felt very sick and had a premonition of projectile vomit forming a perfect heart outline as it flew from him to her.

Determination won the point. He swallowed hard and kept everything inside.

She was standing across the table leaning towards him and tentatively trembling his arm. She was as beautiful as any angel of death might be.

"Sit up," she said.

Was there firmness in her voice? Yes, there was. Was condescension there? Yes, there was. Was detrimental judgement there? Yes, there was. Was there any hint of sympathy? None.

"Drink this," she said.

Only his mother had ever spoken to him in that tone. "Oh!" he said.

"Drink it."

"What is it?"

"A remedy."

"Oh!" he said and realised that he sounded feeble and wretched, so he tried again to see if he could colour his pronunciation with the courageous moan of a man who had fought with too much ale and won. "Oh!" he tried to say, but it came out as a wet and odorous belch.

"Drink."

He took the cup and drank. The taste was nettles and peat and unripe plums. He got half of it down.

Neptune awoke in his stomach, assembled his horses and headed for Will's throat. Will found his feet, found the door, found the yard, counted cobbles, found the corner where his urine from the night before had hidden beneath the morning dew, was delighted it had gone, smiled, and spewed a torrent of undigested everything to redecorate the corner where Alexander de Hoghton's north and east wings butted together.

When he had finished he leaned back against the wall, managing this time to avoid the stain he had made. He felt ice cold and a tremor ran through him. He closed his eyes, and breathed slow, straining breaths.

"Drink."

"What."

"Drink," said Ros.

He shook his head.

She grabbed his head, forced the cup between his jaws and poured the rest of the contents into his mouth. He compliantly swallowed.

"Now go to bed and sleep."

He wanted to tell her he had loved the words but thought better of it, and made his best wounded hero walk over the courtyard. He would do as he was told. His progress was slow and he had to pause part way to steady himself against the wall and to swallow more air. Just before he went inside he looked back across the yard.

Ros was tipping a bucket to swill away his vomit.

"I am surprised that you are not more used to strong ale." Campion's grin was indulgently warm. It was the closest to devilment that Will had ever seen upon his friend's face.

They were in Campion's chamber. It was late afternoon. Will sat on the floor by the fire. He felt weak and fragile but very much better.

"I'm sorry Edmund. Should I find Alexander and apologise?"

"He was suitably amused. He's an old man and seen plenty of ale-sickness in his time."

"For not helping with the harvest."

"There's more to be done tomorrow."

"Late isn't it?"

"It's mostly in. Just the final fruit and tidying up, then they'll be sowing. And brewing." He laughed mischievously.

"I'll work twice as hard tomorrow."

"Are you going to have some supper?"

"My stomach feels tender, but I am hungry."

"Don't overfill it. And sit close to the door. And rehearse your route to the privy!"

"I must make amends to Ros."

Campion leaned against the wall and placed a pause before he spoke. He joined his two index fingers together and kissed them as he considered his words, then said, "She's a servant."

"So am I. So are you."

Campion's new smile was devoid of devilment, but rich with pleasure. Will knew he had passed the test, though there was an afterthought to Campion's appraisal of him that harboured just a sliver of suspicion. Will spotted it in his eye.

Supper was good. It was more of the stew that they'd had the day before, and at first Will thought it might trigger his nausea again but after the first two mouthfuls sank home he felt nourished and fortified and was glad that the taste could be once again associated with benefit rather than biliousness. At the end of the meal he was given added reason to be charged with both anticipation and consternation.

Piers took Will on one side.

"Friday will see a party."

"I know," said Will. "I will be moderate."

"Oh no, you must be much more than that. Moderation is not in our repertoire."

"What do you mean?"

"A play, Will, in which you will play."

"What?"

"My lord wants a play that day and we are his players and you are of our company."

"I will play before all these?"

"And more. It will be a revel to remember."

"What play will it be?"

"The one that we will write Will. You and I."

"What?"

"I will write it, but I can't do it without you."

"Why not?"

"Because my lord wants a play about Father Campion." Will took a step back. "About Campion?"

Piers glanced around the room locating Campion at the far side and at the same time drawing Will close again. "And he mustn't know it. He knows there will be entertainment, he knows you will be part of that, but he must not know that he is the hero."

Will laughed a little.

Piers went on, "That is why I need you to help me to write it. And we cannot delay. We will go to our room and begin it tonight. I must know all you know about his history and then we make our comedy."

"A comedy?"

"While we still can. His ending is still happy."

Solomon and Andrew joined them. Fulk was conversing with Ros who was clearing the tables. That sight distracted Will but Piers blocked his vision. "It must be a

127

surprise. Speak to no one about this other than we four."

Will nodded. "Solomon will be Campion."

His three comrades shuffled slightly.

"I will play Campion," said Piers.

Will swallowed a laugh. "But Campion is tall."

"Not as tall as Solomon," said Piers.

"But a lot taller than . . ."

"I will play Campion."

Solomon spoke. "It is the custom Will. Piers plays the leading part."

"Always?"

"Always," said Solomon.

"That is a small matter," said Piers.

Yes, thought Will.

"It will not be a long play and it will not be the only entertainment. It must have humour and Andrew must find a song to fit, and we must find a jig to fit that. So; to work."

They led Will from the room. He looked over his shoulder to see that Fulk was still with Ros. She was laughing. He was making her laugh. Laughter is a kind of love, thought Will.

Over the next hour Will told the others all that he had learned of Campion. Piers made tiny notes in the meagre pool of amber that his single candle provided. Eventually, Fulk arrived and Piers recapped on everything that Will had said. Andrew was already strumming a quiet sequence on the lute and saying out loud rhymes that he found for some of the words Will had used.

"I think this play should mostly be a song," said Fulk. "A ballad which we enact."

Piers considered the proposal. "Mmm," he said with a favourable inflection.

"An interlude," said Solomon. "We can do one of our tested favourites after."

Andrew nodded. "You could do your Cuckold Miller."

Everyone except Will laughed. The others explained that this was a bawdy comedy and a great favourite of their regular audience, especially Lord Alexander.

"Campion should see that," said Solomon.

Will saw a possible opening. "What kind of part is the miller?"

"A fool," said Fulk and they laughed at the memory of him.

"Played by Piers?"

"It's my finest role, among our comedies."

"Then you should not play Campion."

There was an unsteady settling of the laughter.

"They are different plays," said Fulk.

"We should not confuse people's memories," said Will. "Campion is a champion. He has great good will. He loves to laugh and I'm sure he will do so heartily at your miller but let's set him in strong contrast. Let's not offer any muddling in merry minds."

"It's a well-made point," said Fulk.

"And the Campion play will only be an interlude," said Solomon with just the trace of hope in his intonation.

"Hmm," considered Piers.

"Or a prelude," said Solomon. "A short song about Campion, then straight into The Cuckold Miller."

"Might work," said Piers. "The Miller is a good length on its own. So that plus a prologue would make sufficient cheer to round off the feast."

"Solomon should play Campion," said Fulk. "He's got the height."

Piers wrinkled his lips. "Yes," he said. "Solomon the wise shall be Campion the champion."

"What shall we call the song?" asked Andrew.

Will had no hesitation. "Campion's Brag," said Will. "It is what he will best famed for."

"Good title," said Fulk.

Piers toyed with his pen, which was dry from lack of use. "Got a tune we could put it to Andrew?"

"The Grey Hawk."

"Aye, the Grey Hawk is good," said Piers. "If we get the words right, they'll all sing along. Well, this candle is guttering and so am I. Think on what you've heard Andrew and as you work the field tomorrow start to fashion the singing words. We'll go to the barn before supper and see if we can make the song."

Their gathering broke up. Solomon came over to Will and patted him on the shoulder. No words were needed. Will accepted the thanks in silence. It seemed right. The big man would be the giant.

The following days passed quickly. During the mornings and most of the afternoons Will and his fellow players worked as directed on the farm attached to the manor. The last of the winter food was stored in the barns. The last of the apples and pears were picked. Ploughmen were at work. Next year's crops were sown.

There was much anticipation of the feast and festival that would conclude the week. Friday would be the feast of Saint Dennis, a Christian martyr. The talk was that Father Campion would stay until at least then. He would celebrate a holy Mass and then there would be much feasting and drinking. The manor, the close farm and the all the associated tenants and servants would be there. Everyone knew the danger, but it was the perfect plan because if they had the misfortune to be visited by non-sympathisers, the harvest carnival was a convenient cover for the gathering.

The actors made good progress on their song. Will had heard the tune before and easily assimilated the melody. They soon had all of the words and most of the actions. He had reservations regarding some of the phrasing selected by Piers, but both Solomon and Andrew appeared taken by his particular word-play and with their support he was able to persuade their scribe to adjust the lyric. He found this influence intensely rewarding. Piers would take all the credit, but Will would always know that he had been instrumental in the construction of the song. He would hold some of his more inspirational verses tightly to heart and preserve them for future preaching.

His experience of players had been severely limited. He had seen licensed troupes a few times at fairs and feast days in Stratford. At those times he had been intrigued, uplifted and richly entertained, but what he had seen was the final work, whereas now he got to see the act of creation. He marvelled at the players' inventiveness and how they linked words to actions and to music. They had such instantaneous wit, including Fulk, who held his own with the rest. In fact, when it came to dance, posture or acrobatics he was the master, which was probably how he had merited his place in the company. Will, on the other hand, was there under false pretences. He was a double deceiver.

By Wednesday night the company were almost ready,

but Will was wondering whether he could surreptitiously prise a few more biographical facts out of Campion and so he went in search of the priest. He was thwarted however by the fact that Campion had slipped out of the Tower that afternoon. No one had noticed him go and it was only as a result of Will's frantic search for him that Jane finally confirmed what had happed.

"Don't worry," she said. "He is close by and will be back tomorrow."

Will was relieved to hear it. For a moment he had felt abandoned and vulnerable, but calm returned. Then they had an unexpected visitor.

FOURTEEN

Unbidden guests

Jane, once again, was the bearer of the news. Will was working
with Fulk, stacking straw in the barn where they had met to
devise their song. They were in high spirits and used the ditty to
aid them in their routine, craftily dropping it when others were
close so that they would not overhear the content. Jane found
them. She was flustered.

"Fulk, Fulk."

The youths stopped working and cancelled their
laughter.

"What is it?

"There's someone here. He is waiting for my beloved
step-aunt in the great hall."

"Who is he?"

"I don't know. I overheard bits from above when he
came in. I want you to go and listen. You too Will. I want you
to listen especially."

"Why especially?" asked Will.

"Because he talks like you do."

Fulk and Will made it to the hall with the speed and
furtiveness of boys half their ages. They crept onto the minstrels'

132

gallery and peered between the balustrades. Elizabeth was seated in the armchair at the head of the table. Opposite her, at the far end of the table, stood a man with a woman's face.

Elizabeth was holding court. "Alum?"

"Alum."

"What about alum?"

"I am a trader, my lady, and I have been informed that you have a source of alum. It is, by all accounts a good source of very good alum."

"We would have no dealings in it, should it be inferior."

"I'm sure not, my lady, but alum of any quality is awkward to acquire especially when trade with certain ports is . . . difficult. English alum is not easy to come by."

Jane had caught up with listeners on the gallery but she had to hold her position beyond the door as the noise of her skirts would have betrayed her entrance. She stretched her neck to listen. Will liked her neck.

"I am somewhat perplexed as to why you felt it necessary to come here," said Elizabeth.

"It was on the advice of Mr John Shakespeare."

Will's guts constricted.

"And who might he be?"

"A glover. Stratford-upon-the-Avon. He uses your alum."

"Alum is worked on our lands but it is not necessary for you to speak to my husband. Mr Amcottes will negotiate with you. I cannot understand why this Mr . . ?"

"Shakespeare."

". . . would send you directly to this house, or why the porter felt it needful that you speak to Lord Alexander."

The man with the feminine face leaned towards the table and used a lower tone. "John Shaklespeare sends a message for his son."

There was a thunderous silence.

"His son?"

"His son. William."

The silence spoke again.

"And what would that message be?"

"It is for William."

Will watched Elizabeth. She took a controlled breath

while she fixed her visitor with a predatory stare.

"Well, there is no person of that name here."

"Might you, or your husband, or any of your household, know where I might find him?"

Jane brushed past the crouching pair of players and strode straight to the balustrade. The air announced her arrival and her voice took instant command.

"Who is this person?"

Elizabeth did not flinch. "Thank you Jane."

The visitor looked piercingly towards the gallery and Fulk gripped Will's foot in a signal not to even breathe. Will didn't breathe.

"This is my niece, Mr Thursby."

Jane took the reins of the conversation. "And this is my house. My home. It is not a market stall. If you desire to purchase alum. Go to an alum trader."

"Thank you Jane! I can assure you Mr Thursby that we have no information regarding your Mr Shakespeare's son. As you may have seen, our house is very busy with the last of the harvest and the starting of the sowing. So if I can ask you to return to the gatehouse they will indicate the direction of Alum Scar which is just a few miles to the north and east. Ask for Mr Amcottes."

"I'll see you to the gate sir," announced Jane and swiftly left the gallery.

The visitor drew cautiously closer to Elizabeth.

Will breathed slowly out.

"I understand that this house is a good house."

Elizabeth toyed with the seam of her sleeve. "I would hope so."

"A good house."

"I would hope so."

"Forgive me. I hope I can trust you if I say I crave the ear of a man of the church."

"It is a common craving."

"A man of the good church. The best church. The only church."

"Your faith sir is your own curse and blessing. I wish it serve you weakly with one and strongly with the other."

"This being such a strong house, I wondered if you can draw on the services of a priest."

"We adhere to the law, sir. And I'm sure you know the law."

"Unjust as it is."

"I don't judge the law, sir. The law judges me. I strive not to give cause for that judgement to be made. Here is Jane."

Jane turned on all her charm but as was Jane's wont, she made no attempt to disguise the insincerity of it. "This way sir."

"Alum Scar?"

"Alum Scar sir. The porter knows the way."

Jane led the visitor out. Fulk and Will went to the great keep tower to watch their progress to the gate and the stranger ride away. When Jane returned alone they intercepted her in the courtyard and then all three went to the great hall. It was empty but they could hear Elizabeth's raised voice deep in the upper reaches of the northern range.

Jane sat in the armchair. "Very slimy man, she declared.

"It was a woman," said Fulk.

"I must admit my mind was questioning his masculinity," said Jane.

Will was genuinely puzzled. "Are you sure?"

Jane said, "There was something disingenuous about him."

The fire cracked sending a spark arcing onto the rush-covered floor beyond the hearth. Fulk stamped on it casually smothering it. "He was a she. When you've played as many women as me you know what to look for. The posture was forced, the neck was as smooth as a swan's and her voice was inconsistently low. Her thighs were too soft and she rode like a woman. She was a she."

Something pricked Will's mind but he failed to understand what or why.

Jane was energised but also reflective. She drummed the arms of the chair with her fingers and nibbled the nails of her other hand. "Aye, Fulk, I think you may be right."

"No doubt about it," said Fulk.

The voices of Alexander and Elizabeth were heard getting nearer. Jane vacated the chair. "He's coming down."

Alexander staggered into the room using two hazel sticks. Jane gave the slightest bob, the boys bowed and stepped back. Alex grunted. Elizabeth snapped. "What are you doing here?"

Jane took the initiative. "I made them listen from the gallery."

Alexander slightly delayed his heavy descent into the armchair. He sighed, then grunted an acknowledgement.

Jane continued. "I wanted Will to hear the man's voice."

The old man grimaced slightly as he adjusted his position to face Will. "And?"

"The voice was not known to me, my lord. The sound of it was."

"A Warwickshire man?"

Fulk stepped forward. "Woman, my lord." He repeated his reasoning. Jane was now completely convinced, and Will too, was becoming more persuaded by Fulk's opinion. Even Elizabeth accepted it. She said, "This is more disturbing at every turn."

"Alexander leaned on one arm of his chair and tossed his sticks to the floor. "How in hell's name did she get as far as this hall?"

"That, I shall discover," said Elizabeth.

"That you will," said Alexander. "And you will know so not one moment before I do."

"The porter was pissed," said Jane.

"Jane!" exclaimed Elizabeth.

"He's always . . ."

Alexander cut in waving his hand. "There's more than Rowland to get past."

Elizabeth was quieter this time. "They're in the fields."

"What? Where was Jerome?"

"He's with Campion."

"Where is Campion?" asked Jane.

"With the Arrowsmiths," said Elizabeth.

"Thank the lord for that at least," said Jane.

Alexander slapped the stays supporting the arms of his chair. "God's wounds - how the hell do we know if anyone else has said anything to this . . . person?"

"They didn't on the way out. I made sure of that," said Jane.

Alex shuffled in his seat again. "Thank God someone

has their bloody head mortised on."

"We're all likely to lose ours," said Elizabeth.

"Wait, wait, wait," said Alexander. "Speak to everyone. Find out what has been said by whom. From what you've told me, things were well done once the mistake of granting admission was made. This person may be harmless."

Jane walked towards her uncle and stopped a few feet from him. "Any woman who goes to those lengths of disguise is not honest."

"True enough," said Alexander.

Elizabeth stood behind her husband and gripped the back of his chair. "Campion must go. Today."

Alexander breathed deeply. "Easy! Easy! Frighted bird. Frighted bird. Like my brother."

"Frighted and wise," said Elizabeth.

"He's our guest and this house is safe."

"So safe that this weird woman, who puts on the mantel of a man, knows where to look for him."

"She never mentioned him," said Jane.

"She knew where to seek Will, surely she knows more than that."

"Two considerations," said Alexander. "Elizabeth you may be right. But she may be of good faith. Secondly, whether she is loyal or not, if you convinced her that neither priest nor glover's boy are here, then as far she is concerned, this house is empty of her prize, and therefore is the safer for that. Campion will be all the more secure."

"We are being watched," said Elizabeth.

"And watched over," said Alex. "Now, I want Rowland here without delay, and see someone porters the gate in his absence. And that gate is barred to all save on my word. Excepting Campion and our own – but they must be our own. When I have seen Rowland, I will see all that I need to see in order to find out who saw and said what. During this time, Fulk and Will, you will give extra watch from the keep. When Campion comes back, all that has been learned will be put to him. If he wishes to flee, he goes with our good help. If he is content to stay then we will be honoured to house him."

Elizabeth interjected. "My lord . . ."

Alexander sliced the air in front of him with both hands. "He will make the decision, we will make the hospitality."

Will and Fulk went to the battlements of the keep as instructed. A short while later Jane, wrapped in a grey cloak, joined them and reported that Rowland the porter had been spoken to in severe terms, but he complained that the visitor had known such detail about the de Hoghton's that he had been convinced that it was safe to open the gate. He couldn't recall saying anything about the young master Shakeshaft and was adamant that he made no mention of Campion.

"I believe him," said Jane, "though the man carries so much fluid in his head we can't be sure there's any room in there for such a thing as memory."

"He's the porter," protested Will.

"He's usually under the watchful eye of Jerome, who is without doubt our best man. It's only right he should be at Campion's side."

Will felt a sting of jealousy tinged with the remembrance of the guilt of inadequacy. In addition to that he was much troubled. The visitor claimed she had a message for him from home. The wonder of what that message might be burned deep within him. The prevailing westerly wind had turned cold and Fulk slipped off to get his and Will's cloaks.

"You look troubled, Will."

"She knew of me. My real name."

"The name you were given. You can make any name real. Unlike me."

Will listened with his eyes and saw a woman enclosed uncomfortably in the cloak of her heritage. She shrugged in order to snuggle slightly deeper into its collar.

"What's in a name?" she mused.

"Everything."

"And if we called the west wind east would it blow any less cold?"

He turned his doublet collar up in the hope of a tiny extra comfort. "Wind of change," he said.

"You didn't recognise her then?"

"I didn't even see that she was a woman," he said.

"You should look harder Will. Study with more scrutiny."

"Yes, my lady."

"She had a message for you."

"That's what she said."

"From your father."

"Yes."

"Then she must know him."

"Lots of people do."

"Because of his trade."

"Mostly. He is well known in Stratford."

"Because of his leather work. His gloves."

"And for other reasons."

"If you saw a glove would you be able to tell that it was made by him?"

"Most probably."

"What about this one?" Jane's hand emerged from the vent in her cloak. It clutched a fawn glove. Will was immobilised. He fixed on the glove as a cat on a suddenly revealed rat.

"Hers?"

"It was tucked under her saddle strap."

Will gave Jane a look rich with a blend of disbelief and admiration.

Jane read his accusation perfectly. "Fulk is a good teacher," she said.

He took the glove from her. "Calf skin." He turned it inside out, drew a sharp breath and then another. "Walter stitched this."

"Walter?"

"Father's apprentice."

"Sure?"

Will showed her the stitching. High up the seam was a neat pattern of overlapping thread. "Every glover has a name, and he leaves it in every glove."

"Well she wasn't entirely false then."

Will offered the glove back to Jane.

"Keep it," she said. "Now you each have something belonging to the other."

"I need to know her message."

"No you don't. You live, you breathe, and you are free."

Shakespeare scoured his horizons. "Freedom is temporary."

"So are life and breath."

"True."

"So don't waste them."

Fulk returned. Will slipped the glove inside his doublet and put his cloak on. It diminished the bite of the west wind, but he didn't feel any warmer.

When the light began to fail, Will and Fulk were relieved of their watchful duty. Others were put to that task and it was stated that the night watch would be doubled. After dinner, Jane met up with the players and told them that the word from the Arrowsmith's house was that Campion had suggested that their plans for the end of the week should be unaltered. They would mark the feast of St. Dennis with mass followed by merriment. Jane left the players to their final preparations.

Will's heart wasn't in it. He was a cauldron of confusion. He began to imagine what might have befallen his father or mother, or both. And then there was Ros. God in heaven, she was a glorious creation. And then there was God. God who had created him, who had called him, who would send agents to arrest him, to test him, to end him. God who would revive him, welcome him, celebrate him, smile on him, elevate him, give eternity to him. God who would forgive him.

And then there was the world. A world that hungered for him. By coming to Hoghton Will had seen the appetite the world had for him. It wanted to show him new wonders, new horrors, new joys, new fears. It turned strangers into friends and offered friends that might be foes. By learning to listen with his eyes Will was starting to see souls. He saw those souls in a peculiar light, a light that only he could shine. No one else was him, so only he could see what he saw in the way that he could see it. That notion chimed within him. Its resonance created a vibration that shook his bones.

Whilst telling Piers the tale that was Campion he had discovered a part of himself hitherto hidden. He had found that through his own words, and with song and movement, he could breed a new species of life.

And then there was Ros. Why had God created her? And having created her why did he deposit her in such lowly circumstances?

And then there was Campion. The finest of men. The standard against which all others could be measured. The benchmark. The one to copy. The book made flesh. He knew why God had created Campion. To torture and destroy him.

And then there was Ros.

Fulk kicked him and told him to concentrate. He remembered the words he should have said and proclaimed them without due feeling. Fulk's expression was all that was needed to make him repeat them with more gusto. Andrew struck the strings of the lute and they launched into the song that Piers had written. It was Piers' pride but most of the words were Will's. The structure belonged to the tune that Andrew had brought, but the phrasing scanned so well because Will had an ear for it and orchestrated changes to make it fit more finely.

They played loud. No one else was near the barn and Campion was not even inside the protective wall. Campion was at large. Campion was in increased danger. Campion was closer to God.

They rehearsed deep into the night and when they were happy with *The Brag*, they practised the other pieces they would play. Will was given almost nothing to do in those sections, but he savoured seeing his skilled collaborators busy at their magical craft.

When they finally retired to their beds Will made a diversion up onto the roof of the keep once more. The lookout heard him coming and hence made sure he was looking out. Will looked out too. The west wind was still blowing. It had brought heavy clouds, so even if there was anything there the lookout was unlikely to see it. He would have to watch with his ears.

Will saw nothing and saw everything there was to see. It was too much to take in. And in addition to that, there was Ros.

FIFTEEN

The copy and book

The feast of St. Dennis came. The harvest was all in. The household was assembled for the customary banquet, but this year there was an additional celebration which, in turn, wound up additional expectation. The holy Mass would be held and be presided over by someone that the congregation considered to be much closer to God than they could ever hope to be. Perhaps his sanctity could shed a little salvation on them?

The vestments were taken out of hiding, much to the consternation of Elizabeth, and the great hall was laid out. The table that later would be tested by the weight of culinary excess, was simply adorned with cloth, chalice, wine and bread. Father Campion wore the vestments that the family had treasured for decades. He greeted the congregation that comprised most of those who lived and worked within and close to the tower, plus many other notable locals who were especially loyal to the family and to the faith. He spoke plainly and colloquially.

"Good friends, it is right grand to welcome you here. I thank you on behalf of my lord Alexander for your industry and your loyalty, and I thank on behalf of him to whom we owe all thanks for your fidelity and your charity. Later we will feast on the food that you have farmed, but first we will pray, and we will eat as he commanded us to, by feasting on his holy flesh and his sacred blood." With those words he entered a kind of trance. His presence in the room transmuted. His persona was extended by a visible aura generated by the attitude that he adopted. He willed himself into an elevated awareness, not of his surroundings, but of a place beyond the walls that enclosed them, yet present also within the hall. His eyes looked out and yet saw only his inner vision. His compatriots by witnessing that change were taken with him. They too, left the place where they resided and without moving were relocated in sacredness. The air changed and was charged with unseen but palpable energy. The timbers contracted, tightened and locked out all evil. The smoke from the fire hung as angelic incense. Campion crossed himself. He spoke in Latin. "In nomine Patris et Filii et Spritus Sancti . . ."

The congregation breathed in as one and concurred with gentle thunder.

"Amen".

The Mass surged and all were carried on its tide of communal meditation. To begin with, Will rode the spiritual surf, but the devil came knocking. He caught himself slipping from prescribed thoughts to search out any sign of Ros, and when he could not see her he settled instead for Jane. She was a picture of devotion. She had a seat but chose instead to kneel. Her hands gripped each other so tightly they might have been nailed together. He could see the pattern where blood could not pass so that a halo of paleness delineated each finger and gave her gloves of pure piety. Her focus was the floor but she saw only the future and from her expression Will deduced that it was not a pretty picture. He saw her seeing salvation slip away.

Elizabeth, on the other hand, was a self-portrait of piety. She mostly sat, kneeling only when the sacrament crested at instances of consecration or deep devotion. Otherwise she adopted the carriage and countenance of a bereaved Madonna. She phrased her responses as one practiced in praying but also managing to present as a penitent who was playing with more affectation and hence less persuasion than Fulk, Andrew or Piers. The picture she presented was all surface and no subtext. It was the badge of belief. Shakespeare saw the façade and hence

143

looked through it. He formulated an axiom that a façade could only be seen by seeing that which it disguised. He thought about the prevalence of deception in his troubled country. He lived in a time costumed in disguise.

Alongside the matron of the house sat its true master. Alexander projected peace. He did not appear relaxed, but resigned, to whatever the next hour, day, or night might bring. He remained seated at all times and Will doubted that he had the dexterity to kneel. Nevertheless, he showed sincerity, humility and security. He was the alternate of his wife.

Will didn't like the counterfeit faith he saw in Elizabeth and so switched his attention back to Jane who was still arched in honest devotion as the Mass moved on.

The tide of invocation swelled as the English congregation spoke and sung as a Roman choir. Their Latin liturgy had a Lancashire intonation, but to Will the regional cadence enriched the prayers he'd learned from his Warwickshire compatriots and gave them extension. His spiritual heritage was as strongly rooted a hundred miles from home as it was in the persecuted hearts he'd left behind. He was buoyed on the waves of conviction voiced so loudly in that impromptu church pitched on a wooded hill. His soul was alive again, revived by the ancient vocabulary. His second language, though not as extensive as his first was more ancient, more eloquent, more consecrated. It was the common tongue of saints, the mother of meaning, and the father of faith.

He understood afresh where his ambition lay and how he could crank up his courage to discharge his duty. These people needed him. They would welcome him, they would listen to him, they would revere him. He would be hero and holy man, prophet and pious poet, saviour and . . . saint. Could he fight that fight? Could he endure that trial? Could he conquer death? He could. What would Ros think of him then?

After the consecrated bread became Christ and had been consumed there came a time of contemplation. Fulk sang unaccompanied a plainchant that Will had not heard before. After that there was a kind of relief and release. The hall remained quiet but one by one the faithful slipped from their unity with the host they held within them. Jane looked exhausted. Elizabeth projected invigoration as she anticipated that the tools of the sacrament could now be returned to storage.

A flare of anxiety shot across her features as Campion stood and clearly indicated he was about to preach.

The priest addressed them easily and with humour, but as on previous occasions he was able to rise from the banal to the profound in one smooth switch of pitch and rhythm. Will noticed that when he spoke of higher things hid did so with added gravity signalled by a deeper more resonant tone, or a lighter more musical air and at the same time his words found a beat that struck in time with an excited heart, and coincidently, not far removed from that suggested by the lines he had been rehearsing in recent days. He spoke at length. Most were spellbound but sporadic shuffles and coughs began to precipitate. Among the more restless was Elizabeth.

There were elements of the sermon that Will had heard before, some many times since Stratford. These constituted the timber frame of Campion's campaign and he had crafted them to perfection to touch the heart and pin the memory. The priest simply substituted the name of the county for the one where they were residing.

Campion concluded. "And so good folk of Lancashire, this haven of holiness, keep sacred this blessed county. Foster here the children of the true faith. Teach love before you teach letter. Teach truth: the truth that lies beneath the text. I must entrust you to do this for me for I cannot long escape the hands of heretics. The enemy have so many eyes, so many tongues, so many scouts and crafts. You must carry on when I am gone. I have no more to say today, than to recommend your case and mine to Almighty God, the searcher of hearts who sends us his grace. May we at last be friends in heaven, when all injuries shall be forgot."

He then invited them all to kneel while the farewell blessing was given. The amen was the loudest of all, signalling association, agreement, and welcome conclusion.

Gentle conversation instantly elevated into deafening discussion as overwarm folk stretched their limbs and restored the spirit of the crowd to the secular. Through the polite melee Will watched Elizabeth struggle in her priorities between shepherding her ailing husband, dutifully congratulating Campion and urgently organising the removal of anything that might be incriminating. The room was readied and the feasting got underway.

Will discovered that his appetite was dulled by nerves. He tried to tuck into Agnes' magnificent game pies but only made slow progress. On the one hand he craved a belly full of beer and on the other he knew he must severely pace himself so that his memory and his stomach would hold what was required. This was doubly frustrating because he had not known such a sumptuous spread with pork, venison, swan and all manner of game roasted and in pastry along with a wide selection of the best of the harvested fruit and vegetables, and cheese and eggs, plus rich bowls of jellied potage, and silvered plates of sweetmeats. And all this was presided over by the boar's head centrepiece, roasted and glazed and richly decorated with green herbs and baked fruit.

The solemnity of Campion's Mass was all dispersed now. The room was thick with the vapours of cooked food and spilled cider and ale. Voices jested and laughed and sang and the muddled cries of more than a hundred happy revellers reverberated from ceiling to wall and made everyone shout even more in order to be heard. Will found the strain of conversation difficult, partly because it was so noisy but also because his mind was constantly flicking back to the play he was to perform. In addition, he was looking out for Ros. He caught sight of her several times but she had much to do and appeared well disciplined in the execution of it. She was the target of many menfolk and as the ale in their blood increased so their self-control diluted. On numerous occasions he saw her ambushed and pulled onto the knees of men, most of whom appeared to have few scruples and even fewer teeth. She laughed good-spiritedly and fought off their fumbling affections with kindly firmness. At times she objected less, or not at all, and that caused Will to generate resentment.

Once the majority of the food had been consumed the room was reorganised once more. A space was cleared beneath the minstrels' gallery and the merry makers shepherded to sit and stand in a grand arc facing it. The armed chair was placed as a throne for their honoured guest and two more with high backs positioned either side. Only then did Will realise that it had been some time since he had lain eyes upon Campion, and that Elizabeth and Lord Alexander had gone from the hall too. Now, however, they reappeared in a tiny procession. Alexander came first, slowly and as steadily as he could manage with his stick and uncooperative leg, then Elizabeth in her finest red frock and pearls and jewels, and then Campion who was also dressed anew. His hosts made great show of this. Alexander had made a gift of a new disguise for him. He was now resplendent in red though the hue was more crimson and less scarlet than that of his hostess. Now he was yet another merchant traveller, sartorially splendid but not so showy as to draw too much attention. His entrance brought the greatest cheer of the three and he took that applause with good grace and a self-mocking humility that became instead a kind of generous pride reflecting back the adulation to those who gave it. Behind them, through the door beneath the gallery, Fulk gesticulated wildly to gain Will's attention and summon him to the corridor. Will went, and there found another Campion, for there stood Solomon in the very clothes that the priest had worn only an hour earlier. Will gasped, Solomon grinned and Andrew put his finger to his lips. Clearly very few knew of this switch and Campion himself was not one of them. Will was quickly whisked into the small dining hall where his own simple stage clothes were laid out.

"Put them on," said Fulk.

The doublet and hose were not dissimilar to Will's own but much more brightly coloured with alternate segments of orange and yellow and sleeves more medieval than contemporary, so that he had the appearance of a jester or fool. Meanwhile he heard the hubbub fall as Pier's voice rang out in song. Soon Andrew's lute resounded and his voice harmonised with the chorus of the play master's scene-setting song. Then that was done, and Piers was talking to his audience. Just what he said was indistinct, but clearly successful, as great waves of laugher ensued and burst of clapping signalled weighty approval. Fulk ushered Will to just outside the door where Solomon grinned and did a little jig, then Andrew struck up the introduction to *The Grey Hawk* and the three of them burst into song, and the two youngest into the room.

Friends and dear countrymen, lend me your ears
And of Campion's brag, let me sing.
His tale he won't tell, so you listen well
He's the mark, and the copy and book, my brave boys.
He's the mark, and the copy and book.

The crowd cheered. Will felt slightly dizzy. He was encouraged by their happy faces which were warmly but gently lit mostly by the glow from the fire away to Will's left, and also by a few clutches of candles here and there. They parted to either side of the door as Solomon sang the next verse solo from behind the screen.

In London my father sold books now and then
And in London I first held a pen
In school I spoke well, the queen she could tell
That I was the fellow to watch, my brave boys.
That I was the fellow to watch.

Then Solomon leaped through the door with a flourish, and the audience at once recognising the man that was both Campion and not Campion, bellowed laughter and spontaneously slapped out vigorous applause. Solomon sang on.

And fellow at Oxford, at just seventeen,
And I spoke once again for the queen
I told her of tides, and in March beware ides.
Even Caesar had bad luck with friends, my dear boys.
Even Caesar had bad luck with friends.

The four of them acted out the sense of the lyric with Fulk presenting as an especially pompous Julius Caesar. Piers, Solomon and Will made the actions of Caesar's assassins stabbing him in the back and sending him forwards in a dramatic death throw which evolved into a forward roll that in turn culminated in a leap to his feet that signalled the start of the chorus.

Friends and dear countrymen, lend me your ears
And of Campion's brag, let me sing.
His tale he won't tell, so you listen well
He's the mark, and the copy and book, my brave boys.
He's the mark, and the copy and book

Then Solomon took up the melody again.

I studied so well, I could not trust the book
And from England's sad shore I did sail,
In Ireland I found, the old faith was sound
And I switched to the songbook of Rome, my brave boys
And I switched to the songbook of Rome.

The players played out reading from books then writing on paper and Fulk mimed nailing a paper to the door.

They said I'll be martyr in Prague so they did
And they pinned that brave word on my door
But I would not take scare, and I left it right there
For I'd rather die than live false, my brave boys.
For I'd rather die than live false.

Into the chorus they went again this time incorporating the simple jig they'd worked out. By now many of the onlookers had caught the tune, some clapped in time and even joined in with the repeated phrases.

He's the mark, and the copy and book, my brave boys.
He's the mark, and the copy and book

Solomon moved along the front row of the spectators showing off the costume he wore, and switching to falsetto for the last line of the next verse.

I came back to England, wrapped in disguise
With a fake name and cheap buckram shirt,
And sometimes so grand with codpiece in hand.
But I never swapped hose for a skirt, my brave boys.
But I never swapped hose for a skirt

The tall man took centre stage, recovered his natural pitch and cannoned the lyric to the ceiling.

And although my new name it was changed now and then,
And although my new shape was not mine
My heart it is true, I love God and you
And I'll never leave England again, my brave boys
And I'll never leave England again.

The audience cheered and clapped and the players gathered for the final chorus, but something was wrong. Dominic Arrowsmith appeared on the gallery his face contorted and arms flailing wildly to stop the show. The players were oblivious to the interruption and powered into the chorus at the top of their voices but suddenly Will caught sight of pockets of unsettlement and then Elizabeth was on her feet flapping her arms and shouting something that no one could hear. It took a moment for quiet to settle.

"Please! Please!" yelled Elizabeth. "Mr Arrowsmith what is it?"

"Party at the gate, my lady,"

"What?"

"Magistrate Riley, and a party."

"Magistrate Riley?"

Alexander found a vocal volume that Will had not heard from him before. "Party? How many?"

"Twenty or more."

There was a silence and then a combustion of sound as everyone rattled out their reactions and through this Will saw Elizabeth squirm into a convulsion and emit a scream that bore no resemblance to any uttering he had heard before. What she said next was completely muffled by the animated hubbub, but then she stumbled into a repetitive litany of "What? What? What!"

Jane took control.

"Good people, good people I pray you listen. Remake the general feast. Father and friends disperse and quickly. Not you players, you must replay. The close household - go to your tasks - to your ordinary tasks, in ordinary ways, but with great haste. And hide what must be hidden. With great haste. Haste! Haste! I pray you, all haste! But calmly!"

Jane's expediency inspired Elizabeth to grasp for her authority, though she could not hide her crippling fear. "Father Edmund, to your appointed place. Someone find Nathaniel fast and get him to open up the place. Then everything away . . . no not . . . oh saints the papers . . ."

Jane firmly eased her stepmother aside, and at the same time caught the attention of Ros who had materialised apparently from nowhere. "Take Father to his place, and then you must see to the papers. Bury them well, or you bury us all. Now to our duties each and every one. All else! All else! We must recommence the festivities. Piers – present your play. All else, eat, drink and make merry."

Alexander had risen from his seat. He waved his stick in the air as if conjuring Jane's masterly command into reality. "Players make your play," shouted. "Make your play."

Initially there was some confusion, and Elizabeth looked as if she was about to lose her wits, but Jane calmed her and sat her down. Alexander reclaimed his seat next to her. The house servants were highly animated but everyone seemed to know what to do. Will held the door as Ros went hurrying through with Campion heading for the priest hole. Will's instincts were to follow but Solomon gripped him firmly on the shoulder and pulled him back into the hall. Meanwhile above the raucous exchange of one hundred opinions Will heard Ros calling loud for Nathaniel the carpenter.

"Here!" came the response from close by and Nathaniel the carpenter rushed between Solomon and Will in urgent pursuit of the servant and priest.

Margery, Elizabeth's favoured servant, came to her mistress and did what she could to help Jane calm her aunt, meanwhile Dominic Arrowsmith came from the gallery and went straight to Alexander to give him a report more confidentially.

"Who is here?" asked Will.

"Riley the magistrate," said Fulk. "They'll be holding him at the gate. If he has a warrant they'll have to let him in. If he hasn't got a warrant why has he brought twenty men?"

"We'll go straight into the Cuckold Miller," said Piers.

"I need to change costume," said Solomon.

"No time," said Piers, "play it as you are. Now places, and get Andrew to strike up the first tune, it will quieten the crowd."

Moments later Andrew was playing, and Solomon singing along. There were no words but he vociferously sang the tune and got all the other players to join in. Then they clapped and thumped their feet and got the audience to do the same. Everyone understood why. The priest hole was being opened and resealed and the more noise they made the more it might hide the sound of the concealment of Campion.

Meanwhile Lord Alexander resisted all petitions that his doors be open, but eventually Dominic Arrowsmith relayed a message that their lord could not ignore and a grave single nod of his head signalled that the real life drama may be about to steal the stage from the players.

Three more times they sounded the tune before the hall fell quiet. It did so, not because the song had ended, but because magistrate Riley and his escort had entered through the door beneath the gallery. He found himself in the focus of all, and there was a moment of comic pathos as he stood among the players and made a slight bow to Alexander.

Fulk could not restrain himself and gave the first line of the play. "There once was an unfortunate miller . . ."

Alexander raised his hand, the flattened palm towards Fulk.

Magistrate Riley spoke. "My lord de Houghton." He offered another slight bow.

"Mr Riley."

"I am sorry to interrupt your revels."

"I understand you have a warrant."

"I do, my lord."

"To what end?"

"To apprehend a person on behalf of our sovereign. A person most unwelcome to our shores."

"What person might he be?"

"The Priest Edmond Campion."

A murmur rippled round the room."

Elizabeth breathed drew breath to speak but Alexander prevented any sound by a raised arm. Alexander allowed full quiet to fall before he said, "What reason have you to think that he be here?"

"This paper gives me full permission to sack your house in search of him. I would prefer to save my men the effort and your property the damage. And there will be damage. Unless you simply place him in my custody."

"This is a loyal house, Mr Riley. Who issued this supposed warrant?"

"I will not be stalled by rhetoric, my lord." The magistrate raised his voice. "All here remain so at my pleasure on pain of prison and worse. All the men will be tested." He turned to his captain. "Search every chamber, crack every wall, lift every floor."

The murmur re-erupted as a rumble. Some squealed, some shouted, some proclaimed defiance, but all that was overwhelmed by the shouts of the militia that the magistrate had brought. His escort brandished their swords and strode purposefully to pincer the crowd, while others move off in twos and threes towards the doors. Then one great shout towered over all other sound.

"I am he."

The whole assembly was equally surprised by this outburst and everyone halted their movement and held their voices. The shout was made again.

"I am he."

The moment of confusion persisted while individuals tried to find the origin of this bold declaration. Solomon, who had stepped to one side when the magistrate entered, now strode forward and reclaimed the centre of the improvised stage. He repeated his speech again.

"I am he. I am the man you seek."

A new choral rumble obscured what Riley said next, but he called for quiet and when that was re-established, he called his captain close. Then he addressed Solomon. "You are the Jesuit, Edmund Campion?"

Solomon grinned. "Ask anyone in this room."

The crowed murmured again but the captain hammered his sword on the floor until silence returned. Will scanned the room. His heart was racing, and he saw great confusion on the faces of the crowd. No one knew how they should react. Except for one.

Jane stepped forwards by a pace. "He is Edmund Campion, Mr Riley. We can all bear witness to that."

"If you can then you are all branded by the same crime."

There was a choir of distressed mutterings. Jane did not shirk. She silenced the less spirited with her strident announcement. "The family carries the accountability for this man. He is here at our pleasure."

Riley looked askance at Solomon and entered an unheard conversation with his captain. Will felt certain that Solomon's ruse was about to collapse but suddenly the captain gave a sign and two of his men laid hands on Solomon and ushered him roughly towards the door.

"My heart it is true, I love god and you," cried
Solomon.

Someone in the crowd called out, "The mark and the
copy and book!"

The magistrate said something but no one could hear
it. The captain banged the floor again. Riley addressed
Alexander de Hoghton. "You must come too."

Jane spoke up. "Leave him here. Take me. This was
my father's house. It is my house. Take me."

Riley ignored her and turned to his captain, "Take the
Lord."

There was movement among the crowd and groups of
men surged forwards, but once again a raised arm from
Alexander was enough to restore stillness and silence. "I will go
with you, Mr Riley. But at my pace."

Riley nodded. The hubbub was rising again but Riley
quickly quelled it. "One more," he said. "We must have one
more. Campion was reported with a boy. We must have the
boy."

A tremble ran through Will. He felt goose-whiteness
rinse his face and he was certain his bladder was about to
spontaneously empty. He waited for the warm river to run
down his leg, but it didn't happen. Fortunately, both the
magistrate and his captain were looking roughly in Will's
direction. Had they not been they might have seen the swathe
of spectators that put their focus on him. He knew, however,
that his hour had come. This was his time. This was when he
must prove his worth. He must own up. He drew breath but he
caught the face of Jane and she gave a small but strong shake of
her head, and at the same instant another voice claimed all ears.

"That person is I," said Fulk with a flourish.

"And who are you?" asked Riley.

"The person who pinned the word Martyr on
Campion's door," proclaimed Fulk, but most strangely not in his
own voice, but in an accent much more reminiscent of Will's
Warwickshire drawl.

Riley needed no further persuasion and Fulk was
summarily apprehended by the captain and taken from the
room. General noise rose again as Alexander was urged away.
Elizabeth was seen making token objections, but Riley firmly put

them aside.

The next hour was bizarre. The search party left as quickly as it had arrived. Many of the revellers left the tower while those that stayed and made pools of tense discussion. Elizabeth burst into tears and withdrew to her chamber with Margery. Jane assembled the players in a small room off the minstrels' gallery.

"There isn't much time," she said. "We have to get our guest out. They will not be fooled for long." Ros came to the door and Jane summoned her to join them.

Will's clothes were damp with drying sweat but his heart was settling and he felt that his face may have regained its usual colour. He wanted to admit to his attempt at bravery. "I was about to . . ."

"I know what you were about to do," said Jane. "It was noble but foolish. You saw how they reacted to Fulk's impersonation of you. One speech from you and they'd know you were the genuine Warwickshire man and that would convince them the real Campion was here. They would make you talk."

Will felt pale again.

"They will be back," said Jane, "and they will rip every room apart."

"Let them," said Ros.

They all stared at her, but she did not flinch.

"Let them," she said.

SIXTEEN

One face

The Magistrate Riley returned the next day. He brought his men, and Alexander de Hoghton, but not Solomon or Fulk. The Tower was searched but not in an especially fastidious way. A small amount of damage was caused where they tested joints and floorboards but this was done more out of spite than determination. They knew that if the grey hawk of the counter-reformation had been there, then he had flown.

Only Ros knew how Campion had been spirited away and she blatantly refused to tell anyone. That way, she said, not only the man but the manner was safe. No one in the search party thought to question her.

After an hour the magistrate's men were going through the motions of a hunt but convincing no-one not even their master. He called them off and met with his former prisoner in the great hall. Alexander sat by the fire, its banked logs failing to feed any colour into his face. Will watched from the gallery but arrived too late to hear the first part of the conversation.

"Give him my regards," said Alexander.

"I would rather have given him that for which he

156

hunts."

"Then you will need to look elsewhere."

"Such as?"

"My dear Mr Riley, I can honestly say that I have no better idea than you."

Riley shifted his weight from one foot to the other but made no response.

Alexander did not shift his attention from the fire. "I remember well when you found all you needed in the rites of the true faith."

"I still do, my lord. But the true faith has changed."

"Truth cannot change."

"Campion is not here. Not now. I believe that to be the truth."

"You will return my two men."

"They misled us."

"They spoke not a word of a lie. You made of it what truth you would. That is not their crime."

"I'll send them back."

"By nightfall. And not a mark upon them."

"I fear it may be too late for me to guarantee that. My men do not like being misled."

"None of us do. We cannot tolerate it."

"They'll be with you this day." The magistrate made a small bow and left. Within moments his entourage had quit the castle and the west wind was the only unwelcome guest within the walls.

Alexander de Hoghton took to his bed where he would remain for the next three days. Elizabeth, who had stayed in her own room throughout the search, gravitated to the great hall where she took a meagre supper with Jane. Will did not witness this. The players ate in the dining hall but their appetites were subdued as the fate of Solomon and Fulk still hung in the balance. Will told the others what he had witnessed but Piers seemed unimpressed. Andrew was downcast and did not contribute to the conversation. Ros was the most conventional in her demeanour. She was uncommunicative, but her energetic efficiency did not waver. It was yet another attribute for Will to admire.

Magistrate Riley kept his promise and the captives were returned from custody shortly before sunset. Elizabeth summoned them to the great hall and they soon had an impromptu audience of the majority of the household.

"I see you are bruised, gentlemen," she said.

Both men had the visible signs of a beating on their faces, but the discolouration was shallow.

"The frustrations of victorious men when they find they are losers," explained Solomon with a grin showing at least as many teeth as he had when he last smiled in their company.

Jane spoke. "How long did you preserve your impersonation?"

"In truth, not long," said Solomon presenting his arse to the fire. "Our fortune was favoured by the escort not being local." This remark sent a murmur of uncomfortable agreement around the room. The magistrate had brought unknown faces with him. Understandably these were not from the de Hoghton estate, but it had been a focus of much discussion as to who they might be. Solomon and Fulk could shed no light on that. "As soon as we were at Riley's house we were recognised by some of the household, but we played along as long as we could." This generated communal approval. "When they threatened my lord Alexander, we had to conclude our act. We offered the plate but they chose to put their rewards on our pate." The laughter this raised went some way to alleviate the impact of the beating on the faces of the two. Fulk gave a little bow and a rapid enactment of one of their assailants landing punches, and then himself being dizzy as a result.

Solomon said "They tried us further but their tricks were no match for us. We spoke only of our play."

Jane said, "And did they not question as to how you knew the play?"

"We told the truth, my lady. We said we made it up."

Jane was enlivened with delight. "But from what? Surely they must have asked from what?"

"There my lord Alexander came to our aid. He said that there were no surprises in our tale. The man was already legendary. Isn't that why they were hunting him?"

There was low level laughter.

"Such a remark did not sit well with the Magistrate, and he resolved therefore to try again to find him. So they came back here to look again."

Jane said, "Meantime what of you?

"The cellar," said Fulk. He put on a sad clown face. "The old cellar. No food but cobwebs, no drink but mildew."

Elizabeth asked, "Did they try you further?"

Solomon replied, "There was talk of it. . ."

"And fear of it," said Fulk.

"But it did not happen."

Elizabeth sighed then drew in a thought on the next breath. "Good servants, I scarce know how to thank you for your moment of – creation – that saved something inconceivably precious. You must eat now. And get Agnes to put a balm on those bruises. Our players must be handsome."

With that she summoned an end to the gathering, though couple to continued to hold court on a much smaller basis, continuing to embellish their adventure for the benefit of twos and threes in turn as they chewed on their suppers.

As Elizabeth withdrew to return upstairs she passed close to Will. She looked ashen and world-weary. Jane joined Will.

"What an escapade."

He bowed slightly. "An escape. Where is Campion? Do you know?"

"Only one person does, and she's not telling."

"Elizabeth?"

Jane spurted a laugh. "God's blood no! And if you find out don't tell her. She's as leaky as last year's nets."

"Then who knows? Just Ros?"

"Just Ros. And Campion of course. And God."

"My lord Alexander."

"He doesn't wish to know, because that way it can never be extracted from him. Wise counsel, Will. Very wise counsel."

Will considered what she had said and the implications it had for Ros. He sank so deeply into that thought that the rest of the room was removed from his consciousness. Then Jane said something completely unexpected.

"Come to my chamber Will."

"What?"

"All is well. I just don't want to be alone." There was a vulnerability about Jane that he had neither seen nor suspected possible until that moment. "All is well," she said again. So he went with her.

Jane's room was one of the few that he had not yet seen. It was part of the inner structure linking the Great Keep to the northern range. It was not large, but comfortably furnished with a quality bed and an ornately carved backless chair. It had its own fire, which had settled low. They built it up then Jane took to the chair and Will squatted on the floor added wood, and took a stick to lift it a little higher to allow air beneath it. The chimney had a good draw and the fuel soon caught.

"So when shall we commence our Latin lessons?"

"Whenever my lady wishes."

"Which lady?" asked Jane.

"If she commands it we will go through the motions. If you desire it, we will do it properly."

"You might have noticed, Will, that I am not disposed to carry out Elizabeth's commands."

"She's not very good amid a crisis."

"Whereas you are."

Will shook his head. "I was too scared to do anything."

"Better that than do the wrong thing."

"You were wonderful," he said.

"Rehearsal."

"What?"

"I had rehearsed it many times in my mind. It was bound to happen sooner or later. Once I knew Campion was coming I knew trouble would follow hard on his heels. I thought carefully about what must be done. Played it out in my mind."

"How courageous were Fulk and Solomon!"

"True servants," said Jane. "And hence true masters from whom we can all learn."

"Aye to that," said a saddened Will.

Jane saw his shame. "Your turn will come."

He wanted to boast and show off but all he could portray was his true, and less than adequate self. What magic did Jane weave to put him at such ease and yet solicit such honesty from him? He had quite forgotten the social divide between them, and in remembering it, hated it. "When my turn comes I hope I will be equal to it, my lady."

"The door is closed. My name is Jane."

"My lady?"

"God gives us one face and we make ourselves

another."

"What?"

Jane was caught in some net of deep reflection. She looked at Will but clearly did not want to share the thought she held. He could tell by the way she first held her breath, and then breathed out a sound that had no definition other than frustration. She found a fresh thought between the flames of the fire. "Think of Elizabeth. How devout is she? How true? She calls herself a Catholic but by her deeds she demonstrates a different devotion."

"You consider so?"

"I know so. She waves the holy flag of God from the parapet of a usurper's keep. She is no more Catholic than Cramner's confessor."

"Strong words."

"Truth cannot be otherwise. She is a trapped woman. Marriage to Alexander was a much needed windfall that she grasped with eager arms, but with it came a legacy. His devotion was much less flexible than hers. My family are too fixed in faith to turn their backs on the communion of saints."

"Yet you lament the fate of your brother."

"I do. And I would not wish it on you, as I have already said. But neither would I condemn you for denying your heritage and starting anew."

"Then why despise Elizabeth?"

"Because she makes no such denial. She fakes fidelity. She hides behind the holy."

"And is there harm in that?"

"No one can hide forever. What then? What if she grows weary of hiding? What then for my father's brother?"

"She is much younger than he."

"'Tis true. God's teeth. She's thirty years his junior. Thirty years. He spied her and she spied his purse and counted the wrinkles on his face."

"When your uncle is no longer for this world, what then for Hoghton Tower?"

"A question worth the asking. He has a half-brother, called Thomas like my father."

"Ros told me."

"We never see him. He plays a safer game, but I suppose the Tower will be his. I have not seen Alexander's will.

Have you?"

"Have I? Why should I?"

"It is in the library. Somewhere. You have been working there. Keep an eye out for it Will. Read it. Report it to me won't you?"

"I will."

"You are a treasure. A true blessing." She held her downturned hand towards him in a gesture that might have been supercilious but was, instead, endearing. He took it and kissed it. It was the first time his lips had touched feminine skin since he had left Stratford. Her hands were soft. The flesh was cool to the eye but warm to the touch. She slightly tightened her grip on his.

"Almost all is falsehood, Will."

"Almost all?"

"God gives us one face and we make ourselves another, then another, then another and yet another on top of that. A face for every chamber. A face for every foe, and one for every friend. And when there is no painted face then there is no need for friendship, for there is something far better on view." She gave the slightest of squeezes then slipped her fingers from his.

Will did not know what to say. His mind and heart were racing and he could not determine which was in the lead. He fumbled to form a silence. "Be assured of my constancy . . . my . . ."

"I have no need of your constancy, or of your deference. At least not when we are alone. Out there we must play the pretence. We have our roles, our prescribed painted faces, and the tragedies that go with them. But when we remove our finery, and our face paint, what difference is there then?"

"Birthright?"

"And who taught you that my scholarly schoolmaster? Those of low birth? Or those of high?"

This time Shakespeare let the silence stand. Within it he thought a lot about the lady with him, and how much thinking she must have done. It was not that she was planting new ideas in his head, but rather awakening attitudes that were lying dormant there. The hand that had held his now absently smoothed her skirt against her thighs. She stopped the silence.

"There is something about you . . . "

"About me?"

"Yes." Her stare held him now in an emotional embrace. The way in which she regarded him suspended his awareness in a cone of control. There was nothing to which he could attend other than what lay in that invisible, but not intangible, pyramid of power that she projected. "You are special, young Mr Shakespeare. You are special."

"I try . . ."

"Do not try. Never try. Never try to be what you are not. Be what you are. But learn how to show it. Without pretence. Without lies. With just enough ambiguity to survive."

The final word broke the spell. Survival sent a shiver via his spine to his soul. He thought of home.

"I am worried about my family."

"That's what families are for."

"The message. That man-woman brought."

"Ah the mysterious Thursby."

"She knew my name, she had a message from my father. What should I do?"

"Be who you are. Be where you are. That is all you can do."

It was Will's turn to regard Jane with a loaded stare. "If only you were my mistress."

"I am one third my uncle's age and three times as weary as he. Weary of role-playing. I have been cast as daughter, Catholic, mourner, sorrowful sister, spouse to be and last strand of true family. You talk of constancy Will. I cannot be inconstant. It is not in my nature. I cannot do that which I advocate. I cannot renounce my faith, for my faith is my foundation. I cannot disown my family for I am of that family. I cannot betray this tower for this tower is my name. Yet that woman would have me severed from all those things and grafted to another tree."

Jane's eyes were wet. A moment later the masonry of her deportment shook and she steadied herself by pressing the fingers that he had kissed to her own lips. She breathed slowly and deeply and regained most of her composure. She leaned forwards towards him.

"Help me to save this house Will."

"Where have you been?" Fulk looked dejected.

"Thinking."

Andrew was asleep, Piers and Solomon nowhere to be seen. Fulk's flame danced dull amber as Will closed the door and fell onto his bed. "Thank you."

"For what?"

"Saving me. If the magistrate had taken me I could not have played as you did."

"I played you."

Will sat up sharply. "You didn't give my name?"

"No. What do you take me for? I gave a name you'd given in the tales of your exploits. Oswyn.

"I remembered you'd said he'd left Stratford with you and Campion, so that's what name I said. Didn't work for long. I'd already been recognised by a cooper. He knew me from Lea."

"I'm not happy that you put Campion at Stratford. Did you say my name at all – my father's name?"

"A man can have both wit and wisdom you know Will. I did not mention your name, or any other name or any place name save one: Park Hall at Bromwich. I gambled they knew of that one."

"Well they do now."

"Perhaps they do, perhaps they do not. Because even before our true tale was told they knew us to be false."

"So they beat you for frustration not information."

"It was brief, but it was painful, but it could have been worse. I threw a few practised dips and dives. One hit his fist full on to a timber. That memory I will cherish."

"Thank you."

"It was not for you nor for Campion. It was for Alexander. He is my lord and I am his man. If he is convicted of harbouring your mentor, he will be hanged and I will be assigned to vagrancy."

"Jane would not let that happen."

"Jane has no authority, and Elizabeth hates me with a hunger."

Will pulled of his jerkin and kicked off his shoes. "Why?"

"Because hating is what she does. She hates the house and the household. She thought she was marrying old gold and found she was wedded to steel. Sharp steel. Pointing at her heart, from all directions."

"She's frightened."

"Who isn't? Fear is air - everywhere."

"Then stop my breath."

"Stick with Campion and someone will."

"He's gone. I know not where."

"Preserve that ignorance. It is your salvation."

"He left me no instructions." Will shed his hose and slipped under his sheet.

"You've had half a year of his instruction."

"Two months. Not even that."

"But he crammed a year's worth of teaching into those weeks. You told me so."

"Such is the man. He does not teach. He is the teaching."

"Unlearn the lesson."

"Why?"

"It's the road to Tyburn."

"That's what Jane said."

"Talked much with her have you?"

"A little."

"She's on your tongue tonight. You wish."

Will gave the slightest of sniggers to acknowledge the insinuation, but his countenance stayed serious. "She is a good woman."

"Unlike some." Fulk reached inside his doublet and drew something out. Will could not see what it was in the feeble candle light. It came flying through the air and landed on the sheet on his lap. "Now you have the pair."

Will fumbled for it and recognised it by the feel of the fabric. "Her glove!"

"The other glove. Whoever she was, not only was she here, she was there. At magistrate Riley's house."

"You saw her?"

"No. Either she kept from our sight, or she had been and gone. But been she had. If you confirm it is from the pair."

Will slid from his covers and went over close to Fulk's flame. He turned the glove inside out. "It is," he said.

"How did you get it?"

"I saw it on the table, as we were leaving. It looked

lonely. You can reunite it, with its friend. With its owner."

"Where is she?"

"I'm a player Will, not a sorcerer. But I can read the future. And I predict you will find her. Or she you."

The next morning Will was up early. It was still dark. He had slept badly. So many thoughts and shapes had stocked his dreams and filled the gaps between slumber and the search for sleep. His memory and his imagination wove a pageant too horrible to see performed. He shook it off and wiped away the slight sweat by taking off his shirt, turning it inside out and putting it back on again. He recovered his hose and pulled on his jerkin. Fumbling around he found his shoes but carried them until he was outside the bedchamber. All his fellow players were sleeping.

Ros was in the kitchen, alone, encouraging the fire in the oven. She hadn't heard him approach and let out a squeal when he spoke.

"Good morning, Ros."

Her reaction had sent the glowing splint she was holding tumbling back onto her hand. "Shit!"

"Sorry."

"What do you want?"

Will had a graphic answer to that question but chose not to voice it. "I want to know where Campion is."

"How should I know that?"

"You made good his escape."

"I hope by now he is far away. And I hope he stays so."

"How did you do it?"

"Yesterday's bread is over there. There'll be no other breakfast for an hour or more."

"I've not come for breakfast."

"Well you will not get anything else until Agnes rises. Then she'll give you a mouthful." Ros licked her hand where the burning splint had touched it.

"I'm sorry. I didn't mean to shock you."

"And what do you mean to do master Will? Have you any meaning in you?"

"I mean to discover what my patron wants of me.

What am I to do? Did Campion leave a message for me?"

Ros turned her back on Will and began to reassemble the smouldering kindling inside the oven. She blew on it to encourage it back towards burning. "Your patron is my lord Alexander, you must do whatever he commands." She blew again. Specks of ash billowed around the oven.

Will moved across the kitchen and stood close to Ros. "Did Father Edmund say what I was to do?"

She stopped blowing and turned to face him. "If Campion had given me a message for you, I would refuse to relay it."

"Why?"

She blew her answer into the embers.

He gripped her gently by the arm. She wrenched it free. "Don't touch me!"

That remark, and the spite with which it was spoken, speared Will with more pain than any pike could. He broke from her and went to rip a fist of crust from yesterday's bread. He sat on the table and chewed without tasting.

"Get your arse off there."

Will didn't move. Ros blew. He ate his crust. It was difficult without a drink to wash it down but he was adamant he would disobey her instruction and so remained where he was. The kindling caught and a saffron glow gilded her face.

He swallowed three times, licked the lining of his mouth, and spoke. "You are the loveliest woman I have ever seen."

"Keep looking." She took thicker sticks from the pile at her feet and built the fire.

"Why search when you have found the treasure?"

"Keep looking."

"I am."

"Just don't touch."

Will brushed the crumbs from his lap. "Thank you. For seeing Campion safe."

"He's not safe. He's just in a different danger."

"Off!" Agnes stood in the doorway.

Will slid from the table.

"What in the devil's name are you doing in here at this hour?"

"I couldn't sleep."

"Sleep! What's that?" Agnes waddled past and went towards the dining hall. She called as she disappeared into the half-light. "Clear out."

Will decided it was time to go. He made for the courtyard door. Ros blocked his way, pierced his irises with hers and spoke softly. "If they come back for you. Find me."

"I will."

She returned to her oven.

Will went back to bed. He kicked off his shoes but couldn't be bothered undressing. His roommates were rustling, and starting to wake. A thin daylight was condensing out of the darkness. Before he lay back Will slipped his hand under the mattress to check the calf-skin gloves were still hidden there. As he drifted towards a doze he dreamed he could feel the slight bulge they made between his shoulder blades, and when he was full asleep the dream emboldened in his mind. The gloves clawed through the straw of his mattress, erupted from it, tore through the sheet beneath him, and closed tightly about his throat.

The dawn released him from his nightmare. He located the glove and re-examined it. This was the right hand, and in the seam that joined thumb to palm he found a stain. The stain could have had many sources, but the tight seam had kept the colour on the ruddy side of brown. The bloody side, he thought.

SEVENTEEN

Naked villainy

Frances Thursby stood naked by the window. The town was
blinking in the damp dawn. The air was cold and her skin
tightened into goose pimples. She didn't care. Let the chill do
what it will. It might kill the child. She'd had the scare many
times before. Most women she knew were regular as the moon.
She had never been. The moon played games with her.
Sometimes she went for months, but no infant had made a crib
in her belly. She was glad about that. She loved the thought that
she was barren and dreaded the prospect that perhaps she was
not.

She liked to let the air hurt her. The cold was gentle
pain and Frances felt she ought to suffer. She liked to make
herself hurt. Long ago she had used a knife. Once she had
thrown herself in nettles. Another time she had swam in water
beneath broken ice. She had waited to drown but then struggled
to the side and shivered so hard she thought her bones would
shatter.

When life was warm her blood ran with haughty joy
and she would be who she could be, and in sweaty stupor she

found the confidence to soar in sin. Heat was heaven; cold was life. Cold was from the earthen north. Cold was the confirmation that she was not yet in hell.

She gripped her own waist as her lovers sometimes did, and sank her nails far in hoping they would find blood. She stood tall reordering the sands of time where they were just starting to give signs of gathering where they might start to sag. How much sand did time have in store for her? Perhaps less than he had already given. Her mind's trapdoor opened and she shook at the thought that she might hang like a sack of silt, with quicksand shit stroking the inside of her legs and dripping from her twitching feet.

Satan waited. There was no point in praying. Far too much sin had been spent. There could be no refund. Salvation was priceless. No queen could purchase it. No court could command it. The Devil sat anticipating her living end. His rear tail twitched while the one at the front was spear-firm, sword-sharp and barbed, and gorged with acidic puss. That would put an end to her periods; but what menstrual monster would it put in their place?

Come on cold. Do your worst. Tell me I am still alive.

Down in the market-place the painstaking and the desperate coughed at the cold and started to set up their stalls. Those with too-warm beds or warmer wives were still at home. It was too dark for Frances to focus on their faces. They were distant indeterminate pale masks. She wanted some of them to see her in all her nudity and took half a step closer to the window. She wanted the self-righteous to ogle so that they might add their condemnation to her after-death demise. She wanted the sinners to sin more by staying at their stares and hence she would not be alone in the bonfire that never burned away.

Where now is my smugness? Where now my bigotry? Where now the smiles that let men slip inside me while I work out how to cut their purse? Where now the lick of my lips that asked men to eat me just as soon as they had loosened their tongue and told me how I might benefit from their deals? Where now my shape to drive men out of their minds and into my bed and my wet trap? Here it is. Here I am. See me live. Watch me die.

She went back to bed and snuggled into the fermenting

warmth. She was stinking yeast.

Will thought the ale to be watery. He didn't complain. He hadn't paid for it. Thursby had. The tapster had returned to him with a message that Mr Thursby had taken to his bed, but he would rise and join Mr Shakespeare as soon as he was dressed. In the meantime, perhaps Mr Shakespeare would enjoy ale at his expense. He put the jug in Will's hand.

It was mid-afternoon. The alehouse was bustling but he found a corner with a small settle that was unoccupied but still warm. He poured from jug to cup.

Will was glad of the dilute strength of the beer. He'd purchased his own jug when he'd arrived so now he was draining towards the finish of the second. In addition to that he'd downed one on the outskirts of the town as he neared the end of his five mile walk from the tower. So he now had a good half bucket of beer somewhere in his belly. That he didn't mind, but he needed a clear head for the conversation that he anticipated.

As soon as Thursby brought a cup and jug of ale and sat opposite him the debate over her masculinity was ended. This person was female, yet there she sat bold as a halberd blade but steel-smooth too. That chin had not been shaved and would look no different if it never was. Her face had soft contours and yes, he had seen that type of feature on boys, but this was not an immature person. Fulk was right regarding her neck. It was swan-slender and not dissimilar to Jane's. He held out his hand. They gripped. Her palms were neither soft nor calloused but somewhere mid-way between the two. There was strength in the squeeze.

"Thursby?" said Shakespeare.

"Shakespeare," said Thursby. William?"

"The same."

"Frances."

Will nodded. "Frances."

"What can I do for Mr Shakespeare?"

"I was told you had news for me. From my father."

"Who told you that?"

"Someone who knows the inside of Hoghton Tower."

"Do you know the inside of Hoghton Tower?"

"It is a dangerous place," he said

"Who told you that?"

"The same person who said you had been there."

"And who was that?"

"Someone who was arrested."

"Arrested in mistake for you?"

Will felt his eyes widen. He tried to stop them, but they'd finished before he'd even known they'd started.

"What is the message from my father?"

"How can I be sure that you are his son?"

"How can I?"

Frances sniggered. "You can assure me that you are that person?"

"I can assure you that I am not."

Frances raised her eyebrows and paused in the raising of her ale cup.

Will went on. "I have lived a lifetime in these months since I have been from home. I am a different person now from the one I was before I left."

"Your father sends his love."

"There was no need to send that. I carry it with me. And always will."

Frances leaned forwards and lowered the loudness of her voice. "He wants you to renounce your resolve to pursue the dangerous path you tread."

Will sat back on his stool. He kept his voice low also. "You play him false. He would never say that."

"He said it to me. Your father is ill, and – much troubled. He wants you home to see to his affairs. You must take the business." She filled his cup from her jug.

"My father knows I am the least able of his children when it comes to his trade."

"Which trade, Will? Your father trades in many things, some of which are not his to sell. Wool belongs to the crown. It is state owned. Its sale must be licenced. Yet he dispatched me to source some for him."

"And are you licenced?"

"I am many things."

"And some things that you are not."

Both punctuated their parley with a swig from their cups.

"I can return to your father with wool he might buy, or

172

I can take him something he values far more; to see his son, safe."

"His son is quite capable of finding his own way home, thank you – Mr – Thursby."

"Safely?"

"As safe as any other wayfarer."

"One that is hunted as fervently as you. You are a wanted man, young Will." Frances let that thought ferment. "And no one wants you more than your father. And mother. They regret what you are doing. Those that have pained your family for their faithfulness are tightening the screw."

"How do you know this?"

"I have many friends. I can see you swiftly back to Stratford and help your family escape the unfair forces that are about to be brought to bear."

"They would rather bear those trials."

"Do you know what they entail?"

"I do."

"No master Will. You do not. And you cannot imagine how terrible they are."

"I think I can."

"I know you cannot."

Will slid his tongue around the edge of his lip then sucked on one of the knuckles of a fist that he had involuntary constricted.

Frances stretched the silence then said, "I have another message. From Mr Cottam, at the school. He said he too has seen the true extent of the threat to your family, not only your father, but also your sisters, and your mother. He said you should make that your first duty."

"He would not say that."

"William, you have to trust me. The response to – certain – transgressions is changing. We are talking about treason. And treason can be seen to taint not just the traitor, but also the traitor's family."

"I am no traitor."

"Not yet. Mr Cottam has learned how threats are rising. He has family who have suffered. He knows, as I do, that the threats can be lifted, and even reversed. Your family could prosper again. Higher than it ever has before."

"And how would my return achieve that?"

173

Frances replenish his ale. "You said, William, that you have lived a new life since you left home. I know you have. And I know there are men who would pay very handsomely for the account of your journey."

Will started to get up. "I have no more to say to you."

Frances grabbed Will's wrist. "I am not one of those men. I am not even a man, as I think you can see. I bring you messages and method. And anything else you want from me. She stroked the inside of his arm with slight slithering of her longest finger.

Will swirled in a pool of confusion which was not aided either by his sudden rise to his feet, or the quantity of ale he had consumed. A firm tug by Thursby, along with the arrival of the tapster with yet another jug resulted in him sitting again and trying to assemble his thoughts. He waited until the tapster had been paid and had moved away.

"Who are you?"

"Things have changed in Warwickshire, William. The county is for the Queen and the Queen is in fear of the king of Spain. There is a new ruthlessness. Your family wants you home. So does Mr Cottam."

"You haven't said who you are, or why you disguise yourself as a man."

"Could we sit here and talk like this if I did not?"

"You came to Hoghton in that guise."

"In the hope of speaking with Lord Alexander."

"Why?"

"So that he might let me talk with you."

The inn began to wave slightly about Will's head, but his line of thought was steady. So steady was it that it brought the memory of the stained glove back to mind. The glove that, with its partner, was hidden beneath his doublet.

"Go back to my father; tell him his son is of sound purpose. In truth Mr . . . Mistress . . . Thursby I have not taken any position other than that awarded to me. I am my lord's man. I can do nothing other than that which he decrees."

"Ask him to release you."

"All that I shall ask him is what he requires of me." He gathered himself and prepared to stand.

"You are not in a safe place, William. You think you are but you are not. I found you. Others will follow."

"You didn't find me. I found you." He stood.

"They nearly found Campion."

"Who?"

"Don't be foolish. If you are there, he is too."

"He's not there."

"He was."

"He's not there."

"They'll find him. Shall I tell you what they'll do to him?"

"I think he knows that. Wherever he is."

"And they'll do it to you. And to your family."

He took one more drink. "I need to be back by nightfall." He slapped the cup on the table and turned for the door. The room revolved to catch up with his new orientation. This sent him slightly dizzy so he closed his eyes.

When he opened them there was bright sunlight and a bedroom he had never seen before.

EIGHTEEN

If you have tears

"He went to Preston?"

The players and Ros had located Jane in the great hall.

"You should not have encouraged him, Ros."

"I did not."

"Who knows this?"

Ros shrugged.

"My lord Alexander, Elizabeth?"

Ros shrugged again.

Jane sighed again and tapped the back of her head against the wall three times.

"You should have stopped him, Ros."

"I went to my work."

"Then how can you be sure he has gone to Preston?"

Fulk stepped forward. "I gave him Frances Thursby's other glove last night."

Jane looked quizzical.

Fulk explained, "I . . . found it. In Magistrate Riley's house."

Jane sighed and rested her chin upon a stressed fist.

Ros added wood to the fire. She took the poking iron

and disturbed the settled ashes, making them glow like hope. They faded again almost immediately. A sadness settled on the room.

Jane turned towards the window in search of solace. "Well, you must go and find him."

Piers twisted the fashionable end of his beard. "We cannot leave without my lord's consent."

"It is given," said Jane

"By whom?"

Jane's face tightened. "Consent is given. Go into town. Bring Will back."

Solomon spoke from the rail by the door of the great hall. "How best should we do it? We can't go around shouting out if anyone's seen him."

Jane said, "Ask quietly, and carefully. Start at the Golden Lion. We must secure the safety of Will, and of this house and all the houses of which he can tell. I do not understand why he has broken his rules so rashly. He seemed of stronger mettle than that."

Piers straightened his doublet. "He is a young man with a spirited imagination. He heard news of news. He has the facility to make imagined fact from fears."

Jane fanned her fingers across the grain of the table. "Find him. Or find where he has gone."

"As always, my lady, we will do our utmost to carry out your will." Piers gave a slight bow and led his men from the hall.

Jane and Ros were alone and for several moments neither spoke. It was mid-morning but the early sharp light had been subdued by a rapidly growing bank of cloud and hence the hall was gloomy. The fire struggled to increase and produced more smoke than light. The windows sulked. Now that action had been taken there was a sense of impotency. The mood was sullen.

Ros waited. There was plenty she could be doing and protocol ruled that she should withdraw and get on with it, but her relationship with Jane was more flexible than that. There was a kind of dilute sisterhood between them. There was a de-formalised friendship that they used when alone. At times like this Ros would be at liberty to lead the conversation, something she would not do if others were there, but on this occasion she felt she must wait. Jane's mind was busy. Her pupils moved but focussed only on her thoughts. Her breathing was slightly strained. She looked at Ros.

"He has an eye for you."

"I know."

"Do you encourage it?"

"No."

"He has charm."

"That's why I don't encourage it."

"Why so?"

"He's not for here. He's not for me. And I am not for him."

"Are you for any man?"

Ros made no response.

Jane's lips crinkled. She twitched her torso beneath the bodice and then walked the length of the table to look out of the leaded window. All she could see was grey autumn.

"They've got him Ros, they've got him. God knows what they'll do to him."

NINETEEN

Sigh no more

Will rubbed the ache from his eyes. He could remember nothing of the night. The mattress beneath him was coarse and sank sharp shards into his naked back, buttocks and thighs. The sunlight seared across the ceiling rebounding off the lime wash. There were no familiar scents in the air, but the odours he detected troubled him. One was like sweat, but was not sweat, at least not his sweat. Another was a flavour he recognised but could not name. Another was the taste of hair.

He sensed something substantial close to him. It was a mass without a meaning. It was still. He turned towards it and saw her face incompletely, pale and white, through a shroud of black hair. Her eyes very slightly open. She lay on her side, her breasts slung sideways, her belly, white and starred with a few widely-spaced black freckles, stretched smooth and motionless to the wiry thicket of her pubic bush. One thigh lay slant across the other, with her knee sinking into the bed and propping her in position. She looked slender and lovely and slightly incongruous. Something was missing. Where was her arm? He focussed on her shoulder and traced the line of that limb. It disappeared behind her back. That's where it was. Something else was missing. Where was movement?

He felt cold. A tremble shuddered through him and then a second. His eye itched and he put his finger to it. There was something crusty round the socket and he withdrew his finger to look at it. His whole hand was smeared dark and he strained his pupils to pull focus and identify the stain. A double recognition struck him. The smear on his hand was dry blood; and she wasn't breathing.

Within a bolt of breath he was beside the bed, standing unsteadily and gasping for air. He now remembered the smell that he knew but couldn't name. Blood. That's why she was so white. Her blood filled the bed behind her and spread a blanket on the floor. He realised he was stepping in it and leaped out again, but he had already seen the knife in her back. A second lay on the floor at his side of the bed. So much blood.

His clothes were in a dry pile by the window. He skipped over and grabbed them leaving a small pattern of toe prints. Somehow a smear of blood was printed from his foot onto his shirt. He dropped his clothes again and for the first time started to think logically. He had to get out. But between him and the door was the blood lake. He could not have blood on his shirt, his hands or his face. What should he do? How quickly must he do it? What was the hour? Where was he?

Noises below. Muffled voices. Indistinct shouting. Laughter.

His memory began to work, but he had forgotten how to operate it. Recollections came in disorderly fragments. The tone of her voice. The shape of her ears. The first sight of her nakedness. "We can go to London." The sensation of her tongue intertwining with his. "You could go to court. I know men who will take you there." The wet tightness of her vulva. "You could stand before the Queen."

A blanket lay crumped close to the unsheathed dagger. He grabbed it and rubbed ferociously at his hands and face. Small flecks of the dry stain were taken by the abrasive vigour of his action but most remained. His mind said he could hide his hands but not his face. He found the window and knew the time, for the day was well underway with the market below. There was too much light for the glass to be a good mirror but there was sufficient grime on the glazing to give a slight silvering and show him the contrast between innocence and guilt. There was a stain all about one eye and on both cheeks. A little water could clear him, but water there was none.

An ale jug stood by the wall at the dry side of the deathbed. There was a just a little left in. He poured it on his hands and wiped it all around his face then took to the blanket again and rubbed hard enough to take off his skin and bring his own blood through. After a minute he was dry and another look in the uncooperative window showed his state was better, but he could not see sufficient detail to check he was clean enough to escape notice. There was nothing else he could do, there was no more liquid in the room except for that which would incriminate him. He got dressed. The stain on his shirt could be almost hidden by fastening his doublet tight but one cuff signalled suspicion. He pulled his hat as much over his brow as he could. Dressed and shod he was as ready to leave as an arrangement of clothing could concoct. Between him and the door lay the crimson lake. Beyond the door was the passage and the stairs and then the drinking parlour where he must surely be challenged. He had no option; that was the way he must go.

He threw the blanket on the blood and stepped on it. In a single move he opened the door and, without looking, stepped out onto the corridor then scuttled down the stairs and through the parlour. It was empty, probably. He didn't pause to look and no one called to challenge him.

He was amid the market and edged and bustled his way through the traders and their customers. His urgency made his movements rude, and that in turn brought physical and verbal rebuffs, but he barely felt them and the curses did not register in his mind. Some of the facial expressions did, however. They were ambiguous and might just have been responses to his impudence, or they could have been signs of shock that would fix his face and his guilt in their minds. Their reactions provoked him to even greater haste. He felt sure he must not have eradicated the stain on his cheeks. He tussled with the decision to head towards where he knew the water carrier often was. It would wash him clean, but what about the vendor? And there was always at least a small gathering there. What would be the point of washing his face if he showed it unclean first? He powered on, keeping the Golden Lion Inn at his back. By sheer good fortune, or the benevolence of kindly spirits, he found himself heading towards the shambles, where the butchers turned livestock into dead meat.

Without a pause for rational thought, he executed a Fulk-like comedic stumble and fell slithering onto the stone sets where the slaughtering took place. He made sure his cheek and both hands splattered against the slime, and then in his supposed daze put his palms to his face. The laughter told his tumble had been generously witnessed. A butcher cursed and kicked him but it was sweet pain. He staggered to his feet recovering his crimsoned hat. Now he was truly blooded head to toe, and many could bear witness how it had occurred. He suffered a few more obscenities before gathering his composure and easing his way across the square in the direction of the Stony Gate road.

A few were gathered at the gate and his blood-smeared appearance spawned smirks but they were derisory rather than wary and he acknowledged them with a self-deprecating shrug which seemed to satisfy and then he was out of the town and a mere two hours' traffic from the tower. The way would be infrequently peopled and he was unlikely to meet problems he could not avoid.

His waist was grabbed and he fell tumbling to the roadside ditch.

He rolled in a wrestle of thrashing limbs, his hat was over his eyes, but he crabbed to one side, yanked his cap clear and stood ready to let fists fly, or to leap for an escape.

Fulk faced him.

"Will? What's this?"

"Fulk!"

Andrew, Solomon and Piers emerged from the foliage in the ditch.

"You're covered in blood."

"It's from the market, the shambles. Where were you?"

Fulk pointed to the ditch. "Here. Solomon sharp-eyes saw you coming through the gate."

"She's dead."

"Who is?"

"Thursby."

"Where?"

"Next to me," said Will. "In the Golden Lion. Blood everywhere. Next to me."

Piers said, "Is this her blood?"

"Some of it."

"Come off the road. Over there. Sit round"

They moved fifty yards to sit away from the highway so that any wayfarer would not question their conversation. Solomon gave Will small beer from a goatskin flask and the apprentice actor recounted his nightmare awakening.

"But did you strike her?"

"No, no. No."

"Then how?"

"I don't know. I can't remember. We drank a lot. We talked."

"About?"

Will shouted "I don't know!"

Andrew calmed him. "Easy, Will."

Will swallowed air, took another drink, then said, "She took me to her bed, then I fell asleep, then woke and she was dead. One knife in her back and another near my hand."

Piers questioned. "Whose were these knives?"

"Hers I think."

"She wore one at the tower," said Fulk. "I saw it."

"Blood on my hands and my face."

"Do you remember a fight?" asked Piers.

"There was no fight."

Solomon spoke. "Someone did it while you slept, then made it seem like you had done what they had."

"And that is how it does look," said Will the fear within him building bile and threatening vomit.

Piers said, "Anyone in the inn that you recognised?"

"I know no-one in this town."

Fulk said, "You know one less now."

"But I gave my name to the tapster.

Piers said, "Which name?"

"Shakespeare."

"Well no one knows you're at the tower."

Fulk said, "She and her kind do."

"What do you mean – her kind?" asked Piers.

"I found her other glove in the magistrate's house. When he discovers what's happened he'll be back at the tower."

"Lord Alexander will protect you."

"Even after this?"

"I didn't attack her!"

Piers said, "If they find her now and you're found in that state, that's all they need to know."

Andrew broke his silence. "We should get moving."

"If they send for Riley they'll pass us on the road."

Solomon said, "Why would they send for Riley? There's officers in the town."

Piers squinted as he eyed the Stony Gate. "Riley has his friends in town. He'll hear soon enough and we have two hours on the road with a boy bathed in blood."

Will protested. "Pig's blood!"

Piers exuded condescension. "No one can tell."

"Lea," said Andrew. "Down to the river and if the tide is right we can be there in the hour. Martin would ferry us. He's trustworthy."

The group was quiet while Piers considered. "And if the tide is wrong?"

"Walk the bank path. It will keep us away from the Hoghton road. And if it comes to the worst we push Will in the water. That'll wash things out."

"One of us will have to go back to the tower. Tell the news."

"All of you do," said Andrew. "I'll take Will. Martin is my cousin. He'll keep good peace for me."

"Let's not delay," said Piers.

So Will and Andrew split from the others and hurried down the road to reach the bridge well ahead of them. Then they made their way along the bank until they came to ferry points. Andrew stopped at one and spoke to the boatman. Fortune was with them. The tide had turned and Andrew's cousin Martin, steered and rowed them downstream with speed and ease.

Andrew spoke little but his benevolent rounded face set a tranquil mood which Will absorbed keenly. Martin smiled at Will but made no comment regarding his appearance. The sky was still thickly overcast and set a dull sheen on the surface of the water. Its serenity lulled Will and his recollections began to gather a little more coherently. Parts of the conversation he'd had in the inn came back to him: what Frances Thursby had said about his father and how it had had both a ring of falsehood and a chime of truth about it. He remembered too, the penetrating courage of her gaze, and how predatory and yet compelling it had been. She was a falcon. She was a witch. And now she was neither.

Now she was a ghost.

The river broadened and flattened but at the same time the tide pulled stronger and Martin had to work less hard in order to make progress but needed more skill to steer his course. He kept closer to the north bank and Will reasoned that would be where they would moor. They made swift progress and soon the meandering stopped, their route was straight and the river ahead had no ending.

"The sea," said Will

Martin smiled. "We're not going that far lad."

The bank to their right was further away now and the edge of the water stopped short of it, separated from its grassy turf by saturated mud. Over Martin's shoulder he saw the line of a jetty stretching out into the water. Martin seemed to know its position instinctively, only looking to check when they were within twenty yards or so. They butted gently alongside, as Martin stowed the oars. He gripped the timbers then expertly looped his rope around the short vertical stave and steadied the boat as his passengers climbed out. Will's legs felt strange. They were stiff yet unsteady, and he hobbled along the boards of the jetty a little as his two companions conversed and money changed hands. Will surveyed the silver expanse of the estuary as the salt breeze burned the cheeks between his squint and smile.

"Come on," said Andrew and his feet found a tune from the planks of their tiny bridge over the mud.

Before them was Lea House. It was not fortified and much smaller than Hoghton, but a manor nonetheless.

There was a staff incumbent at Lea House. As Alexander, Elizabeth and Jane were twelve miles away some of the core domestic servants had been shifted there also, but the manor still functioned, and the estate had to be serviced so Will was once again embroiled among a whirlpool of unfamiliar folk. He was introduced to Ambrose the steward of the house. Will felt him to be slightly overdressed for his station, and he demonstrated a distinct lack of sympathy for Will, but did so in a manner that Will found amusing rather than distressing.

"Well he'd better lodge with you until my lord sends word what to do."

"Aye, sir," said Andrew.

"Get him washed find him some fresh clothes, give him something to eat and keep him out of sight."

"Aye, sir."

Ambrose turned away and put his attention back on the paper in his hand, then stopped and half turned back. "And he's a player, that's all he is so far as this house knows. Do you understand?"

"Aye, sir,"

"Do you understand master Shakeshaft?"

"I do, sir."

"Good. Now go and get clean. There will be food in an hour."

And so Will was lodged in the room allocated for the players when they were at Lea. It was above the stables which brought back fond memories of fumbling and tumbling in the hay with Martha. Andrew brought fresh clothes from their playing stock together with something to eat, and as soon as that was washed down with quite the finest ale Will had tasted, he was fast asleep and rolling through dreams that were hyper-vivid while they existed and completely forgotten before he awoke.

A smell of honeyed decay provoked him. It was a scent he did not know; sweet and vinegary, fresh and stale, damp and smoky, pungent and delicate, permanent and ephemeral. For a few minutes he allowed the aroma to toy with his mind. When he rose, the day was in full, but strangely muted, light and the household was already up and at work. There was no sign of Andrew. He wasn't hungry so didn't go in search of breakfast, but rather stole outside and tramped across the yard to a sandy rise topped with sharp long grass and looked once more at what he thought to be the sea, but was in fact still only the expanse of the estuary. His view was far from clear.

The atmosphere was heavy and a wet and cold breeze cut from the west. The air was dense with a fog of sand and saltwater, hence the air scoured his skin and put grit in his eyes. He could not plainly see the water. Instead he applied imagination to perception and decided where the mud became movement and beyond that where surface became sky. In truth it all seemed one to him.

He wandered a little distance then slipped down the landward side of the dune to piss his name in the dryer and more yellow sand. When he shuffled his way back up to the crest Andrew was there.

"Come on," he said and set off westwards along a shore-side sheep track and into the terracotta gloom.

"Where are we going?" asked Will.

"Making a delivery." Andrew was weighed down by a pair of large, bulbous canvas bags one of which he now let slip to the sand so that Will might take it up. He did so and immediately marvelled at how Andrew could have carried two. With difficulty Will manoeuvred it into position across his back. The draw cord cut fiercely into his shoulder.

"Where to?"

"Along the coast. Not far."

The track mostly followed the mud bank edge but sometimes curled up to top the tufted dunes. They were still alongside the gradually widening river with the expanse of the estuary ahead. The panorama did not improve, if anything it grew more dense. Soon Will was sweating and panting. After perhaps half of an hour they came to a place where a number of boats were beached. Though high and dry, each was tethered to a post driven into the turf. Andrew tossed his sack into one and so Will followed suit.

"Wait here," said Andrew and he disappeared landward.

Will sat in the boat and swiped a sleeve across his brow. He thought back to the previous day and the shock of waking up next to a corpse. That image was vivid but now shreds of the previous night came clearer to the front of his memory. He remembered now the way she undressed him, slowly, kissing his young chest and sometimes biting his shoulder. All the while she was talking to him, asking about the places he had been and about whom he had been there with. He could not remember what he had said.

He looked out towards where the sea must be, but still saw only a suspension of sand. Just his luck. The first chance he had to acquaint himself with an ocean and fog frustrated him. Be patient. He would be here some days and he didn't imagine these conditions would endure.

Without warning, within the gloom, he saw a shape.

187

Then it went. Then it returned. It moved slightly. Then it went again. Perhaps he had seen a whale, or a sea dragon?

He felt Frances Thursby's saline teeth in his shoulder, and the wetness of the mouth between her legs where he had put his fingers.

Andrew returned with a pair of oars.

"Out you get," he said, and he put the oars in the boat, and untied its line.

Together they dragged the boat across the pebbles and sand. Then their feet sank in the mud and the aroma that had greeted Will on his awakening returned with added pungency. The tide was on the rise however, and the river rapidly thickening so they didn't have to wade far before the boat kissed water and found buoyancy. They climbed aboard and Andrew took the oars. He pulled like a professional and they pressed into the sea-fog's embrace.

"Is this the river or the sea?" said Will.

"Both," said Andrew. "The river's going one way, the sea the other."

The shape Will had seen from the shore reappeared. It looked like a black barn. It was a boat with a superstructure and a single mast.

When they got close Andrew hollered. "Helloah!"

It was not a large vessel. Will had seen bigger boats than this on rivers, but it was substantial. It was bulky, being wide compared to its length, it cut a deep draft and its rail was above their heads when they stood. A figure appeared on deck, a line was lowered for their sacks which were hoisted from them and then a ladder of a kind, made from rope. After a little awkwardness they were aboard, and a man with a red face and yellow beard invited them below. The hold was open but there was a simple cabin and they went inside to where the smell of the sea was overridden by the bouquet of grain. The light was poor inside, but as his eyes adjusted will made out the simplest of tables and a figure sitting there.

"Well, I was hoping for at least a duke, but I suppose you'll do," said Campion.

The cabin was cramped, cluttered and dark but the friends found a means to awkwardly embrace.

"You're safe," said Will

"Thanks be to God," said Campion.

"And Ros."

Campion laughed lightly, but did not elaborate.

"Are you going to sail away?" asked Will

"Certainly not," said Campion. "How about you?"

"I'll go where you go."

"Will you?"

The priest was tucked in the corner of the cabin. He was snug in a sailor's cape, a raft of papers before him, every tenth of an inch rich with the ink tattoo of his minute hand. Two precious naked pages lay to one side, imprisoned under a smooth stone. Will sat opposite him. The bench beneath him was secured to the deck as was the table between them. Andrew was alongside Campion. The deck above made a low ceiling such that none could stand upright. Somewhere a shuttered port was wedged slightly open. It gave a little air and less light.

"You know I will."

"You must return to Hoghton, remain there, study and pray."

"I've killed someone."

Campion looked marginally disappointed.

"Or so it appears."

"And did you?"

"No."

Campion breathed one full slow breath. "I am your audience."

Will recounted as much as he could remember. He left out the lascivious details.

"And what did you tell her?"

"I told her I knew of you but not that I knew you."

The priest rubbed his fingertips through his beard. "What else did she ask you?"

"If you were at Hoghton. I said you were not there."

"What else?"

"About my route from Stratford. She suggested houses."

"Which?"

"Park Hall, Gawthorpe, Rufford."

"And you acknowledged?"

"I said there had been many stops on my journey. I could not recall them all. She said I had been at those places, and been there with you. I was Peter. I denied you. Many times."

Campion made a gable of his hands and put his lips to their peak. He appeared both lighter and heavier. "They know my footsteps, so why have they not tripped my feet?" He glanced at Andrew but he had no reply.

"I think I know," said Will.

The priest peered at him more in curiosity than in confidence.

"The path seemed almost as important as the quarry to her. She wants you but she wants many others too. Those you bless you also condemn."

Will then experienced a new sensation. He felt both superior and humble. The humility stemmed from his mentor's eminence, the superiority from the satisfaction of his swifter wit, but topping even that was a glow kindled from knowing he had spoken a truth above grace and stated a fact that put piety in a pathetic perspective. He liked the feeling but couldn't comprehend why. Campion, his hero, was both the villain and the victim and was helpless in both roles. For a flicker of time, and it was only that, the living saint was but a helpless casualty of his own campaign.

The boat moved. Campion gently reordered his papers. His renown returned. He shrugged inside his cloak and resumed his mantle. He had been a mouse in a bottle but now he was the falcon dove again. "When it is deemed safe, you must return to Hoghton. I am not sailing away from you Will, but I must move away in order to be closer. I am leaving you in the hope that you will stay with me. I will return, and by then you will know whether you will stay and whither you will go."

With that the formality of their meeting was at an end. The sailor and a second joined their company. They unpacked the sacks of provisions they had brought and drank a cup of small beer. Then it became clear that Will and Andrew were required to leave. Everyone went on the main deck. The sea fog was still about them but there was motion in it and the sailors went about their business with confidence. They prepared to rig the sail. The boat had more movement despite its fettering to an anchor. Campion looked into the fog as if he could see eternity.

"Did you enjoy her bed Will?"

"I think I had drunk too much to enjoy anything."

"The best bedfellows are Italian."

"Are they?"

"And the best bedfellows of all are Italian men."

Andrew laughed heartily as did the sailor who overheard. Campion grinned and clasped Will's hands between his own. "Keep the faith young Will. Fail the boy you are and find the man you must be."

Will felt he was saying goodbye to a saint but wasn't sure if it was the one facing him.

Back in the rowboat Andrew pulled towards the barely visible shore. He didn't have to work hard because the tide was still on the rise, but Will opted to sit beside him and they took an oar each. That way Will could still see the vessel they had left. The sail was slowly inching up the mast. Campion was a grey statue.

The sea fog blew drapes of cloud between them.

TWENTY

Assume a virtue

Will remained at Lea House for another two nights, then word came that he should return to Hoghton. He was nervous as he made the journey but his fears were allayed when he got back to the Tower. Jane sent for him and they met in the great hall.

"We have a lot of influence in town," she said. "People are very loyal."

"Am I safe?"

"Alexander has compensated the landlord."

"But am I safe?"

"Others had been asking for her."

"Others?"

"Others who knew she wasn't a he."

"Magistrate Riley?"

"We've heard no more from him."

"And my lord Alexander?"

"You are charmed Will, because of the company you have shared. You are here at Campion's behest, and that gives you good protection." Jane pulled focus on mid-air. "From those you can trust."

"And who can I not trust?"

192

"That we still have to determine."

Elizabeth was less conciliatory. She made him wait until after dinner then sent for him. Margery conducted him to the bedchamber, let him in and left. For a moment he had to simply stand his ground. A single tallow burned producing a sooty yarn and very little light. The bed was made. Elizabeth, sitting at the small table, had been writing. Will could perceive the poor quality of her hand though he could not see what she had written. It looked inconsequential and a waste of precious paper.

"Quite an adventure master Shakeshaft."

"Yes my lady." Will was surprised. She seemed good-tempered, almost jovial. That changed. Her voice dropped in tone, her face drew tight, her stare took aim.

"Normally you'd be beaten, put in stocks, and turned out of this house."

"Yes, my lady."

"Campion has craved leniency. We can't deny him that. But know this. You are our boy now, and you will adhere to the laws of this house. You will abide by all that is expected of a Hoghton servant."

"I will."

"You will not come and go as you please."

"My intentions were honourable, my lady and, I thought, for the good of this house."

Elizabeth held the palm of her hand towards him. There was ink on two of the tips of her fingers. She savoured the silence she had enforced. Will waited. This was far removed from the agitated Elizabeth he had seen while Campion had been in residence.

"I will decide what is good for this house."

Will wondered if Alexander would agree with that, but dared not voice his thoughts.

"You will learn to play. You will spend three hours of each day in our library. You will do whatever else we require of you."

"Yes, my lady." He waited, wondered, dared, and spoke. "Which texts am I to read?"

His adversary squirmed a little. "My lord Alexander will list them when he is well enough."

"Yes, my lady."

She made him wait still more. Her fingers played on

her lips, her eyes skimmed the table but read the thoughts in her mind and summoned them to her tongue.

"Did you end Frances Thursby's life?"

"I think I would remember if I did."

"You can't remember!"

"I can't remember there being two knives. She had one, but there was no other one until I was awake and she in final sleep and it was on the floor. Though there was something about the dudgeon that seemed faintly familiar. I think I may have seen that knife before."

Elizabeth's composure shifted. "Where?"

"I can't remember. I have seen so many knives."

"You must become invisible here."

"But. . ."

"What?"

"I am a player."

Thunder brewed in her eyeballs. Her cheeks flushed red. "You will stay from my sight and you will not trouble my lord Alexander. You will learn to play and you will prepare to play but I will say if you are to play. You will study the texts that we will prescribe. When the school assembles you will tutor the boys in their writing and in their rhetoric. Should any boy show promise for the priesthood, you are to send his name to me."

She had not mentioned either Jane or Ros. Behind his back Will crossed the first two fingers of each hand.

"You will not converse with Jane without my prior consent and you will stay away from female servants. Especially Ros."

After that proclamation Will wasn't really listening. Elizabeth blustered on but he'd already understood the tone and track of her message. He became much more interested in his analysis of her than in what she said. His contempt of her had been gestating for some time but now it was born. To begin with he felt sorry for her. Here was a woman condemned to a life of fear, and although she was in a state of relative safety she was not courageous enough to hide her anxiety. She had married into what she thought would be security but it had turned out to be vulnerability. Her husband's brother had fled to Flanders and suddenly Alexander was the head of the Hoghtons and the first focus of any persecution that might come their way. The arrival of Campion and Will had amplified that danger. Her lack of composure was in stark contrast to the living saint. His torturous martyrdom was assured, yet he exuded only calm confidence. Elizabeth's danger was far less, yet she never seemed at ease. Her authority was forced and desperate. Her rhetoric lacked logic, her judgement sounded contrived, her wisdom was guesswork in disguise. He was well used to being brow-beaten into deference, but at that moment he deeply desired a pair of daggers to silence this superior.

After he left Elizabeth's chamber he could not remember half of what she had said to him, but a fresh detail of his night with Frances Thursby returned. As his finger found the moist sheath between her legs he had been mindful of the stain on her glove, a blood stain, the blood of Simon Sedlow? The man whose dying words had identified his assassin as 'she'. Was that the thought that had made Will reach for something sharper to sink into his bedfellow?

As autumn began to leave the trees so calm routine returned to Hoghton. There were no repercussions from what had happened at the Golden Lion, though Will never lost the fear that some ramification might suddenly occur. He had dreams about it. In many of those dreams he was guilty. One in particular haunted him. In that dream he stood by the water carriers in the town square and a crowd gathered as he tried for hours to wash the blood from his hands.

His routine was easily established. Mostly he was assigned menial tasks about the house and estate, but a list of texts was forthcoming from Alexander and Will happily retreated to the library each day to read most everything else that was not listed. sometimes children of the household servants or of local tenants, were brought to a schoolroom and Will and Fulk, were tasked with teaching them their letters.

Will learned to act. In the evenings the troupe would gather and go through routines or learn parts of plays. This was not a well-structured procedure. Without a performance being scheduled they had no incentive to practice anything with any sense of reaching a praiseworthy standard, and Alexander was in no mood to play the genial host. Will explained Elizabeth's bizarre decree that he should train as a player but not be allowed to play. Piers dismissed it, saying he would sort out that problem if and when they were required to perform, and in the meantime Will should learn parts and be tutored in delivering them, which he duly did.

Avoiding Ros was a much greater problem. He saw her most days, and this was tolerated by Elizabeth so long as there were always others present and that they did not engage in conversation. As far as Will could tell, Ros was not inclined to converse anyway. Infrequently he would catch her eye, but all she gave in return was a steel stare. He still loved her.

Jane completely ignored her aunt's command and actively sought Will's company. "If I speak to you, then you are obliged to reply," she said. Nevertheless, Jane was wary enough to conduct their conversations away from Elizabeth's sight. Gradually their relationship developed and became a closed bridge between their social strata. His feelings for her were not as strong as those he held for Ros, but he was attracted to her. He loved her wit and her sharp pragmatism. He wished she had been as educated as he, for she was his match in thought-play but fell short on knowledge. She was hungry for other histories and the romances of myth. She continued to have no appetite for the future laid out for her.

He loved the world of letters. He loved the learning he carried with him, the tales from antiquity, and the stories from far countries. He loved the magic of words and how their sound could remove one world and replace it with another. He loved the mysteries of his faith and the promise it offered of eternal bliss or wretchedness. He loved the power that music added. He loved melody, he loved the dance, and he loved the souls of singers and dancers as they sang and danced. His training with the players brought all these loves to higher intensity. At the same time, however, he saw more clearly the difference between the real and the fanciful. He loved the latter, but knew he was condemned to forever face the former.

Playing was becoming his ale. Playing set aside the actuality of the world and created instead a real falsehood. He liked that. In that fake reality was a place detached from the pain of the present, but it was a place too where pain and pleasure could be played out to promote its purpose, or its pointlessness. He could see how the drama was a disguise that revealed all. Piers told him that wherever they played, the ceiling above their heads was called the heavens. Will wanted to play well. He wanted his ultimate sponsor to take him to the heavens where he would see him face to face, where he would shake the hands of brave martyrs who had gone before, and no doubt the first of those hands would be that of Campion.

There was no news of Campion.

In this thinking Will returned to his resolve to become a priest. He would draw from this wondrous year the learning and the means by which he would build a charisma like Campion's. He would be ordained, he would preach, he would bless, he would bring Christ's body to be the bread of hungry souls. He would save others before he surely must be brutally stopped from saving. Campion was confident of doing that, and Will felt he could be so too, but he feared it terribly.

For now he was safe. Or was he? It was Jane who frequently reminded him that some malignant party had somehow discovered that Campion was among them. There was a person or persons in the household not to be trusted, and they didn't know who that was. Campion said he would come back, and should he survive long enough Will felt certain he would keep his word. By day the prize on his head grew higher, and those who wished him harm grew greedier. They also may hold affinity with Frances Thursby, and they may know that the person who had put paid to her was Will.

TWENTY-ONE

Best for winter

Warwickshire was bitterly cold that winter, as was the whole of England. Frosts came early and the soil turned to stone. Farmers feared for their winter crops and so fierce and prolonged were the freezes that they had to break the surface of standing water so their flocks could drink. Snow fell in November and again in December, and between the two the thaw brought shin-deep mud, roads became impassable for carts and waggons and only the most intrepid of pedestrians persevered. Those on horseback fared slightly better but even their progress was hindered with crossroads and gateways becoming treacherous with trodden slime. Travel was to be avoided and the inhabitants of towns and homesteads became more insular. Those who had to journey resented it. Those whose survival depended on evasion found their plight became both easier and more difficult. Hunters were less likely to set out, but those in flight must face the added worry of the weather.

George Eliot made his way to Birmingham. The first freeze had turned to slush and the slipperiness of some sections of the way made his mare wary and skittish. The warm southerly had veered to the east again and sleet showers sliced at his cheeks. He resented having to make the journey but had no option. His fortunes were low, his finances minimal, and he needed income. In addition, a cryptic message that he had received stirred his head and raised his hopes. He had been back at the inn at Solihul, when word of mouth had arrived that a Philip Gyfford had information to his advantage and a possible commission on behalf of the crown. He had been recommended.

The journey took all of the short winter day and it was completely dark by the time his mare was stabled and he was welcomed into the cosily panelled dining room of Gyfford's house. The property was proudly presented with many ostentatious features and good examples of the latest trend in side boards, chairs, and chests, but Eliot formed the impression that though extravagant on one hand, his host was thrifty in other ways. He lived alone and kept a meagre staff. The cook was good. He was served with a splendid game pie, and delectable wine.

"I understand that you got close to Campion," said Gyfford.

"Briefly."

"And Frances did."

Eliot paused his chewing while he considered his tone. "You know Frances Thursby?"

"We've met."

That didn't completely answer the question Eliot had asked.

"She occasionally furnished me with information. Invariably good information."

"That's one of her skills."

Gyfford laughed. "Yes. One of them. When were you close to Campion? And why?"

"You will forgive me Mr Gyfford . . ."

"Philip. You must address me as Philip. In our business friendship is vital. It is the foundation of trust."

Eliot rinsed his mouth with wine. "Our business is what I need to clarify. Trust is a dangerous commodity. Use it foolishly and it transforms into treachery."

Gyfford raised his glass. "Mmm. Fascinating thought."

"We live in treacherous times."

"Indeed we do. Treason is our business. Yours and mine."

"I must clarify that I am loyal to the crown."

Philip laughed again. "You are loyal to your purse. There is nothing wrong with that. The crown, my dear George, is the best friend to have in your purse."

"How is it that you know of me?"

"By repute; and good repute. I understand your fears, but know I am aligned most firmly with our state. You need not fear me. I too have been on the trail of Campion, but indirectly. It is frustrating. I supply information, others act on it, others of great purpose and influence and many at their command, yet he slips through their fingers. It is time for me to be a little more direct."

"You want me to hunt on your behalf."

"In partnership."

"Then you will claim the reward."

"In partnership."

"I am already in partnership. With two others."

"Who are they?"

"It is of no matter, since both appeared to have deserted me. One left me for dead when I was in fever, the other . . . has just left."

"Frances."

"You know a lot."

"That is what I bring to the table." Philip consumed the last of his pie.

"And what is it you expect me to bring?"

"Campion, of course. How close did you get?"

"We were in his company at Park Hall in September. He went north. I was stricken by sickness. Frances went after him. I went after her, but she had vanished."

"Where did you look?"

"For Frances? Wigan, Preston, Lancaster."

"No news of her?"

"None.

"Not at any place?"

"No one I asked had anything to tell of her."

"And I was informed that you were a good spy."

"By Frances?"

"Frances is dead."

Eliot froze.

"Tragic, isn't it? She was a lovely lady."

"She is dead?"

"Stabbed. In the back."

"By whom?"

"A boy named William Shakespeare."

"I met him."

"He bedded her. Then deaded her."

"Where?"

"In Preston. At the Golden Lion."

"I asked at the Lion."

"And?"

Eliot thought hard. "They said nothing. Nothing of consequence."

"Cagey. That's lions for you."

Eliot wasn't laughing, but he was trembling. Philip filled his cup.

"Eat up. Drink."

"I feel sick. I loved Frances."

"Everyone did."

"I met him. His mother is an Arden. I met him at Park Hall."

"I thought you might have."

"I want him dead." Eliot leaned back. "I want William Shakespeare dead."

The smaller, fatter, older man toyed with his cup of wine. "He's sixteen."

Eliot's stare remained fixed on the candle flame on the table between them. "I'll kill him myself if I have to."

The fatter man pushed the debris of his dinner to one side. It was his turn to lean back. He breathed and sighed before he spoke.

"We'd better find him then."

"You don't know where he is?"

"He was lodged with the de Hoghtons in Lancashire. Some report him to be still there but others say he's gone, cleverly replaced by a player of similar appearance."

"I'll kill them both."

"And how will that benefit you? Or me? Or the crown?"

"Shakespeare must die."

"He will. One day. What we must discover is whether or not the fellow at Hoghton is he."

"Why?"

Gyfford swilled his mouth with Rhenish wine and swallowed. "The story is that he is remaining there until Campion returns, but we don't know when that will be. We can waste the winter chasing a fox that's gone to ground, or lie in wait for it to come back to its cub. The bigger question is what is he doing there? He is an educated boy. There is talk of a seminary."

"Frances spoke of that."

"A school for Jesuit priests. Now imagine the reward for uncovering that."

"Meanwhile Campion campaigns. Others could beat us to the main prize."

"It's Advent. Christmas is upon us. No one is in the mood for chasing shadows. Who knows where Campion is? Some say he sailed away, to Ireland. Could have. He's been there before. Lancashire looks towards Ireland. It's a short sail."

"I don't think he's in Ireland. He's too intent on his purpose."

"Well, it's not a good time for persuading men to ride long distances, and it's my view that if we play a cleverer game by being patient we can be first to the prize."

"I need the trophy now."

"No you don't; you need money now. I can see to that. This is a wager, a gamble on my part. I will place the bet, by supporting you. Fear not. No debt will be incurred. I owe it to Frances."

"So what exactly do you want me to do?"

"You are trusted by the Catholics."

"I am a Catholic, when I'm with them."

"Exactly. Go to Lancashire and get involved. Find out what is happening at Hoghton. Exercise control. If you act too rashly you'll get revenge but nothing else. It's Campion we want. Young William is a bonus. If he's preparing to be a priest the crown will kill him for you."

"I'll do it myself."

"George, see the bigger plan. The Hoghtons have a

library. A Catholic compendium for all we know. What's in there? Has Campion added to it? It could be a casket of seditious treasure. All the crown needs to condemn Campion and who knows how many more?"

"Whatever the crown needs the crown can create."

"But better if it doesn't have too. Many influential people will be pleased with us if we can serve up not just a dish, but a banquet."

"If all this is known why hasn't the house been overturned?"

"The local man is a fool. There was a raid, but Campion escaped, and they were not learned enough to look properly at the papers. They've had time now to stash them more safely. A second attempt will have to be much more thorough, but the timing has to be right. If we keep troubling the place, Campion will be warned and stay well away. We must be patient."

Eliot finally finished his food. Thoughts of Frances still sent pangs of nausea, but the possible scope of the boon that Philip Gyfford projected set his mind racing. The rewards for commanding the capture of man and manuscripts could indeed be high. He studied the calm self-assurance of his host.

"How is it that you are so well informed?"

"Before Frances approached you she came to me. I have not been idle. I know many people and they know many others. There are few Catholic houses in the country where we haven't got a person paid."

Eliot doubted that.

"I have such a person in Hoghton."

"Who?"

"For the time being it is safer that you do not know."

"If they have told you all this, why do you need me?"

"The person is a caged fox. It can see but cannot catch."

Eliot drained his cup.

Gyfford went on, "I need a man who has the guile and the guts to act decisively – but at the right time. You can slay your player-boy, but first bring me his hero, and his texts."

TWENTY-TWO

Deaf pillows

Advent brought new terrors. There was talk of the de Hoghtons going to Haigh Hall but Alexander was not thought well enough to travel, so the reverse was suggested, that the Bradshaws would come to Hoghton.

The full realisation of what was suggested sent Elizabeth into exasperation. She set about finding some way of backtracking. While she was keen to accelerate the prospect of a wedding of Jane to James, the submission of Roger, James' father, that the whole family might descend on Hoghton for the festive season sent her brain into a whirlwind of panic.

It was the end of breakfast when Elizabeth bustled in to the dining hall. She was there in search of Jane, who was in turn seeking Margery, because she had heard that a dispatch had come the twenty miles from Haigh.

"We could not possibly cope!" declared Elizabeth.

"No question," said Jane who was doubly disturbed, though ten times as composed.

"It would be difficult," said Margery.

"You are right Margery," said Elizabeth. "Now give me reasons."

Margery shuffled her weight from foot to foot as she

formulated excuses.

In the corner, Will, Andrew, Fulk and Solomon kept a low profile but hungered after every word. This could mean they would be needed to perform.

"I've known the larder be fuller, my lady. With my lord Alex being how he is we were not expecting major revels. Half of Advent is gone and we'll need to set to. We'd need everyone from Lea. The Haigh household is large; five daughters, five sons. One is a priest."

"What?"

Jane looked askance. "Surely you knew that?"

Elizabeth faltered. "I knew he was contemplating."

"Ordained," said Margery. "That's what I've heard."

"But surely he won't be at home?"

"At Christmas? His first as a priest. He might."

Now Elizabeth's and Jane's horrors were merged in opposing delight and dismay.

Jane's mind got to the point first. "Do not even contemplate what you are thinking. There have to be banns, they have to be posted in good time, and that time has passed if there was to be a yuletide ceremony."

"There will be no banns, Jane. Lord Alexander has decided. We cannot advertise the possible presence of a priest."

"Without banns I would not be married."

"You would in the eyes of God."

"Glory be," said Margery. "Are we to have a wedding as well?"

"No!" said Jane emphatically.

"Let's not sacrifice our serenity . . ."

Jane could not prevent herself from interrupting Elizabeth with a breathy sneer. For a moment the two women were locked in a bitter fusion of facial storms. The whole room suffered the pause. Elizabeth inhaled deeply.

"We cannot risk another priest in this house so soon after what occurred in October. I will make that plain in my reply. I will also state that due to my lord's disposition we feel that we cannot accommodate the entourage from Haigh Hall." Everyone relaxed. "However, we would welcome a visit from James, his sisters, and one of the un-ordained brothers of the Bradshaw family."

It was Jane's turn to draw breath, but no more was

said, and Elizabeth withdrew to fight with her pen and compose her response.

Advent advanced gloomily. With the days at their shortest and the freeze biting again there was little that could be done out of doors save for the sawing and splitting of wood. Time was given to maintenance and repairs of tools, of garments, and of the indoor fabric of the buildings. There was talk of a second priest hole being made, but Elizabeth scuppered that idea as being too risky. The trees were naked now, sleeping but watching. Evergreens were pruned and coppiced at the solstice and wreaths of rosemary, bay, holly, ivy and mistletoe were made to decorate the great and small halls.

A reply came from Haigh. The Bradshaws would stay at home for Christmas itself but a deputation of James and two sisters, Alice and Mabel, would come for the New Year and stay until twelfth night.

Jane shared her relief with Will while walking the estate gathering mistletoe among a small party of woodsmen and some of their womenfolk. She'd selected one of her plainer cloaks, sage green. He didn't hide his delight in meeting with her. The cold diluted the colour in their faces, and also worked its winter magic, so that the fainter the background hue the greater was the foreground blush of their cheeks.

"I don't expect you can escape the marriage."

"All decided before I was born, Will. Fate. We discussed that in our Greek lesson."

"We did."

"Were we always destined to have that discussion?"

"And this one."

"So is that all we are ever at liberty to do, discover our predetermined destiny? Where is the test in that?"

Will tried to balance the long-handled billhook he was holding on one finger.

"The test is in the dealing with it."

"How is that fair?"

The woodcutters reached high with their hooks. The mistletoe and a brittle branch of the host oak fell heavily, lashing one of their number. Laughter erupted.

"Fair?"

"If we are all given different destinies where is the fairness in the test of how we deal with them?"

Will chuckled in admiration of her remark. "James Bradshaw is a lucky man."

Jane's cheeks swelled briefly as she first celebrated then mourned the sentiment. She collected an armful of the mistletoe. "So where is the test for him in dealing with his destiny?"

Shakespeare said, "I think I'm talking to it."

Jane laughed a little. The men by the tree went to work again. No one objected that Will wasn't helping. He used his billhook as a walking stick. Jane led him away from the others.

"I know I'm going to have to marry him," she said. "Aren't I?"

"Marriage is a contract," said Will. "Love is . . ."
"Luck?"
"A disease," he said
"An infirmity."
"A curse."
"Or cure."
"Never healed me yet."

They had separated from the wooding party. Jane stopped and stared at the white and sapphire sky. "Maybe that's because those who might administer it to you are too scared to do so?"

He turned to her but she stayed secured to the sky. "The problem with my mind," he said, "is that it walks without bounds. I see several futures, all of which could happen, and none of which will."

"Tell me the ones that won't happen for they'll surely be the most entertaining."

They were edging around the south-eastern corner of the curtain wall. They could see the Darwen river and between them and it a thread of smoke rose from a hovel. Outside, a frail figure reorganised his pile of firewood.

"Have you met that fellow?"

Jane looked. "Everyone knows Poor Tom. Except Poor Tom himself."

"He scared us half to death the first night I came here."

"Quite mad. Sometimes in summer, when the water is low, he spends days on a tiny island in the middle of the river."

"Have you ever been to an island?"

"Aren't we on one?"

"I would like to go to another."

"What would it be like?" she asked.

"Ruled by love, not by hate."

"Is that what rules us? Hate?"

"It's what governs us."

"Does the Queen not love her subjects?" There was thread-of-gold sarcasm in her voice.

"When I get chance I'll ask her."

"Isn't that what Frances Thursby promised you?"

"I didn't believe her."

"Perhaps it wasn't a promise. Perhaps it was a prophecy."

"Witchcraft?"

"Or worse."

"She had powers. But so do you."

Jane sniffed the scent of the mistletoe she held. "We all do," she said.

"I wish to God that we didn't."

The solstice sun was sinking low. Dendritic shadows lengthened. Trees took light from the west. Soft voices giggled and harder ones laughed, a short distance away. Branches snapped and fell to earth. "We can harness our powers," she said. "As Campion does."

"God gave him more."

"Why?"

Will shrugged. "Because he asked him to."

"Would have been kinder to refuse."

"Do you call God cruel?"

"Yes Will. I do. And if that damns me, then so be it. I see in Campion a lovely, loving, wise and giving man. He is a man without hatred, even of those who hate him. And do you know what Will? I don't even think they do hate him. I think they fear him. They fear him because he loves and he creates more love. Love for the thing they fear. So God takes this lovely loving man, and he says - you'll do. I'll give you the power to love much more than others, and that love and that power will bring you more pain than you can imagine."

"But think of the rewards."

"If you are thinking of the rewards Will, it's not love, it's greed."

Will shivered. "We should join the others."

"I have love for you William Shakespeare."

"Do you?"

"But it cannot be shared, because I do not want the rewards. For me, or for you."

He stepped closer to her. The sun was in the hedgerow. Her face was the hue of pale snow. Her lips a bay leaf. She held a cushion of mistletoe between them. She did not move away. He did not move nearer. The world waited.

A woodsman broke cover twenty yards away.

Will and Jane re-joined the party. Soon they were inside, sipping spiced wine. The longest night began.

The scent of the aromatic shrubs filled the small hall in the east wing. Garlands and wreaths were manufactured and stacked in readiness to be hung the next day. Will made a small posy of some of the remnants and took it to his bed where he lay on his back unable to see anything other than its outline shape due to the lack of light, but he inhaled deeply the perfume, smelling especially the sweet spice of the mistletoe. He fell to sleep. His dream imprisoned his limbs but unlocked his memory.

Frances Thursby sat opposite him in the saloon of the Golden Lion. She was a golden lion with the lamp light catching her tumbling hair, hungry eyes and wet mouth. Her mane fell to her unbuttoned shirt. She leaned forwards, her cleavage soft-contoured and swollen with invitation.

His erection ached.

She put her hand on his wrist and leaned towards him as if to whisper but instead kissed his cheek just beyond the border of his mouth. She leaned back with a grin that said she had so much she could show, could teach, could bestow.

His erection ached more.

She leaned forwards again stopping just short of his mouth. She breathed deeply inhaling him towards her. He pressed his mouth to hers. She split, and her tongue surged to find his. She put her hand about his neck and pulled him from her lips so she could slide her teeth to nip the lobe of his ear.

"Come," she said, and she led the way through laughing eyes, toothless smirks and beams of timber that had stood still for a century but swayed now as if he were on the

Spanish ocean.

Once in her room she pinned him to the door and sent her mouth on a mission to find his soul somewhere underneath his tongue. He was sure he was about to shed his seed but somehow kept it in store.

Her clothes fell to the floor. A part of them fell too heavily, and he knew it was a belt with sheath and dagger.

She expertly unstitched his doublet and his hose slid to earth and his erection was against her naked belly, and then wrapped by one of her hands.

The room was sweat, and the song of nymphs, and they were now entirely naked and she pulled him to the bed and spread wide the longest thighs he had never seen.

What if she had the pox?

He looked for the pox but saw only pubic mane, wild, feline and impossibly familiar. He cupped her breast and she pulled him closer in encouragement. He mounted her awkwardly and began to probe pathetically with his penis, but she wasn't ready for him yet, and instead found his hand and led it to her groin and encouraged him to dip his finger. Then she took his shoulders and turned him so that she was on top, and for the moment the movement was all stopped, except for the room, which revolved like the night heavens, only faster, and slower, at the same time.

"So," she said, "to stand before the queen."

His reply was to take a third of her drooping breast into his mouth.

"Park Hall?" she asked. "Rufford? Gawthorpe?"

He opened his mouth still wider in order to stop it, but her tone was not questioning, but confirming. Surely he had not confessed that had he?

"Knowsley? Speke? Lathom?"

He had the most succulent of gags. He wanted her nipple in his throat. He must soon explode.

Her voice lost inquisition. "Ferdinando Stanley. Sir Thomas Hesketh. Ashton, Molyneux, Weever."

Names he knew. Persons he had met. He could not have told her. He needed to be sober. Perhaps her breast milk could do it? He sucked harder. She plucked her nipple from his gums and replaced it with her mouth. Yet still her voice spoke inside his head.

"Giles Colby."

How could she say that when he had her mouth?

Her wet vulva capped his crown and she slid down his shaft. Two thrusts she made and on the third the heavens and all their stars fell through the roof and entered his pelvis where the torrent split in two, one half shooting into her, the other making star powder burst inside his head.

She squealed in dubious delight, then laughed as she fell upon him. And then there were three of them; the two in the bed and the one remembering it. The one remembering suddenly recognised the dudgeon of a dagger, and where he had seen it the first time. The one being remembered realised the Shakespeare seed was now inside an intimate stranger. But had he given her more than that? Had he given her a litany of lives whose were now listed for traitors' deaths?

The one being remembered recalled the dagger that had fallen to the floor with her frock. He considered what it could do. The one doing the remembering suddenly saw again the other dagger, and knew where he had first set eyes upon it.

And now he was awake.

He had to tell someone. He tried to sit up in his bed but realised he had already done so, and for a moment he rocked back and forth slightly. He surveyed the room. It was the depths of the night and nothing could be seen except dark mounds where his fellow players slept. He would wake Fulk, but Fulk would not appreciate that. Andrew would be sympathetic but sleepy, Solomon would be reluctant to wake and Piers would sneer.

He got out of bed, leaving his hose behind but slipping his doublet about his shoulders. His shirt fell to his thighs so his lower legs immediately felt the December cold, but he went barefoot, because there was some urgency and he wanted his progress to be quiet. He was going to tell Jane.

The floorboards were cold but not painfully so. By now he knew their pattern. He knew the places where they creaked, where they gave quietly, where they were smooth or abrasive. He shivered slightly and his breath was warm and wet on the tip of his nose. He crept westwards along from room to room of the first floor of the north range until the place where it butted to the west wing. He found Jane's door and tapped at it.

Nothing happened. He tapped harder. Still nothing. He was scared to knock more vigorously in case he woke the wrong sleeper. He was about to wonder what to do but his mind had already decided and he was turning the handle of Jane's door.

All was shadow. The room, the bed, its drapes. He crept nearer. His hand reached forwards and parted the curtain drawn about it. There she slept. A slightly moving sculpture of shadow. Only a quarter of her face was apparent, the rest being tucked beneath the covers. Her breathing was slow; he could just hear it. The covers breathed with her, marking the rhythm of a life in pause.

He wondered what he should do. Should he speak? Should he shake her?

He touched her forehead. It was warm. She did not wake. He had not touched her face before. He stroked her forehead. She did not wake. He stroked it more. She shifted in her sleep and more of her face appeared. Now her nose and mouth were visible. He was sorely tempted to wake her with a kiss. Instead he stroked her cheek. Her eyes opened, found focus. She inhaled and his hand was over her mouth before she had finished the gulp.

"It's well. All is well. It's me Will."

She ripped his hand away. "What . . .?" Her voice was sharp but whispered.

"I know whose dagger it was."

"What?"

"In the Golden Lion."

She saw his legs. "Will, you cannot be here like this."

"I remembered. In a dream."

His legs trembled. It was the cold; and the memory.

Beyond the casement a night bird called.

She emerged more from the bed. Her nightshirt was solid shadow in the nearly no light. She reached down to where her cloak was spread as extra warmth. She gathered it and passed it to him. "Wrap this round you."

He did so.

"Now go down to the great hall. The fire will be there. I'll follow."

"I just . . ."

"The great hall Will. I'll follow."

It was the cloak she had worn for wooding. He tugged

it about himself. The absence of colour made the contrasts of her form more distinct. She was living stone.

"Go on."

He left her and made his way to the great hall, treading on iced stone while passing the priest hole on the way. The big room was freezing and now his feet had trodden rush beneath. It was damp and cold. There was more light because of the towering windows, but still no other colour than shadowy grey. There was no moon but nevertheless the windows shed a pattern of themselves on the floor and walls. The fire was in, but low. The long bench from the side of the great table was before it. He sat there and cantilevered his legs so that some radiance from the smouldering embers gave feeble comfort. Dare he add some of the smaller logs left there for the morning? Perhaps Jane would.

He waited.

Presently the door opened. No one came through. He could sense someone beyond it. He could hear breathing. No one entered. The door moved slowly, not shutting but closing to the jamb. He waited.

The door opened again.

No one came through but he could hear muttering. Someone was talking. The sound was soft. It was a child or a woman. To whom was she speaking? To herself? To another? To him? More breathing. Then a moan. The door swung violently wide. Then she came in.

Elizabeth wore a long white night smock. Will took a moment to confirm it was her. Her hair, normally completely ensconced in her headwear fell free. It was copious and fell in a heavy tumble of wavy grey. Her feet were bare. Her eyes were open but staring and focussed on empty air. She did not acknowledge Will, in fact he quickly understood that she did not even see him. She stopped just inside the door, muttered inaudibly, walked another six paces, stopped, muttered, found her way to the end of the long table, waited, effortlessly took a place sitting on the bench at the table, said "Such toys", and fixed her stare midway between herself and the fire mantle.

He moved cautiously towards her, sliding along the bench at the fire side of the table. He stopped half way. He didn't know whether to speak or not. He said softly, "My lady?"

She did not react, but spoke. Her voice was emphatic

213

in tone but low in power, and so it sounded both urgent and yet resigned. "Sleep is so seductive."

"Aye," he replied.

"Before the dreams."

"Aye . . ."

"Before the dreams"

"Aye, before the . . ."

"I have such dreams."

"I too."

"My hands are of your colour."

"My lady?"

"Screw your courage with your thumbscrew and you'll not fail."

"Thumbscrew?"

"My hands are of your colour. They do God's work. God's work."

Will was not convinced that this was a conversation, but the topic engaged him nonetheless. "God's work is so hard. Why does he need me to do it for him? He is a tower."

"Who?"

"How to make a tall man shorter? Stretch him, 'till he snaps."

"Who?"

"And when he's caught, the search begins. And if they do it, we'll all go to it."

Will was sure she was speaking of Campion. "He will keep you safe, he will not say he has been here."

"You will. You will. You will."

He was shaken by this response. He was now completed perplexed. Could she hear him? Was she conversing or was their interchange accidental? Was she sleeping? He had heard stories of such night movers but never seen one until now. Or was she possessed? Had she been infected by a spirit? From where? Good, evil or lost?

She angled her head in his direction but her focus did not change. What she saw was not in the room with them. Not yet.

"Have you seen the instruments child? Have you seen the tools of the torturer's trade? They are such craftsmen. There's such an artistry in sorrow. But all that's for tomorrow. And tomorrow. And tomorrow. I must wash my hands. I must wash . . . my . . . hands . . ."

She rose so suddenly that it made him jump. For a moment she stood stock still between bench and table. Then her hands moved, but bizarrely. It was if they washed each other but whilst still apart and by her sides. She jerked her shoulders, trying to force them together but they remained apart. The frustration contorted her face, then it was gone, replaced by a vision of a fear. She stepped from the table and stood still. There was the sound of water drumming. She was urinating where she stood. When that was done, she walked to the door stopping clear of it. He considered going to open it for her, but her fingers had found the handle. She opened it, waited, and then went. The door gently thudded behind her.

Will exhaled. He suddenly remembered cold, shivered, then shook it off. He couldn't resist padding across the rush floor to where Elizabeth had vented her bladder. He felt around with his toe searching for dampness.

"Not the first time."

He leaped back as if he'd seen a snake.

"She does it a lot." Jane was above and behind him, in the minstrels' gallery. "So I am told. I've only witnessed it once before. But the servants at Lea are always putting her back to bed. She's a terrible sleeper. Perhaps that's why she's so tetchy when she's awake. Add wood to the fire. I'm coming down."

Will did as he was told. Adding hazel twigs and branches first to reinvigorate the flames and then putting oak logs on top.

Jane came and sat next to him on the long bench. "Come, move it closer to the warmth."

They did so. Jane had donned another cloak. He recognised it as scarlet but saw it only as pewter and russet in the fire glow.

"Was she asleep or taken by a spirit?" he asked.

"Is there a difference?"

"Do spirits enter us when we sleep?"

"If your mouth is open," she said.

"When Campion returns he must bless her."

"Didn't work the last time."

"Some demons are strong."

"Are there any that are weak?"

The rising fire crackled erratically. Will stretched his

toes towards it. "Truly I know nothing of demons."

"Truly, we all know nothing at all. Except what we decide we know. Then we know it for sure. Then we know it to be good or ill because we have made up our minds. Nothing is good or bad but thinking makes it so."

"What?"

"I know that to be true. I have decided."

Shakespeare thought hard about what she had said. "I think you are right," he said.

"You have decided that have you?"

"I have," he said. He memorised her words. "Nothing is good or bad but thinking makes it so."

The hazel twigs were well alight. The flames began to lick the logs.

"So, why did you wake me?"

He suddenly felt ashamed, but put it to one side. "I had a dream, in which I remembered the night at the Golden Lion."

"Was it a damp dream?"

He looked quizzical but evaded her provocation. "I saw the dagger clearly and suddenly knew where I had seen it before."

"And where was that?"

"At Park Hall in Castle Bromwich. On the belt of a fellow called Rondel."

"Who is he?"

"He was known to Hugh the gardener."

"Hugh the priest."

"What?"

"My brother knows him. He's in disguise as a gardener. He's a priest."

"He vouched for this Rondel fellow."

"And the knife belongs to him?"

"Hugh is a priest?" Will thought back to his conversation with the gardener and how he had thought there was more to him than his appearance suggested.

"The wisest kind," said Jane. "Not all priests want to be martyrs. You are sure this knife belonged to the man called Rondel?"

"I saw it on him."

"Not all knives are different."

"Simon Sedlow was concerned about Rondel and his accomplice."

"He had an accomplice?"

At last the burning logs exuded sufficient heat to warm the soles of Will's feet. "Man called Eliot. George Eliot. They only let them in because Hugh vouched for them. Simon seemed troubled by them."

"Who is Simon?"

"Simon Sedlow from Stratford. He's the one that was killed at Colby's . . ." Will's voice trailed off. The wood smoke coiled in the arch of the fireplace and Will breathed deeply drawing some of its charcoal taste into his chest. "This is why I woke you. This is why I had to tell you."

"Why?"

"The servant who found Colby mortally wounded said his last words were 'she was a spy'. She. *She*. I'd seen her wear a knife. I'd heard it hit the bedroom floor. The glove that Fulk found had a bloodstain on it. I feared she must be the assassin and perhaps she'd do to me what she did for him, and I remember reaching for the side of the bed and grasping for her clothes to find her knife."

"And did you find it?"

"I can't remember."

"What is it with your memory Will?"

"It was the beer."

"More than the beer I'd wager."

"What?"

"Talk to Ros. She is has rare knowledge of such things."

"What?"

"To the point of enchantment. I don't mean that unkindly. I love Ros more dearly than any other. She knows her remedies. And her maladies."

"You think the beer was spiced?"

"Richly. I know you fight ale poorly Will, but I doubt the Golden Lion serves that rich a brew. I suspect more likely your bedfellow knew her midnight mushrooms and slipped some in your cup."

Will's admiration of Jane found new heights. "You are so wise."

"When men realise that, they burn us for it. Did you

217

stab her?"

"I don't remember doing the deed, but I carry the guilt that goes with it."

"It doesn't explain the second dagger."

"That's my hope."

"Mr Rondel's blade."

"Why would he arrive?"

"Perhaps he was always there?"

"How?"

"The room was dark and you were more than drunk. He could have witnessed all you did."

"And all I said."

"Yes."

"A list of names and places," said Will from beneath a blush.

"And possible destinations. If he thought he had Campion in his grasp, it would be enough to stop her and move to claim the prey for himself."

For a while they fell silent. Slowly the rising fire gave sufficient heat to make their closeness cosy. Unwittingly each edged closer until Jane's two cloaks touched. He could feel her arm through four woven layers, and she did not move away. What a day it had been. The afternoon in the woods was a romance through which he saw what could be, except that it could not. The night brought dreams that unlocked more of the sealed caskets of his slow-burning nightmare, and in Elizabeth he had seen and heard an un-woken sleeper.

"It was as if she was trying to warn me," he said suddenly.

"Who?"

"Elizabeth."

"We are all trying to do that Will."

"All?"

"Listen. Be a priest. Thousands will thank you. They'll kneel before you, drink your blessing, adore your homilies, and hold you in their hearts. The saints in heaven will smile on you and the angels will polish your seat in the seraphim. But be clear on one thing Will, the ones who need to hear you the most will not be listening."

"What are you saying?"

"That so long as we have priests and prosecutors all we

will ever have is pain."

"Until the priests persuade the prosecutors."

"Haven't you noticed Will? It works the other way."

Soon the wood on the fire had burned through and the cold began to creep around their cosy cove. They must either rebuild the conflagration or return to their beds. The tower murmured as distant draughts played at ghosts.

Jane stood. "Thank you for telling me your remembrance. Perhaps we now know how Frances Thursby died."

"Perhaps." Will stood too, and she faced him.

"I do not think you killed her Will, but even if you did, then that was probably no bad thing, depending on what you may have told her."

"And what another may have heard."

"We may never know. As for Elizabeth's dream, there was talk at the table tonight that Campion has been caught."

"Where?"

"Oxford. Pay it no heed. It's the third such story in as many weeks."

"I heard the others."

"I doubt they keep letting him go. It's just fear and speculation. It spoils my lady's sleep, so that's fine by me," she said.

"If they do catch him and he confesses being sheltered here they will come back for lord Alex. Perhaps for Elizabeth. Perhaps for you."

"Let's hope they come by Christmas and save me from James Bradshaw."

She planted a soft swift kiss on Will's lips.

"Remember that for ever," she said. "And forget it straight away."

She left the hall. He stood by the fire but it gave no heat so he headed off for bed. As he circumnavigated the great table he trod in the wet patch where Elizabeth had spilled her urine.

Pete Hartley

TWENTY-THREE

No other medicine

All work stopped on Christmas Eve. There was sadness in the
house that a priest was not in attendance but the family gathered
in the chapel at midnight for prayers and to sing the *Coventry
Carol* in English and *In Dulci Jubilo* in Latin. There were mugs of
mulled wine served in the small vestibule hallway that linked the
chapel to the eastern end of the great hall. The family and the
household servants, including the players, then made their way
into the great hall which was now richly hung with the green
shrubbery they had harvested.

Alexander had been the first into the chapel and he
urged everyone out before him, as his movements were awkward
and slow. Will felt an inclination to wait for him. He offered his
arm and the old man gratefully took it. He trod carefully, his
trusted ash stick in his other hand. He was thickly garbed in a
rich black wool coat edged with sable. Will could barely feel his
arm through the layers. They paused at the arched doorway.
Alexander tapped the masonry with his stick.

"From Whalley Abbey, you know," he said.

Will did know because he had asked Andrew. The arch

220

was incongruous being unfashionably Romanesque and the stone was the only part of the tower not quarried from the very hill on which they stood. "I believe so," he said to his host.

"We have so much to thank old king Hal for," said Alex.

Will chuckled, not so much at the irony, but it pleased him to see the jovial spirit of his host. Through most of his long life Alexander de Hoghton had celebrated a reputation for merriment, and joy. He had eschewed the more serious concerns of his Catholic peers, though he had always remained quietly faithful to the cause. His spirit and easy-going attitude meant that the Queen's local agents had looked favourably on his acquisition of Hoghton once his brother had fled to Flanders. With the burden of the tower, or perhaps with the onset of the winter of his life, Alexander had adopted a revised temperament. He became much more serious. He was the custodian of not only the estate but the family heritage stretching back to the conquest of England by William from Normandy. Virtually all the land visible from the tower when looking west or south, was his. There was even more beyond the horizon. He was a very wealthy man but as they shuffled along Will felt he steadied a person of great poverty. Age and antagonism had robbed him of his prosperity. All he had left was spirit, and Will detected a deterioration of that faculty too, but he was warmed by the gusto with which the lord had sung and prayed during the service, and by the gleam in the old man's eye and the sharpness of his wit as they wobbled towards the great hall. Jane stood in the door, clutching Alexander's favourite stag horn cup, steaming with warm mulled wine. When she passed it to her uncle she also passed an unseen basin of warmth to Will, filling him with her smile and wishing him the blessings of the Christmas feast.

The fire had been stacked high while they sang and that, plus the seventy people there, made for a homely gathering. Genial faces turned in their direction as they made their way to the arm chair and Will knew that he would soon lose the privilege of being the primary escort of their host. Alexander sensed this too and drew Will closer to him with a tightening of his looped arm.

"I hear you had an adventure with a dangerous lady," he said with his best attempt at confidentiality.

221

"I did my lord."

"Take my wisdom young man, with regards to dangerous ladies. There is no other kind." He laughed throatily.

Will laughed too, accepting not only the jocularity but also what he interpreted as the forgiveness of his overlord. He eased him gently into his chair.

"The peace of Christ be upon you, Will."

"And on you, my lord."

"Now go and drink deeply. But not too deeply."

Will grinned and bowed. He stepped aside and turned to find Jane with another cup. "I've tested it," she said. "It is spiced but not with a treacherous recipe."

"How can you be sure, my lady?"

"I drank some before we went to chapel, and I can remember every word."

Will grinned. It seemed that everyone was grinning. There was a swell of chatter and laughter and everyone looked glassily at each other from faces flushed with wine, candlelight and fire glow. Beyond and above them the great lattice of the windows formed a cage to keep the secular world in its place.

"Well, my priest, are you ready to be a player later today?" asked Jane.

"I think I shall be a sailor."

"A sailor. Here's new courage."

"Cowardice I fear."

"Why a sailor?"

"To find that island of which we dreamed."

"When you do, then send a ship for me."

"I will."

The merry making that night was respectfully muted and lasted less than an hour, then all went off to their beds. The main feast would follow the next day, and last for twelve more.

Christmas Day should have begun back in the chapel with a Mass but no priest was available so once again it was a simple ceremony of prayers and songs. Then as noon approached once again the household gathered for feasting in the great hall.

The centrepiece was a pig's head pickled with ale and vinegar and stuffed with chopped pork and raisins and surrounded by pies and game and sweetmeats. The feast was laid out on a long table at the east end of the hall then carried to the great table where it was eaten. Andrew played his lute and Solomon his drum while Piers and Fulk blew pleasing melodies on their whistles and pipes. Will and Fulk sang, but not as sublimely as Solomon whose wassailing carols solicited lusty joining in, and brought thunderous applause. Alexander was central again, and he made sure that the players were well furnished with food and drink. Will kept an eye on Jane who sparingly shot him nods of approval. Elizabeth made a great show of celebrating, and after several cups of wine her spirit was liberated and she laughed almost continuously and very vociferously. The servants shared her joy, though Will felt that they had two characters to their mirth, the real when genuinely distracted and the fake when in conversation with their mistress.

In the late afternoon the players managed to perform two of their stock comedies, one that was new to Will plus a reprise of lord Alexander's favourite, *The Cuckold Miller*. He laughed so heartily Will thought his lord's heart might not hold out for the duration of the performance. When the show was done, Alexander made the gatekeeper Rowland, Lord of Misrule for the rest of the day. To the minds of many this signalled the final forgiveness of Rowland for his less than scrupulous execution of duty when Frances Thursby had been admitted. The porter revelled in his role and much hilarity was had as he gave ridiculous speeches and orders and everyone became more and more drunk.

Ros was a constant delighting irritation. Her presence was frustrating for Will, for the more intoxicated he was the more he wanted to court her, but she kept her distance. Never drunk, but not quite sober, she laughed and cajoled and allowed herself to be teased and embraced by a succession of men. Sometimes that behaviour was so blatant that Will saw it as provocation aimed directly at him.

The day did not so much end as become dovetailed into the next: the feast of Saint Stephen. Some folk went to bed as the night rotated; others curled up in warm corners and snoozed until dawn. It was a sleepy day during which Will saw nothing of Ros and little of Jane. By mid-afternoon he was exhausted, went to bed and did not rise again until the following day which was the feast of John the apostle.

The revels continued in disorderly fashion as the yuletide season matured. Very little work was done about the estate but the kitchens began to gear up again in anticipation of the next wave of feasting on New Year's Eve and Day. Ros was much engaged with baking. Jane grew more sober and palpably tense as the New Year drew close. It would signal the arrival of James Bradshaw.

At dusk on the fifth day of celebration, the feast of Saint Thomas a Becket, Jane sent for Will.

"She wants you in her chamber," said Fulk. "Would you care to borrow my codpiece?"

Will ignored his jape and hurried to Jane's room. Ros was there, sitting on a chair. A second seat had been brought and set for Will, next to Ros. Jane stood at the casement in the last of the light.

"I trust you both," she said, without looking at either. "More than any others."

Neither servant spoke.

Jane studied the horizon. "I have a plan. No it is not a plan; it is a dream. A fancy that might become fact. My father went to Flanders. Supposing I followed his lead?"

There was silence.

Jane said, "Well?"

Ros said, "This is your home my lady."

"And always will be. But soon I will not live here. Soon I will abide in another man's house."

Will asked, "Does James Bradshaw plan to go to Flanders?"

"No, I plan to go there. To avoid him. I want you both to come with me."

The two servants looked at each other. Ros' face filled with incredulity and distaste in equal amounts.

Jane still aimed her attention through the window. "It would be without my uncle's consent, so I cannot command you to come."

Will thought very hard. "And when there what would we do?"

Now Jane looked at him. "I might marry you."

"Might?"

"You'd have to agree."

"How would we live?"

"I have jewels, I have clothes. Could you copy Campion and play the merchant?"

"Play?"

"Your father is a dealer. You must have seen him deal."

"I will copy Campion and play the priest."

Jane came and stood before him. "I offer you this other path. It is the wise way, the way we can save each other."

"And Ros?"

"Ros slipped Campion from this house. She can do the same for us. If that is all you do Ros, then I thank and bless you, but I would much prefer it if you came with us."

Will's mind was in a turmoil. Ros was breathing audibly. Jane's hands were clamped so tightly her fingers were visibly discoloured even in that feeble light.

"What say you both?"

Ros was at once calm. "If you wish to slip from this house, send for me and I will show you the way. But I am bonded here. I cannot go with you without my lord's say."

Jane sat on her bed. "Thank you Ros. You may leave us now."

Ros stood, bobbed a curtsey and left. As she shut the door its latch unlocked Will's pulse.

"What say you Will?"

"I say the future is full of fear."

"And I say you are right."

"We cannot fight it with fantasy."

"But now you are wrong. We cannot live our dreams unless we dream them first. Go and sleep with that thought, and if you dream a better answer, share it with me in the morn."

Will did not sleep well that night. He kept churning what Jane had said in his head but it refused to solidify into a shape he could comprehend. He saw a lady he admired and a woman of strength who was suddenly shaken by vulnerability. He tussled with her motives. Could her fear of marriage be that strong? By her own admission she hardly knew her prospective husband and it was a woman's Christian duty to accept the best marriage brokered to her. The Bradshaws were a reputable family of strong foundation. They were rich. They were of the old faith. They even had a priest in their number. He could not accept that apprehension alone was sufficient to shake her sense of duty. Did she really therefore, have deep feelings for him? Was the elopement a serious suggestion? Would this paragon of the old heritage slough it all away for the sake of a poor player? Could she abandon reputation, prosperity and eternal salvation at the behest of a romance of her own imagining? He doubted that. Then what was she doing?

Was she simply trying to save him from himself? Perhaps that's why she tried to involve Ros? Jane knew how much Will was attracted to Ros. Did she think her inclusion would be enough to draw Will away? Surely not. She had sought his presence continually despite Elizabeth's disapproval. Their conversations were easy and punctuated by frequent laughter. He loved her depth of thought. He loved her speed of intelligence. He loved the way her eyes sparkled when she sparred with him in their dialogues. He loved the way she laughed at him when he played on the stage. He loved the way she listened to the verses he penned. He saw how his words could send her mind into stasis. He loved the way she sometimes had to draw a deliberate breath to break from the spell his speech had cast. He loved the way she had been compelled to set aside their differences in station, and seek out the human in him. He loved the way she loved him more than he loved her. Could it be that she loved him more than he loved Ros?

He surely could not rebuff that love.

She had shown him what she had dared to dream and asked him to make it live. In short she offered him a myth. This would not happen again in his life. He must accept.

He thought about the body beneath the bodice and the warmth it would give. He had tasted her lips and longed to try her tongue. He imagined how she would cling to him and how he would know that lust and love could be one. He longed to know that.

He could be a merchant. He could buy and sell. He could live in Flanders with a wife who'd snapped herself from one of England's oldest vines and spliced herself to a Warwickshire weed. They could grow in peace, and in prayer, in a place where the Pope was still revered. They would make family. He would make money. She would make him happy.

It seemed a simple choice. The closer he edged towards sleep the more he grew to see the possibility. It all seemed so much more rewarding than running from priest hunters. He could love Jane de Hoghton. He *would* love Jane de Hoghton. He resolved that he would tell her so. There was a terrible guilt over his betrayal of God's calling, but this new life was suddenly overwhelming in its attraction. He simply knew it was the path he must take.

It was a pity then, that when James Bradshaw arrived, he brought not only his two sisters, but also a male guest who was lodging with them for the festive season.

Will recognised him as soon as he saw him dismount in the courtyard.

TWENTY-FOUR

The purpose of playing

"It's James Rondel."

"I know who it is." Ros bustled along hurriedly taking lavender rushes via the underground passage to the great hall.

"It was his knife."

"So you said."

"I told Jane."

"So she said."

"She has to be wary of him."

Ros dodged a puddle in a depression of the underground tunnel floor. "She seems quite taken by him."

"That's just an act."

"Well you should know."

It was the sixth day of Christmas. The guests had arrived in the late afternoon. The welcome meal was to be relatively simple, but there was to be some celebration. The players would play. Will had kept a low profile but now he would need to dance, sing and act before the man he suspected had slain Frances Thursby as she had slept next to him. Will suspended their conversation as Margery approached and passed them. The weather was bitter with a savage easterly blizzard thickly coating the ground outside. The yards were treacherous so the underground passage was in full use. Once Margery was well clear, Will blocked Ros' path. "Rondel is a very dangerous man."

Ros gave a scornful grimace and used the bulk of the sheaf of lavender to lever her way past him. She accelerated away and skipped up the steps towards the hall.

"You be careful," he called after her.

She halted and looked down at him. Just for a moment there was tenderness in her face, as if gratitude had taken her by surprise, but as soon as she recognised it, she banished it. Something terrible took its place. She leaned slightly towards him and her voice lost almost all of its power. "Do you want me to fix him?"

"Fix him?"

"Well?"

"I don't know."

She didn't wait for Will to make up his mind, but carried on up the stairs and disappeared towards the hall. Shakespeare was left stunned and puzzled, but ever so slightly pleased.

The tower had found a new vigour with the arrival of their guests. Will witnessed the urgency of the household as the visitors were accommodated. He also observed from the fringes how the family went about its fawning. Elizabeth adopted her ingratiating geniality and gossiped vicariously about all kinds of subjects of which she had little knowledge. She told of the reconstruction of the tower and how her husband's brother had taken the trouble to ensure this or that feature in order to enhance its fashionable status. She spoke at length of the family pedigree, though Will surmised that James Bradshaw knew it far more accurately than she did. She talked of the extent of their land, though it was unlikely that she had ever set eyes on most of it. Will deduced that no part of this conversation was necessary. Everyone knew just how prominent the de Hoghtons were and how much wealth they commanded. Will considered that James needed no persuasion to consider allying himself with the auspicious family. Furthermore, he seemed strongly attracted to Jane.

There was something about Jane's demeanour that troubled Will. Either she was an exceptional actor or her disposition towards her suitor had radically changed. She laughed easily and there was a vivacious quality to her conversation that he had not expected. She seemed genuinely interested in what he had to say and was relaxed in her responses. Will wanted to talk to her, and tell her of his decision to accept her proposal but protocol dictated that he must keep his distance unless summoned.

James Bradshaw portrayed a formidable presence. He was a man very much at ease with his position. Dark haired, of a strong stature, athletic and lean yet sturdily muscled and with a propensity to project approval to all irrespective of their station, Will began to wonder if Jane's rebuttal had been founded on a premature evaluation of her suitor.

James' two sisters were gracious. Will considered Mabel's face the more agreeable but Alice had a more immediate warmth in her disposition.

Even just a few guests had changed the dynamic of daily interaction. It was as if the whole household had become subtle players by reverting to the strictness of the unwritten rulebook of domestic propriety. That evening however, his troupe must demonstrate their special dispensation to break the decorum. The players must play, and to do that they had to spread joyous disorder by enforcing the subversive and irreverent.

They played *The Cuckold Miller* once again and while the guests laughed audibly they were restrained in the duration and volume of their mirth. The household chuckled politely having seen it too frequently and too recently. Alexander had declined to join them for both meal and play, and his absence cast a shadow over the evening. Elizabeth did her best to fake merriment.

Will's words came easy enough during the playing, but he was acutely aware of the presence of new watchers. In particular, the attendance of James Rondel cut him to the core. He caught his gaze at several points during the play. Rondel was grinning in what appeared to be genuine amusement, and at no point did he make any sinister acknowledgement. There was blatant recognition though. They had met at Park Hall and there was no doubt that the Bradshaw house would know that Campion had recently been at Hoghton, so it would not be a surprise to find Will here. Nothing about Rondel's demeanour suggested any implication in the business at the Golden Lion.

After the show the guests and players mingled. Rondel was warmth incarnate. He sought Will, slapped him on the shoulder and shook his hand. Although his congratulation seemed overcooked in the light of the somewhat flat audience response it did not sound insincere.

"Such fun," he said.

"Campion enjoyed it," said Will.

"The great man has a great humour by all accounts."

"He does."

"You no longer accompany him."

"He deserved better."

"There is more important work for you here."

"Is there?" asked Will. He sipped his spiced cider, carefully.

"So my lady Elizabeth tells me."

"What has she told you?"

"That she presides over a school for Campions."

Will's heart took a different dagger. Was his hostess this free in disseminating the detail of the enterprise that so terrified her only a few weeks earlier? "She told you that?"

"We already knew." Rondel slapped Will's arm again. "We wish you well, young William. You, and all who follow the courageous path of the true cross."

"I may not walk it," said Will, shocked by the speed and honesty of his instinctive riposte.

"Why so? Do you falter?"

"Others may stop me."

There was an almost imperceptible tautening of muscles in Rondel's cheeks. "What do you mean?"

"As you suggest, the priest's path is treacherous."

Rondel gave a slight nod. "Isn't that what warrants the reward?"

"The reward cannot be earned if the questor expires before the campaign is launched."

Now Rondel's eyes found renewed lustre. "Trust in God. He may have already sent angels to protect you." He slapped Will gently again on the upper arm and his hand remained there for a moment and executed a reassuring grip. Then, laughing warmly, he moved away into the festive swarm. Will was left isolated amid the crowd.

Ros came bustling close. "Follow," she said.

Now Will was doubly stunned, but Ros had a strong natural authority and he found himself snaking in her wake even before he was conscious of a decision to comply. She led him through the door beneath the gallery and on to a nook in the corridor not far from the priest hole. She was clutching a tray with half a dozen empty cups on it. "Well?" she said. "Do you want me to fix him?"

"Fix?"

"Just enough to keep him out of trouble while he's here."

Will breathed a sigh of indecision.

"Or would you rather I served that condition on James Bradshaw?"

"Not unless my lady Jane requests it."

"She hasn't, and I don't think she will."

"If you get chance, tell her I would speak with her. Privately."

"And Mr Rondel?"

"He's no threat to me here. Perhaps he never was." He stepped back towards the great hall. "Why would you do this for me?"

The empty cups jostled on the tray as she went on her way.

The revels, though modest, went on until after midnight. A bleary-eyed Ros found Will slumped beneath the gallery not far from the fire. "Small hall," she said, then hurried away.

Will made his way whilst on the perimeter of sobriety, and one third asleep. He expected the small hall in the east wing to be jovially populated and staggered in without ceremony but found he had disturbed a moment of intimacy. As soon as they heard him, Jane and James Bradshaw put space between them. Will spluttered an indecipherable utterance that might be understood as an apology and turned to leave. Jane stopped him.

"Will?"

He approached the pair trying to counterbalance the awkwardness with deference. "My lady?"

"This is Mr Bradshaw. He greatly admired your performance."

James' countenance glowed. "I was richly entertained."

"I will convey your gratitude to the troupe, my lord."

"I already have spoken to them, Will. I want particularly to encourage you."

"I'm not entirely sure my future lies in playing, my lord."

"That's not the future I seek to encourage." Will discovered that in close company James Bradshaw exuded a powerful warmth. "Our faith needs brave squires to rally to the standard."

"I doubt I have sufficient bravery, my lord."

"I doubt few do, but what you have, beyond question, is the power to play it. Perhaps that's all bravery is? Perhaps that's all power is?"

Will glimpsed Jane. She was as transfixed by James' rhetoric as she had been by Will's. The silence of her listening shouted inside his head. Meanwhile he heard his own voice playing the precursor of his thoughts once more, as he spoke as much to himself as to his compatriots. "Playing brings no real pain, my Lord."

James screwed his lips in thought, and then said, "Overleap the boundaries and I'm sure it would."

"Isn't that the purpose of playing, my lord?"

James considered again.

Jane filled the gap. "The purpose of playing is to hold a mirror up to nature."

Both men were now silenced. Eventually, James said, "I have a brother who is a priest. He dearly wanted to be here with us, but my lord Alexander sent word that it would not be wise, so soon after your escapade when Campion called. Edward, I'm sure, would support you in your ambition. As a brother I mercilessly teased him. Since his ordination his words have chastened me in ways I would not have imagined. Before he went to study he played the pious valiant. He pretended the courage, for I know he had his fears, but he is beyond bravery now, Will. He is not playing, he is possessed."

Jane spoke very slowly. "Perhaps one leads to the other?"

Once again neither man had a response, though each gave due consideration to what she had said. After a moment James continued, "God needs men like you, Will. Start by pretending. That way you will learn to wear the disguise. The deportment will follow. Then the spirit will speak through you."

The spirit was not speaking through Shakespeare. What reverberated in his head was an entirely human perspective. He was unsettled by the congeniality of James, which was out of joint with the image Jane had generated prior to his visit, but what disturbed him all the more was the transformation in Jane herself. Gone was the reluctant suitor and the dissuader of martyrdom. She was enamoured of her most feared guest and conspiring to turn Will back to the road to Tyburn. No doubt the romance of scandalous elopement had been cast from her mind. He was in shock, but he didn't catalogue her as fickle. This was something much stronger. Four hours in the company of the brother of a priest and the wise woman had reset her course. What was at work here?

"I'm grateful for your good wishes, my lord." Will bowed slightly and began to edge away.

James stopped him with a quieter but insistent tone. "Will, you must know that James Rondel is not a close acquaintance of mine. He is known to our family."

Will wasn't sure what to say. "I met him some weeks ago."

"At Park Hall."

"Yes."

"The one in Warwickshire."

"Close to Castle Bromwich."

"Where you also met Hugh the gardener."

"I did."

James checked the shadows of the hall and lowered his voice. "He is a secret priest."

"I had heard the rumour. He vouched for Rondel at Park Hall."

"So Jane told me earlier this eve. He came to us with introductions from Gawthorpe, Knowsley, and Speke."

The recently dreamed memory of his night with Frances Thursby came rushing back into Will's brain. "Park Hall?" she had asked. "Rufford? Gawthorpe? Knowsley? Speke? Lathom?"

Will asked, "On what business did he come to Haigh Hall?"

"In search of Campion. He made no pretence

otherwise. He said he wanted to hear him preach again. He told me he had heard him first at Park Hall." James' voice was still low, his eyes still vigilant of shadows within shadows. He leaned even closer to Will. "Jane has told me of your night at the Golden Lion."

Will shot Jane through with a bitter glower.

Jane leaned into their huddle. "He needed to know about the knife, Will."

Will snorted an exhale. "He's not wearing one tonight."

"It is his manner to carry one."

"It was his blade. I am convinced."

"Convinced?"

"The knife was very like his, or the exact same. I did not see him wield it. And if he did that night, he chose not to rest it in me."

"But left you for the hangman," said Jane.

"Or saved me from a sweet assassin."

"What?"

"Frances Thursby slew a Stratford man."

"Are you certain?" asked James.

"I think she did. And she may have been about to do the same to me. If Rondel was in the room with us that night he may have been my guardian."

Jane said, "Then why not wake you and take you with him?"

Will shrugged. "I know not. It may just have been simple robbery. She had money."

James said, "Was it taken?"

Will shrugged again. "I didn't see it. Neither did I think to look for it."

James breathed deeply and turned out from their huddle. He took a few paces into the dark and checked once more the depths of the deep night shadows. He kept his voice soft and low. "We need the measure of this fellow. He may be the Holy Father's closest confederate or Queen Elizabeth's most dangerous infiltrator. Either or neither, we need to know."

Will said, "Could you not question him?"

"Questions can be answered without knowledge being gained. We need a surer way."

Jane said, "Then we must use deceit."

235

"What?" asked James.

"Deceit is often the best route to discovering the truth. What we need is a true liar, and that is what we have. A player."

For the third time both men were silent.

Jane's focus was on Will. "When will you next play?

"New Year's Day."

"What play will you give? Pray not the *Cuckold Miller*."

"There is still argument," said Will, "but it will not be that."

"Could it be a new play?"

"In two days? Why a new play?"

"A new play with a scene very like one you have played for before. Played for real. In the Golden Lion."

The frost bit deeper. The barn was far too cold for play-making. The players stacked their mattresses at one end of their bed chamber and used that room. Though well away from the main gathering places and thoroughfares of the Tower it was not as withdrawn as the barn so there was more difficulty in keeping their practice confidential. Will relayed Jane's idea to the troupe. It caused much consternation.

"A new play in a day?" Piers was incredulous.

"A new part of a play," said Will.

"It has to be a comedy," said Solomon. We can't go killing people on New Year's Day and expect folk to cry.

"Better then than on twelfth night," said Andrew. "We'll need a comedy for that."

"Has to be a comedy," said Solomon.

"But we need to kill Thursby," said Fulk. "Or a witch like her."

"It can be funny," said Will. "The trap would still work wouldn't it?" He looked to Piers for his expert reply.

"If the mouse is in the room the trap will work. But the mouse might be rat, or even a cat. Rats are cleverer than you think and cats give nothing away."

"We should be doing this in the barn," said Fulk. "All three are there."

Piers was getting agitated. "We've got a day! It can't be done."

"Campion's brag," said Will, suddenly. "There's a

killing in that, and it's funny. *I told her of tides, and in March beware ides. Even Caesar had bad luck with friends, my dear boys.* We stab Caesar."

"That's not going to prick anyone's conscience," insisted Piers.

"We add another verse," said Will.

"Yes," said Fulk enthusiastically. "With Will as himself, and me as Frances Thursby. Then we just need someone to be Rondel." He looked at the remaining trio. Two were too fat and one far too tall. "Hmph!"

"Perhaps Jane would play Frances," said Will. "She was very comely."

Fulk said, "Get Ros to do it. Eh Will?"

Piers was sternly serious. "Women do not play."

"No," said Will. "They do not."

"I'll do it," said Solomon. "All I need is a blond wig and shoes on my knees and I'll creep in on them."

Everyone laughed except Piers. "You are Campion. This needs expert playing. I'll be the guilty one."

Andrew settled his bulk on the floor. "And so we play the scene, what do we expect Rondel will do?"

Will said, "Jane and Bradshaw will watch him. See his response."

"And what if he does not respond?"

Fulk plucked a straw from one of the mattresses. "I can insert another twist."

"What?" demanded Piers.

"Leave it to me. We should work out the new verse."

Solomon leaned against the door and spoke softly. "What about my lord and lady? Are they part of this? They saw the first version. They'll wonder why we changed it."

"I'll speak to Alexander," said Piers. "He'll want to know the itinerary anyway."

"And Elizabeth?" said Solomon.

"Don't tell her," said Will. "She'll give the trick away before we've played it."

The matter was settled. Will composed the new verse and they worked out the action, whilst keeping careful tags on the whereabouts of James Rondel. It was reported that he and the Bradshaws were conversing convivially in the great hall where Elizabeth held another affected court.

When it was his turn to keep watch, Will took the opportunity to secretly scrutinise Rondel from between the spindles of the balustrade of the minstrels' gallery. He was wearing his decorative dagger. The scabbard, though suspended from the girdle with leather, was constructed from ornamented metal. The hilt and handle of the dagger were also elaborately fashioned. Even from ten yards distant, Will could see that the patterns did not match.

The rest of the tower household went about their yuletide business. The kitchen staff were close to frantic, getting ready for the next round of feasting, that night and on the following day, the first of 1581, the year in which Will would turn seventeen.

In the late afternoon, when their practice was done, Piers went to inform Lord Alexander, Fulk announced he was going to tease Ros, and Jane sent for Will.

Jane looked especially appealing in the half-light from the casement of her bed chamber. So did her pristinely made bed.

"Leave the door open, Will."

"You sent for me." He inserted a very long pause, then added "My lady."

"Last time we spoke here I was filled with fear."

"Were you?"

"Of the future. Of the man I thought James Bradshaw is."

"And you were mistaken."

"He seems completely unlike the man I remembered."

"We change."

"Yes," she said. "We do."

"I am ready to go with you."

"No you are not."

"I will risk everything to start the adventure you described."

"You are ready to go with the Jane that was, not the Jane that is. As you say, we change. I have changed. My fear is lifted. I am what I was again."

"And what is that?"

"Jane de Hoghton. Daughter of this house."

"Which you will leave."

"The house. Not the family."

"When you were frightened of James Bradshaw you loved me, and now you love him you are frightened of me."

"I don't love him. But I might. I am not frightened by you, Will, but I remain fearful for you." Her mouth captured the last of the sunlight. "I have love for you, and I give it to you to carry with you for ever. Yes, my fear of James is lifted but I am not without all fear. I have reverted to that which is imposed on all of us. Perhaps we do what we do not because of love, but because of fear."

"Love is the antidote of fear."

She came and stood directly before him, just out of reach. "If James Bradshaw was a truly fearful man, I'm sure I'd be scared enough to love you very deeply indeed." Will made no reply. "He would have you a priest. I still say no to that. You have too much for a short life."

"Too much what?"

"Fear."

"Fear?"

"Find the antidote. Find love, Will. It may take you a long time, but while you are looking who knows what those in your company will discover."

"Your mind is made up?"

"Is your New Year's play ready?"

That night songs were sang and wassailing spiced ale was downed until midnight had passed. No one was quite sure when the transition happened. Jerome was the appointed time-keeper and the great game was to get him so drunk that he would never declare the hour, but he was far too wise for that, and he made regular excursions to the roof of the keep to observe the movement of the stars. That was to no avail, because the sky was completely overcast, so he went instead to a specially marked candle that had been lit at sundown. That was to no avail either, because on at three of the inspections that he made it had been blown out. In the end he waited on his best judgment which derived from a blend of instinct, personal weariness and an assessment of when the mood of the merrymaking was at its optimum. Cheers went up, songs were sung even louder, and within an hour most folk had tumbled off to sleep. Some even went to bed.

New Year's Day, the eighth day of Christmas and the feast of the circumcision of Christ, got off to a tardy start. There was little movement until mid-morning. Will was ahead of the trend. His mind was filled with the plan they had made, and he went to the great hall to prepare the performance area. This time they were to use the north window recess as their stage, and a curtain was to be set up behind which they could change quickly. Amazingly, in addition to a blond wig, they had found a leaf-green doublet remarkably similar to that sported by James Rondel. Piers could just squeeze into it, provided he did not attempt to hook the fastenings. There was little that Will could do by himself except bring what they had out of storage and put it ready in the place that would be their stage. Solomon strode in a little later and they rigged the curtain with a length of rope. Will tucked the Rondel costume into a corner behind the drape.

Hosts and guests assembled at noon. Gifts were exchanged. Alice and Mabel had brought oranges studded with cloves which they gave to Elizabeth. In return she gave them each a pair of calfskin gloves. She regarded them as the finest crafted, though even from a distance, Will questioned that. A rich Flemish blanket was presented to Alexander, by James Bradshaw on behalf of his parents. In return he promised a basket of especially fine canary wine.

More spiced ale was produced and consumed and the wassailing songs sung again. Then came the food. Capons, pheasant, duck and venison tested the table. The fowl were stuffed with thyme, hyssop, parsley and hard roasted eggs, plus raisins, pepper, cloves and ginger. Pears, apples and newly baked sweet pies followed: apple, cherry, damson and mulberry. There was creamy cheese flecked with ground mint.

As the light began to fade, the fire was re-stacked and seats arranged in arcs facing the makeshift stage for the show. This was not as comprehensive a gathering as when Campion had called but a good number of the whole tower household were made welcome. The principal guests joined the hosts on the front row. Alexander had the armchair and was flanked by his wife on his left and his niece on his right. Next to Jane was James Bradshaw, and next to him an ebullient James Rondel.

The show started to great applause and the older company played three stock sketches which Will had not seen before. The Hoghton entourage laughed loudly and their visitors even more so. These episodes were stitched together with seasonal songs, led by the players but known by many and so there was much joining in. The day darkened. It was time for Campion's Brag. Piers made the introduction.

"My lord, lady, good friends; and foreign invaders from Wigan."

Raucous laughter.

"It is no secret that last year this tower was blessed by special hands. We pray for the liberty of those hands so that they may continue to bless so many others."

Unanimous choral approval.

"This is the story of that remarkable man. What happened before he came here, and some things that have happened since."

A slight quietening in the room.

"We have presented – most - of this before, but this time master Shakeshaft will play himself, so that if the magistrate should interrupt again at least one right scoundrel will be taken into custody."

Laughter returned.

"We give you Campion's Brag!"

Applause and cheering.

The troupe erupted into song:

Friends and dear countrymen, lend me your ears
And of Campion's brag, let me sing.

The play was re-enacted but with Will in his actual role as companion to Campion. All else was as normal until the point when the original song was done. Then came the new section.

There came up through England, wrapped in disguise
With a fake name and good flaxen shirt,
And sometimes so grand with codpiece in hand.
For she had swapped hose for a skirt, my brave boys.
For she had swapped hose for a skirt.

At that point Fulk made his entrance. He had made a change from earlier and for those who had seen Frances

241

Thursby the mock likeness he had assembled was breath-taking, though it was clear as ever that he was Fulk beneath.

The audience didn't know quite how to react. Some bellowed their mirth, others squealed, some were hushed but all went quiet as Andrew changed the key of the tune, played more slowly, more sinisterly and the singers put stress into their voices.

> *She took knave to town, and poisoned his ale*
> *And up to her bed did they ride,*
> *And they rode so grand with his codpiece in hand.*
> *But she had a knife by her side, my brave boys.*
> *But she had a knife by her side*

Fulk displayed the dagger he had brought. He flourished it wildly but then swiftly hid it on the far side of Will as he lay on the floor, Fulk straddled him and began to thrust with his groin. Laughter erupted again and the players waited for it to subside. Will was watching Rondel carefully.

> *He feared for his master, he feared for his life*
> *He feared for what he had said,*
> *But he need not have feared for in came another*
> *And left the hard rider cold dead, my brave boys,*
> *And left . . .*

The song stopped, the action stooped. Piers had entered melodramatically and paused. There was a gasp as he was instantly identified as the man in the front row of the audience. Elizabeth squealed and choked. Piers carried on. He took the dagger Fulk had hidden and mimed stabbing the female love-maker in the back.

Andrew played three discords on his lute. Silence fell. Piers sang a cappella.

> *I need one more knife to be sure, my brave boys,*
> *I need one more knife to be sure.*

He approached the front row with outstretched hand. He stopped before Rondel. The mood of the room was still very uncertain, but Rondel held his composure. He locked fake mirth in place and gave his dagger to Piers, who ceremoniously sank it into the female figure portrayed by Fulk. There was a moment of heavy pathos, then the whole troupe, including Fulk leaped up into the final verse and chorus.

> *My heart it is true, I love God and you*
> *And I'll never leave England again, my brave boys*
> *And I'll never leave England again!*

Everyone cheered and much light was made of Rondel's contribution. Fulk pulled him up into an embrace and made him bow along with the players. Rondel beamed widely and the audience cheered, and Fulk kept him there until Piers had called quiet.

"We'd like to thank our armourer."

"My honour," said Rondel.

"Here's your knife back," said Fulk.

Rondel took the hilt. "Thank you," he said, but when he tried to return it to his scabbard he could not, for there was already another knife there. It was the one Fulk had brought into the action. Rondel was stunned.

"Oh, you already have one," said Fulk. "And look the pattern on the hilt matches the one on your scabbard." Fulk said all this with flamboyance as might a market place magician.

Rondel drew the knife. His face was pale. "I lost one like this."

"I found it," said Fulk. "At the Golden Lion."

A sore mood descended. It was as if the tower itself had been taken ill. Alexander declared an abrupt end to the revels. There was great awkwardness while the remaining food was taken through to the small hall. The servants were shooed through, but the players were told to remain, as they had been so involved in what had gone before, and their youngest recruit was at the heart of it. A kind of impromptu court was assembling centred on Alexander. Elizabeth strutted like a wounded game bird.

"This is not the time," she said, and no one was quite sure what she meant.

James Bradshaw sent his sisters through to the other hall and Elizabeth dispatched Jane to host them.

"I wish to remain and hear this," she insisted.

Alexander spoke with a firmness they had not heard from him for some time. "Jane, you will play the host."

Jane heaved a breath through flared nostrils and left the great hall.

In addition to the remaining family members Jerome stayed and Margery lingered in the shadows. Alexander told Solomon to shift the arm chair closer to the fire, where the lord then sat upon it and angled his feet towards the flame. Rondel leaned against the table board in an undignified and nervous manner, but projecting a countenance part pleading part defiant. Quietness settled.

"Your knife?" asked Alexander.

"Yes."

"Young Fulk fetched it from the Golden Lion. On my instruction."

The fire spoke. Everyone listened.

Rondel was still half sitting on the table. His grip tightened on the edge of the board. "I had one like it."

"That same one," said Alexander.

"It is very similar."

"The same."

"It could be. I lost mine."

"Where?"

"At an inn."

"The Golden Lion."

"No. The Red Lion. At Solihul. It was stolen from me. As I slept." The fire chattered on. "I swear."

"Swearing is so easy," said Alexander.

"My lord?" Will implored. Alexander nodded his assent. "I saw that knife at Park Hall."

Alexander nodded.

Rondel said, "I lodged at the Red Lion."

Everyone in the room knew it was an impasse. Elizabeth shifted. Alexander raised a finger inviting her comment.

"Mr Rondel, what is your true faith?"

"Unshakable."

Alexander said, "Would you die for it?"

"My lord I would."

Jane's voice came from the door. "Would you kill for it?"

"I already have."

"Where?" Jane walked into the room. Alexander gave her a disapproving glance but did not object.

"In Norfolk. To protect a priest."

"What priest?" asked Alexander.

"Hugh Hall."

Alex said, "Hugh Hall is at Castle Bromwich. Warwickshire."

"In the guise of a gardener, my lord."

"I know that."

"He was almost captured in Norfolk. I killed the person about to betray him. Hugh gave me absolution. Then made good his evasion. Write to him, my lord. He will voice for me."

The impasse was secure. Some wanted to continue the inquiry for this drama was more entertaining than any that could be played, for the simple reason that the audience were now the players and the consequences real, but Alexander had lived too long to be drawn into pointless spirals of argument with no possibility of a clear resolution. He raised his hand to summon silence.

"Mr Rondel, I know not whether you saved Hugh Hall's life, and I know not whether you ended Frances Thursby's."

"My lord . . ."

Alexander raised his hand again. "What I do know is, my welcome for you under Hoghton's roof, is at an end. You will leave our company at first light."

Rondel looked crestfallen and awkward. His countenance was contorted. He looked as if he had concocted reasons to plead his stay but knew it would be neither politic nor productive to voice them. He bowed formally. "My lord."

When Rondel had left the room James Bradshaw stepped forward. "My lord, I'll see him back to Haigh."

Alexander twisted in his seat in readiness to rise. "You'll stay until Twelfth Night. I'll send men to see him on his way. They'll take letters to Haigh. I am not sure that's where he will want to go. If he does, so be it. If he doesn't, we'll take interest in his direction. Jerome, get those knives off him, until such time as he parts company with all those who enjoy the protection of this house."

"My lord." Jerome went in pursuit of Rondel. Alexander reached towards Fulk who helped him to his feet. Well done my boy." He gave a throaty chuckle, then turned to Will. "And master Shakeshaft, a real player now. Survived two stabbings young man. You are charmed."

Will smiled and bowed.

Elizabeth breathed to speak but caught her husband's eye and that was enough to make her think better of it.

"I have letters to write," said Alex. "Send Ros to me to collect them."

Elizabeth nodded. Once Alexander had left the room multiple muted conversations broke out. Will found Fulk.

"How long have you had that knife?"

"Alex sent me for it while you were at Lea. I went with Jerome to compensate the publican. We were sworn to keep the details of the deal secret. My lord kept the blade until I told him of our plan for the play. You may or may not have proved Rondel's guilt. But you verified your innocence. Your tale was true. The knife matched."

When he went to bed that night Will was once again a bundle of emotion. The plot, the play, the distancing from Jane, the cunning of Alexander, the connivance of Fulk, the ambiguity of Rondel, all tumbled together in his head. He had trouble getting to sleep, and he was sorely in need of it, yet he was anxious not to miss the dawn departure of Rondel.

He need not have worried, for when the household rose the next morning, Rondel did not.

TWENTY-FIVE

Wills and fates

The disposal of James Rondel's body caused some consternation. In the end Alexander ordered it to be taken to the river bank and burned. The ashes were then put into the water.

The manner of his dying was never determined. He simply did not wake. Some said God had judged. Some said he had been poisoned. Some said he had taken poison. Rowland the Porter said he had seen the ghost of Frances Thursby pacing in the outer yard.

Alexander had to write more letters, but they were not dispatched. James Bradshaw said he would take them when he went home. The twelve-day revels were stalled by the incident, but once cremation was done they began to gear up again. Alice and Mabel Bradshaw were the most unsettled, for they had formed an affiliation with Rondel. In general, though, the feel at Hoghton was that justice had been delivered.

After several failed attempts Will managed to get Ros alone. She was flattening pastry and in a sweat.

"Was it you?"

"Was what me?"

"Did you do for Rondel?"

"I only do what I am told."

"Were you told to do it?"

"Go and learn your playing, player boy."

"Ros!"

"What?"

"Did you stop James Rondel?"

"I don't know," she said. "Did you?"

There they left the matter. Alexander made no moves to determine what had happened. He declared that some angel of God had done the will of God and that was that.

The festivities of Twelfth Night loomed large. Will learned a new play, and once again he had a hand in modifying it. *Heartsease* was based around a popular dance tune of the time but it contained a servant character with similarities to Rondel in that his appearance and demeanour were similar so Will penned new lines based on a blend of Jerome and Ambrose, the steward at Lea. He also penned a drunken porter scene that allowed Andrew to deliver a very fine irreverent parody of Rowland.

The fifth day of January and the eve of the feast of the Epiphany dawned crisp and sharp and was filled with preparation and anticipation, a combination that quelled all question that the death might dampen the revels. The stage, complete with curtain, was set up again. Music began in the mid afternoon with more Wassails sung and some dances, and then the feast was brought out. Agnes did them proud, and against all odds the banquet topped the excesses of Christmas and New Year. Roasted lamb was the mainstay meat but the table groaned with even more game, and even more sumptuous sweet and savoury pies than they had demolished the previous week. She had been furtively thrifty with dried fruits secretly stored, including Lancashire pears that had been peeled and kept in fortified wine since September. Those pies were the most popular of all the sweet dishes. She had correctly predicted that, and when all were gone, she proudly produced another four the size of small shields. Alexander publicly commended her and proclaimed her banished from the kitchen for that night and three more days. She laughed blissfully, got very drunk and turned distinctly ruddy in colour.

Will enjoyed his acting more than he ever had thus far.

He was nervous but less so than the previous times, and those watching exuded great warmth which gave him confidence. The play was cheered jubilantly which was small surprise for it was fast-paced, tuneful and bawdy, and by the time it was presented there was not a sober soul in the tower, excepting Ros, who either drank with caution or had a spirit stronger than the brew she imbibed. Will kept his eye on her when he could but she played the space supremely, disappearing and reappearing on the pretence of service whilst in reality taking sustenance and enjoyment when she would, but at the same time using self-control to keep a pragmatic perspective. Will pondered her demeanour. Why could she not embrace the saturnalia like others? Why must she always hold that final safeguard?

After the play, there was dancing almost until dawn. Jane was inseparable from James Bradshaw. In the small, dark hours they slipped behind the curtain of the stage and kissed at some length. Will watched from the wings.

The feast of the Epiphany was no revelation for Will. It brought only recollection and a realisation that nothing had changed. The day started late as the sleepers awoke sporadically and invariably nursing the cursed crania of too many cups. If Jane rose she chose not to descend. The lower yard percussed to the irregular clicks of iron-shod steeds as the Haigh Hall party gathered to depart. Elizabeth made the formal farewell in the Great Hall. Will and Fulk were unfastening and folding their stage curtain.

"We will hope for Easter," she said.

James, sallow with a headache, grinned gamely. "Not just hope for, but long for, my lady."

"At Haigh, if my lord Bradshaw consents."

"I shall plead until he does."

"I'm sure he will." She turned the generosity of her dismissal to Alice and Mabel. "I trust you both have cherished your visit, shadowed though it was by the unforeseen execution of God's will."

Alice said, "We will always accept his will. And if it was such, we were blessed to witness it at work."

Mabel said nothing.

Elizabeth said, "We thank you again for your presence and your gifts. I wish you a swift, warm and safe journey home."

With that the party, minus their hostess, made their way to the yard. Will made it his business to carry the curtain that way en-route to its storage. They mounted with little fuss and, in the company of a small escort, walked their horses through the gate and cautiously over the icy exposed stones of the track. Will watched the benevolent thief of his romance retreat into the dank uncertainty of the mist.

He took the curtain back inside to the trunk where it was stored. He stuffed it in then lay on top and daydreamed.

So, he was priest pupil still. Amid the turmoil of yuletide, the year had turned, and in doing so it had returned him to his appointed station. Servant to the de Hoghtons, acolyte of Edmund Campion, student of the true faith, martyr in waiting. He felt the weight of condemnation on his chest and it pained his breathing.

This year, in April, he would be seventeen. His mind raced with triple imagined futures. The piety and weird empowerment that would grant him such grace that he could make wine into sacred blood, bread into godly body, create Catholics, confirm Catholics, and commit Catholics to wondrous eternity. But that way lay the test too: to die on their pikes. Slowly.

A second path sprang open: a player. He liked the playing very much. He liked the thrill of giving joy and the glow from admiration. He liked the sound of laughter, and strangely, the greater sound of silent concentration. He was enchanted by the way a word from his mouth made more than life in the minds of listeners. He knew too that God had gifted him a rare enchantment. He could divine the finest word. When given to a player, the word could be made flesh. That flesh could be eternal too, even though it lived and died only in the moment. It spoke man to man, soul to soul.

He loved the power he had to make permanence from the passing. The living could debate and even the dead could call out. Had not Frances Thursby called her case from the grave through their play? Even in the infancy of this necromancy he saw the glory of history retold, and of futures that might unfold. The player was a preacher too, playing with the truth to give falsity the lie. That thrilled him as much as the powers of priesthood. It shouldn't, but it did. And it wasn't nearly so dangerous.

As always there was a third alternative narrative. He would melt the heart of Ros. Nothing more than that. That melting would be the portal. Once she thawed and let him warm her then no matter what followed. He'd take any future with her. This was the impossible route. However, Campion's escape had seemed impossible, but Ros had granted that. She could do the impossible. He was convinced.

TWENTY-SIX

Golden lads and girls

The news of the death of Rondel hit George Eliot hard. It came swiftly on the heels of good fortune. Philip Gyfford had not been idle and through his representations Eliot had been summoned to Kenilworth Castle where he had entered the service of Robert Dudley, the Earl of Leicester. Dudley now possessed the document Frances had sold to Gyfford, and he was eager to have more of the same. He was even keener to have their author. For the purposes of priest-catching Eliot was now Dudley's man. Although this was done in secret it gave Eliot a certain legitimacy should he need it. The downside was that he felt double the pressure to succeed. However, he did now have more funds at his disposal and more authority.

The mourning he experienced for James was more than that he felt for Frances Thursby. She had been a delightful lover, but James Rondel had been a long-standing friend. They'd shared adventures, downed countless yards of ale, fallen out, repaired splits, wasted time, gambled incessantly, and kept secrets. Rondel had left him to sweat away his life, while Frances had nursed and repaired him, but strangely, he did not view the former as total treachery or the latter as lasting love. Eliot was convinced that ultimately Rondel would have returned, and Frances would not. As it transpired, neither did.

It looked now that Rondel had been more than one step ahead of him. He had got to Hoghton first and done so without confiding in him. Eliot understood why. He knew Rondel well. James had been uncomfortable about the three-way split they had agreed with Frances. This was his way of cutting her out of it. He would claim the Campion prize. He would have shared some with Eliot, but not on the basis of the deal with Thursby. Now there was no need to share. There was no one to share it with. If Eliot could bag the quarry he would know the reward, and it would be more than financial. The Earl of Leicester had hinted at a pardon for prior capital crimes alleged against Eliot. The spy would have his money and his freedom to spend it, Dudley would have the prestige and even more approval from the Queen many said he had once suited, and Philip Gyfford would know noble, and perhaps royal, gratitude.

Despite the perspective the news of James brought him, Eliot still wished revenge for the loss of Frances. He would never know her affections again and that riled him. Despite the understanding that she would almost certainly keep their liaison on an intermittent basis, he had a deep and strong admiration for her. Her life was romance. Her murder was more than the death of person. She had been the corporeal fusion of spirit and adventure. Her destruction was more than murder. It was supernatural robbery. He would even the balance. He had much more security in conducting that now he was Leicester's man. However, he knew that he must make Campion his priority. He could not go galloping off to Lancashire if the traitor was not there.

Gyfford's spies had no secure knowledge of where the wanted man was, but they were hopeful. They had learned of Rondel's downfall from sources in the north. The details were imprecise but there was no doubt the man was dead. Other facts came with that news. There were rumours of a possible marriage between the de Hoghtons and the Bradshaws, two very Catholic families. Surely they would want a priest to officiate. For some time now Gyfford had thought that Campion would return to his fledgling seminary. Might he not coincide his sojourn with a consecration of matrimony? What blessings that might bring to those two noble strands of treacherous loyalty? What curses? What rewards?

If he could discover when the wedding would be he could gamble on netting mythical prey and weighing a legendary payload.

At the same time, he might slice the odd sprat.

TWENTY-SEVEN

Kindness in women

The wedding was fixed for the Spring. In 1581 Easter Day was relatively early on the twenty-sixth day of March. Jane could not be married before that as the six weeks of Lent prohibited it. Everyone would know when the wedding could not take place, but only a very few individuals were told precisely when it would happen. Jane was not one of them. There was deliberate confusion. The banns would be read but not until the last minute and only to those whose ear could be trusted. Preparations were made but the people doing the preparing did not know exactly when the fruit of the labours would be called upon.

"At Easter?" asked Will.

It was the first day of lent, Ash Wednesday. They were in the walled garden. Will was walking with Jane at her request. They risked the wrath of Elizabeth, but Jane brazened off the concern in her usual bullish manner.

"I presume so."

"And you are happy to be so wed?"

"Oh Will! Happiness is not a state I can embrace."

"You seemed happy at Christmas."

"I like James. I think he will be a good husband. I only hope I can be a good wife."

"You shall be."

"If I survive it."

"You shall."

"James wants sons. Their births could be the death of me."

"Pray."

"Thrice a day." She scuffed a pebble beneath her shoe. "Don't you?"

"Not as much as I used to do."

They walked a little further. The sun found spaces in breaking cloud and gave the first hint that warmth would return again this year.

"God loves you," said Will. "He'll spare you."

"There's little sign that he spares those he loves."

"That's the Jane I used to know."

"The one you tried to court."

"I didn't try very hard."

"I enjoyed the romance while we had it."

"I wasn't aware we had one."

"A dream and no more."

They turned the corner and Jane's steady but measured pace signalled that she thought they should sustain their walk.

Will breathed deeply. "Will it be Campion?"

"God forbid. There's enough risk getting any priest who will do it properly. Last thing we want is England's most treasured traitor."

"You'd be more than married, if it was him."

"Now, it's you that speaks the way you used to."

"We've walked full circle," he said.

"Full square," she said alluding to the garden.

He breathed a slight laugh.

She said, "How could it be Campion? No one knows where he is in order to invite him. The date is fixed Will. We can't wait on Campion."

"Unless he has sent word, and hence you have a predestined hour."

"That would be foolish. Someone in this house is for

256

the Queen. Should that person learn the date of my nuptials, whichever priest it be will get a bigger fee than he expects."

"Who is that person? Who is the spy?"

"It's horrible; mistrusting every smile, misreading every mood. Could be anyone. Could be you."

"Not anyone. Not family."

"Who is family?" asked Jane.

Somewhere, a crow replied.

"Frances Thursby found me, not Campion."

"She was looking for him. Somehow she knew to look here."

"Chance," said Will. She traced me because of Father Cottam."

"And how did she find him?"

"She'd spoken to my family."

"See what I mean? There is no family, only individuality, and no person is perfect. Flaws are nature's nearness. Weakness is natural. We weave that weakness into the fabric that should hold us, but sooner or later it will snap, whether we intend it or not. The Bradshaw family is already fragmenting. James told me. He said I will make it stronger. I think, perhaps, I will simply make it more brittle."

"Riley's raid was probably due to loose tongues. Campion stayed too long. That's not a spy, but simply a slip."

"He had men that none of us knew. They had been sent, and in good time."

Now a crow flew across their sight. It landed in a tree close to another. The one that had been at rest there took to wing and landed on another branch further away.

They turned another corner, where thorny stalks threatened to snag them as they passed. Will said, "So who would you name as the flaw in this fabric?"

"I have no idea, Will, and that is my honest truth. But when my wedding comes we may find out. And if we do not, I will go from this place, and leave the threat to you."

All through Lent the tension built. The subject of the wedding was not taboo, but neither was it discussed. It became a narrative ghost. It was seen everywhere but acknowledged by none. In formal speech it was referred to as "the Bradshaw visit" or

257

"when Mr Bradshaw comes back", but informally it was simply "Mr Bradshaw's bed".

The players were duly charged to create a programme of entertainment for "Mr Bradshaw's feast". This was a bitter prescription for Will. The troupe revised the nuptial songs they knew and set about tweaking the wording and making up new flourishes for the jigs that went with them. Comedies were the order of the day but *The Cuckold Miller* was definitely off the agenda. Much as Alexander loved it, the salacious content was not felt appropriate for the sealing of new marital promises. Piers knew a play from his youth that he felt would stand revival, but there were gaps in his memory, and he turned to Will to help fill them. This commission was seen as flattery by all except Will. Whilst savouring his acceptance as a prime poet in their company, he had little desire to pen words celebrating the marriage of Jane to another. The fact that in reality she had always been unobtainable did nothing to soothe his disappointment.

He began to transcribe the tale that Piers told along with the lines that he could remember, and then set about adding phrases and lyrics of his own. Unfortunately, while the vocabulary and syntax were strong, the sentiment was frequently at odds with the required mood. Solomon took him on one side.

"This is about you Will, not about the wedding."

Will had never shared his thoughts about Jane with Solomon. "Is it that plain?"

Solomon nodded. "Think as the bridegroom."

"I am."

"No you are not. You're thinking as the loser. Don't put your words in his mouth, put his words in our mouths."

Will tried, but found it very testing. He struggled for several weeks, wasting much precious paper. He began to realise that playing and the poetry of play-making were easy sometimes and impossible at other times. He could craft words, he could shape verse, he could sing and play, but those things would not come to order any more than the materials of any wright would. Apprenticeship was seven years in duration, and in this new discipline he had not yet had seven months. He'd been practising for priesthood much longer. He'd been praying since before he could speak. He'd thought of God every dawn and dusk. Now he saw the disappointment on the faces of his fellow players, and he read the unsatisfactory sentiment of his scribbling. He was no better at play-making than he was at preaching, and preaching had the payoff of eternal prosperity. He should return whole-heartedly to priesthood. He was good at that. He was pre-ordained for that. This play he could not write proved it. He was unable to put himself in the perspective of others' souls.

He resolved to resign from play-making and playing and writing verse. The play itself had defeated him. Or so he thought. Suddenly his mind was reopened. Suddenly he knew the joys that Jane's new husband would surely feel. Suddenly Jane was loved all the more but he no longer knew the need to desire her. This was because in Holy Week, the darkest of all days in the Christian calendar, Ros did something miraculous.

She took Will to bed.

It happened at the moment he least expected. All during Lent Ros had been increasingly hostile towards him. She had a steel stare that cut right through his ever-hopeful soul. She could radiantly flash a generously jovial expression, unleashing her own delight and evoking raucous laughter in others, then catch Will's gaze and switch instantly into a stony blankness, pinning him with iron pupils. It was a look that both locked and repelled him. By Spy Wednesday he'd had enough and had cast all thoughts of any association with her completely aside.

It was after dark on that day and Will was descending the stairs in the north range. He was going nowhere in particular. Rumours had intensified that the Bradshaws might arrive at any day, so there was increased activity about the place. Will was snooping to see if he could glean a little more insight, and in part he was casually scouting for Fulk, because Fulk usually knew more than others and generally more than he was supposed to know. By coincidence Ros was right behind Will, but he determined to not acknowledge her. It was after dark and neither Will nor Ros had a light, each finding their way from memory and by rippling their fingers across familiar contours of the patterns of stone in the wall. There was a pool of feeble grey at the foot where moonlight slid under the door. Will stepped steadily but slowly. Suddenly arms slid about his shoulders and neck. There was a momentary shock but this was an embrace not an assault. He stopped. Her hair and cheek met his. She gripped him more tightly. He did not know what to do, but instinct was his overlord and he swivelled towards the warmth of her skin. She allowed this move, adjusting her hold on him to accommodate it. He could see almost nought in the near total darkness, but saw enough to see her eyes were closed. By the time the thought of that had registered, her lips had found his, and he accepted the kiss.

The second was more luscious than the first for she opened her lips to let his tongue find hers. At the same time, she eased her soft body more securely against his and held the back of his head as he pressed her towards the wall. She was still one step higher than he, but during this embrace he levered himself to the same level and, as she was smaller of stature than he, kissed down to her. She clung to him still. She was warm and welcoming. They broke and she held him while he played soft kisses on her cheeks and eyelids, using this manoeuvre as means of verifying that this was indeed the Ros that had rejected him so strongly for six months now.

They kissed a third time, and he pressed harder with his groin so that she might know how excited he had become. She broke from him and he presumed his favour was over but instead she slipped her hand to find his, and gripping it she led the way to a space that he did not know existed.

She expertly found her way through the unlit underground tunnel and into the eastern range and then straight to Lord Alexander's bedchamber. She opened the door silently and eased Will inside. No candle flame burned but a rose of log ash glowed in the hearth. From that glow Will could make out his overlord in his bed slumped mid-way between lying and sitting. He could not tell if the old man slept but he made no acknowledgement of their presence or their passing, for Ros did not falter in her progress and led will directly across the room to the panelling at the far side which was obscured by a wall hanging of a hunting scene. She slid behind it taking Will with her, and then, she somehow opened the panelling and squeezed behind it dragging Will into a gap between the wood and the wall that was barely broad enough to accommodate them.

"Climb," she whispered.

He couldn't see but sensed her elevating from him and by fumbling with hands and feet he discovered that there were sufficient ledges protruding from the wall to enable him to scale it. Arms came down towards him and she hoisted him the final few feet until he tumbled onto fabric and straw.

"Where are we?"

"Between wall and wall, ceiling and roof."

"In the attic?"

"A box within it."

"Priest Hole?"

"Campion spent two days in here."

"When?"

"When Riley searched the place."

"You said he'd gone."

"That's why they didn't find him."

Will worked it out. "Because they knew what you had said."

"Because they knew what I had said."

Ros was rustling. There was a soft thud as she closed the trap through which they'd climbed. There was almost total darkness in the hiding place but a sliver of lighter shade sliced through the wall bringing with it a blade of ashen air from outside. It was not enough to see by but just sufficient for Will to catch glimpses of Ros as she slipped her smock over her head. He could not see the nakedness she had revealed but sensed it strongly.

"Are we beside my lord's room?"

"Above it, partly."

"Partly?"

"Don't make any noise." She reached for Will's head, found it and drew it to her own. She kissed him eagerly. He reached for her and his hand collided with her bare breast.

They kissed for a while and by manoeuvring to find the best embrace he discovered a little more about the hide. It was taller than he thought and tucked in the apex of a roof gable. They were tight against the roof tiles and right up against the outside stone but a wattle and daub wall kept them from the attic proper, so should any inspector arrive that way he would presume he had travelled the full length of the space.

"Get undressed," she said.

The only way he could do so was by standing up. She stood too, in order to afford him more space. He dearly wished he could see her, but he could not. When naked, he pulled her to him.

"Do what you wish," she said. "But don't put it in me."

For a while they stood and he enjoyed feeling the smooth warm weight and firm suppleness of her body as their tongues hooked and danced.

Awkwardly he pulled her down to the rough priest bed and instinct took over as he wormed between her thighs. She complied with this until the stronger instinct made him probe towards an entry into her, but she firmly distanced him, but at the same time made no indication that they should stop their other interaction. Their passion intensified and once again he made a try to impregnate her, and once again she made her insistence clear. This time he accepted her condition but the urge within himself was overwhelming so he thrust hard and rapidly against the outside of her vulva. Her panting told that she shared the thrill and that spurred him on all the more. Their motion must surely be heard by Alexander if he was awake, but so overwhelming was the sensation combined with knowing that this willing, willing lover was Ros, that Will cared not at all if the price of his action would see the termination of his employment, his liberty or even his life. Ros sank her fingers into him. Her gasping was now so insistent that she could not kiss, and clamped his face into her neck. His seed sprayed out between them.

Somehow they lay side by side. He was sated, she dissatisfied. Will waited for them to be discovered, but no one arrived. There was no sound at all from below.

They both became calmer, he more than she. After a few moments he heard her fumbling for something. She found fabric and discarded it. And then found another. She wiped herself with it then passed it to him.

"Here."

It was her apron. He cleaned his sperm from his stomach and side where it had slid and was drying cold.

"Why?" he said.

"Why not?" she said.

They didn't say anything else, but lay in almost blackness and for him in blissful bewilderment.

She pulled their garments over them because in their stillness they grew cool. They kissed more and continued to touch with tenderness and affection. She taught him what to do with his hand between her legs, and although his arm ached and ached he persisted until her body jolted thrice and she gasped a sustained breath and then sank to complete relaxation.

Still they did not speak, and some moments later, he realised she was asleep.

He woke. At least he thought he woke. So strange was his environment and so incomplete the content of his sight that he could not be sure he was awake. In addition, his memory of what had transpired was so dreamlike that he doubted it had happened at all. But he felt warm flesh alongside and the coarse weave of her smock against his chest, his arm, his leg, confirmed his own nudity. His foot was cold so he drew it up beneath whatever lay over that part of their too small bed. It felt like his jerkin.

What hour was it? He could not know.

Should he wake her?

His arm was going numb so he withdrew it from around her. She murmured but settled again, so he decided not to nudge her. He lay there for a very long time, continually resolving that he should move, somehow find his clothes. He was just about to do that when he woke again, and could only presume he had returned to sleep. Indeed, he had, for now the miniscule light let in through the slightest gap in mortar was clear white. It cast a shape no larger than a carpenter's nail upon the inside of the false wall. Now at least he could see some small outline of the space that enclosed them and he could just differentiate between different piles of shadow in order to guess at which might be his clothes.

"Where you going?"

"We must get out of here," he said.

"No we mustn't."

"Why not?"

"Listen."

He listened and heard muffled movement.

Ros shifted sleepily. "It's daylight. Margery will be with Alexander. We will have to wait until she's not."

"How will we know?"

"I'll know."

She stood on the mattress and reached to where the air

and the light came through. She slid out a slice of mortar and the hole trebled in size. Then on tip-toe put her eyes to the gap.

"What can you see?"

"Two rooks."

"What are they doing?"

"Waiting."

She replaced the mortar wedge and slid down to sit hunched in the corner. He drew himself close to her and put his hand on her knee, but she brushed it off.

"Dying for a piss," he said.

"Die."

Time waited with them. Twice she eased the trapdoor ajar and listened, and twice returned it to its recess.

More darkness.

She lifted the trap again. "No noise," she breathed and carefully positioned herself with her feet through the gap. Slowly with just the sound of smock on wood she slid away. He followed and somehow found foot and hand grips on the wall. Then they slipped through the hinged gap in the wall board and were behind the tapestry. Ros carefully edged around its end. She gripped Will and eased him into the chamber. He sensed that Alexander was in his bed, but now curtains were drawn about it, at least on their side.

Ros indicated that Will should remove and carry his shoes. When he held them she mouthed that he should now move fast and not stop, and instantly set off for the door, which she opened, and held, and immediately stood as if she had just entered through it. Meanwhile Will slipped past her and out onto the corridor where he danced a few steps away before re-donning his shoes. He heard Ros in conversation with her lord, but did not linger to discover the matter of their speech.

He made his way quickly into the yard and then to the stables where he urinated in the sweepings of hay. The stalls were mostly empty.

"Where've you been hiding?" Fulk stood in the doorway.

Shakespeare though fast. "In my lord's room."

There was a long pause. "All night?"

"I believe so." Will shook the final drops from his member and slipped it away. "Who's gone riding?"

"Most of the house."

"Where?"

"There's going to be a wedding, haven't you heard?"

Will quickly understood. "At Haigh?"

Fulk shrugged. "That's the gossip."

"When do we follow?"

"We're not needed."

"Not needed?"

"My lord Bradshaw has his own men. We're being sent to Lea."

"To Lea?"

"Not you. You're to stay here. Didn't Alexander tell you? What did you talk about all night?"

"I need some breakfast," said Will and strode off. He was thankful that Fulk did not follow, but understood too that his player friend knew deflection and half-truth when he heard it. That, after all, was his trade.

The house was four-fifths empty. Jane had gone. He doubted he would see her again. He would certainly not see her wed, and he was glad of that. Neither would he play at her wedding feast, and that too was a relief, though he had taken increasing pride in crafting parts of the play they had made. He could keep those words for another time.

He took porridge from the kitchen and while he quaffed it down, Ros appeared and slotted straight into her routine. Strangely, Agnes the cook said nothing to her, and Ros said nothing to Will. She did not even look in his direction.

TWENTY-EIGHT

Minutes hasten

On Good Friday the other players left for Lea. They set out on foot. It would take them all day. It was raining, but despite the downpour Alexander de Hoghton and his entourage also left for the same destination, though on horseback and breaking his journey in Preston. Word was sent ahead to the Golden Lion. He would have dinner there.

Hoghton Tower was empty. Agnes and Ros stayed, as did a handful of other domestic servants. Margery had gone with Elizabeth. The rumour was quickly out that the family had relocated to Haigh Hall for the wedding while Alexander had returned to his favoured, and warmer, residence at Lea.

Jerome was left in charge of the premises. He kept himself very much to himself, but on Holy Saturday he sent for Will and told him that at midnight he should attend a secret Mass in the chapel.

"There is no priest," said Will.

"There will be," said Jerome, and there was.

It was Campion.

Will shuffled in reluctantly, much preferring to be in bed, but there kneeling at the altar was his former companion.

266

Will dare not speak for the priest was deep in prayer, so he simply knelt by him, crossed himself, and began to pray also. They remained that way for some time. Campion incanted a Latin litany, but just as it seemed it might perpetuate indefinitely, he suddenly fell silent, breathed deeply and embraced Will.

"William!" said Edmund.

"Father Edmund," said William. "Welcome back."

"I promised."

"You did."

"I have much to relate, but the hour of Our Lord's resurrection is upon us and we must celebrate. I have sent for . . . ah!"

"At that moment Jerome came into the chapel with Dominic Arrowsmith, and also Ros. Dominic carried the box of vestments, chalice and plate. Ros brought bread and wine. They were joined by four men from the stables and farm and this tiny throng celebrated together the Mass of Easter Day. Afterwards they were joined by Agnes and by Rowland the porter and breakfast was consumed close to the third hour of the day.

Will experienced a most peculiar week. He had many conversations with Campion, but also spent many hours simply in his company as the priest worked in the library. Everything was very relaxed. There seemed to be a quiet consensus that the fugitive was there in absolute secrecy and there was very little fear that they would be visited. With hindsight Will could see the cleverness of the ruse of arranging the wedding for this festive time, and combining it with the very public removal of Alexander back to Lea. The fact that the players went too, reinforced the sign that he would celebrate Easter there. All eyes were taken off Hoghton. If there was a spy in the household, then hopefully that person was some miles south or west of the tower and unaware that England's most wanted man was there.

The degree of deception was only fully clear three weeks later when Elizabeth returned to Hoghton, walked joyously into the great hall and stopped dead, flushed white and stared as if she looked upon a ghost.

"Father Campion!"

She began to palpitate visibly, and swayed awkwardly, until she steadied herself against the table. She didn't lose consciousness but all the men were ushered from the room while Margery and Ros fussed about loosening the laces of her

bodice and enforcing her to lay her head on the table and
breathe slowly and deeply. Later that hour she retired to her
room, and changed into a less restraining dress. Will, Campion,
and Jerome gathered by the fire. She eventually returned to the
great hall and sat in the armed chair.

"I had no conception."

Campion grinned graciously. "What you didn't know
couldn't endanger you."

"My husband is aware that you are here?"

"I am here at his invitation. I will leave if you desire it."

They waited for Elizabeth's objection to Campion's
proposal, but it did not come. Instead she perpetuated a pause
by laboured breathing. Margery brought a little watered wine,
and then remained close by her. Campion and Jerome
exchanged nonplussed expressions. Neither knowing whether or
not arrangements should be made for a rapid departure by the
priest. Even when Elizabeth had settled her poise she chose not
to speak or remove her focus from the grain of the table.

Protocol decreed that Elizabeth should lead the
conversation but Campion filled the awkward gap. "Was Jane
well married?"

"She was."

"You secured a priest."

"He remained only the one night."

Will's mind leaped to Jane who no longer had any claim
on Hoghton, nor could ever hope for one. She was now a chattel
of her husband. She had heritage but no chance of inheritance.

This time Campion observed etiquette. Though Will
thought the priest was now deliberately extending the
uncomfortable pause.

"I fear we have failed you, Father" said Elizabeth
eventually.

"I am never failed," said Campion. "I have hopes, not
expectations."

"We have not recruited a single novitiate for the sacred
army of our Lord."

The campaigner slightly steepened the sideways tilt of
his head. "The harbour master is not required to catch fish."

"Following the visitation we had during your last stay,
I'm afraid I could not stomach the establishment of a seminary. I
made my feelings plain to my husband."

"It was never intended to be a seminary, but simply a sheepfold, for lambs."

"Well, we have none."

Campion sustained the silence. He finished it with a deliberate intake of breath which he held for a moment before saying, "None were sent. Because the gate here is broken."

There was undischarged lightning in the room. Everyone felt its terrible pregnancy.

Elizabeth's face was blushing strands of deep pink against the ghastly velum-like texture left over from her earlier near-faint. "If the fold can't hold lambs it is not secure enough for England's prize ram."

Campion said simply, "I shall leave in the morning."

The tower was infiltrated that night.

TWENTY-NINE

Violent delights

The confusion was total. The infiltration was much swifter than
the previous raid. By the time Will was awake, a cacophony of
shouts, slams and rattles reverberated the very fabric of the
tower. By the time he had found his hose, someone was already
at the door of the room where he alone had been sleeping. It
was flung open and Will's eyes were seared by sudden light and
pricked by hot splinters as a torch swung by his face. A rough
hand took him, threw him to one side and lifted his bed.

"Where's the priest?"

"What?"

"The priest?" he yelled.

"Not here," said Will.

A fist hit Will's stomach, expelling all breath from his
lungs and leaving a boulder of pain, but then the light and the
searcher were gone. With panic-driven momentum Will hunted
for his shoes and for air and found neither for far too long.
Meanwhile the percussion of turmoil tortured his ears. Suddenly
his fingers discovered familiar leather and at the same time his
diaphragm remembered how to draw in breath. One shoe on,
he decided to cut his losses and make what escape he could.

As he hobbled across the yard it was clear that the tower was in chaos. Light danced beyond the glass of the windows of the great hall, the doors to north and south ranges swung open. Armed men strode across the space, the wind of their motion adding sound and glow to the torches they bore. He was sure he heard Elizabeth's voice strained and wailing in the distant middle of the commotion. His progress was dream-like, propelled by instinct, steered by inquisitiveness, redirected by fear.

He found himself at the foot of the stair in the small hall in the east range. Ros was there, and in the unlit space beyond her he sensed Campion.

"Delay!" she whispered. "Delay!"

Then she was gone, and gone too was whoever was with her. Will presumed she had taken him upstairs towards Alexander's room and the place where he might hide. At that instant another presence came from the stairs below; a stranger bearing fire. This person caught sight of the higher stairs and made to gain them.

This was the moment that a glorious yet terrible transformation surged through Will. In an instant he was soaked in the shame of cowardice that he remembered when he mistakenly thought to be under threat while riding from Giles Colby's house, and at the same time a new energy arose, which might have been courage, but it was too strong for courage. So powerful was this feeling that no other sensation was needed or would be tolerated. Impelled by a force he had never known, Will launched himself at the figure and not caring where his fists and feet fell, he flung his entire form upon him. The burning torch went spinning across the ground shedding sparks and splinters as its cone caught against the rushes on the floor. The two of them hit the floor in one combined tumble, and Will's head smacked hard against the padded ground. Momentum then separated them and Will slid into a sleek rehearsed recovery motion that brought him neatly, if unsteadily, to his unevenly shod feet. The room was restored to near darkness but there was a minor glow from the redness of the remains of the fire and the guttering torch, and there was a sufficient contrast of greyness from the widows to determine some physical shape. His opponent filled the gap delineated by the window and Will saw an arm swing. The sword came down, but landed only a glancing blow that he felt as a dull, heavy shock, but without sharpness. Somehow the figure was upon him, but once again his stage fencing practice instantly precipitated and a turn and sidestep to let the invader roll off and fall once again, and the clatter told that he had landed among fire irons close to the hearth.

Will's mind was moving faster than thought. By the time he had named the implement, his hand was already firmly grasping the poker. He swung it as a sword and struck only the fireplace mantel. He swung back and cut air, then swung again, but by now the other man had been alerted and his sword was brandished in defence. The collision of their weapons was ugly and dysfunctional, gaining no advantage to either, but now they were in recognised semi-formal combat. Will blessed the lessons that Fulk had instilled. Although his weapon was unconventional and his vision significantly hindered, Will went at it as if this were a stage show but with no attempt to ensure the safety of his partner.

Their interaction continued as a haphazard series of collisions, but nevertheless Will's balance and coordination let him avoid getting hurt and at the same time he managed to manoeuvre into a position where the feeble light showed a better outline of his opponent. At that moment he swung the fire iron at the other man's head and it hit hard. A half-moan stopped all motion.

His adversary's head lay close to the fire and Will could see his face for the first time. His eyes were shut, but he lived, there was no doubt about that. He lived, he breathed. Many times after this, Will would remember those breaths. Now came a monstrous moment. No longer was he moving prior to thought, but neither was he free from instinct. There came an eternal instant. Time stopped and waited while aeons raced. A consideration was made, but too late, for while Will was wondering what he should do, his arm was already hammering the poker against the fallen man's cranium.

The snap was sickening.

Will looked and tried not to see. He threw the poker into the embers as if that would rid him of the deed. He thought of Satan smiling. He thought of God but could not comprehend his face. He thought of Ros, and went in search of her.

The fact that he wore only one shoe meant he had a

limping gait, but in the darkness no one could see that, and within his own awareness it conjured a half-animal conception for while his left leg gained purchase through the well-worn leather of his shoe, his naked right foot felt the cool grain of the almost invisible floorboards. He envisaged himself as part human-part reptile, half-transformed a terrible dragon whose picture he had seen drawn on a document in the library. He felt he was not going to heaven any more, he was escaping from hell.

As he approached the doorway to Alexander's room he heard a voice he knew well.

"Over here is the place," said Fulk.

Will paused at the jamb and looked in. Fulk held a torch and was heading towards the far wall where Ros had led the way to the secret place. Between the two players were two other persons, one more heavily built than the other. That person had a drawn sword, the other possibly a knife. Fulk moved the position of the torch and Will saw more clearly the dagger and the figure who held it: it was George Eliot. Fulk now reached for the wall to reveal the way to the priest hole, and in an instant the demonic conception in Will's soul flared again scorching away all rationality and replacing it with action. His unshod foot turned toes to talons and launched him through the air to land on the man-at-arms and cannon him into Eliot. As all three sprawled Will saw their shadows swirl while Fulk turned.

"Will – no!" yelled Fulk.

"Will?" said Eliot already recovering.

The third man lurched his weight back and Will was first pinned against the wall and then winded as an elbow found his stomach and knocked the satanic dragon out of him. He strained to find human breath but already the soldier was standing and arching back his sword hand. Will waited for the worst, but it did not come for Fulk ran and kicked deflecting the man's attack.

"William Shakespeare," spat Eliot, and now the attack came from that direction, but Will's intuitive animalism returned and he rolled free to hear a sharpened point sink into wood. Eliot's weight was on his leg however and he knew another stab would follow. The terrible worm in his head wriggled and thrashed. Now the other man was cursing and lashing out, hitting something, perhaps a bed post. Then he shrieked in agony. Fulk must have done something with the torch, for what little light they had was suddenly dulled, but then the direction of it changed and showed Eliot to be the one possessed as he dived, dagger in hand, towards Will's eyes.

Will kicked and his naked foot found Eliot's face.

"Out, out," shouted Fulk and Will felt a friendly claw hoist him towards the door and they were outside the room. "Out!" yelled Fulk again pushing Will one way whilst running with the torch the opposite way.

The animal spirit wanted to turn back and deliver or take death, but a new instinct was on the rise and after the briefest hesitation, Will chose flight. Then he realised that if Campion was in the hide he must be surely now discovered, so he stopped again. He could see nothing but knew that the moaning man was still in Alexander's chamber, and while Eliot was not moving, he must be listening.

Will deliberately slapped the door jamb. There was a storm of noise but Will was already on the move, energised not just with animal power, but also with the scent of victim becoming victor. Follow me, he thought, follow me and I will lead you away from my master martyr. He was heading back the way he came intent on reaching the small hall, but Eliot gave more than chase, he also boomed commands.

"Stop the boy! Hold the boy! Stop him!"

Persons ahead responded.

"Oi!"

"Boy? What boy?"

"Stop the boy!"

This is no boy thought Will. This is pure will.

The steps to the small hall were ahead, and from down them orange shapes told of men holding fire. He was heading for certain arrest but did not care. He embraced suicidal sacrifice. Catch me if you can, he thought, but in doing so you will not catch the better man.

Will leaped down four steps at a time, hot foot, cold foot, hot foot, cold foot. His eyes saw half a dozen persons there, some with flames, all with blades, except for one - the one he knew, the one he loved - and her torch burned brightest of all.

A tumult of shouts went up as he appeared. Feet were triggered and eager hands reached, but Will was too wizardly and avoided all. Ros too, was on the move and Will swung towards her aspiring to be the tail of the comet. She was holding him with her starlit eyes and soon he was close behind her, his cold foot, colder now as they descended from the room, down the steps that led to the underground passage that ran beneath the yard.

Someone tumbled on the steps behind and above them and that gave the escapers glorious time.

They were underground, but now she stopped, fixed Will with the sharpest steel of her eyes and pushed him back against the wall that was not there. He sank into a space.

"No breathing!" she insisted, and slammed something across before his face.

Then she was gone. He heard her race away while he existed in complete black coldness. Then man after man came near and went, but he neither saw, nor smelled any of them. He locked himself stock still and waited for this prison puzzle to unravel or encase him for ever.

He had only touch to tell of where he was, and touch was not able to tell him very much. Behind was cold rock, above the same, before a wooden door, beneath stone, cold on one foot and even colder on the other. The only heat came from his exhaled breath. The warm moisture rose, teased his nose and eyes and left a web of wetness across his face. He did not dare to explore the door in the hope of finding a latch. He must wait, because for all he knew, there may be unkind blades just waiting for him to emerge.

A kind of madness came. To begin with it was a welcome calm as his pounding breath slowly settled. Then some spontaneous deeper breaths juddered in. These were few, but urgent and unexpected, and slightly too noisy for his liking. When regular respiration returned it brought with it a crushing sense of claustrophobia. Suppose the door was locked. Suppose the door could only be opened from without. Suppose Ros had been killed and no one knew he was there. Suppose Ros was at liberty, but did not care to return there, ever. Incarceration was a horrible enough prospect, but to be so condemned by the one he loved so much would be beyond unbearable. Was this what it meant to be a follower of Christ? Was this how he felt on the night before the crucifixion? Abandoned by all the love there was.

He could shout, but would not shout, for the only

shout he could make would be with a Judas voice. He would betray himself. He could wait and shout. But what if he waited too long and the tower was razed, or Elizabeth ordered its abandonment? Who then would hear his shouts but the owls and rooks and rats? Would he freeze? Would he shiver to death? Would his flesh turn to frostbite and to gangrene while his throat tightened with thirst and his belly burst from the broiling gasses of eternal hunger? Would he ride the satanic stallion of fever? Would he be tended and tortured by the ghosts of disappointed martyrs?

This madness came upon him quickly and took root. So distracted was he by it that he had failed to make the soldier's count and estimate the passage of time. Had he been there minutes or three hours? His fragile guts said minutes, his unshod foot said a quarter of a day. He tentatively touched the cupboard door. He slid his fingertips across the grain, feeling not only the plank but the tree from which it came. Its reply was to infect his brain with the memory of the imagined cross to which his god had been nailed. He put his other hand to the same task, taking care to make no noise but hunting for a handle or a latch. None was found.

His thighs gave way, not from fatigue but from despair. Only then did he discover that the cupboard which was barely tall enough to stand up in was far too shallow for him to sit down. He was condemned to be slumped to death.

Movement in the tunnel. Feet at a pace, drawing near. Should he speak? The steps were too heavy for Ros. Should he speak? He could sense the bulk of the person. How? By the sound of air? By the echo of the person's passage through the tunnel? He couldn't really do that, could he? He could. He was. Did that make him supernatural? Was he blessed with senses others did not have? Did that make him martyr material? Was he already dead? Half of him hoped so. Was life after death an eternity of neither standing nor sitting? The whole of him hoped not. He should shout from this premature grave. He dared not. The person about to pass was friend or foe. There was an equal chance of each. The odds were stacked half way between rescue and condemnation. Surely any chance was better than none? No. No chance was best if there was certain probability of capture. But he had surprise on his side. He could force the door as soon as the bolt was drawn. Friend or foe would be shocked, and forced aside, while he ran to increase the possibility of escape. He should shout now, before the movement and the moment had passed. But what if the foe did not unbolt the door, but went to get a posse of foes? No chance then. He must hold his breath.

The noise went by. That hope faded, but brought the unlikely companion of relief. He was still at liberty and safely locked away.

Almost silence returned. Distant muffled movement, yells and shrieks stifled to whispers by distance, by stone, by a heavy door that he was sure no sixteen-year-old boy could unhinge.

Somewhere a drip marked circular time. A lethargic drip. So long was the delay between drips that it seemed the next would not come, but it always did. He thought of counting them but what would be the point of that? And what would he think if they stopped? What would he think if they increased and became a trickle, then a gush? They didn't. They just dripped. Eventually. Lazy water. What if it wasn't water?

Then the distant muted sounds ceased. No more shouts, no more movement. Just the drip, and the draughts. His naked foot was painful now. The cold that slipped under the door was a spring of invisible fluid that found skin but wanted bone. It penetrated his flesh and delivered ice to his ankle. The chilled ache ascended his shin. When it found his knee he would know more time had elapsed, though he would never know how much. He would wait for that. It would pass the passing time.

He prayed. He prayed first to Saint William of York who, they said, had been poisoned by someone who had contaminated the chalice of wine at Mass. Imagine that. The archbishop had thought he had changed wine into the everlasting life-giving blood of his saviour, and drank instead the hemlock that killed him. Surely the saint would have known instant bliss, and thought it to be a miracle of the consecration, not slaughter by sacrilegious subterfuge. Will wondered if God ever told the assassinated archbishop the truth or let him live forever enjoying an afterlife lie. Perhaps in making his prayer and thinking these thoughts Will had given the game away? He felt the all too brief heat of a blush, and then chose another saint.

Saint John was his next choice, the evangelist, not the

Baptist. This was his father's saint. More significantly this was a man of letters, a man who spoke through his written words. Campion had pointed out how John's gospel differed from the others and stood alone because of its style. Will saw what he meant. John's language was unique. He was also 'the disciple whom Jesus loved' and whenever Campion had referenced him in that way he had looked Will in the eyes in a manner that was both uplifting and unsettling. Will asked Saint John to send a liberating angel to free him.

Then his mind switched to Saint Peter, because he too had been a prisoner and an angel had come unto him, and the chains had fallen from his hands and feet, the prison doors had opened, and unchallenged he had walked free. He asked Saint Peter to spare that angel for just a few moments of everlasting time so that he might repeat his mission.

No angel came.

A devil did.

So ensconced was Will in prayer, or in stupefied sleep, that he heard nothing of the approach but was jolted to consciousness by the slam of the bolt and a drenching of even colder air upon his face. At the same time a feeble but also searing light of a single flame in a lantern box stung his dark-sodden eyes. A fist clawed at his tunic and yanked him out and in the same move slammed him against the wall of the tunnel. Then his rescuing assailant pressed against Will with his whole body weight, as the hand unclenched him and blocked Will's mouth before his shocked breath could become a sound. A face pressed almost too close for focus and said, "Shh!"

"Fulmmm!" said Will.

"Shh!" whispered Fulk. "Nothing! Nothing! Now come on."

But Fulk had turned traitor. Will had seen him leading Eliot to the priest hole. Should he follow? He thought of running the other way, but something told him that this was Fulk, and Fulk was always someone he was not. Fulk had no reality, only role. Right now he was playing rescuer, or so Will hoped. He followed.

They ascended the stairs to the small hall, and as they neared the top Fulk paused, crouched low and tensed like a wild cat close to starvation and to a kill. Will copied the posture. Seeing the state of light beyond them he deduced, correctly, that dawn was near. Nevertheless, Fulk did not deposit his lantern. He peered around the balustrade at the rim of the stair and then slipped down with feline silence until his lips almost kissed Will's ear.

"The Chapel," was all he said.

Will knew this meant they had to traverse the small hall and then the even smaller vestibule hall that linked the great hall to the chapel. By his catlike posture, pained face and thin voice Fulk conveyed all that was necessary regarding the danger of their proposed movement. He crept back to the rim, peered again and was gone. Will hitched onto his wake, and flit across the space, hobbling from uneven soles and from the stiffness induced by his incarceration. By the time he reached the vestibule he found full acceleration and flexibility and with it came a surge of welcome energy to make him light of heart and fleet of foot. Then they were in the chapel . . . but there were others there. Will stumbled and almost stopped.

It was Jerome and a second person who disappeared completely and magically as soon as Fulk whispered something inaudible.

Before Will had time to question or survey the scene, Jerome had grasped him and was propelling him towards the altar, and only then did Will see the disorder that made sense of so much. The stone altar had been set aside, along with its plinth, and beneath that was a gap. The space was but two feet square, and before he could object Will was thrust down it. All his nature dissented. Only minutes after being freed he was to be imprisoned again, but the sight of good Jerome prevented any protest. A boot on his head pushed him low and the slab was slid back in place above his head and beneath the altar. More scraping and stone thuds suggested all of the floor had been replaced. His heart almost refused to beat, but once through the hole he discovered the space was not quite so restrained, furthermore he was not alone, and there was light. Fulk's lantern was there, and clutching it, was Ros.

Even in all this confusion she looked gorgeous. She was squeezed against rock, contorted to less than half her height, and with most of her delight invisible, caressed by the darkness of their shared cave. The front edges of the curtain of her hair glowed, and her face, up-lit and hence masked in macabre shadow, should have looked fierce, but shone instead with the glory of a gospel illumination. A finger on her free hand made a crucifix with her lips.

How he wished he was that finger.

He determined to move, to grasp and to force a kiss, but the space was too confining. Then it wasn't confining at all, for Ros was gone, leaving a gap that he could fill, and before he knew it he was crawling and the cave had become a tunnel. Ros' scuffling sounded the way and Will's soul made certain his body followed.

Will tried to fathom the direction they were headed but could not. The tunnel rarely kinked however, but in places impenetrable rock forced a diversion. It was never high enough to stand upright and most of their progress was made crouching, but for long stretches they were forced to crawl on all fours. Will was both reassured and concerned by the occurrence of timber shoring. This passage had been properly mined. Very infrequently it widened and there was sufficient room for two persons to squeeze past each other. In one such location Ros stopped and Will squeezed into the feeble circle of light her lantern shed. They were panting and took a few moments to calm their breathing.

Ros said, "Got a gift for you."

"Have you?"

She reached inside her frock and from between her breasts she produced his shoe. He looked upon it as if it was a purse.

"Put it on."

The contortion was difficult but his foot sang with gratitude.

"Where does this lead?"

"Out."

"I've heard stories of a tunnel all the way to Salmesbury."

She looked at him as if he'd suggested they might emerge in France. "Come on," she said, and set off again.

This time the journey was dispiriting. It seemed relentless. What must the digging of it been like? In reality it wasn't that far, but hidden from reference points and bracketed by fear at the rear and the unknown ahead, anxiety brooded within him. Also fatigue was starting to bite as much a result of the emotional turmoil as the physical exertion. He banged his head on the roof and the agony sent the sound of the sickening crack his poker had made straight back into the place where his guilt was manufactured. He was crawling now, not just through the soil of the Hoghton hill, but also through remorse. He had killed a man. There could be no doubt. But now all there was, was doubt. He had slaughtered his own sanctity. He had stained himself with mortal sin. And for a Catholic, mortal meant death after death.

He stopped. Ostensibly it was to catch breath and summon new strength, but in reality he had chained himself to the floor with self-pity.

Ros did not stop. She did not even pause. The sound of her slipping away swiftly faded, dulled by narrow distance. He was alone again, with the world's worst jailor: himself. There was no light whatsoever, and his head swam so much he was no longer sure that he was not actually spinning around. When he eventually urged himself to step forward he did not know whether he was moving on or going back.

After moments, hours, or days he heard shuffling ahead once again and a filigree of straw said there might be light. There was. It was the lantern flame, and as he drew closer to it he sensed clean air and realised that Ros was stationary. When he caught up with her she said one word, "Care!" Then she stood stock still and listened. Then she moved, wriggling very awkwardly through rocks that almost interlocked. Half way through she stopped again. Then she blended a whisper and a shout. "Tom!" "Tom!"

Nothing came back.

"Tom! Tom!"

Nothing.

Ros wriggled more and slipped from Will's view. He followed and there was much freshness now, and a sense of greater space. There was light too. It was feeble but natural daylight, yet Will's gradually adjusting eyes could tell they were not yet out in the open. Ros was scrambling over a pile of rocks and as he followed he smelled the thinnest of strands of carbon. Suddenly he could stand, just about, and he saw a gaping hole ahead, and in its mouth the embers of a well-used fire space.

"Tom," he said. "Tom's hovel. Poor Tom."

"Sssh!" said Ros. She edged towards the entrance.

The fire was out and looked as if it had not burned for

some time.

"Tom's not here," said Ros with deep distress just beneath the veneer of matter-of-fact. She stood peering into the dawn mixing scrutiny with contemplation. She seemed to have slipped from the mundane into the mythological, purely by her attitude. In an instant she was back. "We need to get you away." Without waiting she was gone again, out into the dawn and down towards the river bank.

Will went after her.

"I thought you were taking me to Campion," said Will as they ate.

"You will never see Campion again," said Ros.

The cheese was exquisite. The bread was still warm.

"Is he safe?"

"Who knows?"

Will paused his chewing. The kitchen smelled of rosemary. The cook, called Joyce, continued plucking the pheasant.

Cheese crumbled from the corner of Ros' mouth. She caught the crumbs and fed them back whence they had emerged. She took a swill of buttermilk, and then spoke. "He was safe the last time I saw him."

Will continued with his breakfast. Joyce was known to Ros, who said Joyce was secure as jailor's strongbox. Even so, Will was cautious and leaned forward and lowered his voice. "This is not a safe house."

"It's the safest of all," said Ros as stoutly as ever. "No one will look in a protestant stronghold. Joyce is the bravest Catholic in the county. But we can't stay here long for her sake."

Joyce tore feathers and let them fall to the curled sack at her feet. "Stay as long as you want. His lordship never comes in here."

Ros inclined her head towards their hostess. "Joyce is steel. She has a score to settle. They hanged the priest she was fucking."

Will stopped eating again. Ros did not falter in her munching and Joyce plucked more vigorously.

"If he is safe, why will I never see Campion again?"

"We've talked all that through before. He's on a suicide mission and you have brought his executioner to the tip of his tail."

"I have?"

"Thursby found you, and through you found him."

"But he's safe?"

Joyce spoke up. "He was sitting in that chair three hour ago."

Ros sucked her fingers.

Will said, "Where is he now?"

Ros shrugged. "East or south. Who knows?"

"Which way am I to go?"

"Back to Hoghton. When Eliot has gone."

"He's still hunting for Campion?"

"And for you."

Ros brushed crumbs and the remnants of underground clay from her frock. Will took another bite. The rhythm of Joyce de-feathering the fowl presided. Ros swigged more buttermilk, then burped.

Will swallowed and said, "How did Eliot know that Campion was here?"

"I told him."

"What?"

"Well, I told someone who told him."

"Who?"

Ros' reply was one of her penetrating stares.

"Why?"

Another stare.

"Why risk Campion?"

"Campion means nothing to me."

"Then why help him to escape?"

"His papers are enough."

"Enough for what?"

The third stare was the sternest yet blankest of all.

Ros finished her drink and stood up. "Someone will come for you, when it is safe."

Will's grabbed her by the wrist and halted her. "The first raid. Magistrate Riley. Did you bring him?"

"Someone will come for you, when it is safe." She snatched her wrist away and left.

Joyce gathered the stray feathers into the sack, and then

hung the pheasant in the cold room.

It was Fulk who came. He refused to discuss his actions on the night of the raid. It was dusk two days later and they made their way back to Hoghton beneath spectating stars.

"Ros said you were at Lea," said Will.

"I came back."

"To meet Eliot?"

"To serve my lord."

"Eliot?"

"Jesus, Will!"

"You were leading him," protested Will.

"I was misleading him," said Fulk. "And now I'm leading you."

"Misleading me too?"

"No more to be said."

And no more was said. The journey was done in silence until the dogs heard them approach and Rowland admitted them.

The tower felt bruised. Somehow the semblance of normality slowly healed to become its old self but with scars. Elizabeth remained in perpetual tension and set everyone else on edge whenever they had to encounter her. After a week she left for Lea to be with her husband and the mood settled but remained sombre.

There was chatter among the workers but no one pointed fingers at Fulk and Will wondered if only he knew what his fellow actor had been doing that night. He did not reopen the discussion and their relationship was re-established on a plinth of distrust.

Ros kept her distance too. Elizabeth had warned them both that Jerome was charged with keeping them apart. He would report any liaison between them and that would signal dismissal of one or both. Will was keen to try surreptitiously, but Ros made it clear she was not interested so he gave up trying, but not dreaming.

One Sunday at the end of April he suddenly realised that the previous Thursday had been his seventeenth birthday. He told no one.

THIRTY

Weird sisters

Alexander returned to Hoghton tower on the tenth day of July 1581. He was no frailer than when he had left several months earlier, but his homecoming signalled the start of a terminal decline. Day by day he grew more lame, more incontinent and more erratic in his moods and behaviour. He also grew thinner and weaker. A kind of mild madness roosted in his head.

Seven days after Alexander's return Edmund Campion was captured at Lyford Grange in Berkshire. George Eliot made the arrest. The news of this did not reach Hoghton for several days and it remained an unconfirmed rumour for several more, by which time Campion had been tortured on the rack and a list of places he had visited had been extracted from him.

On the twelfth day of August, Will was summoned to Elizabeth's chamber. Ros was also there. Elizabeth was seated at the small table. Ros and Will waited. Daylight was fading. Elizabeth kept her gaze downcast. She arranged a set of two pens and an ink jar. Spread before her was a large square of paper. Alongside there was a pile of smaller cuts of paper and on these were written lists. As usual with Elizabeth the hand was untidy and there were many deletions and corrections. When she was happy with the arrangement on the table, she drew a careful breath.

"My lord's health has worsened."

Will nodded. "My lady."

"His speech is slurred. His hand unsteady."

"Yes," said Will.

"I have a task for you, Master Shakeshaft." Will waited to be enlightened, but instead, Elizabeth looked directly at Ros. "Campion's texts . . . where are they?"

Ros, in her softest and most youthful voice said, "My lady?"

"They cannot be found in the library. Where are they Ros? Jerome tells me they were handed to you. Where are they?"

"Safe my lady."

"Safe where?"

Three heartbeats passed.

"If I said that, they would not be safe."

"You have them?"

"No."

"Then who does?"

"Hoghton."

"What?"

"There are places in this house that only I know. That's where they are."

"You must tell me. If you do not . . ."

"What will you? What will you do my lady? Turn this table into a rack and wrench it from me?"

"If I have to."

"I will not speak. I will never speak even under torment – and I am no stranger to torment."

Elizabeth's face flushed scarlet. "You have been kindly used here."

Ros' voice took on a tone Will had not heard her use before. It had authority and rebellion in equal parts.

"Outwardly kindly. This hall shelters me from storms but in the hovel that is my head a tempest rages. There is no greater torment than the torture of the mind. It is a game without conclusion."

"You must say where Campion's testament is lodged."

Ros stared into air.

Elizabeth banged the table. "Where are Campion's texts?"

"God knows, my lady."

"God knows everything Ros. But I don't and I must. You must tell me."

"God saw me hide it, and if it is found, then it is God's will, and whatever torment might follow, then that is God's gift. So, my lady, I leave it up to him."

Elizabeth took one of her deepest breaths. "You will leave this house, Ros."

"If I do, my lady, then more people will learn where those texts are. And they will visit you and they will find them in your keeping."

"I will grant you one more chance to tell me where they are."

Ros said nothing.

"You will leave this house. Do so by dawn tomorrow."

Ros curtsied minimally, and left the room.

Will waited for Elizabeth to regain some composure. Eventually she looked up and smiled but her eyes were closed. She said, "My lord Alexander is sore confused."

"Yes, my lady."

"I fear he is close to death."

"Yes, my lady."

She opened her eyes and looked directly at him. "You will transcribe his will."

"His will?"

"His will. His last will. The one he wrote before is . . . lost. You must write it anew. Neatly, but with haste. He cannot live long. You will know that Campion is under examination. If he has spoken of . . . certain things, the officers of the crown might descend at any minute."

"I should write it?"

"He is clearly too ill to do it himself. I know his mind. I know what he wants."

"Then, my lady, you must write it down."

Elizabeth changed the position of the ink jar. "I have attempted to do so but my . . . hand . . . my secretary hand . . . is not good enough. I was ill taught."

"There are plenty here who can write well."

She used a slow blink to evade the suggestion. "I never

wanted Campion to come. And when he came, I did not want him to stay. And now he has gone his danger remains with us. I know what my lord Hoghton wants for me. It is here. Transcribe it to a better hand."

She passed her lists to Will who skimmed over them with disdain. He read some words out loud. "Plate, bowls, spoons, salts, also all her . . ?"

"All her apparel, rings and jewels. All her jewels. Sufficient furniture. And twelve oxen. And a bull. And horses enough for her convenience."

He couldn't make out the next words. "And. . .and. . ."

But she wasn't paying full attention, and was lost in her own thoughts. "And to sleep peacefully in her bed. The whole night through. For such winters that God will grant me."

Will could have left her in her reverie, but he took inspiration from Ros and became assertive. "There is no mention here of players."

"What?"

"There is no mention here of players."

"Do you not know? Andrew, and Solomon and Piers have gone to Knowsley."

Will did not know. He thought they were still at Lea.

"What of Fulk and of me?"

"Add what you will, master. . . Shakespeare. Do not over play it and I will not strike it out. My lord will add his mark. I will see to that."

"And Ros?"

He waited in total tension. Elizabeth's face flushed through scarlet to find creases of purple, but then it relaxed. She drank a slow shallow breath, and then said, "There is no such person."

"Do you wish me to write the will here?"

"I do."

"It will take some time. It must be written carefully."

"Then write it carefully."

"I would prefer to do it in the library. There are other wills there. I have seen them. It would help with the wording."

Elizabeth gave a dismissive flick of her hand. "Bring it to me in the morning."

Will gathered up the papers, and the pens and ink, and went to try to find Ros.

His search was frantic, but there was no trace of her. No one had seen her. He was afraid that she had already left, though Rowland the porter assured him that she had not gone via the main gate. A curious thought then befell him. She might have left via the secret escape. It was an absurd thought, but Ros could be absurd in her behaviour. He went to the chapel, but the altar was in place. It did not look like it had been recently moved.

He made his way towards the library but felt very uncomfortable about executing the task he had been given. He doubted just how much Alexander knew about it. Alexander was his lord, so long as he lived. Not Elizabeth; Alexander. He diverted his route and went to Alexander's chamber, and there he found Ros, standing by Alexander's bed.

She did not hear Will creep through the ajar door. The room was dark but a candle separated the two figures, casting light on Alexander and radiating a glow about Ros.

"My mind is not completely gone," he heard Alexander say. His voice was strained and had a wetness to it. "I will read it, provided I can see it. My eyes do not always comply with my requests."

"Get Will to read it to you. Not Jerome, not Fulk. Will."

"Jerome is trustworthy."

"Trust in you will die with you."

"Go and fetch him. I will make sure he knows that it is not my desire that you are dismissed."

"What does that matter? She will dismiss me as soon as you are gone. But I want you to know, that when I go, the Queen's men will come. They will find Campion's papers."

"Fetch Jerome. Fetch Shakeshaft."

"I am here, my lord."

Ros snapped around, sending shadows dancing crazily across the walls as the candle she held fought the draught of the turn. "How long have you been there?"

He loved and hated the fierceness in her face. "Not long."

"What did you hear?"

But before he could reply, Alexander had summoned him. "Young master Shakeshaft?"

"My lord."

"I understand you are to re-write my will, Will?"

"I am so commanded. Unless my lord instructs otherwise."

"On the contrary. Do you have paper?"

"And ink."

"Then draw up a chair. If it is my will, it should be I who dictates the content. Ros – fetch Jerome."

And so it was done. Will found it difficult to write neatly on his knee or the bed, so he spread the paper on the floor and Alexander dictated the testament. Will read Elizabeth's lists to Alexander and he granted all of them without exception. They were interrupted after a short while when Ros returned with Jerome.

"This woman is to remain in my service, do you understand?"

"Yes, my lord."

"And this boy is transcribing my final testament. See it?"

"Yes, my lord."

"Now go away, Ros."

She stood her ground for a moment, and then said, "I was never here." She turned and left.

"Take the chair Jerome. Witness this."

It took some time. Alexander fluctuated between sharpness and sleep. In fact twice Jerome had to forcibly wake him, though on each occasion he made it seem accidental. Will was delighted when he himself became a bequest. Along with Fulk, and also musical instruments and play clothes, Will was bequeathed to Alexander's brother Thomas. Should Thomas de Hoghton not want those items they were to go to Sir Thomas Hesketh at Rufford Hall. So that would be Will's destiny. Continuing with the Hoghtons seemed unlikely as Thomas de Hoghton was keeping his distance. It was close to midnight when Alexander dictated the most surprising clause. He settled endowments on all his servants, thirty in all. Alexander was careful about one clause in particular. He endowed a significant sum to Margaret, wife of Roger de Crichelowe. Margaret was to be described as a 'bastard daughter'.

Will, still crouching on the floor, knelt upright at that point. Alexander met his gaze face on. His expression was not that of a confused man. This was a moment of deliberate decision. Will wrote it down.

An hour or more later Will read it all back to its author, and there, on the bed before the young player, and before his steward Jerome, Alexander signed it.

Will deposited the testament with Jerome and went off to his bed.

Fulk slept and lightly snored a few feet away. Will watched him for a few moments. This was a young man Will had admired. He had learned so much from him. Had he not done so, he doubted that he would have survived his encounter with the men at arms. He doubted too, that he would have slain one of them. It was an act that was known by many, but only he, and God, and all the dead of all of time, knew that he had perpetrated. He may have escaped judgement for it in this life, but he must face trial in the next. He must carry that weight for ever. This and his other secrets were his bedfellows. He had penetrated three women: his father's servant Martha, Anne Hathaway of Stratford, and Frances Thursby. And now he had killed a man. Four great sins. He had enjoyed each one.

He agonised over his judgement of Fulk. He had seemed so trustworthy, yet he had been leading Eliot to the priest hole. Did he really know it was empty? Was it a decoy? Or was this most faithful of players always acting? The better actor he was the less chance there was of knowing the true man.

The next morning Ros was not in the kitchen. Will gulped down a hurried breakfast and set off to search the tower for her. No one had seen her.

"Lady Elizabeth sent word to ask if she had gone out," said Rowland in the guardhouse. "But she aint. At least not past me."

Will was learning though, and his knowledge provoked instincts that had paid off the night before. He tested them now. "Well I'm going to have a look for her," he said, "so let me out."

"As you will, Will," grunted the big man and he opened the pass door.

Will went straight to Poor Tom's hovel. Tom was sorting his wood pile.

"Tom?"

"Poor Tom is cold."

"Tom, have you seen Ros?"

"I have a fire."

"Have you seen Ros?"

"I have a fire!" said Tom giving the phrase pride.

"Ros. I'm looking for Ros."

Tom locked his stance at an inclined angle and raised a learned finger. "She brought very fine bread."

Will left Poor Tom to his woodpile and hurried to the beggar's hovel. A small fire burned.

"How did you put the altar back?"

"Don't be a fool," said Ros. She sat on the far side of the fire, cupping one of Tom's drinking bowls in her hand. "Do you want some milk? Don't take it all. I brought it for Tom."

Will noticed a pack of gathered fabric behind her. It was a bundle of belongings. "Rowland said you hadn't gone out."

"Rowland is an honourable man."

"What are you doing here?"

"Complying with my lady's order."

"Your lord overruled it."

Ros shrugged.

"I wrote out his will. There's money in it for all the household."

Ros did not take her eyes from the fire. She made no acknowledgement of what Will had told her.

"There's even provision for a bastard daughter. It's for one named Margaret de Crichelowe."

"Doesn't make her legitimate."

"I will go to Thomas de Hoghton."

"He won't want you."

"Or Thomas Hesketh at Rufford."

"Rufford is agreeable, from what I've heard." Ros drank from the bowl. A sliver of milk ran down her chin. She wiped it away with her sleeve.

"Come back Ros."

"Why?"

"It's where you belong."

"More than you know."

"What?"

"Why bastard?"

"What?"

"Why is bastard bad? The world is populated by

bastards. We work the world."

"We?"

"Lusty things, we bastards. Made by lust, and so fired with lust. Lust is good. Lust is strong. Lust is noble. Don't give me a love child; give me a lust child any day."

"Any day," said Will. "I nearly did."

"That wasn't lust."

"It was love."

"Can't have been."

"Why not?"

"Cause I'm unlovable."

"I say no to that."

"Say what you like, Will, but don't say it was love."

"I say it was love."

"And I say it was weakness. So learn a lesson from me. Do what weak men do, Will, and strongly hide your weaknesses. Call them bastards. Give them nothing. Not even in your will."

There was a distant clunk as Poor Tom stacked his logs. Ros drained the milk from the bowl. A draught danced with the wood smoke, and through the twirling confusion Will saw the truth.

"You are Alexander's bastard?"

"Twice over."

"What?"

"Same seed, different hens."

"Who was your mother?"

"What's a mother?"

"You are in his will – we all are. All the household."

"His will is what I am. I need no more from him. What do you mean: *twice over*?"

"Work it out Will."

Will had already worked it out. "He fathered your mother and then he fathered you on her."

"Well done."

Will sank back against the stone of the hovel. Quite close by, a tumble of logs rattled. Poor Tom cursed. Will studied Ros through the wood smoke. "How do you know this to be true?"

"I knew it. My grandmother confirmed it on her deathbed." She sipped more of the milk. "My mother brought me to the tower and left me at the gatehouse. Her breasts were full, my belly was empty. It was the old tower then. Thomas was here - Jane's father who fled to Flanders. He was starting to rebuild. The new tower was an infant, like me. He let the servants nourish me. They say his wife gave me some of her own milk. Made Jane and me cousins, and sisters of a sort. Weird sisters."

"Jane knows all this?"

"Jane knows lots of things."

"You've been here ever since."

"Before I could speak he sent me to Lea." Her intonation became sarcastic. "To my lord Alexander. I belonged to him." She put the bowl down and looked out from the hovel as if scanning the space for something; her past, or her future.

"Where are you going?"

"Away."

"Vagrancy is death."

"He'll take me."

"He will?"

"He promised." Now she looked straight at Will's soul. "And I promised him."

"Who?"

"Someone."

She was already looking away, and Will could see what she could see. She saw security, she saw comfort, she saw prosperity, she saw love, she saw legitimacy. He hoped that when she found the place where she imagined it to be, that it would still be there for her. His heart was not broken. It was demolished.

"Why did you go to Alexander last night and get him to reverse Elizabeth's command?"

Ros smiled a little, but conveyed a great deal of glee. "She knows I'm more of a Hoghton than she'll ever be. Leaving is my choice. Not hers."

"Come back inside."

"I am well out. And you will be soon."

"You threatened to tell where Campion's papers are."

"They are safe. Except for one."

"Which one?"

"The one I gave to Eliot."

"What?"

"In exchange for your life."

"What?"

"He was determined to find you Will. The paper was enough to put him off your chase. It was your writing. The Brag."

"Well he'd see that sooner or later anyway. Campion said he would print them."

"Until then he was determined to find you. It was personal. He had celebrated lust with Frances Thursby."

"How could you possibly know that?"

"James Rondel told me."

"When?"

"While I was fucking him. Just before I poisoned him."

Another wooden thud was underscored by Poor Tom's mutterings, and the rattling alarm of a disturbed blackbird.

"What did you poison him with?"

"The same potion that is killing my father."

"You are poisoning Alexander?"

"Not any more. But Elizabeth will finish it for me. She pretends to think it is medicine. She knows it's not. She'll be terrified that I will have told her husband last night."

"And did you?"

"Alexander needs to die, before they come and tear this tower apart. Next time I won't be here to save you. So he needs to die and then the will you wrote for him can save you. You will go to Rufford."

Will impulsively grabbed Ros' wrist. "Stay."

She snapped it free.

"I have given you more than any wife ever will. I have saved you. I have seen in you what you can do. Jane saw it too. We talked long about it. We talked long Jane and me. She saw my baseness, my bastardy, but refused to colour me with it. We are after all, twisted sisters. She made her escape. Now I make mine. Together we have given you yours. I will find my nobility, and you, will find yours. That is my gift."

"You do not know . . ."

"I know. I know all you are about to say, but I cannot hear it. I cannot hear it because I have promised someone. And he promised me. And we will fulfil our promise."

She leaned forward and planted a wet kiss inside Will's willingly parting lips. She tasted of milk, warm milk, and with that specific taste came a memory that Will did not know he had. It was a memory of suckling, of nourishment, of human strength. It was the flavour of future. This was something above and beyond love. This was a passing of the lactose of life. This was woman giving man the energy to climb the edifice of existence.

She made the kiss last a long time. She paused the parting of their mouths so that it was gentle, and lingering, but final. Then she said, "You have promise. Preserve it. Meet it."

She picked up her bundle and strode out of the hovel. A few yards later and without breaking her stride, she turned back and shouted.

"You are the wisest man in the world."

She might have been saying it to Will, but he could see quite clearly that she was looking at Poor Tom.

Summer was busy. Will and Fulk were drafted into the rural workforce to tend the animal winter feed, vegetable and fruit crops. Fulk became sullen for extended periods. Will began to appreciate how much his friend had valued Ros' presence, and he suspected that the they had had a much more intimate relationship than either had wanted known. Several times he broached the subject, but Fulk was unwilling to talk about it. Will could see there were secrets there, and he felt foolish for not realising at the time. His own infatuation had cloaked his powers of observation, and meanwhile Fulk had been doubly discrete, for not only had he not betrayed his lover, he had spared Will the pain of knowing that he was frequently celebrating the passion that his fellow player so achingly wanted.

Of course Will raised the matter of Fulk's apparent treachery of Campion with him, but he was reluctant to discuss that either.

"Just know, Will, that I am and always have been true."

"You were leading Eliot to the hide."

They were in the barn, unloading the first of the August hay from a cart. There was no one else there.

"Listen Will, what is done is done. It was well done."

"Well done? My lord Campion will be well done."

"He was not captured here. He was not in the hide. We got him well away."

"And did you also bring him here?"

"Where would be the sense in that?"

"Was Ros the one in touch with Eliot before he came?" Fulk paused in his pitchfork labour a little too long and Will knew he was close to levering the truth from him, so he pushed harder. "They had good knowledge of the tower, and seemed confident that their prize was here."

"What does it matter? Campion preached for another three months. He knew his hour would come. It didn't come here."

It was Will's turn to be trapped by a moment of trance. "I loved a traitor."

"You didn't love her. I loved her. Three times a week."

Will was spurred into action, aimed his pitchfork and lunged at Fulk. Their play-fencing skills leaped to their mutual defence as an exchange of stabs and blows passed between them culminating in Will being pinioned to the hay with one prong of the twin-spiked pitchfork on either side of his neck.

"I loved Ros, Will, I loved Ros." Fulk's face was so close that Will could taste stale breath. "I loved Ros, but Ros is incapable of love. Ros cannot love back. But as well as loving her I also fucked her. And she fucked back. She was a shit lover, but a supreme fucker."

Will rammed his knee upwards and into Fulk's groin. He tried to break free, but despite being pained and crumpling Fulk managed to keep his hand and his weight on the fork, so Will remained trapped.

"Well I fucked her too. And I loved her."

"No Will, she fucked you. And you were in love with someone like her."

"Someone like?"

"Yes. The one in your mind's eye."

"What?"

"She didn't love you, but she did save you twice."

"Twice?"

"Twice." Fulk was through the piercing peak of pain in his pelvis, and his weight was crushing Will against the hay again. "Once when she shut you in the cupboard in the passage, and again when she sent Eliot to find the page of Campion's brag she had placed for him, while we got you through the chapel."

The enormity of Ros' actions washed into Will. He was suddenly without feeling and let his weight slump so that his chin bit into the curve of the pitchfork.

Fulk backed off and let Will lurch against the pitchfork while he limped away and took deep breaths to finally dampen the ache in his groin. Will could have removed the fork but chose instead to remain imprisoned. Neither man spoke for several moments. Eventually Fulk ambled over and extracted the fork. Will stayed exactly where he was. There was more quietness. Distant voices and the rattle of wooden wheel rims told of movement in the yard.

Will said, "Did you know that Ros is Alexander's daughter?"

"I know who she is."

"And granddaughter."

"Does it matter?"

"It matters to her."

"There are bastards everywhere."

"That's what she said."

"Well in saying that she says what is true."

"Are you a bastard?"

Fulk rammed his fork into the hay again, "Ask my mother." He began to shift the pile sheaf by sheaf from cart to stack. His motion was now calm and methodical. His exposition followed the rhythm of his work. "Ros is a wise woman. She should be queen. And the Queen contacted her. Not directly, but the Queen has agents everywhere. Somehow someone found out that Ros may have a grudge against her host. Ros did, because of what Alexander had done and not done. He had made her a double bastard, but not acknowledged her or her mother, though he let her work at Hoghton."

"Rich reward."

"Exactly. And that's what she has gone to claim."

"But she didn't deliver Campion to her paymaster."

"She's kinder than that. She has no argument with Campion. It was Alexander she wanted."

"She could have poisoned him at any time."

"And be the first accused. We all know who did for Rondel."

Will thought long, and then said, "She told me she has been poisoning Alexander."

"That's Elizabeth."

Will recovered his own pitchfork and leaned on it. "How do you know?"

"Ros told me. Ros gave the potion but made sure Elizabeth knew what it contained. Enough to make him ill but not to kill. Until he'd remade his will."

Will now worked it out. "That's what they both wanted."

"Alexander will die within days. Mark my words. The potion will have changed, but not at Ros' hands."

Will sank his fork into a sheaf. "Hoghton will be raided." He lifted the sheaf from the cart and launched it onto the stack.

Fulk followed his example. "Let's hope Alexander dies first. For once his will is proved we can be out of here."

Will stopped work again. "Thank you Fulk."

"For what?"

"For not betraying Campion."

"Why would I do that? He's a good man. He taught me useful tricks."

"Like what?"

"How to kiss like an Italian."

Alexander died three days later. His will was proved on the twelfth day of September. One week later Hoghton Tower was visited again. By then Elizabeth had moved to Alston Hall, the residence on the north side of the Ribble bequeathed to her by her husband. She took Margery and Agnes with her to add to the small household already installed there. Jerome brought news of the raid. No one was arrested but some papers were taken away.

Edmund Campion was extensively tried during that month. Though terribly weakened by the torture he had endured, he gave a virtuoso defence of himself and even those who opposed his views were certain that he would be acquitted. He was, however, sentenced to be hanged, drawn and quartered. His execution would eventually take place at Tyburn in London, on the first day of December.

Will Shakeshaft and Fulk Gillum were installed as players at Rufford Hall midway between Hoghton Tower and the Lancashire coast. There, Shakeshaft became Shakespeare once again. After only a few months Will moved to joined Lord Strange's Men at Knowsley. His stay there was even shorter, for he made a trip home to Stratford. He rekindled his friendship with the sheep farmer's daughter, Anne Hathaway, and she became pregnant, so they got married.

He was very fond of Anne, but he frequently thought about Ros. Rosaline. One day he would write her name in a play, but no one could ever truthfully portray Rosaline.

The real Rosaline would only ever be a dream.

*

If you enjoyed this book, please consider helping other readers to discover it by putting a review on Amazon.

Thank you.

The Chapter Titles

The titles of the chapters are drawn from the following quotations:

The very substance of the ambitious is merely the **shadow of a dream**.
Hamlet Act 2 Scene 2

Fair fruit *in an unwholesome dish, are like to rot untasted.*
Troilus and Cressida Act 2 Scene3

I have no spur
To prick the sides of my intent, but only
Vaulting ambition, *which o'erleaps itself*
And falls on th' other
Macbeth Act 1 Scene 7

Ay, **in the catalogue** *ye go for men,*
As hounds and greyhounds, mongrels, spaniels, curs,
Shoughs, water-rugs, and demi-wolves are clept
All by the name of dogs
Macbeth Act 3 Scene 1

And loathsome canker lives in **sweetest bud**.
Sonnet 35

Sir, I am made of that **self-mettle** *as my sister*
King Lear Act 1 Scene 1

When sorrows come, they come not **single spies** *but in battalions.*
Hamlet Act 4 Scene 5

Infirm of purpose!
Give me the daggers. The sleeping and the dead
Are but as pictures.
Macbeth Act 2 Scene 2

I am no **breeching scholar** *in the schools.*
I'll not be tied to hours nor 'pointed times
But learn my lessons as I please myself.
The Taming of the Shrew Act 3 Scene 1

Hamlet: But what, in faith, make you from Wittenberg?
Horatio: **A truant disposition**, *good my lord.*
Hamlet Act 1 Scene 2

Enter the **PLAYERS**
Hamlet Act 2 Scene 2

Lord Polonius: What do you read, my lord?
Hamlet: **Words, words, words**.
Hamlet Act 2 Scene 2

Macduff: What three things does drink especially provoke?
Porter: Marry, sir, **nose-painting, sleep, and urine**.
Macbeth Act 2 Scene 3

Unbidden guests *are often welcomest when they are gone.*
Henry VI, Part I, Act 2 Scene 2

He was the mark and glass, **copy and book** *that fashioned others.*
Henry IV, Part 2, Act 2, Scene 3

God has given you **one face** *and you make yourselves another.*

Pete Hartley

Hamlet Act 3 Scene 1

And thus I clothe my **naked villany**
With odd old ends stol'n out of holy writ,
And seem a saint, when most I play the devil.
King Richard III Act 1 Scene 3

If you have tears, *prepare to shed them now.*
Julius Caesar Act 3 Scene 2

Sigh no more, *ladies, sigh no more,*
Men were deceivers ever,
One foot in sea and one on shore,
To one thing constant never.
Much Ado About Nothing Act 2 Scene 3

Assume a virtue, *if you have it not.*
Hamlet Act 3 Scene 1

A sad tale's **best for winter**.
The Winter's Tale Act 2 Scene 1

Foul whisp'rings are abroad. Unnatural deeds
Do breed unnatural troubles. Infected minds
To their **deaf pillows** *will discharge their secrets.*
Macbeth Act 5 Scene 1

The miserable have **no other medicine** *but only hope.*
Measure for Measure Act 3 Scene 1

O'erstep not the modesty of nature: for any thing so overdone is from
the purpose of playing, *whose end, both at the first and now,*
was and is, to hold, as 'twere, the mirror up to nature; to show virtue
her own feature, scorn her own image, and the very age and body of
the time his form and pressure.
Hamlet Act 3 Scene 2

Our **wills and fates** *do so contrary run*
That our devices still are overthrown
Hamlet Act 3 Scene 2

Fear no more the heat o' the sun,
Nor the furious winter's rages;
Thou thy worldly task hast done,
Home art gone, and ta'en thy wages:
Golden lads and girls *all must,*
As chimney-sweepers, come to dust.
Cymbeline Act 4 Scene 2

Kindness in women, *not their beauteous looks, shall win my*
love
The Taming of the Shrew Act 4 Scene 2

Like as the waves make towards the pebbled shore,
So do our **minutes hasten** *to their end.*
Sonnet 60

These **violent delights** *have violent ends.*
Romeo and Juliet Act 4 Scene 2

The **weird sisters**, *hand in hand,*
Posters of the sea and land
Thus do go about.
Macbeth Act 1 Scene 3

*

By the same author

Ice & Lemon

A novel

Not being able to get his luggage from the plane is the least of Dan's troubles. Heathrow is in a state of chaos. There are lifeless people everywhere but not one bears any sign of trauma or injury. Global communication freezes. London is gridlocked and burning. Mains power fails. Phones fall permanently silent. Life has simply stopped. Only those who were airborne when it happened have survived.

Ice and Lemon chronicles Dan's fraught expedition into a Lancashire blighted by extreme climate and thinly populated by desperate survivors in a desperate attempt to locate his family. What he discovers there could have truly cosmic consequences.

"An excellent novel. Stunningly assured, gripping from the off."

"Brilliantly told and full of humour and pathos, dealing with grand themes on a localised level."

"The story moves at a tremendous pace with shocks and surprises around every corner and a truly mind blowing conclusion."

Untitled

A novel

She presumed their first meeting had been coincidental, but then discovered that he had already painted her in intimate detail. They agreed not to reveal anything about their previous lives to each other, not even their names. They became lovers and planned to marry, but then he disappeared and she had no means of discovering what might have happened to him.

A decade later she received a postcard that enabled her to start the search but, in doing so, she discovered that she could be the most hunted target of the Cold War. She hoped she could survive long enough to find out why.

The unseen and unthinkable escalating nuclear arms threat is the dreadful umbrella overshadowing this story, that riddles beneath the ideological standoff that dominated the middle of the last century, but there are other tensions here too, just as dangerous to the individuals involved.

National security vies with personal fidelity, integrity with identity and nature with legality in this psychological thriller; and for the protagonist at the heart of it all is the perennial quandary: who really is the person that she loves?

"An exceptional mystery."

"The more I read, the more intrigued I became."

"This is a book I truly recommend."

The Atheist's Prayer Book

Short stories in search of the super in the natural.

These stories are a quest to reveal the spiritual in the secular, the exceptional in the ordinary and the eternal in the momentary. Its blend of orthodox narrative and magical realism cuts into the darkness of misfortune and misadventure to intrigue the thoughtful and enchant the curious.

The prose has been compared to that of Christopher Priest, J.G. Ballard and Alan Garner, and this collection is very much in harmony with the philosophy of the latter, who has suggested that the purpose of stories is in serving *our need to make sense of the natural world and of the hidden forces in ourselves.*

Christmas Present

Seven Seasonal Ghost Stories

This Christmas Present is a compendium of seven short ghost stories from northern England. These subtly told tales serve just enough chill to spice up winter evenings by the fireside or lonely commutes during the hours of darkness. Five were first published or broadcast in the 1980s while the opening and closing tales have been crafted especially for this compilation.

ABOUT THE AUTHOR

Pete Hartley is based in northern England where he taught drama for three decades. He has written extensively for the stage. Some fifty of his plays have been performed by professional, amateur and student companies. Six have won prizes, and one was broadcast by BBC Radio. He has also had short stories published and broadcast.

Printed in Poland
by Amazon Fulfillment
Poland Sp. z o.o., Wrocław